On the Trail of the Myk

Book 2 of the After the Atoms Fall Series

I0771521

By Casey Robert Swanson
With Jessica Dailey

On The Trail of the Myk

SageAuthor Books

Also available from the author

The Order of the Sage
Beyond the Fears of Tomorrow

Coming Fall 2025
Branches

All people, places and incidents in this book are a piece of fiction. Any resemblances to any incidents from today's world events are purely coincidental.

ISBN #979-8-9986992-1-4
eBook ISBN# 979-8-9986992-0-7

Printed in the USA

Dedication

This book is dedicated to our little puggle, Xena, who passed onto Dog Heaven this last year as I was finishing the writing of this book. She brought tremendous joy to my wife and myself both at home in in our many travels with here. She joins our other dogs, Luke, Dottie, Taz and Tucker in Dog Heaven along with all of our dogs that have meant so much to us in life.

Table of Contents

In the beginning, there was man, a human, from whose form we came.
Then amongst us a change evolved, a new race of this world.
We became as high above the humans as they did among the cattle they breed.
Finally, even among us of the highest form, a new evolution began.
No longer of the human, no longer of the White,
We stand above both, as they provide us nourishment. We are the myk.

Always in the aftermath of war it is often the stream of refugees from one place to the next that is the biggest challenge to the victors. The united army's victory over the White was no different, except in one respect. The importance of finding the fleeing foe had taken on a new importance.

The White, those who followed of the 'Old Ways', could no longer find welcome nor refuge in the Northern Valley, once their home, with the defeat of their King, The Myk, a son of Nourne, who fled the conquerors. They no longer had a home.

In singles, pairs, small groups they traveled to the North and the East to join their king. They fled from the liberators of their slaves, of their food source. They traveled at night, past the Myk's Valley, where once stood the proud Palace of the Myk. Past the Great Swamp and its Jal-Beast, something even the White feared. Past the desolation of the North they traveled, where few of the humans now dwelled. Always they were fearful of who followed, of being found.

To the cavern of their God, Hydron, the father of their form, they fled.

Most carried the proud mark of the greatest of the White, a second head, developing as they tread to their new home. And as they marched, these second heads had the time to mature, to achieve dominance.

Once in the Cavern, a ceremony, of late creation took place. The Myk and his chosen few were all who stood witness. Two of the myk (no longer of the White), each carrying a broad sword, stood on either side of the new member of the Cavern. At a nod from their leader, the Myk, both swords flashed as one and the first head sliced off, cleanly above the shoulders. The second head now gave life to this form. Sometimes rising within the cavity where once stood the old head, at other times from any part of the creatures shoulder. From this the Genesis of a new race was born.

And in unison they shouted, "WE ARE ONE! WE ARE MYK!"

Chapter 1
The Skeleton City

Zircon hesitated as he reached the crossroads of the Ways. While it seemed clear that this was the pathway that led to the distant Skeleton City laying just over the horizon, something seemed out of place to Zircon. Then he noticed it. He should have seen them sooner, but he was preoccupied with Gar's final words to him about this trip. 'That is a good way to get us all killed,' Zircon thought to himself. Just over the hilly rise, to one side of the way, his eyes followed carrion birds, vultures of some kind, circling something that was just out of sight of the caravan. They were landing in large numbers in the distance. Something had happened out there and not too long ago.

The rest of the expedition noticed Zircon stopping to watch the vultures and their circling and they stopped as well. Word had passed quickly over the winter of Zircon's value. He carried an almost second sight, an unusual awareness of everything around him. This second sight had stood him well since he had landed on these shores amongst them. Even in those earliest days, when Zircon's personal torments worked against those feelings of awareness.

This was a trading expedition, joint Jall and The Hold, sent out to gather from this ancient pre-war city the value of its metals. As was wont on these expeditions to the Skeleton cities, security was the primary concern. The menace of the countryside that surrounded these trading parties was primarily the danger of the Great Bear population and the tremendous wolf packs that lived near these ancient cities. A small party would have no chance here if either bear or wolf were run into.

Six wagons, slow, ox-driven, meant for heavy loads of cargo, were driven by the Jall. Accompanying them were 100 of Shieldmen of The Hold and a dozen outriders on horseback hired for the trip from the Southern Valley. Nevertheless, it was the man from across the sea, Zircon, with his long-rifle, that the Trader-King had insisted lead the expedition.

Gar had sent Zircon to go on this expedition for a reason and the Trader-King had learned long ago not to ignore the advice of the Sage he had known and trusted since he was a child. Gar had been one of his teachers in his youth and now was his most important advisor in these troubling times. When Gar had suggested that Zircon be the one to lead this party to the ancient city, that advice to the Trader-King was as good as an order. When the Trader-King asked Gar the reason for this suggestion, Gar was his usual close-mouthed self about the reason. That mattered not to the Trader-King. Zircon would lead this caravan on what The Hold and the Jall considered an ordinary, if not important, trading expedition. They sorely needed the metal in the rebuilding of Twror and wealth was to be made by those who could supply the rare commodity.

Zircon looked into the distance. A new mantle of responsibility now surrounded him. He was no longer the bitter scourge who had landed in this New World almost a year ago. The White (Twrorians he reminded himself) now considered him almost a saint for protecting them after the war. With this newfound self-respect had come a peace with Thorium and within himself. Those around him looked to Zircon now for the newfound strengths he possessed and his innate abilities had moved him to the forefront of this world in everybody's eyes.

* * * *

Before this expedition, Gar had sought out Zircon in secret, finding him in a small tavern at the City by the Lake. Zircon had traveled there to escape for a time the adoration of the Twrorians. They had already built a home for him in Twror, even before they built one for Gant, their Mayor.

Zircon looked up as he saw Gar approach him. How had he found him here? Zircon had tried to keep his coming to this place a secret. At times he craved isolation as he tried to fit his still muddled thinking into this new context (of his place) in this world he found himself in.

Zircon stood as Gar reached his table. How he had found him didn't matter, Zircon now welcomed visits from Gar. The two men shook hands as friends. Zircon smiled to himself as he thought back to their first meeting in the Jall City. Gar motioned Zircon to be seated and the two men sat across from each other at the small table. The proprietor brought a beverage for Gar whom he recognized as a Sage.

"You smile, Zircon, that is a thing I am happy to see," started Gar.

"I was thinking back, briefly, to our first meeting. I trusted no-one then."

"And now look at you. At home in a land where the people know, trust and love you."

"Feelings that at one time I would have run away from. I am a new man, yes, but there is still the old within me. And at times it still tries to come to the surface."

"The reason for your retreats?" asked Gar, knowing the answer.

"Yes, before I lash out at the innocents who now look to me for protection," Zircon answered.

"You still have much too learn, Zircon, but you are becoming the man you are meant to be."

"Once I would have taken objection to those words."

"You have learned much," Gar continued without pause stating to him matter-of-factly, "Zircon, I have a job for you to do with an expedition of the Jall and The Hold,"

Zircon spat on the floor upon hearing this. He briefly showed his old flash of anger, seething, before settling down, repeating within himself with a mantra taught to him by one of the followers of 'The One True God'. "Use this when your old ways come to the surface," he had been taught. "Let the calm of the words bring you relief from your pain."

He had little respect for the Jall, those bio-engineered creations of the Teachers, whose only real contribution to this world was the concentration of wealth through their trade dominance. Nor did he hold much respect for The Hold, who lorded over their selection by the Teachers to wait out the dark days in the safety below ground. These two peoples, selected or engineered by the Teachers, were failures in Zircon's eyes, wasting what the Teachers had given each. They had been the first to break on the battlefield and then after the battle, they took out their anger on the defenseless White.

Gar remained patient. He knew the inner turmoil that Zircon still fought on an almost daily basis. Gar had arranged the meeting between Zircon and the priest who had taught Zircon the first steps of meditation. A strong man he would become. A tool for what was coming. But as yet Zircon's abilities were still being forged by the events that he stood very little control over.

"This is important, Zircon or I wouldn't ask you. This expedition is going to a city that hasn't been visited successfully before. I don't know what you'll find there, but I have a feeling, a recollection, of something. Something of importance will be found there. And I need you there for me."

"Why not another, why not you?" Zircon responded, still simmering with his anger just beneath the surface, saying his mantra silently to himself. At peace with himself most of the time, he was still volatile as well. Total peace would take time he had been told too many times by the Order of the Sage.

Gar spoke again, quietly, in a voice so as not to further inflame Zircon's inner turmoil. "As for myself, there is much I must do as yet to prepare for what is coming. You, Zircon, have certain skills that the Jall value. It is the Jall-King who makes such decisions on trade mission matters. You will be in charge of the security of this expedition and the men of The Hold have agreed to answer to you."

"Those weaklings, will they run again if trouble arises?"

"That is why I need you there. They will listen and follow you," stated Gar.

"Why not Thorium, he's the leader, not me."

Gar smiled at that. "It was not so long ago that you wished to challenge him for that."

"That was the old me," Zircon answered, eye to eye with Gar. To answer the Sage directly, looking him in the eye, that was something the old Zircon would not have been unable to do. There had been too much envy, bitterness and anger inside him. Then he had seen the family of White burned alive inside their home by the men of The Hold. Something had snapped inside him then, while holding the dead bodies of the family he had dragged from their burning home to try to save them. He looked at the scars he now carried on both arms from that fire. They reminded him of the fundamental change in the way he saw the world around himself.

"You are remembering how you felt when you saw the White family killed?" Gar asked Zircon quietly.

"Yes," answered Zircon, a tear in his eye.

"Do you remember how you used to feel about Thorium?" Gar asked the man.

"Yes, though I try to forget. That White family I will never forget." Zircon was trying to understand Gar's line of questioning.

"The feeling you once had for Thorium is how the people of the Hold and the Jall feel towards him. Though Thorium makes his home in the City of The Hold, the people there consider him an interloper. He is a constant reminder of their failures, in both battle and the aftermath of the battle. Thorium could never be successful in this mission and there are other more suitable jobs ahead for him as yet."

"And me?" Zircon asked, puzzled.

"They saw you at the battle, unyielding, giving the others a chance to survive with your skills. They saw you at Twror, outnumbered, standing up to them, protecting the helpless. They may not like you, but they respect you. And they will follow you."

Respect and honor, these were new feelings to Zircon that he was trying to deal with and absorb.

"Is it that important? I have other plans for myself," Zircon asked of the Sage, looking straight at Gar who sat across from him.

"Yes, I think it is. Something is there, something forgotten. I just don't know what it is," answered Gar, holding up both hands in a helpless gesture.

"Then I'll go, for you. When do I leave?"

"We leave now for the Jall City. I'll tell you more, what thoughts I have, on the trip."

* * * * *

Zircon held his hand up, motioning for the expedition to come to a stop. He got off his horse, unslung his long-rifle (always loaded) and motioned at two of The Hold's shieldmen to follow him.

"Quiet," Zircon said to the two men as they came forward and joined him, "Something happened over that rise."

Zircon held his long-rifle at the ready as he moved up the side of the hill towards the top of the rise. One of the two warriors who was accompanying him armor jangled. "Silence!" Zircon whispered. "Leave your shields here as we climb to the top. A battle happened over there."

"Who fought?" one of the men whispered back.

"That's what we'll soon see. Afraid?" Zircon couldn't help taunting the men a little bit. There was still the old Zircon just below the surface.

"No," the two men whispered back to Zircon in unison, but Zircon couldn't help but notice that each of them now held back an extra step behind Zircon.

Near the top of the hill, Zircon dropped down to his hands and knees and crawled the rest of the way to the crest. The two men who accompanied him remained some distance from the top of the hill. Zircon looked over the valley before him and saw the carnage. The carrion birds were in a feeding frenzy over what lay dead on the field of battle. Zircon had never witnessed what he now saw before him. He stood up and motioned for the two men to join him.

"Bring my horse," he told one, "and then tell the caravan to continue on quickly. I want a closer look at this."

$$* * * * *$$

Zircon remembered briefly how he had received the horse and another gift, a wooden shaft with a light on the end. Zircon and Gar were about halfway to The Hold from the City by the Lake, riding in a rough if not comfortable wagon Gar had obtained in the City by the Lake for the trip. A pair of horses pulled it.

The two men were sitting quietly at the front of the wagon, each in their own thoughts, when they heard the sound of a pair of horses galloping up quickly from behind them. Brigands they both thought. Zircon readied his long-rifle and Gar pulled his staff from where it was stored behind their seat on the wagon. Gar pulled the wagon off the road to a clump of trees. From the sound of the horses, they couldn't out run them in the wagon. Gar looked behind them as a rider came into view, rapidly leading as majestic a horse as Gar had ever seen.

"Jamen of Kiln, we thought you brigands, coming from behind us as quickly as you did," Gar exclaimed as Jamen approached.

"I bring gifts for Zircon to enable his success in what is coming. Tor, your fellow Sage, told me that I would find you on this road from the City by the Lake to The Hold. I was told to bring these gifts as quickly as possible to you."

"And always you take the words of the Sage so deliberately," Gar laughed.

Jamen dismounted from his horse and approached the wagon as Zircon and Gar got down. The three men clasped arms as one in greeting. Jamen was a man Zircon could respect and he was honored by the friendship that Jamen showed towards him.

Jamen handed the reigns of the second horse to Zircon. It was light brown and stood half a head taller than Jamen's own stead. The horse's nose was White as was each of its feet. One eye patch was White and the other black. The horse nuzzled Zircon as if he was its long lost friend.

"Mine," was all that Zircon could say. To be given such a fine horse by Jamen of Kiln was more than he could imagine. Jamen's ranch was known for its fine horses and Zircon couldn't imagine one greater than this stead.

Jamen continued to speak to Zircon. "Tor told me of the journeys that you will be taking. Here is a friend that you will need for those. Strong, loyal, brave, unyielding, as steadfast as you yourself have shown us to be. Behold, the champion of our champions. Few are the men that he will allow to ride him. Already he has claimed you as friend; a gift of Kiln and the people of Twror."

"And what is this?" asked Gar as he reached inside the saddle of the gift of the horse. "A tool of the Sage?"

"The light-rod is a gift of Tor for Zircon," answered Jamen. "I am told that he will find it useful in the times to come."

"Stay and join us for a meal," suggested Zircon, humbled by the gifts he had just received.

"I cannot stay. The council is meeting tomorrow on a matter of some concern and I must be there."

With that, Jamen got back onto his horse and began his rapid return to the City by the Lake.

Zircon removed the saddle from his horse (was it truly his?) and couldn't help but notice the fine detail work on the leather of the saddle; another treasure. He tied the horse to the back of the wagon.

"We still have far to go," said Gar as he reboarded the wagon. "We will eat as we travel"

* * * *

The three men together looked out over the battlefield below them.

"Where are the fighters? I see only dead beasts below us," the first to arrive asked. "Have the carrion birds already devoured them?"

"Who fought here, what armies?" the second man asked Zircon as he arrived.

"Just bring me my horse and get the caravan started again. Close order by the shieldmen. Something has happened here and I must see more. Two armies did fight here. Over food or territory, I can't tell. I will rejoin the caravan shortly." Zircon began moving down the hillside as he gave these last orders, his mind contemplating what he saw before him. Could this be what Gar had in mind when he sent him on this trip?

One of the two men hesitated before turning back to the caravan now over the hill from them. "But the armies you speak of, where are they?"

"Those that died, they lay before us," Zircon answered.

"But I see no armies, only bear and wolf."

"It was the bear and the wolf that fought here, in great numbers. Quickly now, my horse. I'll be below, among the bodies of the dead beasts. Get the expedition under way again, with a close watch to the horizon."

Two vast armies had fought here and hundreds of bodies remained about the field of battle, but not a man among them. Countless bear lay before them and maybe a few hundred wolves. What could have brought them here in such numbers? Even the wildcats would have been helpless here.

Zircon began moving down the hillside as he gave out his orders. His mind was trying to comprehend the carnage he saw before him. No sign of weapons or armor could be seen. This was a battle of tooth and claw, between armies of the wolf and the bear. Very few of the wolf remained. As he wandered through the surreal battlefield, he saw bear and wolf lying side by side, jaws still engaged with flesh. The two enemies met here in fierce combat to the death. Who had won? His mind traveled back again to Gar's words, "Something of importance may be found there." Could this be what Gar had anticipated? The journey had just become that more dangerous.

The expedition was almost an hour further along the route to the Skeleton city when Zircon finally caught up with it, riding rapidly on his tireless horse. He was happy to see the outriders close on either side of the caravan with a squad of soldiers on foot before and after the wagons and a third in reserve riding a middle wagon's. The warriors of The Hold were cowards in Zircon's eyes, but at least they were prepared cowards.

Zircon rode up to the first wagon and the Jall in charge of the expedition. "We march through the night without rest. Have the torches lit on each wagon as nightfall approaches. Rotate the warriors, two hours riding, two hours marching, throughout the night, using all of the wagons to transport them. We may need them fully rested before we reach the remains of the skeleton city. With daylight, all will ride the wagons, except those on horseback. The outriders must remain in close contact, all within the light of the wagons lanterns. Those on horseback will rest as well; three hour shifts." Zircon delivered his orders in a crisp tone to the Jall who commanded the wagons. He was growing quickly into this newfound leadership that was thrust onto him.

The Jall leader looked alarmed at Zircon' words; his first thought was the White. It was known that many had survived the war and fled north. Moreover, as the double-heads came to life, more fled everyday to wherever the Myk was hiding.

"No, not the White," said Zircon in answer, "maybe worse."

"Worse," the Jall leader quivered. He quickly passed on Zircon's orders to the caravan while he thought to himself, 'What could be worse than the Myk?'

Zircon now rode in front of the caravan. Two great armies, neither of them human, had fought near-bye, not a half days march from where they now traveled. The battle was fought only a day before, the dead on the field of battle still fresh. Where were the victors, the survivors?

Zircon looked around him, low ridges rose a short distance from the way on either side, clear but for scrub trees and brush. A fire had come through here not many years before. Would there be an ambush during the night? No, whoever won the battle had suffered some pretty grim casualties. However, were they being watched, even still? There wouldn't be any sleep for the expedition this night.

The daylight turned into twilight and then the dark of evening fell. The last of the weary shieldmen clambered laboriously onto the now crowded wagons for what rest they could garner. Torches lit the four corners of each wagon in the eerie procession. The outriders drew in close to each wagon, their horses weary as well from the march.

"Outriders, dismount, tie your horses to the middle wagons," Zircon now ordered the outriders of the Southern Valley, "and then board the wagons with the rest." The horses had to continue the march, tied off on the back of the wagons, but at least they were free of the weight of their riders.

Zircon was still ill at ease. He could feel the eyes watching them as the wagons slowly moved along the way. He had done all he could to prepare them for what he knew was coming. Would it come during the night? At first, he thought naught. Then he put himself in the place of the victors of the battle. Night would provide the best cover for a diminished force. The men did what Zircon asked of them without objection. Was it enough? They all felt the unease of Zircon.

Only Zircon remained mounted now. He carried his long-rifle in a sleeve on his saddle where it was available in a moments notice. The horse he rode seemed tireless. Jamen had mentioned that it was one of the prize stallions of Jamen's family's breeding farm; a horse of uncommon bravery that would never tire nor panic in battle. Zircon could feel that in the horse now. It was dark brown with a patch of White across its nose and it stood about half a head taller than any other horse Zircon had seen. The light of the Sage was in another sleeve of the saddle as well.

"This horse will do you well," Jamen had told him as he handed him the reigns. Zircon reached up and patted the powerful neck with the palm of his hand. "Stay with me now Friend, we both know something is out there," he whispered to the horse's ear.

Zircon rode well in front of the wagons now carrying in his hand the cane light given to him by Tor. It seemed that each person he met as he started the trip had something of value for him. Even Gar had given him the shard of wood he kept in a pouch on a chain around his neck. "The words are unknown, but its use I think will become clear to you," was all Gar said about it. The importance of the trip had become increasingly clear to all the parties aware of it.

The light cane's brilliant light shown on the cracked and rutted way that they followed and that lay before them to the skeleton city. Zircon tried to listen for the nighttime noises around them but the noise of the ox-drawn wagons made that next to impossible. From the light of the wagon's torches Zircon could see maybe thirty-five to forty feet on either side of the way. However, that distance could be traveled in seconds if either of the battle's combatants should attack them this night.

Zircon rode further ahead, beyond the torchlight of the wagons, and then back and forth across the soft ground on either side of the way. He stopped briefly to take a quick drink from the carafe of the Sage's beverage, another gift, this time from Gar. And this time the beverage was sweet. Not at all like the time he had tried it in a tavern in the City by the Lake. Not a tavern frequented by the Sage, that time it had been bitter.

They were not alone, that was certain now. Wolves, the bear, or something was out there just outside the light of the torches. Then Zircon heard the howl, answered by others on either side of the way. Zircon flashed his light to the side and briefly caught sight of a wolf, giant in size, its eyes flashing briefly in the canes light as it looked directly at Zircon. 'There is intelligence in those eyes,' Zircon thought.

Zircon turned his horse and rode quickly back to the others. How much time did they have? The wolf he knew did not hunt at night. Nevertheless, these wolves, he had seen those eyes. Not the eyes of a predator, but the eyes of a General, ready to give a command.

"Out of the wagons, all of you, horse and oxen in the middle, wagons on there sides. Hurry, time is short!" shouted the watchful Zircon as he rode Friend back to the wagons.

In seconds, the shieldmen were out of the wagons and moving into position to defend the wagons. As quick as they were, the time allowed was not enough. The first of the wolves struck and two men fell, dead, their throats ripped open by the wolves' claws and teeth. They heard howls on either side of the way. Then silence. Zircon flashed his light on either side of them, still riding the steady Friend, his horse, and dark shadows could be seen on either side, just beyond the lights reach.

The wagons, with the oxen released, were tipped on their sides, the torches now mounted on the upturned sides. The wagons now formed two short sides facing out on the narrow way. The Jall stood watch with the mercenaries of the Southern Valley behind the wagons at the ready. The shieldmen now formed two outward bowed crescents facing up and down the way on either end of the wagons, one crescent facing back hence they had come and the other forward towards the skeleton city. The oxen and horse now stood safely in the middle, tethered to the way with stakes driven into the ground. If the attack were to continue, they were as ready for it as they could be. However, already two were dead.

More howls were heard all around them. There seemed to be hundreds, or more, of the wolves. What were they waiting for; daybreak?

A light on the back end of one of the wagons went out, leaving an area in the dark. "Relight it quickly!"

Zircon heard the shout, then a scream. That quickly and one of the Jall was gone, dead, his body shredded by the wolves claws in seconds. The wolf attacker was gone before any could react. Silent assassins; these were not the wolf that any on this expedition were familiar with.

On it went that way throughout the night. Six times, each time a different wagon, a lantern was extinguished and a Jall killed,. Panic began to spread among the men. The shieldmen, exhausted, tightened their ranks, but they were left untouched during the night of terror. They only attacked the Jall when the lanterns were extinguished and now a third of their number was gone.

It was approaching daylight when Zircon, still riding his horse that seemed without fatigue, caught the sight of a lone wolf, crawling silently along a ravine that approached the way, slowly moving towards the wagons. Zircon readied his long-rifle for a shot. His horse stopped, its head raised, as if understanding the importance of the moment. The wolf showed an amazing burst of speed as it dashed towards to wagons from the shallow ravine. The wolf sped towards a lantern on the wagon nearest to the wolf and the Jall standing by the light. The wolf had used the irregular terrain along the way to approach as near the wagons as possible and at the slightest break in the diligence of the Jall, took that moment to launch its lightning attack. Zircon's shot caught the wolf as its immense paws, covered with mud to protect them, first extinguished the light before turning on the Jall. Zircon's shot had saved the Jall's life as the lifeless wolf tumbled over the wagon and fell at the Jall's feet.

"Stay awake or we'll all be gone by full mornings light," shouted Zircon to the startled Jall whom relit the lantern. Zircon got off his horse, leaving it untethered inside the enclosure made by the wagons, and approached the dead wolf. Zircon could not mistake the signs of intelligence in the wolf's attack. Now Zircon looked over the wolf's body. The paws and claws commanded Zircon's attention. The ground on either side of the way was dry and dusty. Yet this wolf's feet he found caked in a coating of thick clay-like mud. Its claws were sharpened, the tools of a soldier. More like a cats claw than a canine. This was a trained warrior not unlike The Hold's own shieldmen.

With the death of the wolf, the attacks stopped for the night. 'Had the attacks all been the work of this one highly trained assassin?' Zircon thought to himself.

The morning sun rose to expose a macabre sight around the expedition. The men looked out past the way and found themselves surrounded by thousands of the wolves. Standing to one side, half again as large as the other wolves, Zircon saw the leader. Instinctively Zircon knew, this was the wolf whose eyes he had caught in his lantern before the attacks had begun. Its intelligence as it watched Zircon impressed the man. The wolf and Zircon stared at each other for several minutes, each trying to size up the other.

The wolves standing on the way leading away from the skeleton city moved back up the hillside, leaving an opportunity for the expedition to leave. The meaning became even more apparent when more wolves gathered in the front of the expeditions and on either side of its wagons on the way. They could leave the way they had come in peace, but no further towards the ancient skeleton city would they be allowed to travel.

Not really knowing why he did it, but understanding he must, Zircon left the wall of shieldmen and walked towards the low hill to one side of the way, to where the Emperor Wolf stood, watching over the scene below, under a lone tree. Zircon put his long-rifle back in its sheath on his horse's saddle and motioned for his horse to remain behind. Friend looked at him as if to say, 'It's my job to be at your side.' But the horse obeyed the unspoken command. Zircon called to the men of The Hold and the Jall and told them not to fire, no matter what transpired.

As Zircon approached the giant wolf, the wolves on either side of the Emperor lay down, their eyes never leaving the sight of Zircon. Zircon noticed their sharpened claws. It was as if to say, our weapons are still for now as well. The Emperor Wolf, slowly with deliberate steps walked down the hill toward Zircon as well, its ears and tail held up. Zircon hoped this was a good sign.

Zircon stopped about halfway up the gently sloping hill and waited. He wasn't sure what was happening but he understood that they stood about as much chance in battle as the bear clan had. He held his hands loosely at his sides in what he hoped the Emperor Wolf would understand as a peaceful manner. Those at the wagons just looked on in nervous amazement at Zircon's actions. He was either the bravest man that they had ever seen or a fool. They waited anxiously to see which it was.

The Emperor Wolf approached Zircon and stood face to face with him, the wolf's nose just inches from Zircon's face as Zircon stood motionless. The Emperor Wolf held his head up high and sniffed Zircon's face. Zircon struggled to hold himself together. Zircon felt the wolf's nose touch his cheek and still he didn't flinch as he stared eye to eye with the wolf. The wolf backed up several steps and sat on his rear haunches, with its ears up, still facing Zircon. Both man and wolf then remained motionless for what seemed an eternity to the men below. The eye-to-eye contact between man and wolf never wavered. Zircon felt a chill run through his body; every nerve of his being told him to run. Nevertheless, he remained standing, facing the wolf, unmoving.

Zircon eventually reached up with this right hand and pointed to the skeleton city, its remains visible in the hazy distance. The Emperor Wolf shook its head as if to say no and looked in the direction from hence the men had come. Zircon pointed towards the ancient city again. He noticed how gaunt the wolves looked. He had noticed that in the assassin wolf as well when he had inspected the body. They needed food! This both made Zircon nervous and at the same time led him to think of this as an opportunity.

The Emperor Wolf picked up its right paw and put it down three times, looking directly at Zircon. Then the wolf looked towards the city and picked up its paw one more time.

Once more, Zircon and the Emperor Wolf stood looking, staring at each other, unblinking, for a long second. The wolf's ears and tail remained up. A grin almost seemed to be on the Great Wolf's face. Then it came to Zircon. The Wolf demanded a tribute for them to gain access to the city. The wolves needed food.

Zircon slowly turned his body away from the wolf and motioned to the wagons for somebody to approach. Zircon held up one finger on his right hand and the left hand he held palm out. A single man was to approach, unarmed. The men inside the wagon fortress looked around at each other for several minutes before a Jall stepped forward from the wagons, approaching Zircon and the Emperor Wolf, his hands open and outreached before him. When he reached them, Zircon instructed him, "Take half of the meat supply, cooked and uncooked, and have it brought here," he ordered the man.

"What?" the Jall responded, bewildered by the request. Unnerved enough by the giant wolf's presence, and now this, what seemed to him a crazy request. 'Who was this Zircon to give away their food supply,' he thought.

"It seems a tribute is demanded for us to continue," Zircon quickly responded.

"A tribute!"

"Yes and we must hurry. Whatever happens next no weapons must be fired or burnished. Or we are all dead. Have the soldiers put all of their weapons in the wagons," Zircon firmly ordered.

"But we'd be left helpless."

"Even with them we would stand no chance if the wolves were to attack us. Look at the hills around us. There must be a thousand of these wolves, all hungry. But it seems a treaty has been reached. We must act quickly to do our part and show our value to the wolves." As Zircon said these words to the bewildered Jall he thought back upon his growth this last year since the mutiny he had so gleefully taken part in and the events that had transpired since he had reached this land. A year ago, he would never have given that order. He would not have understood the opportunity presented before them. A year ago, he would have gladly led them all to their deaths, taken as many of the wolves with them as possible, and enjoyed it. A wry smile crossed his face and the Emperor Wolf noticed it and seemed to smile back.

The Jall hurried back to the wagons to pass on Zircon's orders, happy to be clear of the presence of the Emperor Wolf and his lieutenants. He saw Zircon stand there next to the Great Wolf, his body half turned away, and marveled at the man's bravery. After a brief hesitation, the men of the caravan, seeing Zircon standing there alone among the wolves, began righting the wagons, restocking the goods that had fallen out and piling their weapons onto one of them. As Gar had understood, Zircon was a man these people would trust and follow implicitly. After the job of righting the wagons was finished, the oxen were reattached, and the men transferred half of their meat to one wagon and began to move it off the way and up the rise where the Emperor Wolf stood on next to Zircon.

As this was happening, Zircon sat down on the hillside and watched the activity. 'Had he gauged the action of the wolf appropriately,' Zircon thought to himself. The men here were at the mercy of the wolves at any event. The Emperor Wolf moved along side of Zircon and stretched out its immense length. Trust was established. Two of the Emperor Wolf's lieutenants themselves lay down, ears up, alert, on either side of Zircon and the Emperor Wolf. It seemed that the giant wolf had offered his protection to Zircon. 'Did that extend to the rest of the caravan?' Zircon thought.

Understanding what had transpired somehow between the two, man and wolf, Zircon placed his hand on the shoulder of the giant wolf and rubbed it gently. He could feel the bone beneath the loose skin. The food was the key. This wolf clan was tremendously undernourished and it seemed the Emperor Wolf was no better off than the others. The wolves on either side looked at Zircon with seeming approval. The Emperor Wolf turned its great head; twice the size of Zircon's own head, to face the man and Zircon felt the Emperor Wolf's soft tongue brush across his face. A deal struck, an alliance made and it seemed a friendship sealed. The two, man and wolf, now friends, waited together until the wagon arrived.

Two Jall drove the wagon halfway up the hill. The oxen would go no further. The Emperor Wolf seemed to nod to Zircon that that was far enough. As Zircon stood to walk to the wagon and help unload it before returning to the caravan, the Emperor Wolf stood as well. A friendship formed. The giant wolf returned to the crest of the hill to wait with the other wolves for the men to empty the wagon. As the now unloaded empty wagon returned to the other wagons of the expedition, now all fully loaded with the men and their remaining supplies, the wolves moved to the delivered meat and began to eat their fill, before returning themselves to the skeleton city. Only the Emperor Wolf remained in place, sitting tall on his haunches, surveying the scene before him. He would eat only after his troop had had their share. Moreover, the wolves brought back any extra meat to the city with them.

The way to the city cleared for the men as the wolves parted before the wagons.

"Everybody rides on foot or in the wagons. Tie the horses off to the back of the wagons as well," Zircon ordered the men who now quickly responded when he spoke. Now on horseback once more, Zircon saw several of The Holds warriors go to retrieve their weapons from the wagon where they had been stored. He quickly rode up to the men and loudly ordered them to stop where they were. "We go weaponless from here until the time we reach this point on our return from the skeleton city."

"But we'll have no protection," one of The Hold's warriors objected.

"That is all of the protection we need," Zircon said as he pointed to the wolves traveling towards the city as well on either side of the way.

"We'll stop just before we enter the city for more instructions," Zircon instructed the men as he rode along side of them. Zircon was the only man on horseback as all of the others rode in the wagons to reach the city more quickly. Zircon rode to the front of the wagons and led the way to the skeleton city, escorted by the wolves on the ridgeline on either side of the way. 'What new order of things had they found in this skeleton city,' Zircon thought to himself.

The caravan slowly made its passage along the way to the skeleton city escorted by the wolves on either side. The number of wolves escorting them seemed to have dwindled, but there were still hundreds. For their protection? From what? Zircon had his ideas on this having seen the battlefield but kept them to himself.

Where the fallen remains of the Skelton city seemed to begin, the Emperor Wolf appeared again in front of them with several of his lieutenants. "What is this now?" Zircon scowled as he rode up to meet them. Zircon dismounted from his horse, letting the reigns fall, and walking the short distance to where the Emperor Wolf stood. Zircon briefly looked back to where he had left his long-rifle in its saddle holster and saw his horse, free of control, just standing proud and brave among the wolves. No fear did the horse show in its eyes or manner. He understood now very well how extraordinary his horse was. Strong, fast, brave and now Zircon's companion in what was to come, in peace or war.

The Emperor Wolf did not move as Zircon approached. There seemed to be no malice in the Wolf's eyes whose ears and tail remained up while the fur on his back remained down. A misunderstanding (on whose part?) it seemed.

Zircon pointed to the wagons and then the city. The Emperor Wolf did not move. 'What could it be?' Zircon thought, 'What had I misunderstood?' Zircon found a piece of the metal that they had come to find a few steps away. The piece was about two feet long and Zircon picked it up, carried it to the first wagon and placed it inside. Then he walked back to the Emperor Wolf who had never taken his eyes off him.

As Zircon faced the Emperor Wolf again, just a few paces apart, the wolf looked to one of its lieutenants and then back at Zircon. Zircon could feel the tenseness in the eyes of the men of The Hold and the Jall in the wagons behind him. A wolf walked to one side, picked up another chunk of metal, placed it at Zircon's feet and then returned to his position by the Emperor. The giant wolf then repeated what it had done on the hillside, patting the ground three times with its immense paw.

Looking at the gaunt features of the wolves around them, especially their leader (had it even eaten the food the men had delivered earlier?) Zircon knew the food was the key. In Zircon's mind, a completely new level of understanding arose. These wolves were in dire need of food. The first payment had just been for passage to the city. A new payment was expected for the trade. The question was, how much would the wolves demand in trade for the metal?

Zircon got back on his horse, which had never moved nor quivered in the slightest among the wolves, and rode back to the Caravan to speak to the Jall. This was their business, trade, not his. He had gotten them here, now it was their job.

Zircon called the leader of the Jall over to him as he rode up to the first wagon. "This is where we stand," he told the Jall. "The first payment was the road toll to get here. Now more meat is expected in trade for the metal."

"Trade with wolves, this is madness. We have nothing more to give them," the Jall said briskly back to Zircon.

"We have the remaining food."

"Then what do we eat on the return?"

"We hunt. You're the trader," an exasperated Zircon said. "See how much they want for how much metal."

"How do I communicate with a wolf?"

"You communicate with your gators. You should be able to think of something."

"Communication with the gators was a gift of the Teachers when they created us."

"Well take that gift, combine it with your trading knowledge of dealing with other cultures and figure this out. I got us this far but the danger isn't over."

The leader of the Jall called the rest of the Jall over to him and they talked animated with each other for twenty minutes. The Emperor Wolf now sat facing them at the entrance to the city, blocking their entrance by his mere presence. Only a few wolves remained around the caravan. Most had left for other duties. 'At least the wolves no longer consider us a threat,' thought Zircon, back on his horse.

Finally, the traders decided that the wealth of the trade here was worth any short-term hunger or discomfort. Moreover, if a trading partner (no matter how novel the partner) was found at this Skelton city, the trading glory that would come to these Jall would be immeasurable. A new banner would be raise in the city to them and a new trading clan would be born.

Each of the Jall gathered what food he could carry and brought it to lie in front of the Emperor Wolf and his party. The Emperor looked at the offering and then at his lieutenants. They then walked up to the first three wagons and the last three and stood between them. The meaning was clear. That was enough food for just the first three wagons worth of metal in trade. The Jall walked back to the wagons and brought more food. Two more wagons would be allowed to pass into the city. The last would remain there until it was time to leave. With the trade agreement, accomplished to the marvel of the Jall, the expedition moved forward into the city.

The forth wagon in the row had carried the expeditions weapons. As it reached the cities boundary, the Emperors lieutenants stopped it by standing in front. They growled at the wagon and the meaning was clear. This wagon would stay behind. The Jall quickly brought up the last wagon and loaded whatever they could into the wagon that would stay outside the city. The warriors of The Hold voiced their displeasure through their disgruntled objections to going weaponless in the city. Zircon silenced them with a single look, symbolically leaving his own long-rifle as well. If Zircon could go weaponless so could the soldiers of The Hold.

The five wagons entered the city carrying all of the members of the trading expedition except Zircon who continued to ride his horse in the front. The oxen and the horses tied to the wagons were all skittish with the strong scent of the wolves permeating the air and the Jall had to concentrate on handling the wagons; the fear of the wolves was strong. It seemed that Zircon's own horse, riding in front of and alongside the other animals with Zircon in the saddle, did much to calm the animals as they entered the city. As Zircon rode his horse past each wagon in turn, the livestock seemed calmed by the presence of Friend and became manageable. The value of this horse grew in Zircon's mind, 'What a gift they have given me.' Zircon reached forward, patting his steed's neck. The horse looked back at Zircon as if to say 'thank-you.'

The men would have a lot of work to do to fill the five wagons with all the metal the wagons could carry. Trade had begun and terms reached for trade in the future, one wagon of food for a wagon of metal. The Jall were ecstatic.

The wagons entered the city with the men riding inside them. As they passed through the entrance of the city it seemed almost set up as a fortress without a gate. Dozens of wolves were patrolling the entrance. A small escort of wolves remained with the caravan. While there seemed to be trust between the two disparate groups, man and canine, it seemed little understood by either group. Four wolves walked alongside Zircon and his horse leading the way for the men to where they could mine the metal they seeked.

Not far into the entrance of the city a disgusting, to the men, site greeted the caravan. The men smelled it before it came into view. Off to one side, in a small, open enclosure, dozens of dead animals lay on the ground, including more than a few of the bear from the battlefield. That answered Zircons question on why there had appeared so few bear at the battle. As the men watched, several of the wolves dragged another large bear into the enclosure along with some of the meat from the caravan. Payment for the trade was beginning to arrive. Wolves were working in the enclosure, tearing the carcasses into smaller pieces. Other wolves, primarily female, then collected the food with their jaws to distribute it further into the city. This was a primitive system to the men, but for the wolves, this was a huge step in their development.

Even Zircon's horse seemed skittish as they passed by the food dispensary of the wolves. They kept the oxen under close reign as the hungry wolves in the enclosure looked on at them with hunger and desire. The escort wolves snipped at one that tried to approach the caravan, herding it back to the enclosure.

"There is a hierarchy here,' thought Zircon as he kept a close reign on his own horse that was very uncomfortable near this food pen. It seemed their escort was as much for their safety as that of the wolves. They saw more of the gaunt wolves patrolling the streets. Food was needed here in great supply, and quickly, before this new trade agreement could unravel.

Zircon rode up to the wagon where the riders from the Southern Valley were riding. He motioned to one of the riders. "Gather your horse and ride as quickly as possible to The Hold or the Jall City, whichever is closer. Food must be brought here quickly or all that we have gained will be lost."

It took no encouragement for the rider to leave. He rode his own horse back out of the city as quickly as possible, stopping only briefly to regain his weapon under the watchful eyes of the wolves. The Hold was a hard three-day ride away. Moreover, he had seen himself the hunger in the wolves' eyes.

A little further into the city and the men saw the first pups proving their dominance and submission in the hierarchy of canines, playing in an old orchard. The pups both played with and ate the fruit on the ground, all of this done under the watchful eyes of the packs matriarchs.

Zircon got down off his horse and walked over to the *play area*. Two of his guides came with him and the matriarchs eyes never left him. Zircon reached down and gathered some of the fruit. "Apples," he said aloud to no one in particular. One of the pups, a more adventuresome one, came up to Zircon and sat before him as if to say, "Who are you and what are you doing in my kingdom?" The pup's ears were up and there was no growl. Just several chirp like barks. In addition, a look; a look Zircon had seen in the Emperor Wolf's eyes. Zircon took one of the apples and threw it a short distance away. The pup chased it down, taking a bite, before bringing it back to Zircon. Zircon sat down, the large pup climbed onto his lap and the two wrestled briefly.

The caravan had stopped and the men aboard the wagons looked at Zircon like he was mad. There was work to be done and this man, Zircon, was playing with a wolf–pup as if he was his pet back home.

Another stage of friendship reached between Zircon and the wolves. Finally, one of Zircon's escort wolves nudged his back with his nose. 'It was time to move on,' Zircon understood the wolf to say. The wolf's thoughts seemed clear in his mind, was that possible?

Zircon stood and threw an apple again for the pup to chase. This time one of the matriarchs intercepted the pup before he could return to Zircon. The wolf-pup sat down, watched Zircon first give an apple to his horse, and then climb onto the saddle. "Good apples, "said Zircon to Friend as they each ate their apple.

Under the lead of their wolf guides, the men of the caravan traveled deeper into the skeleton city. 'Where are they leading us,' thought Zircon. The men had all assumed they would be doing their mining near the cities edge. They passed a large briar of wildberries, bluish-black, that grew in clusters. As the men passed they looked on at the site before them, once again amazed at the behavior of the wolves of this city. As wolves, young and old, male and female, passed by the berries they would stop and carefully, lips pulled back, with their front teeth they picked only the plump ripe berries and ate them. The green and still reddish berries they left alone. The wolves seemed to chew and savor the flavor of the berries. They would only pick a few before moving on with their day, leaving more ripe berries behind for others to enjoy.

A short distance beyond the briar patch, well away from any of the wolves' activities, the caravan, still led by the wolves, turned a corner and came to a stop. A large rich mound of collapsed steel structures lay before them. The wolves then turned and left. Trust now seemed complete. But in the distance wolves wandered by just in view. There was no doubt that they were still being watched.

In the two thousand years since the 'Great War' all of the cities of the 'old' time had collapsed into ruin. Some destroyed in molten and ashen heaps, only now safe to visit, others just weathered by time. This last group, scattered throughout these lands, were the skeleton cities, mined for the metal by the people of this land. Few of the ancient spires stood more than fifty or sixty feet in the air. Most were just piles of rubble, colored red by the rust of age. The pile that the wolves led them to was one of these, not destroyed by war, but by time. Huge pieces of metal, larger than a man, remained intact. Even the metal dust, as red as blood, was valuable and would be quick to load as well. In this one deposit here, there was enough metal to support a hundred such trading missions. As the Jall gazed over the heap of rusted metal, they smiled. They knew how important it would be to solidify this trade agreement. No more searching for mineral wealth, there were more riches here than even the Jall-King could imagine.

'And if this city could be taken from the wolves,' the men of The Hold were thinking.

The men clambered out of their wagons and went to work. The Jall walked around, through, and over the mound of collapsed metal, picking up small pieces as they walked. These men knew metal and looked for specific items. They loaded these carefully selected items on the first wagon and continued with their search.

The men from the hold on the other hand took out shovels, pry bars, and just started filling the other wagons as quickly as possible with whatever was closest. This was as rich a pile of metal as any of these men had seen in their travels searching for it and the work went quickly. The second wagon had been filled by the men of The Hold and they were starting to fill the third when something solid was struck. A scholar from the library was with them, sent by Gar on the expedition to aide Zircon, and he came running over to the site. As the scholar ran to where the men were working, he called for Zircon to follow him there as well. It seems Gar had been right in his hunch.

* * * * *

Like with the need for Zircon of this trip, Gar had had a vague feeling that something of great value that had been lost to time was about to be found. It was something from the beginning of the Order of the Sage, something of importance, forgotten in the thousand years of the Order. He needed a scholar who could keep a secret to accompany Zircon and Gar knew just the man. Over a cup of *presso* at the bar that held the secret opening to The Holds library the two men had discussed what might be found.

"Are you sure, Gar?" the student asked the Sage.

"It's very hazy, over eight hundred years ago and only mentioned in passing by the Teachers," Gar replied to the Scholar, looking him in the eye, studying the young man. He had grown to know him well, but even still, this was beyond what most Scholars would know.

"And that's the need for Zircon on this expedition as well?"

"Yes," Gar answered, "he will have a natural affinity for the Wolf Clan."

"Does he know what lies in front of him?" asked the young Scholar.

"No, I just mentioned a vague recollection to him. It is best for what is to come that he encounters the Wolf Clan on his own, without pre-judgments."

"And I am to accompany him?"

"If the hints of recollection are true, it's very important that the

Sage have eyes there. Eyes we can trust," spoke Gar, with a strong measure of discomfort. The timing of all of this was bad, just bad; it should be him going with Zircon, not this young Scholar. "I wish I could remember more."

"And the wooden piece that you gave Zircon, to wear around his neck..."

"I remember even less of that; it was given to me by one of the Teachers. Petrified wood, it will hold its shape to the end of time."

"An unusual shape."

Gar finished as he got up to leave. "You'll travel separately to the Jall City and meet the expedition there as it leaves. Give this note to Zircon and he will recognize you as my eyes. If something is found there I am depending on the two of you and your discretion."

* * * * *

The Scholar hurried to the worksite with Zircon joining him there from the other side of the mound. Not all of the ancient building was gone. Safe, intact, under the rubble, was a large metal door, rusted through but what lay beyond it seemed untouched. Vague writing from before could be seen on the door, but it was too weathered to read. What was unmistakable to the Scholar was the sign, a more recent addition to the door; the mark of the Teachers. Gar had been right in his suppositions.

Zircon took over at this point. "You with the pry-bars get this door open," he called to the workers from The Hold. The men went to work with renewed vigor. Here was something unexpectedly found, another treasure to share. More wealth in each man's pocket they thought as they attacked the door with their tools. As rusted as it was, it didn't take long for the first holes to appear in the door by its hinges and lock. Zircon brought his lantern up to one of the larger holes the men had made and tried to look through. What was inside remained hidden to his eyes.

"The hinges," The Holds leader of the expedition called out to the workers, "Break down the hinges."

"Try to keep the door in one piece," the young scholar called out, "I want to take that back with me."

Two of the strongest of The Holds men put their combined strength onto the rusted out hinges of the door with their pry-bars. The doors weakest spot, it didn't take long to break open. Several of the other men then tied rope onto whatever part of the door they could. A dozen of the men pulled on the door with the rope, and after several minutes of struggle, they removed the door, mostly intact, from the passage it has been hiding and protecting. The Jall quietly loaded the door onto the first wagon while the expedition waited to see what they had found.

Zircon stepped to the exposed entrance and called the Scholar to him. The others he ordered to wait at the base of the mound. They walked through the entrance with the door removed and found a short hall covered in bright ceramic tile, mostly in place. The floor was dusty but free of debris. The metal outer door had done its job. Outer door? The short hallway led to another door, unweathered, of a material with which neither Zircon nor the Scholar was familiar with. Zircon walked back to the entrance, called the closest Jall over to him, and then took him to the door.

"Are you familiar with the material of this door?"

The Jall looked at the door in wonderment. Never had he seen a material like this in the dozen or so expeditions in search of metal he had joined. Should he tell Zircon, the Jall thought to himself. He might as well; the Scholar was here as well. He looked at the door with scrutiny before answering. It was unpitted, unblemished by time, not really shiny nor polished.

Not dull either. In the middle of the door there was a symbol with which he was unfamiliar. Below that appeared to be a keyhole.

"No, Zircon, I don't think that any of the Jall is familiar with this material. I'm not even sure if it is metal or what it is."

"Pass word onto the expedition. Finish loading the wagons quickly. We leave in the morning," Zircon ordered the Jall, who then left the two to hurry the expedition. The loading was already going quickly; there was so much easy material to mine here. This gave the leader of The Hold on the expedition a chance to enter the short hall. He saw the door and thought to himself; 'More complications, but it proves that this city is too valuable to leave to a bunch of wolves.' The man approached Zircon to give pretense to this being the reason he had entered the hall and approached the door. "We'll have the wagons filled by nightfall."

"Nice work," answered Zircon as he continued to study the door with the young Scholar. "Tell the men that tonight we feast on what food remains. We will hunt for food on the way back. That will leave more room in the wagons for the metal."

After the man left, Zircon approached even closer to the door. He used the light that he carried and with the scholar looked over every inch of the door.

"Is this what I suspect?" Zircon asked the Scholar as he looked at the symbol on the door.

"It is the sign of the Teachers," the scholar replied to Zircon, wondering how much he should tell. The scholar decided he would only answer Zircon's direct questions and not volunteer any information. Gar could tell Zircon what he wished later when they returned.

"And look at this keyhole, below the sign, its shape matches the shard that Gar gave me."

"It seems that you now possess the key to what lays behinds the door, in a literal sense. A secret the Teachers left behind for us to find."

"This is not the time to open this secret," Zircon stated to the obvious relief of the Scholar. Zircon surprised himself when he made that statement. The old Zircon would have rushed blindly into the opening of the door.

"This is for another trip of the Sage," the Scholar answered.

"We must keep secret what we know here until we meet up again with Gar," Zircon stated to the Scholar.

"Agreed," answered the Scholar with more than a little relief. He had expected Zircon to ask more questions. The old Zircon would have.

Only one more thing of note occurred in the skeleton city of the wolves. Almost whimsical compared to what else had happened on that important trip. The next morning, as the men prepared to break camp and while they were cleaning up the remains of their feast from the night before, thousands of pigeons came swarming over the mess, grabbing any food remains or waste that lay about the men. At first the men thought that these were some kind of daytime bat, there were so many. The men ducked for what cover that they could find; under the wagons, or into the pit that they had dug into the mound. Fortunately, the horse and oxen were still tethered. Then it was over; the pigeons gone and not a spec of food or waste remained behind. The laughing among the men continued for a good long time until they finally finished the job of harnessing the oxen to the wagons and beginning the trip to the Jall City.

Chapter 2
Assassin in the Dark

A solitary figure walked through the silent street in the early morning mist. He kept his large hat low over his face, not so much because of the chill of the early spring air as wanting the concealment of his still forming face. It had been almost four months since he had been reborn. His vision remained poor, though it was improving and unlike other Myk, his vision was at its best after dark.

Four months, the time had passed so quickly in the hidden lair of the Myk far to the Northeast of Twror. He remembered clearly his rebirth. He had returned from his diplomatic trip to the Castle Nourne, to try to gain a peace so that the White could once again grow in strength. He had returned to the Myk's Palace a failure. Nourne had turned its back on its children. On his return Kat had expected anything but what transpired. Called to the side of the Myk after his failure, Kat had watched as two of the Myk's guards approached on either side, swords drawn. Such was the consequences of failure among the White; executed and added to the food chain. He saw and he felt as the swords cleanly removed his head from his shoulders. However, he did not fall. Rising through the opening from beneath his shoulders was his second head, primitive, still forming and waiting awakening.

Rebirth!

Four months he spent in hiding in the cavern, gaining strength as the head grew and formed. He was often at the side of the Myk. First his teeth came back; still feline Kat was happy to see. Then his ears returned; able to pick up the slightest sound in the cavern. Last to fully form were his eyes and in his blindness Kat's mind had the opportunity to remember all that had come before. What he remembered the most was the betrayal of Castle Nourne.

A new talent arose as well. With all of the myk's thoughts interconnected, Kat learned how he could shield his thoughts from even the Myk without the other knowing. The Myk, whose cowardly actions to flee the battle brought about the fall of the White. Whose every weakness enabled those around him to gain influence over the matters of the White's return to greatness. That would never happen as long as the Myk remained. A strong voice; needed to guide the White to a victorious future. Moreover, that Myk was not that leader, who could be the voice of a new, stronger, all conquering White. Nor could this Myk's counsel remain. A rule by one Myk, the strongest of the myk, and all would follow that strength.

Such were the hidden thoughts of Kat.

The village of the White, this Twror as the invaders called it, was more crowded than he remembered it. No longer a village at the crossing of two dirt roads, it was now a large town, seeming set to grow into a small bustling city. So many here were not of the White. Someday, in a not so distant future, that would change. A bitter smile crossed Kat's still forming lips. He treasured his now fully formed feline teeth. He had thought them lost with his first primitive head.

Because of the daytime crowds, he preferred to do his scouting at night. He would sleep during the day. Kat was forced to use his bedding to try to stifle all of the outside noise from all of the construction going on in this town. His hearing during the day was proving to be a disadvantage. New marvels were arising throughout this town, rising daily from the muddy plains. The noise; how could they stand it? Kat formed earplugs from the wax of a honeycomb he purchased. The honey was like an elixir to his tired hungry body, the wax a godsend to his tormented hearing. He could remove the wax at night when he needed his hearing, but with it during the day, at least he could rest.

He was not alone in the night with his strolls through the village. There were many walking the streets at night conducting business, legitimate or not. Patrolling the city were the damn wildcats! It was, however, enough to render him invisible to those who might be watching for someone like him.

His feet were sore from the confines of the boots he was forced to wear. However, if he removed them it would give away who he was to too many. They wouldn't recognize his new head, but he feared discovery nonetheless. He had this new assignment from the Myk. He had done his best to place the thought in the Myk's mind without the Myk's awareness of it.

Once again, he was in the land of those that had defeated the Myk and conquered the White. This would probably be his last trip to the land of the humans and his new head was craving any knowledge it could gain of these enemies of the White. He would need it when he overthrew the Myk. Then, in the near future, he would need it as he led the myk in the redemption of the White and the conquering of all their enemies. Kat's thoughts were bitter and he tried to control them. Such thoughts would not be helpful on this mission. He himself had been a child of Nourne. Though his bitter thoughts did not make him stronger, he briefly let them dwell in his closely controlled brain. The humans of Castle Nourne had turned their collective backs on their children, the White, in their time of greatest need. Now they would pay the price for that treachery. Like a cat, he would stalk his prey. Soon all of Nourne and the Two Valley's would mourn their loss.

The small White settlement had changed to beyond his recognition since Kat had had his own primitive abode here; a small hut to rest and breed his mate. Moreover, the humans, where had all of the humans come from? Kat had already been through several close encounters with the wildcats that freely wandered the streets of the village; they should all be hunted down. He had one wildcat come right up to him and smell him. Incensed Kat had almost torn off his boots and shown this juvenile wildcat what he possessed. He had wisely withdrawn the idea. He was under orders of the Myk and the now collective leadership of the reborn White. Orders that Kat had so easily placed in their thoughts. The Myk's death would come soon enough with completion of this task. Collective leadership? The White needed one strong hand and they would grow powerful again. Kat, cousin of the first Myk, would leave this revival.

* * * * *

When he had left the cavern that was now the home of the Myk, their big debate was not the restoration of the White, but a philosophical one. When a myk died would it be reborn once again and if so, as what? Was their even a higher order than the Myk? Kat would try to bring up the topic of the restoration of their lands and the others would motion him away.

The myk were debating the subject of rebirth when he headed south under their orders, debating it between their spells of coughing attacks that plagued the Myk. "Just an effect of so many reborn heads," they told him.

* * * * *

Kat turned down a small side street in his wanderings. It was important to him that he know the entire new layout of Twror before it was time for his assignment. What chance he had to escape was dependent on that. What happened to the agents he would hire mattered little, if at all. The streets were paved with flat stones quarried from the mountains to the south of the Hold. What need had the White had of paved roads? New construction was going up on either side of this street. At the end of this block was a large new dwelling place, mostly finished, that would be the home of the installed governor of these stolen lands. With the governor will live his soon-to-be-bride, Theresa of Nourne. Another weakness of these humans, females were for breeding stock and then when passed the age to litter, to be added to the food chain. That was all.

The street ended at a streetlight, something new brought by those accursed Sages. What need was there for light during the night. That was the time of rest and healing. They made his movements more visible. He must remain hidden, undiscovered, until it was time, and even thereafter if possible. There could be no sign that Kat had visited this now human town of Twror. His new intellect would make sure of that. Kat's mental cloud would continue to block the minds of the Sage. The fault would lie solely with the Myk and the Myk would be delivered to Nourne.

Ah, the beauty of his plan.

Where would he find his agents? They must be of the White, preferably in the pre-Myk stage with a forming, but yet with an unconscious second head. There were still places.

Kat turned down a muddy side street, not yet paved with the stone. He longed to take his boots off and release his feet. On either side of the old village street, more an alley, were old taverns and eating-places dating back to when this village was still the center of the White's lands. Kat knew of one that still welcomed the old ways of the White. He hoped to find his needed agents there. In a backroom, there they would serve him the meat he craved most; human, fresh and raw. He was told of another before he left the North, but upon arrival in Twror he had learned that the wildcats had found it and the Holy Place was burned to the ground.

Now just one Holy Place remained. A last refuge, catering to the old ways in the White, hidden behind burning incense, spices and the fresh roasted meat of the lesser species, meant for human consumption. This combination of smells seemed to confuse the wildcats. The aroma made his entry uncomfortable, but his cravings he could control for now.

Myk's advisors warned Kat to stay clear of any place associated with the White of old. However, Kat's mind, already stronger than any of the Myk, told him he would be safe if careful. Moreover, he had to find his agents, soon.

Kat entered the brightness of the eatery and the first thing he noticed was a Nomad with his wildcat sitting in the corner. These wildcats always made Kat uneasy. To enter the secret room he would have to walk past them. Kat's growing mind recognized the danger immediately. 'Walk on by them,' it told him. Kat took a seat in another corner of the room, away from the establishments lighting and ordered bread and ale. Not satisfying but it would help him blend in. He kept his large hat over his head. Even this tended to help him fit in as the Northern Valley, the Myk's stolen property, was overrun with foreigners, many of whom wore headwear of their own. The shadows in the corners told Kat that he was not alone in not wanting to be seen in these chaotic days.

Shortly after they served Kat his loaf and ale, several more of the Nomads and their wildcats entered the eatery. Along with them entered several soldiers of Nourne. Kat recognized one of them from his visit to the Castle Nourne. This was an advantage of his new second head. Not only would they not recognize Kat's face, he could now recall any face or event in his memory in an instant. There were still some blank spaces but they were filling in as his new brain and head finished their development. Already mentally stronger than any myk, Kat momentarily thought about how strong he would become. Even now, he could affect the Sage. A dangerous thought that he quickly pushed to the back of his mind.

Was he discovered? Recognized for who he was? That was Kat's first thought and he sat back further into the shadow of the corner and watched. As he watched, the soldiers congregated at the back rooms door. He felt some relief. He wasn't the one they were after. The back room was discovered. Kat thanked Hydron that he had not arrived earlier and been caught in the trap. Could he warn them? This was the last hold of the Myk, their last Holy Place in the Valley, in the occupied lands and was important to their plans. There was some slight telepathic communications between even the weaker of the second heads, but he recognized none in the back room that he could reach. He looked at the two White behind the bar. One would soon be of the myk, his second head almost fully developed, out of sight, above his right arm. They were terrified. But Kat could do nothing for them. As important as this place was, Kat decided his best course was to watch and wait. His assignment was too important.

The two soldiers of Nourne left, to cover the back door Kat assumed. That was good at least, no one left inside that might recognize him. The Nomads moved to block the front door. They allowed no more entry into the Holy place. If there was a White who followed the old ways in the eatery, it mattered not to the Nomads. Let them see the consequences of the actions of those that still did.

With the outer room under their control, the Nomads heard a whistle from the outside at the back of the eatery. The signal the backdoor was closed and sealed. With that, the three wildcats got up from where they had been laying, stretched and made their way to stand by the door to the secret (no longer) room. The two White at the bar, the proprietors, could only watch in their horror at what was about to transpire. They were as guilty as those in the backroom were. They arranged the kidnappings of those humans who would become food source to the White. They practiced the old ways as they served in secret the fresh human flesh to the others of the Old Way.

Kat could only watch what was transpiring in his own agony and terror. To do anything now would be to reveal his identity. He could easily kill all of the Nomads and their wildcats inside this place. To what avail? All would be tracked down again and he, Kat, would be forced to flee. What he had planned was more important than any single White or myk he might save here.

Three of the Nomads drew their short swords (now as marshals of the town of Twror they carried the blades as a symbol of their rank) and approached the proprietors. One fell to his knees, pleading (the coward!) while the other stood tall and defiant, a true myk. As he stood, he tore off his tunic, his primitive second head now exposed, a proud myk! As yet to young to communicate. It mattered not. He raised his weapon and they knocked it from his hand. They escorted the two White to the door of the secret back room and threw them in. As the Myk fell into the back room its second head opened its eyes and flashing recognition of Kat, seemed to plead, 'Why are you not helping us? Why do you do nothing here?'

With the door closed tight behind them Kat could more than imagine the panic of those trapped inside. He began to feel the first plaintive cries of the still unborn second heads. How many of the White would die here? The humans accused the White of being the barbarians. He could hear the cries and pleading of many of the White inside the room, obviously not of the Myk.

The Nomads now came to each table and escorted the customers out. Kat was not the only of the White in the eatery escorted out. Many, traitors, had given up the Old Ways. Kat outwardly calm, inwardly in turmoil, stood and left when his turn came. He could not afford a close examination. The claws on his feet threatened to extend and tear through his heavy boots. His anger boiled at what was about to happen. He had to control the urges that he kept deep inside.

All of the White knew the penalty for indulging in human flesh; death at the claw and teeth of the wildcats. Nevertheless, the desire had remained strong in many, those of the myk and those still true to the Old Ways of the White.

With the room emptied, the rest of the action would be over quickly, in a manner of minutes. The wildcats would be the judge, jury and executioners. The fate of those in the back room sealed the moment their actions were discovered. These occupiers of the lands of the Myk, the home of the White, would pay dearly for this, Kat told himself.

Kat slowly wandered back to the rooming house where he

rented a room for his stay in Twror. With clarity his ears he could hear the screams of those torn to bits by the wildcats. Twelve, no fifteen of the White, he could hear each voice in its clarity. Then it was over. The wildcats didn't even feast on the remains. They left the building to clean themselves in a shallow pool brought for the occasion. The building burned to the ground after the food source, or at least what was left of it, was removed to be given a proper funeral. To 'cleanse and purify' they said.

"They will all pay for this, soon."

It was now daybreak and Kat walked past the center of the new city and its park. Already those accursed riders of the South were playing their sport with a ball and clubs from the backs of their camels that they were riding. 'The Shiaps, without them victory would have belonged to the Myk,' thought Kat. A small ball, hit by one of the players clubs, flew out of the park and towards Kat. Without thinking, Kat reached for the ball and crushed it as he caught it. He threw the deflated ball back at the camel riders in anger. 'Dumb' thought Kat as the Shiaps stopped play to look at him. It had become almost a joyful tradition for people walking by the park when the games were going on to throw the balls back into play. The people owed so much to the courage of the Shiaps. Kat hurried on to his temporary residence.

Tomorrow he would begin the search for the agents he would need. There were still spots where the myk might assemble. Two he would need, of the myk, with second heads almost fully developed. He would have to be more careful though. If the Shiaps reported what he had done and it reached Nourne, they would come looking for him.

Kat made it back to his room without further incident and lay down to rest during the rest of the daylight hours. He kicked off his boots and let his claw-like feet stretch to their full length. He even let his toenails extend, careful not to tear the bed coverings. Then he retracted them again before he fell asleep. He had a busy night ahead once the sun set with little time to complete his mission.

Chapter 3
Twror

After finishing the morning meal in his office, Gant, now Mayor of Twror, got up from his desk, stretched and looked out his window. It was in times like this, his quiet times, before the busy day began, that he most often thought about his wife, Mora. How she had been lost in the daylight, trying to find food for those hiding in the caverns beneath the Myk's Palace, captured by the White as food source for the Myk. He remembered the torment of knowing where they held her, but without the power to go and help.

Finally he, himself, was taken captive by the White, while searching for food for the caverns as she had been. They brought him to the pit where they held his wife, now food-source himself. However, she was gone, taken into the palace itself, to be the not-dead, not-living, food source of the Myk's closest advisors.

Then came the rescue by the men from across the sea. And always the thought of Mora was on his mind.

The taking of the Myk's Palace and the walk of the damned, as the not-living walked, crawled and carried each other from the darkness of the Castles holds to the sunlight of the courtyard.

Gant remembered the exaltation as he found what remained of his wife; the faint glimmer of recognition in her eyes before dying in his arms; then his madness of which he was slowly crawling upwards from.

Mora; his wife taken from him by the evil that was the White, or more properly, the Myk. He had to keep telling himself those White which remained in Twror were not responsible, sometimes an impossible task. He now lived for Mora's memory, to make something worthwhile from the evil that had come before.

It was still early, as Gant was wont to start his day. The quicker the cities business began to him the less waking time he had to dwell on the bitterness of the past.

Gant gazed out of his second floor office window where he could look out over all of the activity of the rapidly growing, now City of Twror. Almost nothing remained from the time of the Myk. Barely four months before, the Myk's army had been defeated and this village, which at that time carried no name, was liberated from the tyranny that was the Myk. Four months since the Palace fell with all of its horrible discoveries. Any normalcy to Gant was still a realm in the future. Gant swore a silent dedication to his wife and all of those killed by the madness of the Myk.

Gant's office was in a just finished section of the city. A park, dedicated to all who were arriving to make Twror a great city, was being built to dominate the center of the city. Government buildings and markets spread out from the center of the city. Moreover, not just out, but up. Scholars, architects from The Hold and its Library, were bringing new technologies and techniques into the building of this new City of Twror. No longer was it sufficient to just build wide, but with the population boom in the Northern Valley, to build up was just as important.

This was due in a large part to the actions of the Nomads and their companions the wildcats. It was expected that a few of the Nomads would remain in Twror. Very few thought Reed. It was now apparent to all that Twror would instead become the first city of the Nomad culture.

Reed, one of the Nomad leaders, saw the changes happening all around him in Twror and was both pleased and discouraged at the same time. While he was glad that, through their blood in the battle against the Myk, the Nomads had a place to call their own here, at the same time he saw the changes that were happening to the Nomad culture and that saddened him. His ancestors had kept them safe for the centuries, and now... Now Reed fought hard to preserve the Nomad way.

The Lady Ruth introduced Reed to Loren. She had seen a hole in his life the Reed refused to acknowledge. In a short visit with Loren of the R'mon's, Lady Ruth had seen the same thing.

Lady Ruth arranged a dinner in Twror. She invited Gant, Theresa, Wade, Reed and others. She arranged it for a time when Loren was visiting Twror and Lady Ruth made sure she came. Quietly she arranged a crisis among the White that would take all but Reed and Loren from the meal. While not apparent at first, it soon became clear, with Loren's frequent visits to Twror, that a connection between Reed and Loren was very real.

Gant looked out from his office window in the new city. It was the richness of the *Treasure of the Myk* that was making all of this possible. Everyday more people arrived to make this valley and Twror their home; most of them good, strong people. The damaged roads that the White and the Myk it their ignorance had left untouched were being repaired by the Jall. Already a new way was under construction to the south and castle Nourne to replace the old trails.

The Jall, in partnership with the traders of The Hold, had begun a new business; supplying the Northern Valley with its paving material for all of the road construction. They were removing entire sections, unused now, of the ancient pre-war ways and transporting the flat concrete sections in the building of the new way from Nourne to Twror and Erson, and then down to the City by the Lake. Already the section from Erson to Twror was completed and the connection to Castle Nourne was almost done. These new ways were speeding up both the trade south of the *Myk's Treasure* and new immigration. The next section to the city by the lake was now under construction as well.

Another offshoot of this incredible rate of growth in the northern Valley was the need for metal. Any metal, especially iron and steel, was needed to reinforce and build the structures beginning to rise into the sky in Twror and Erson. While the buildings of the Jall City and the Hold were fine there, with plenty of space for the large concrete structures, here in the Northern Valley space was already at a premium. Here what was needed, and it presented the opportunity, to bring back the building techniques of before the Great War. Tor started to bring students north from The Hold and its Library to introduce these new construction ideas. New factories were being built throughout the Two Valleys.

Gant tried to remain in control of the Myk's *Treasure*. A new 'gold rush' was taking place regarding the *Treasure of the Myk* and everybody wanted a piece of the action. Too often Gant was seeing The Hold Traders take advantage of the North. Now it was their turn.

He put the Nomad traders in charge of the *Myk's Treasure*. Not a party to any trade agreements, the Northern Valley was free to set its own trade terms. Moreover, the Nomads were shrewd traders. They estimated that Twror and the Northern Valley had over 100 years of the fertilizer to sell beyond its borders. Moreover, if the Nomads could squeeze another decade or two out of it, that would be so much the better. The profits went to all of the new construction in the North and its peoples. And the Jall and The Hold did not like it.

With this influx of new people and strange cultures came an increase in crime. Crime was almost unheard of under the White. Now the bad came with the good. Gant had barely taken office as mayor when large shipments of the *Myk's Treasure* started being stolen freely and in daylight by The Holds traders. The bounty of war they proclaimed as they blatantly stole the fertilizer. These 'trading' parties came well armed. The new confederation had proclaimed that this was the property of the Northern Valley to help in its rebuild. However, without enforcement, what good was the proclamation.

Reed ended that, assisted by a contingent of archers from the R'mon, along with the wildcats patrolling the streets and the passes to the remains of the old Myk's Palace. This brought crime and the illegal trade almost to a standstill. A few parties tried to engage in theft at night, very few.

Word had quickly spread to the neighboring regions of the Northern Valley and beyond. The almost empty Northern Valley would be a sanctuary to all, welcoming the new settlers in a place of refuge and safety, where all of the *lost souls* of the world could find a secure life and home. People were arriving from places never heard from before, even from the north, and with these came new whispers and stories of the Myk. Defeated but not gone, where were they now?

Gant called a meeting with Reed regarding the new arrivals. They had a lot to cover, from laying out the homesteads and farmlands for the new arrivals, to the security concerns of the North.

Before the meeting with Reed, Gant's assistant entered the room. Gant smelled the meal brought to him. Like so many of the Northern Valley, he craved the seafood that the Coastal Peoples brought in trade. He especially loved the large crab in their hard shells. Served with herbs found throughout the Northern Valley (A growing trade commodity for the North) he found the flavor beyond belief. He knew in his heart that Mora would have loved it as well. Eateries opened throughout the Northern Valley that featured chef's from the Coastal Peoples who worked to out-create their fellow chefs. The result was an outburst of flavors throughout the Northern Valley as ingredients from both regions combined to reach new levels.

The Coastal People were not yet a member of the confederation, however their close trade ties were drawing them closer every day.

In the meeting with Reed, farmland was marked out. Those who fought in the battle with the Myk received first claims to the land. The plots of land were quickly filled and new homes for the settlers built as quickly as possible. The Jall were in high demand with their building skills and the North couldn't get enough Jall Logs for building. Those who had been this lands *lost souls* were now the farmers and builders of this new land.

Entire forests were clear-cut to the north of the Valleys to meet this need for building materials. Questions arose as to what this would do to the land and a new policy was put in place where they planted a new tree for everyone cut down. A young scholar, working with a group of refugees from the east, established the first tree farm to fill this need.

The only thing that seemed to slow the growth of the Northern Valley was the winter storms, now clogging the passes to the north and the east.

The Northern Valley paid what seemed an exorbitant price for the building materials. The roads, ways and paths through the mountains were crowded throughout the winter with supplies and new settlers. Moreover, while The Hold and the Jall controlled the movement of the swamps logs and other building materials, the Northern Valley now controlled the more valuable of the commodities. The monopoly of The Hold and the Jall traders was broken and they did not like it.

New schools were going up, taught by both scholars from the Library and the followers of the "One True God'. There was a competition in thoughts and deeds in their teachings. It was important to Gant that the people of the Northern Valley be well educated. These new schools, combined with the Nomads idea that people were equipped to make their own decisions, led to an explosion of idea's in the Northern Valley. Already this was bringing some views into conflict in the disparate cultures of the refugees streaming to the Northern Valley. Gant worried about this new conflict of ideas.

The stories of the Nomads; the North Valley saw them put down in writing for the first time to the dismay of Reed, himself of no formal education. However, at the same time he saw that it was important that others know their stories as well. In addition, each person made their own choices. Reed understood that to process the raw materials brought to the Northern Valley new skills were needed. There was an abundance of workers that needed the skills and knowledge the Scholars brought forward.

Reed, and others of the Nomads, now saw a schism growing among the Nomads between their traditions and the new opportunities. More and more Nomads were attending the schools of the Scholars. He was starting to feel out of place in the meetings regarding the new cities and the Northern Valley. He alone of the leaders of this new land could not read the documents before him and had to have these read aloud.

In the park, Gant watched as Shiaps on camel played the ball game that they had brought with them from the South. It was growing in popularity among the people of the Northern Valley and there was talk of forming teams, something to help break from the desolation of the past. Gant thought back to the struggles to survive in the north during the time of the Myk. Just trying to survive had been the only motivation of the people then, so many had died. Now the heroes who had survived looked for new ways to share and enhance their lives. People walking past the park often stopped to watch, or at least half-watch, the riders as they struggled to hit the small ball into the netted goals on either side of the park. Often, as Gant watched, the ball would leave the glade-like field the riders used only to be thrown back into play by the spectators walking past. It now seemed part of the play and the Shiaps welcomed the interaction with the Twrorians.

Except now, as Gant watched, a passerby caught the ball and crushed it with one hand instead of throwing it back. Gant tried to study the distant figure as it hurried away. Who among Twror would have done such a thing? A fairly large hat had covered the head of this person and he wore a non-descript cloak. 'He would have to be watched for,' Gant thought. More turmoil wasn't needed in Twror right now, not with the preparations for the wedding of Wade and Theresa of Nourne scheduled for not even a month from this day in that very park he was watching.

Gant tried to get his thoughts engaged on the day's activities, but it kept drifting back to the long years in the caverns. So many had died, so much indifference from the South. The refugees of the Myk's wars were all heroes to Gant and now they just tried to find peace and a new life in this new chapter of Twror.

The first thought of many who had felt the direct wrath of the Myk's depravity had been reprisals against the White who remained. Even now these reprisals continued, though most now knew that even the White had suffered under the Myk's dominion. There was still so much hate, so much animosity towards the White. Even Gant still felt it at times. He had brought a family of the 'lost souls' who had found their way to Twror into his home. To learn from others who had felt such loss. Mora would have approved. Mora, thinking of her, brought tears came to Gant's eyes.

A knock at his office door interrupted Gant from his inner turmoil.

"Yes," asked Gant through the closed door, not yet ready to begin the day.

"A petitioner, your honor," his aide said from the other side of the door. "One from the followers of the 'One True God," he said as he opened the door a crack.

"Who are they, this early in the morning for a meeting," Gant stated, still wanting some more private time for his thoughts of Mora.

"A family of the White," the aide stated. "They were here when I arrived and they say it can't wait."

"The entire family?" (Unusual thought Gant, more mysteries to start the day.) "Give me a few minutes and bring them in. Did they give names?"

"Yes your honor, names given to them by the Lady Ruth; Jonah, Atarah and their three children, all normal."

'A complete White family, even more unusual,' Gant thought to himself.

"Five minutes and show them in yourself. And then stay. There might be something important here."

Five minutes to get his head together again; his memories of Mora would have to wait. "Someday, when things are settled in Twror, we'll be together once more," Gant said aloud to the empty room.

Gant washed his face of his tears in a basin of cold water.

Gant's aide showed the White family in. Jonah and Atarah stood by Gant's desk across from where he stood. The aide took the three children to sit on a sofa on one side.

"Quiet, children, we have things to discuss with these men," Atarah quietly ordered the children. They quietly sat still, without smiles, which the aide quickly noticed.

"Gant, may I take leave for a moment?" the aide asked as he motioned with his eyes to the children.

Gant had seen the sadness in the young children's eyes. "Be quick, I want you here."

Gant had stood when the White family had come in. He motioned for them to be seated as his aide left the room for his brief errand. As they all sat down the woman began. Even where the male had survived, it seemed the females were coming to dominate the White. A matriarchal society was forming and Gant had mixed feelings about that.

"I am Atarah and this is Jonah, my mate. We are considering getting married by one of the Priest of the *Followers*."

"A good thing," Gant answered, picking up a pen to make a note of this on a sheet of paper in front of him.

"Our children are normal, human. We plan that they should go to school."

"Another good thing," Gant responded, wondering where this conversation was going. "Would the two of you and your children like a drink?" Gant said as he reached for a pitcher of cold water and glasses.

"Children, are you thirsty?"

"No, mother," they answered in unison.

"I would," said Jonah, looking at his wife. 'Things are not as tranquil as they seem,' thought Gant.

At that point, Gant's aide re-entered the room with three large stuffed animals; wildcats, now almost sacred to the White for their protection of them. The children squealed, smiling finally, as the aide handed the toys to them.

Atarah objected to the gifts, standing up, "We cannot accept such things."

"Let the children have them," Jonah said, "The wildcats spared me in battle to let me come home to you, so few they spared. I saw many of the Myk's army torn to pieces by them. They seemed to know, just by looking at us, who among the army had no love for the Myk!"

"Your return was a gift from God for the children" the aide stated.

"Yes, God," said Jonah. "A thing within reach of us all," he finished, having become a convert of the Priest.

Atarah seemed shaken, but she continued with Gant once more.

"When the battle ended, before my mates return, I had a visitor. I had five children then, not three as you see now."

"Five? You seem well spoken as a White."

"I was schooled in Erson. It wasn't until late I was found to be a White."

"A late formed deformation?" asked Gant. He had seen such thing in the caverns, something that only appeared at puberty.

"No, hidden under my hair by my parents, a remedial ear. When discovered accidentally by our neighbors, they sent me north to live under the Myk, a horrible plight for any child. I was lucky to find Jonah."

"I was the lucky one," replied Jonah to her, holding her hand. "You have taught me so much." The love between them was apparent to Gant and reminded him once more of Mora.

"You said that you had a visitor and five children," Gant spoke, continuing the story, looking from Atarah to Jonah and back.

"Yes," said Atarah, looking both relieved and defiant. "I was ordered to tell no-one. Finally I told Jonah last week; I could keep the secret no longer."

Jonah now spoke, "The Myk visited my home as he fled north and took two of my sons, both of the myk, with him. Though young I am afraid both were already forming the double-heads."

"The Myk!" Both Gant and his Aide jumped to their feet on hearing this. "And you only now tell us?" Gant almost shouted at the now cowering White female. Jonah now stood as well, holding his wife and looking directly at Gant as he spoke.

"She was ordered by the Myk Himself. There could be no betrayal of such orders. Only now, through the graces of my new found God are we here."

Gant sat down, ashamed at his behavior. "I am sorry; I lost my wife to the Myk's madness. The Myk kept her as food for his depravity and she died in my arms when the Palace was taken."

Atarah now stepped forward around the desk to hold Gant's shaking hand. "You are forgiven by me and now I ask that you forgive me as well," she said to Gant in her quiet voice. Gant could only look at her, still shaking from his memories.

Jonah came around the desk and stood next to his soon to be wife.

"Tell him the rest."

"The Myk spoke these words to me when he left. 'You will see your sons again someday as a once again powerful Myk returns in strength to reclaim his lands.'

"'Where are you taking them?' I asked.

"'To a cavern in the North, dedicated to Hydron, our great and powerful God, others already wait for me there.'"

"And he left with our two oldest sons."

Gant sat down heavily, looking at the two beside him. This only confirmed the fears of those who had fought the Myk; he had survived and was growing strong again. "Do you know any more, either of you?"

Jonah now spoke as they moved back to the front of the desk, taking their seats. "There are many among the male White who consider themselves the *True White* and who look forward to the time when the Myk returns. Always it seems more second heads are appearing among my brothers of the White."

"Brothers?" questioned Gant, worried over the connotations.

"All male White were brothers under the Myk. Atarah had shown me how many of my beliefs were wrong," he said, holding her hand. Atarah smiled at Jonah as he spoke again, quietly giving him the strength to carry on. "It is said that those born with the second head can communicate with each other at distance without words. And that a myk, those who are reborn when the first head is removed, can sense the beginnings of the second head even in its earliest stage."

"And you, Jonah, do you have this second head?" asked Gant.

"Thanks to my new God, no. Only one in ten or so carries that infliction."

One in ten, that was far worse than they thought. The Sage had thought the deviation to be rare. That meant thousands of the second heads were in Twror at that moment, in their various stages of development. They had seen the tracks heading north and had thought that most had left over the winter. Gant now knew that this wasn't true. The Sage, Thorium, and Wade would have to be informed of this as quickly as possible.

"This is all more important than I think you realize. Do you know any more?"

Alarmed at Gants tone Atarah rushed to her children and gathered them in her arms. "Are we in danger? I have heard rumors that the Myk has sent a spy here to Twror."

"A spy, do you know who?" Gant's thoughts briefly flashed back to the lone individual who had crushed the ball by the park.

"Only that he has been reborn and was a personal advisor to the Myk."

Gant had heard enough. "Thank-you for this important information that you have brought me." He looked to his aide and the aide quickly escorted the White family from the room and the building, the children carrying their Wildcat toys. He returned to Gant's office to find the Mayor, head bent over his desk, cradled by both hands and his elbows on the desk in deep thought.

Gant looked up and called to the aide. "We have work to do and quickly. Get me Wade, Thorium, Reed, and any of the Sage that are available. Put that word out quickly. I need them all here by tomorrow, the next day at the latest."

The aide rushed out of the room to summon couriers to carry the request from Gant to all corners of the Valleys and the Lake.

Gant, and everybody else, knew that those who followed the *Old Ways* were still in Twror. It would take a long time to eradicate those who followed the Myk, especially those with strong craving for human flesh. Kidnapping had been common in the earliest stages of Twror and eateries that catered to the 'Old Ways', for a price, had been common. Only last night another burned to the ground, along with those responsible. The debate had continued over the barbarous nature of this law imposed by Reed, the Nomads and the wildcats. In the Nomad's eyes with so many of those kidnapped as food being from the *lost souls* it was the only real justice for the crime. As the followers of the 'One True God' tried to preach forgiveness, even among them there was debate and question on whether those who committed these crimes and who partook of human flesh even had souls to protect. Diligence remained high among the Nomads and their wildcats for when the next eatery would open. The White (the myk!) was getting more secretive about these places even as the kidnappings continued. Now Gant new the reason why, the silent communication of the second heads and there were so many of them. They were dealing with thousands, not the tens or hundreds first thought. He needed more help for Twror and the wedding was happening so soon, so very soon.

Chapter 4
Communications

The Sage always assumed that the computer system of The Hold was a storage system of the knowledge from before the 'Great War' and just that alone; a place where most of the Pre War world's books, documents and information had been stored. There were still huge parts of The Hold's Library that had yet to be studied by any of the Sage or the Scholars they trained. Nobody thought that there could be anything else and that became ingrained in the Sage and the Scholars *group think*. After all, The Teachers would have told them if it was anything else.

As Thul began his exploration of the computer and its capacity, he was not yet polluted by this *group think*. To Thul it was a new universe opening up to him, of unlimited abilities and a toy to exercise his rapidly growing intellectual curiosity.

New windows opened up for Thul as he explored the computers systems. As he tried to follow these new links he was repeatedly blocked. The lines seemed to contain (Nothing!) every time.

Thul asked Locklear about these anomalies and Locklear just shrugged it off. It was just bits of the information the Teachers had tried to store in the final moments before the brief War and failed or just bits of information lost to the depth of time.

"What else could it be, Thul?" Locklear stated. "If it was anything else the Teachers would have told us."

Thul was not convinced. There had to be something more here, something the Teachers had kept hidden from the Sage.

The links had to lead somewhere. Thul tried to follow one as he sat before the computer screen. Like had happened so many times before to him as he tried to follow the ethereal links the screen went dark and the computer restarted itself. Thul regained sentry to the system by putting in his new code. He had changed it from what Locklear had given him. In his work, Thul found he needed a way to keep his research safe from the prying eyes of Locklear and the scholars of the Library. He was searching for something that he wasn't sure would be (appreciated?) by the Sage. What had the Teachers kept hidden from the Sage? Moreover, Why?

Thul had found dozens of these computer pathways to follow, but just how to follow them. It was too much work for just himself. Finally, Thul found a young scholar that he could trust. He set her up with her own password and directed her along one of the pathways Thul had found. Argonia; where he knew the rest of the survivors of the mutiny had landed; a knowledge that the other Sage stressed to him he must keep to himself. "They will find out at the right time," they told him. Argonia seemed to play a part in this. A single clue pointed there. Thul set his young student in that direction while he continued his exploration of the rest of the vast system that was the Library.

Milne and Kristof sat together day after day while Jozef looked on. Kristof and Jozef had made a lot of progress figuring out how the computers worked but they had reached a point where they could go no further. The system had to be more than just a collection of the texts of the past. It had to do something, something more, to have been worth all of the trouble to bring it to this Island and protect it.

Communication, that had to be the key. However, Chuak knew nothing of that component. Because of Chuak, Milne and Kristof now knew of the immense Library of The Hold built by the Teachers. However, here Argonia's people, the elite of the pre 'Great War' world, had built this. Like the Teachers, it had been the purpose of the Founders to preserve humanity from what was coming, the catastrophic end of the world; Nuclear Armageddon.

There had to be a connection between the Founders and the Teachers. How could each have been working without any knowledge of the other? Chuak himself had said that the Teachers knew of the entrance of Argonia and the Founders had approved of the Teachers work. That's why Chuak was assigned to the Island so very long ago. His efforts had begun and preserved the 'Sect of Knowledge' throughout the dark times of Argonia's past. More than a few times Chuak, sometimes with help of another of the Order, had covered up the tracks of the Sect from the Priest Kings of Argonia. It was Locklear himself who had come to Argonia briefly to train a new scholar when the one had died unexpectedly in a fall from the rocks without an apprentice. The High Priest almost caught Locklear, only the intervention of Gar had saved him. To Locklear, like Chuak and the rest of the Sage, the computers were only a source of knowledge from before the Great War. If there had been anything more than that, the Teachers would have told them, so went the logic of the Order of the Sage.

Only Gar seemed to question the motives of the Teachers. And he knew little of the computers and their workings.

Milne brought up with Kristof the idea that communications could be the key missing component of the computers that they had been missing. Both were without the preconceptions of the Sage. The key had to be the ability to communicate between computers. If the Teachers and the Founders had known each other, as the Sage implied that they had, then the two groups would have left some way for the survivors to find each other. The computers had to be that way.

Kristof gave the job to Jozef. They had found clues in the past pointing towards something called The Hold. Now that they knew what The Hold was, Jozef started following the clues, the links that pointed towards The Hold. However, each time he thought he was getting somewhere with his investigation something inexplicable would happen. The computer would shut down and restart.

"Teacher, come here quickly," the young scholar called to Thul who was sitting a short distance away, working on his own computer screen.

Thul was slowly getting used to being called Teacher by the Scholars of The Hold's Library. They had tried to keep it a secret, Thul's DNA marker, but word had slipped out. Thul, the son of Simon, the 'Lost Sage', also carried the marker of the Teachers. Thul had tried to get the young scholar he had chosen to call him by his given name. The young woman, chosen by the Sage not from The Hold but from the Coastal People, seemed almost embarrassed to do so. The young women of the Coast did not call men by the first name; it was a matter of culture. In the end, Thul relented. He would get used to the title rather than offend the young scholar he had selected.

When Thul walked over and stood behind where the scholar was working, he was surprised at what he saw on the screen in front of them. Something new was flashing he had not seen before. A single word was on the screen in the language of the Teachers and beneath it was a small blank area that Thul did immediately recognize. The computer was waiting for a new password.

"Teacher look, I tried a new technique to block the computer from shutting down and this is what I got."

Thul knew how hard the young scholar had been working on the problem that he had given her. A new screen reached, a new avenue of research found. Now what? One wrong move by the two of them and this moment could be lost.

Thul sat beside the scholar and pondered what was in front of them. The answer was just waiting for them to find it.

"You have been sitting here long enough. Go get me a 'presso and come back. Tell no one what you have found. Bring yourself one as well. You have found something important, new, and we must be careful from this point on."

"Yes, Teacher," and she hurried away.

Thul sat back starring at the screen, both hands held together behind his head for support. There had to be a reason for all of this. It couldn't just be lost links leading no-where. There were too many of these links and they all seemed to call out to him; purpose. He had seen the word in front of him before, in the language of the Teachers. One of the Sage would probably know the meaning. However, he wasn't ready to bring the Order into this yet. There was another way. In his search of the Library's books Thul had found and pocketed, a small, handwritten book with some words of the Teachers written language defined. He knew that he had seen this word before and if he was lucky, it was in the journal. It would be tedious, there were thousands of words in the journal in no particular order that he could fathom, but it must be there. Where else could he have seen it? Thul walked back to his private office after leaving a note for the scholar. He would be right back and she was to wait for him there.

The journal was where he had hidden it; small, worn, hand-written, the work of one of the earliest lost Sage, Calderon, who had died shortly after the opening of The Hold in an accident.

The Scholar returned from getting the 'presso for the two of them to find Thul sitting in front of the computer screen flipping through a small book. She had delayed by going to her quarters, showering and getting into a change of clothes. Thul did not seem to notice how long she had been gone. His eyes were flittering back and forth between the screen and the book.

"Your drink, Teacher. I saw Locklear at the beverage stand. He requests your presence as soon as possible."

"That can wait," Thul spoke back, acknowledging the Scholar and taking the offered beverage from her hand. He took a drink then moved his concentration back to the book.

"Locklear said that it was important, Teacher," the Scholar implored Thul, nervously fidgeting as she sat down next to him. The Scholar wasn't used to Locklear's requests being ignored. She reasoned that since Thul was a Teacher he could do that. Nevertheless, it still bothered her.

Thul was driven by what was in front of him. The word had meaning. As if he was possessed Thul's eyes continued to dart back and forth faster and faster from the screen to the book and back again, his fingers running down the list of words. Then …

"Argonia, that is the word," Thul, exclaimed, pushing his chair back.

"Argonia, what is that Teacher?" the Scholar asked.

"A myth, a legend in my home land," said Thul back to the Scholar, a smile coming to his face. He carefully set the book back down and looked straight at the young Scholar, noticing maybe for the first time, the inquisitive nature of her eyes. "And maybe a lot more," he continued. "Go to Locklear, I'm ready for him now. Tell him the Teacher requests his presence." The Scholar rushed off to find Locklear as Thul stood up and looked around the room. There were only a few Scholars at their screens.

Thul walked over to each Scholar and spoke the same words. "As of now this room is closed to all except me and those whose permission I give. Finish your work quickly and leave. And spread this word among the Scholars." Thul wanted to take no chance of interruption.

As the Scholars left the room, they immediately started passing on Thul's instructions. As a Teacher his word was final to them. In a very short time, the room was empty except for Thul.

By the time the young Scholar working with Thul found Locklear in a small eatery by the entrance to The Hold, the rumors were rampant and had already reached him. 'What is Thul up to,' thought Locklear as he rushed to the computer room with the Scholar in tow. 'Or maybe more important,' Locklear finished his thought, 'what has he found?'

When Locklear and the young Scholar reached the Libraries computer room, they found a small hand-written sign posted on the door:

'Closed until further notice by order of Thul, Teacher'

Locklear looked at the sign with dismay. The Library had always been his domain and now Thul was asserting his presence, reiterating his gene pool. They had tried to keep Thul's heritage a secret and now Thul himself had confirmed the leaked secret. This would soon reach the surface. 'With what consequences,' thought Locklear as he opened the door and walked into the Libraries computer room.

The scholar hurried ahead of Locklear, leading the way to where Thul was once again sitting in front of the screen. He had attached the word Argonia to the top of the screen on a piece of paper.

"Teacher, Locklear is here."

Locklear was dismayed at the scholar calling Thul Teacher but there was little he could do about it. Thul had handpicked her and Locklear had no authority over her. As he approached Thul, he saw the hand-written paper tag fastened above the screen.

Thul looked up on hearing the steps of the two approaching him. Locklear spoke, quickly and loudly, "Argonia? What have you found out here, Thul?" Locklear was puzzled and dismayed by the sign. Then he saw the worn book by Thul's side. "Calderon's book, I always wondered what happened to that when he died. Where did you find it?"

Thul looked up at Locklear. No longer did he see the Sage as his superiors. Now he stood as an equal, maybe more. "First, what is Argonia? Is it a place or a thing?" questioned Thul of Locklear.

Before answering Locklear ordered the Scholar to leave.

"Wait, I want you here," Thul told the young woman. For the first time Locklear found an order to a scholar not carried out.

"I am, sorry, Locklear, but Thul is our Teacher."

Locklear looked from the scholar to Thul and once more at

Thul after a quick glance at the screen and the image on it. What was Thul discovering, what was he becoming?

Finally Locklear spoke. "Argonia is a place, an island. I have been there."

"You mentioned it in passing, that it holds the rest of the surviving crew of *The Proctant*. Is that true?"

"Yes."

"And the Teachers knew of Argonia?"

"They worked with the Founders in the final selection of who would pass through and go there. They also worked with the Founders in saving the knowledge of the world."

"Argonia; that seems to be the key here. I type in the word and a password box opens up. What comes next?"

Locklear only shrugged his shoulders. He was visibly surprised to see the link here on the computer between The Hold and Argonia. "I know nothing of what you have found, Thul. I never thought the Teachers would keep such a thing hidden from us. We know so many secrets we protect from their time here."

"It asked for a password, any ideas?'

"The only thing of relevance I can think of is a single phrase. It was so long ago, but the Teachers told us to remember it. The time would come when we would need to use it. 'When the pathway is found the 'Blue Light' will hold the key.'"

"The Blue Light, what is that?"

"You have missed some of your studies, Thul. The Blue Lights is an area to the east of The Hold where the Teachers resided. Even now, so long after the Teachers left they are not safe to travel."

"Blue lights," Thul mumbled to himself, "When the pathway is found."

"Teacher," the scholar exclaimed. "Have we found the pathway of which the Teachers spoke?"

"The Sage have always thought that the Teachers were speaking of a way either into or through the 'Blue Lights' lands," Locklear said, his eyes widening. 'Just *what* had Thul found?"

Thul stared at the screen a second and then at the box below the Teachers word for Argonia. He took a few minutes looking through Calderon's book. "Blue Lights, it must be here, the residence of the

Teachers. It must be in the book. Yes …here …the Abode of the Teachers. The Teachers word for their home." He typed in. The screen flickered, paused and a new screen opened; nothing cryptic, no more password boxes and just a few words in the common language.

"Communications open. What is your destination?"

The three just looked at each other for a short time. Finally, Thul typed 'Argonia' into the computer.

"Communications now open, waiting for a response from the destination."

Waiting for a response? Locklear smiled and then quickly removed the smile from his face. However, Thul had noticed it.

"What more do you know, Locklear? What are you hiding? You say that you have been to Argonia. What's there?"

"Everything and nothing it seems. It is time to wait now, Thul. And you were wise to close this room."

"And the response?"

"We must wait for Argonia now. I hope that all is still well there. The effect of your lost ships crew continues to send ripples throughout these lands."

"Lost crew, the others, Founders, Teachers, the island they landed on …" Thul almost stuttered the words.

Locklear finished the thought for him. "Argonia, yes that is the next stage, the circle set by the Teachers will soon be complete."

"How long must we wait?" asked the Scholar of both men.

Thul looked to Locklear for an answer.

"Days, weeks, years? I will try to get word to our Sage there, but it is difficult and dangerous to all involved," Locklear stated.

"Then you will do nothing to further endanger what is happening. We will wait, for however long this takes, the three of us. We will take turns here until the link opens," Thul ordered.

"Yes," answered the scholar. Locklear looked at the new confidence in Thul; no longer the frightened man who had first arrived upon these shores. 'What else had he found out?' Locklear wondered before answering, "Of Course."

"None but the three of us will know of this for now. That includes the other Sage," added Thul.

"I will make this room my home," said the Scholar in reverent tone towards Thul.

"That only makes sense," Locklear stated before leaving the room. "We need answers before we have anything to report to the Order. We wait on Argonia for now."

Thul and the young Scholar now sat together by the screen, each waiting in their own private thoughts. Locklear, however, had a destination of his own; his office. There, in a secret safe, were the so-called 'lost' files of the Teachers, found by a Scholar who had died in an accident shortly after giving them to Locklear. It was time for Locklear to once more review and study what was in those files.

In the secret cavern that lay hidden under Argonia three men sat in the semi-darkness of the chamber. Something lay hidden just beyond their reach. A secret, lost to time. There had to be a connection between the people coming to Argonia, their Founders and the Teachers. The computer that seemed to hold the key would lead them partway through its links and then inexplicably shut down and restart. What was the computer hiding and how could they find the hidden pathway.

"I need to talk to Chuak again," said Milne aloud.

Chuak arrived about an hour later; the scrutiny above was getting intense with Milne clearly missing and a breakdown occurring between the Priest Cult that had ruled Argonia for centuries and the people of the village who found the travelers more interesting. Everything was simmering just below the surface and a gradual separation was taking place in secret between the Sect of Knowledge and the rest of the people of the Island. Now that the Sect knew its numbers rivaled that of the followers of the Priest-king, they were growing bolder.

Moreover, Chuak knew that the Priest-King would do anything to preserve his power.

It was near twilight as Chuak made his way down the dangerous path along the cliffs face to the caves entrance. Was he followed or just being paranoid? There was one point in the trail where he could make sure. A protruding rock, made to look natural, was the only handhold at a particularly dangerous spot. Chuak could loosen it as he used it. Anyone of the Sect would know and refit the safeguard. Anybody else; well it was a long way down to the rocks below and the pounding surf would cover up any screams.

As Chuak went by, he gave the 'stone' a half-twist. If the person following him was of the sect they would know to turn it forward again as they used it. Chuak traveled a short distance further along the trail to wait for what would happen next.

The stalker reached the narrowing of the trail, reached for the only handhold available and Chuak heard the scream drowned out by the oceans noise; another priest whose disappearance would be noticed. The time was very near for the Priest-King to be overthrown.

Kristof, Jozef, and Milne were sitting by the old computer terminal, staring at the screen that had remained somehow intact over the centuries; in part do to the unnatural dryness that somehow overtook the natural humidity of the cavern. A wall of air at the entrance seemed to keep out most of the oceans mists. The sect carefully maintained the machinery that created the wall, though the spare parts that brought to the cavern two thousand years earlier were almost gone and the ability to manufacture them lost.

Milne got up, stretched and walked over to greet the much shorter Chuak. He started up the conversation where he had left off with Kristof and Jozef. "Communications is the key and the connection between Argonia and The Hold seems paramount. There has to be a link between here and my homeland as well. The Founders came from there."

"If it was a communication system the Teachers would have told us," Chuak responded, following the 'company' line of the Sage that the Teachers told them everything. Milne was starting to get a good idea of how little the Teachers had indeed told the Sage.

Milne and Chuak sat down in front of the screen. A line of code was flashing on the screen, waiting for a response.

"There must be something, forgotten in the passage of time. The confederation, the Hold and Argonia are all connected. All joined by events when the Great War happened. Think back, Chuak, there must be something, no matter how trivial."

"The war came so quickly," Kristof said. "Once it happened, Argonia, as the Founders had envisioned, was not yet finished. When the war came, most of the Founders perished, unable to reach the shelter of Argonia in time."

"And the Teachers?" Milne asked of Chuak.

"Though it seems that the Teachers must have known of the Founders, and they had the tools to do things much faster, it seems the Teachers left the Founders to suffer their fate without help. It is said that The Hold was finished and filled in hours, not the years as the Argonia project was taking. The Teachers transported People from throughout the world instantly from where they stood to inside The Hold as the missiles fell. Great art works collected and the library filled in the blink of an eye. Nevertheless, even the Teachers did not have enough time. The madness came to the world that quickly."

"Your order was founded at the beginning?"

"No, Milne, the Order of the Sage was created by the Teachers when The Hold was reopened, one thousand years ago. The selection based as much on mental stability as anything else and after the first selection from The Hold, no new Sage were added.

"Why were the Sage created," asked Milne.

"You know the reason, I've told you before. We are here to guide the future rebirth of this world and to prepare the world for that rebirth."

"To prepare the world for what?" This was a new phrase he heard from Chuak and he grew excited on hearing it. "Prepare the world for what? Think back to the beginning, there must be more, something, if only a brief recollection, lost, forgotten or just not considered important."

"We were just to watch, teach and introduce new science and technology at pre-selected times. I remember the phrase. We were to do this so that when the people awakened and a pathway is found, the 'Blue Lights' will hold the key," Chuak spoke quietly.

"The 'Blue Lights'?" asked Milne.

"The 'Blue Lights' were the region to the East where the Teachers lived during their time on Earth."

"Milne," Kristof spoke, raising his voice in alarm. "The screen, the path, we have found it."

As Milne, Chuak, and Jozef turned their attention back to the computers screen, a new element had indeed appeared on it. A solid blue screen with a single word, 'Destination' and a dialogue box below it.

"How!?" They all spoke almost as one.

Milne fell back into his chair as the computer itself responded.

"This is Master Computer One, as created by The Founders. Voice recognition and code words accepted. Modification by the Visitors is accepted. Network is on-line and pathways opening."

The three men just looked at each other with amazement.

"Code words, network modification, what is happening", said Milne as he stood and picked up his chair, which had fallen backwards in the excitement.

"Who are the Visitors?" asked Chuak. "Was there another at work here as well."

Milne answered that one before the computer could respond." To the Founders your Teachers must have been the Visitors."

"I have never heard them referred to as that," Chuak seamed incredulous as he spoke.

"This was at the beginning, one thousand years before your Order was formed, when the 'Great War' happened."

"Correct," answered the computer, "Why I do not understand your reference to the Founders, it is indeed those who you call the Teachers who made the modifications to the computers to enable me to become online once more."

"Milne," Kristof called, "The screen, there is a face on the screen."

"A face," Milne stated as he turned to face the computer.

"A young woman," Jozef exclaimed.

"Can she see us?" asked Chuak aloud as the four men all faced the woman on the screen.

"Yes I can," came the answer from the screen.

"Where are you?" was Milne's first question as he reached the computer.

"I'm in the Library of the Sage in The Hold," she answered.

Chuak stepped in front of the computers screen on hearing this. "Do you recognize me? I have been gone from The Hold a long time."

"I've seen your picture in the halls and have studied all of the Sage under our Teacher."

"Teacher, you have a Teacher there," Chuak answered back

loudly in astonishment. Had the Teachers returned during his time on Argonia and he not informed? "This Teacher, you have met it?"

"He chose me for this job, to open the communications before us."

"He chose you?" Chuak seemed incredulous at this news. Would a Teacher choose a young student of the Library over a Sage?

"Yes, Thul chose me from several candidates he had before him. Thul knew that he could trust me with his secrets."

"Thul," Milne almost laughed as he looked at the screen. "Thul of *The Proctant* is there."

"Of course," She answered. "He is our Teacher."

"What heresy is this? The Teachers left our world long ago. We of the Sage follow their instructions," Chuak spoke agitated. Had this Thul somehow co-opted the Teachers work? What they had brought to this world when they saved the people, in the aftermath of the Great War?

"Strange," Milne spoke, "He always seemed somehow a little off. He was late arriving on the ship when we left port. It was never clear if he was a stowaway who worked himself into the Captains graces or a member of the crew. He was always alone from day one on deck, but he worked hard for the opportunity to sail with us." He turned to face the other men in the cavern. "It seems a man from my world is now your new Teacher."

"What do you know of this? How did this Thul assume the position of Teacher?" asked Chuak of the young scholar on the screen before him.

"Thul and Locklear will be here shortly and you can learn more of this from them. I only know what has been whispered in these halls. Thul is the son of Simon, the Lost Sage, and he is said to carry the DNA marker of the Teachers. I am not allowed to say more, maybe I have already said too much."

Chuak fell back almost crestfallen. So much had transpired since he had arrived here to save Argonia, under the instructions left behind by the Teachers and now this.

Chapter 5
Lands United
The Marriage of Lady Theresa and Wade

The Night Before: The Sisters

Theresa leaned back in her large soft chair facing the warmth of the fireplace. She had placed the chair between the beds of her two sisters, Christina and Cynthia. Theresa had been telling them a story of the *before time*, when great cities of millions had populated the world. Her sisters loved Theresa's stories; half filled with things she had learned from Tor, half made up of her own fantasies of what that time must have been like.

Now Theresa was dreaming her own dream of tomorrow. She would be marrying Wade, the man from across the sea who had captured her heart, where so many had failed, with a glance at their first meeting at Castle Nourne. Who was this man, that yet, she knew so little of and yet was marrying? He seemed so little like other men she had known.

"Theresa, you're dreaming again," her sisters chimed in together, sitting up in their beds. They had been listening intently to their older sister's story when Theresa had stopped for a few seconds with her thoughts, so deep was her thinking. Who were these men from across the sea that had so changed her world in such a brief time? Castaways, survivors, even mutineers if you could believe the stories, from a lost trading ship, *The Proctant*. And now she was marrying one of them. Wade, now the governor of the Northern Valley, and with marriage to Lady Theresa he would become Lord Wade, the new lord of Castle Nourne.

"Finish your story, Theresa,' the sisters spoke again as one. Three and four years younger than Theresa's nineteen years, they were inseparable, like twins, and they often spoke together, at the same time, like it was one voice for the two of them. "Finish your story of Paris; we love your stories about that city."

"Paris..." Theresa quietly spoke. "It was the City of Love, they say, before the Great War." Theresa's thoughts drifted back to Wade.

Over the last three years, she had many suitors, but none had caught her eye, until her heart fell with her first sight of Wade. "Yes, the story. Paris; it was the city of lights and now where were we? Oh, yes." Then Theresa felt herself becoming very tired. She finally said to her sisters. "Girls, I'm sorry, but I have so much on my mind I need to rest for tomorrow.

"Oh yes," they said together, "of course."

Theresa then covered them, put a last log in the fireplace for warmth, and quietly walked to her own room and climbed under the piled blankets and furs to get what little sleep she could.

Revelry

The city of Erson had begun to reclaim some of its former glory as the men of *The Proctant* gathered in their favorite tavern in the former capital of the Northern Valley. Picking up the overflow of the refugees streaming north to Twror, Erson had already regained its former population and a friendly rivalry was developing with Twror over what the cities had to offer in food and entertainment.

The tavern they gathered in which had been founded after the *War with the Myk* by one of the Captains of the Army of the Coastal People. He had not wanted to return to their closed society after the conflict, so, like many of his comrades, he stayed behind in Erson. His dream had been to prepare the best foods that the waters of the Inland Sea could provide.

A large fire was burning in the central hearth of the tavern and the men of *The Proctant* shared a table near it, for light and comfort, as they drank their ale and shared their stories. Especially stories, real and made up, of their shipmate Wade, soon to be joined forever to Theresa and this country in the 'morrow.

"Remember the pirate women we met in the South on that one trip. Wade thought that they were just local women looking for a good time," Mendy almost laughed as he told the story. "If the rest of us hadn't showed up at that tavern, Wade would have been shanghaied for sure."

"Yeah, I remember, some big old pirates waiting outside for the women to bring him out," Alum added.

"You remember their shock when we showed up with Davis. The giant towered over them. I have never seen someone run so fast as those pirates ran."

More stories like that one continued well into the night, Wade the center of most of them. Finally, the shipmates called it a night and returned to their rooms.

Assassins Feast

In a still dark corner of Twror they stood, sat and lay in a dimly lit, dirt-floored hut. No longer were there any warm sanctuaries of the myk that used to exist after the fall of the White. All destroyed by the Nomads and their despicable wildcats. This abandoned hut was the best Kat could do for his warriors.

The three Myk ate with abandon the feast before them; little remained of the bounty now, just the partial remains of two Nomads, chosen at random by Kat and lured here by a story of a surprise that Kat needed help with for the couple to wed in the Central Plaza of Twror the next day. Once in the hut, Kat quickly silenced them with a quick slice from his claw across their throats; not enough to kill them at once, but enough to make them silent to the outside world excepting a few last gurgles. Better alive for the feast of his two assassins.

"To the Myk!" they shouted to each other as they savored this now rare respite of fresh human flesh.

"To the Myk! For tomorrow we will have died in revenge for his honor."

One Day Before
A cavalcade of sound

It was the day before the ceremony joining Lady Theresa and Wade. On a stage opposite the dais where the wedding would take place in Twror's Central Park, musicians of the many lands that had been touched by Wade and the men from across the sea, practiced and tried to bring some order and semblance of harmony to their many different instruments and styles.

Lord Perth of Nourne had chosen a conductor for his

daughter's wedding. Somebody he had known since childhood. The conductor had begun his task two months earlier, finally choosing these sixty musicians from the hundreds that had applied. They represented each of the people who had fought in the war with the Myk. Now, a day before the ceremony, a more unified style was beginning to take shape. It would be a challenge tomorrow, but the conductor had put together a package of music that he hoped would bring out the best of each region.

Two days before
The laying of the circles

There was still dew on the early morning grass of the Central Park of Twror. Two circles of stone, representing the union of Lady Theresa and Wade were taking shape around the dais where the two would wed. Originally, just one large circle was laid out in the lawn, the raised dais where the ceremony would take place to one side. However, with so many people arriving to rejoice in the wedding, a second, smaller circle, was laid out in chalk, a mere twenty yards across, with the platform in the center. Here in this inner circle only close friends and family of the two would set a stone that would represent them and their homeland. Even this wall was growing tall, with a second and third layer placed as so many considered themselves friends of the bride and groom. On the outer wall the stones now lay 4 and 5 layers high, many of the stones nothing more than a rock taken from the sod floor of a Twrorian hut of the Whites who had been freed of the Myk. Intermingled in these two walls of common stones were precious and semi-precious stones and jewels from far distant lands. Traders from the east, upon hearing the occasion, left their own gifts on the outer wall.

Two singular stones were set down but two days before the ceremony at the opening of the Walls away from the dais. The stones were fairly large, though they seemed common in their nature. They did have an unusual color to them, however. One side of the stones was much lighter, a quartz line running through it. The town's guardsmen watched these stones being laid by the two men who had brought them on a cart. 'These two must truly love the couple to be wed' thought the guardsmen. The men labored in their placement of these stones, one set atop the other. Once they were done, they turned and nodded at the guards as they left.

Kat watched these stones laid from a distant rooftop. 'He had selected well his assassins,' Kat thought as he watched the men carry out his instructions to perfection. Cloaked in their own visibility the guards would remember them as friends.

Three days before
The office of the Mayor

Gant and Wade met with as much secrecy as possible in Gants office. Gar, with his headaches, and Thorium joined them. It was late in the evening.

"Do you really think something could happen at the wedding, Gar?" Wade asked, somewhat taken aback at the suggestion.

"Call it a premonition, but the Myk hasn't been destroyed; only driven away. He seeks revenge and we know he has spies here," Gar answered, staring out the window at the preparations below for the festivities.

"It will be pretty chaotic at times, Wade," Gant said, looking up from his chair at the others in the room. "And remember the White family and their story. There are far more double-heads, myk, than we first thought."

"But my wedding to Theresa, would they dare," Wade stated with concern facing Thorium.

Thorium placed his hand on Wades' shoulder. All the survivors of the mutiny had become close friends. "Can you think of a better way to bring terror and hurt to the people of this newly unified Northern Valley and the Two Valleys, now joined as one nation?" Thorium responded to Wade's plea. "This would hurt Castle Nourne; bring suspicion upon all the White and help to shatter our newfound unity and peace. What better target could they have?"

"What can we do?" Wade asked his assembled friends with angst. "Should I postpone the wedding out of fear?"

"Then we give in to our fears. We did that once, we cannot do so again," Gant answered, getting up from behind his desk. He walked to his window and stood beside Gar. He looked out at the almost finished work in the park to prepare it for the wedding. The two stone circles stood as a beacon of all they had overcome in such a short time. He saw where the survivors of the caverns beneath the Myk's palace had built their own special memorial to one side of the park; a symbol of the future that would remain, like the monument on the site of the former Palace. "We just have to be diligent," Gant finished.

A quiet came over the room as the men contemplated what might happen. Finally, Thorium spoke. "I will take Tri onto the stage with me. I will be standing alongside Wade as his escort into his future life. No, we cannot give into our fears. However, we must be prepared for everything. And we carry our weapons."

"Weapons, then people will be alarmed," answered Gant to this.

"We will tell them that the weapons are a tradition of our land. Then let only the Myk's spies and agents fear them," he said, grasping the hands of Gant and Wade. Gar looked on with wonder at this one-time stranger's strength and force.

"Any more sign or word of our mysterious visitor you saw, Gant?" asked Gar.

"No, nothing. My description was vague as it was. And there are still some, not many, a few, who would protect an envoy of the Myk," Gant answered, still standing by the window. "We will be vigilant. Most visitors bring stones for the circles. The guards will recognize them as friends. Only strangers, those not taking part in the building of the walls, do we need to be fearful of."

Both Thorium and Gar saw the hole in Gants reasoning as they looked at each other. Gar's headache was severe as they looked at each other. All they could do now was prepare for the worse and hope it did not happen.

One week before the wedding
Theresa and her Mother

Lady Alyce firmly knocked on her daughter's door. It was still early evening and Theresa had retired after the evening meal. She knew how nervous her oldest daughter was about the wedding that was soon going to be here. Lady Alyce thought to herself, 'Just who was this man who has stolen her daughter's heart; he came ashore with the shipwrecked crew and had been heroic at the Battle with the Myk. Nevertheless, what else did she know? So much about him was a mystery, but she knew that he was a good man and would treat her daughter well; Wade, soon to be the Lord of Castle Nourne, soon to be the husband of their eldest.

When Theresa didn't immediately answer Lady Alyce knocked again, a little louder this time. She wasn't worried about her daughter, but she had words of wisdom to give to her that had been handed down, mother to daughter, for generations.

Finally, a sleepy Theresa opened the door. "Mother, I didn't hear you. I have so much to do."

Lady Alyce walked into the room and sat on her daughter's bed. She motioned Theresa to sit beside her. Theresa sat beside her and put her head on her mother's shoulder. "I am so tired, mother, and so worried. What kind of wife will I be for Wade? What will he expect of me?" She started crying and the tears ran down onto her mother's shoulder.

Lady Alyce put an arm around her daughter's shoulder. "You'll be fine as his partner in life. He is a strong, good man. I have watched him work so hard for our Nourne and fight with his life for our people. I like him very much. I believe the two of you will be a wonderful pair in the running of Nourne." Lady Alyce held her daughter tight and told her not to worry that everything will turn out as it should.

"There are words I need to give you now. This is from the conscious and reflections from the women of our past; no truer words ever have been spoken;

> *"There are no lies or secrets in a true journey of two souls,*
> *Be true to him as you are to your own heart*
> *For your heart will never lie to you*
> *And you can never lie to your heart*
> *Love comes from within your soul*
> *Remember to always listen to your heart,"*

Theresa looked at her mother and sighed.

Lady Alyce gave her daughter a big hug.

"What wonderful words those are. I will cherish this forever.

Thank you mother." She then gave her mother a big hug.

"You have much to come before you. Now rest, everything will be as it should be," were Lady Alyce's final words for her daughter as she softly closed the door behind her.

Two weeks before the Wedding

Wade approached Castle Nourne with some hesitation. This would be the last time that he would see Lady Theresa before the wedding, when this castle would become his as the new Lord of Nourne.

He felt the trepidation throughout his body. On board *The Proctant* he was just part of the crew, an apprenticeship that his parents had arranged for him. Then the mutiny and the new land were found. In two weeks, he would be the presumptive head of Nourne, building upon the legacy of helping give birth to this new confederation. He gulped a deep swallow as he approached the door.

Theresa's two sisters, who had been waiting anxiously for him, giggled and laughed as they greeted him at the doorway to the interior of the castle. "She's waiting for you in the rose garden," they jointly said, giggling more. Then they ran off together back into the castle.

Wade knew his way throughout the castle by now; he had been a frequent visitor courting Lady Theresa. He made his way through the hallways, at one point passing through the Hall of Portraits, where the portraits of all the Lords and Lady of Nourne hung going back almost 1000 years. Soon they would hang his and Theresa's portrait on the crowded walls. Lady Alyce had already commissioned an artist for the painting. As he gazed at the portraits he walked by, he wondered about this past that he knew so little about.

He reached the entryway to the castle's inner gardens, tended with such care by Lady Alyce. Looking through the entryway's small window, he saw Theresa standing by a rose bush in early bloom. She looked so beautiful standing there. Wade almost lost his confidence looking out at her. Then he gained his courage and entered the gardens.

"Wade," Theresa called as she heard the doors open and her fiancé enter the garden. "Come here and sit by me," she said as she pointed to a nearby ornate bench.

Wade walked over to the offered seat, smiling, sitting down next to Theresa. They just looked at each other for several seconds before Theresa spoke.

"There is still so little I know of you and your world," she began. In their whirlwind romance, she had always pulled back when he hesitated to talk about his homeland. "Tell me again about where you came from."

Wade reached for her hand and held it as he answered her, unsure of what to say. "It's not much different than here," he began.

Theresa showed a little pout as she heard this. It was the same way Wade always answered her. "Wade, you have seen so much of the world," she responded, hoping to get a little more from Wade this time.

"Not really, Theresa. This was my first voyage as an apprentice seaman. I took the voyage out of a feeling of being lost. I didn't know my place in the world, but I knew that my future didn't lie in the small seafaring town I was from. My parents arranged with the ship's captain for me to join the crew."

"Then your world was different," Theresa laughed. "Castle Nourne is a long way from the sea."

Wade laughed with her. "I guess a small seaport is a lot different than this castle. No rose beds for one."

"No roses?" Theresa questioned, having followed her mother's love of roses.

"None. We have other flowers; none as beautiful as these roses; it is too cold for them to grow there."

"Colder than here," she shivered at the thought.

"Yes, the ice remains just north of the seaport year-round."

"Oh," she stuttered. "And now have you found your place in the world?" she expectantly asked Wade.

"Now I have a home and I know my future lies with you."

Theresa blushed at the answer. "Your family?" she asked Wade.

"My parents who raised me, who adopted me, were not my birth parents. They died together in an accident when I was very small."

"An accident, how horrible!" she exclaimed.

"When I was old enough to understand at 17, I was told that it happened very quickly. Such accidents are common where I am from."

Theresa looked at Wade in loving anguish over his loss. "How horrible, do you have any other family?"

"My adoptive parents had no children of their own. I don't know if my parents had any brothers or sisters. Maybe someday I'll go back and ask that question."

"You weren't ever curious about other family there?" she asked incredulously.

"Not until I saw all the portraits on the wall here. It's common to be adopted in my old homeland. So many accidents, sometimes it seems that life is moving too fast there. My parents adopted me when I was just five. They were unable to have any children of their own; so many of my friends were adopted as well." Wade had a serious look on his face when he thought back about his childhood.

She sat quietly looking to find out more of Wades past.

Then Theresa got serious again. "Wade I do not know your last name."

Wade looked at her with surprise, "I didn't tell you my last name. Well, it's Emiliani. I carry the name of the orphanage. All that pass through the orphanage carry the same name. The orphanage was named after St. Jerome Emiliane the patron saint of orphanages and lost children."

"Wouldn't you carry the name of your parents or your adoptive parents?"

"That is the tradition from where I come from. It reminds us that everybody from an orphanage is a brother or sister of the others who have passed through that orphanage. That way we are never truly alone."

"Oh...," she said. "Then you do have a family."

"I had never truly thought of it that way, but I guess I do."

After a few moments of silence, she asked Wade another question, relishing finding out more about him. "Do you have any recollection of your parents, before they were killed in the accident?"

"Only bits and pieces," he solemnly answered her. I was just five when I was brought to the orphanage. I remember a feeling of sadness in the eyes of the couple that brought me there. They had been friends of my parents but were too poor to adopt me."

"Friends of your parents, how strange," she answered. "In Nourne, as well as most of the lands around it, it is family or friends of the parents who would adopt a lost child without regard to wealth."

With a brief show of anger Wade answered her, quickly calming down as he did so. "They were just the people who brought me there, who abandoned me there. I remember crying when they left. 'Uncle don't leave me.' The pain I felt deep inside me still hurts at times." Theresa felt his pain and anguish when she heard this. "I was lucky in who raised me. Others were not so lucky."

"They were your family then, who left you there."

"I guess they were. Why...," Theresa just held him then as pent-up emotions came out. A memory from long ago had left its mark deep inside of Wade's heart. "Why didn't they adopt me?"

This was a question that Wade had often thought of but kept hidden throughout his childhood. He never had a good answer and the orphanage had been vague about just who brought him in. Now, with Theresa at his side, he felt free to voice it.

"I am sorry..." Theresa said, holding his head into her shoulder "I can feel and share your pain about this."

The Wedding

The weather broke clear and warm on the late spring day. Clouds lay scattered in the sky and the sun burned bright.

The people decorated Twror as if it was a holiday celebration; for it truly was; the joining together of Wade and Lady Theresa; the joining of two lands; the bringing together of the world. The city streets were decorated with lights and flowers. Music blazed throughout the city.

R'mon balloons were tethered all around the central area of the city, each with two or three R'mon onboard. To the people of Twror these were all about adding color to the festivities. To Gant, Wade and Thorium they were much more; a hopeful warning to those who might attempt some evil during the ceremony. What the people couldn't see from the ground, each R'mon had an arrow notched into their crossbow.

The central park was fully decorated. Ice was brought from the northern mountains at great cost and carefully sculpted into a myriad of fanciful creatures. Food vendors from throughout the known world, and few from the unknown, lent their aromas into the air. The flags and pennants of every family, large or small, flew throughout the park. Even the Shiap camels and the Nomads wildcats wore decorations for the festivities.

Towards the western edge of the park lay circles of stones. A tall stage was set up for the ceremony itself. Only here, in the stone circles, was there a strong sense of the security that lay about the park. At the entrance to the outer circle, about ten feet across, six armed soldiers from Nourne and several Nomads with their wildcats stood watch. They carefully looked over every person as they entered the stone rings. Every entrant who was not recognized by one of the guards from the laying of the stones, and there were very few, was pulled aside and searched. A few of the White with remedial double-heads were turned back by a few snarls of the wildcats.

Kat watched all of this from a distance, his perch on a distant rooftop with others, those who were unable to get into the park for the wedding festivities. He had pulled his wide hat down over his face, as he told those around him, "to protect his eyes from the sun.' As expected, his two assassins, having made a show of laying their large stones on the outer circles, were recognized and allowed to enter, unsearched.

A procession now began from the mayor's office to the stage. Shiaps on their camels lined either side of the route, their own banners flying at the tips of each pole they carried. The R'mon balloons showered the parade route with flower petals, gathered from the many lands of the confederation. In the lead of the procession was Lord Perth and Lady Alyce of Nourne, dressed in traditional garb with a rose prominently features on both costumes. Their two youngest daughters walked on either side of them, also featuring a rose on what they wore.

The Sage, each solemnly stepping in time to the music being played, each carrying their personal symbol of the Order, followed them.

The Sage were followed by the crew of *The Proctant.* They had been through so much anguish together, but now able to stand together for this wedding; Thorium, Zircon, Mendy, Alum and Pluto.

Next came the couples friends from so many lands, whose lives the crew had so quickly touched since the arrival of *The Proctant* on these shores; Jamen of Kiln and his son Raymond, both of them with their wives; Gant, the mayor of Twror; Loren of the R'mon's; the mayors of Erson and the City by the Lake; The Mayor of The Hold and finally all those remaining council members, dignitaries and princes of Jall who could fit into the procession.

Finally, bringing up the rear of the procession, were the priests of 'The One True God' in their flowing robes, in so many colors, representing each of the lands they preached. Each carried on a short swinging chain a small container of burning incense.

As this procession entered the park and approached the stone rings, the great mass of the people from all the lands touched by the crew of *The Proctant* made their way into the park.

Stands had been set up between the two circles of stone to accommodate as many people as possible. People sat next to others from lands they didn't know of a year before. Even with the stands, there just was not enough room to accommodate everybody. The park, streets and rooftops around it were filled to overflowing. It seemed the entirety of the lands of the Confederation had emptied for the ceremony.

Once everybody was settled into place, or as close an approximation of that, music trumpeted the arrival of Wade and Lady Theresa. Two flower girls, selected from among the children of the White accompanied them, each holding one of their hands. Behind the flower girls walked a ring-bearer, chosen by lot from the over 100 who applied through their families at Castle Nourne for the honor.

As the couple entered, first the outer ring of stones and then the inner, cheers erupted throughout the gathering, none louder than Kat's two assassins, who quietly inched closer to the inner ring. Inwardly Kat seethed from his rooftop vantage point. 'The beginning of the end', Kat thought to himself.

Phelix, the oldest of the remaining Sage, stood behind a podium facing the crowd. On either side of him stood a priest from 'The One True God'. The ceremony would combine elements of such ceremonies of all the lands present. Phelix would preside over the ceremony.

On one side of the Podium stood Thorium, Mendy and Alum, weapons clearly visible. On the opposing side stood Jamen of Kiln, accompanied by his son Raymond and Zircon, all visibly armed with weapons. The story was circulated throughout the city of Twror that this was traditional for weddings in the lands across the Western Sea. Sebastian and Reed, with their wildcats, adorned with collars carrying Nourne's rose symbol, stood on either side of the steps leading up to the Stage. If anything was to happen, they were all as prepared as they could be.

Kat saw all of this from his rooftop seat. It was all as he expected. It did not matter if the assassination was successful; damage would be done to this fragile alliance against the Myk. It was time for Kat to leave the rooftop and the city.

Kat got himself up from his seat, excusing himself. When those around him questioned his leaving, he answered, "I have to get closer, this is too important." Nobody suspected the double meaning of Kats words.

Important to the tradition of Castle Nourne, the parents of the bride and groom were to jointly solemnize the ceremony. Since Wade had no parents here, he chose Thorium and Lady Ruth to represent him in this tradition. The two families held hands to symbolize the creation of a new family, created from the old.

Wade brought with him the tradition of the exchange of wedding rings. The one he chose for Lady Theresa was one handcrafted by a jeweler of the Coastal People; two whales joined by a sapphire from a pendant he carried from his mother who raised him.

Lady Theresa had for Wade her father's ring, which represented his title as Lord of Nourne, now celebrating the elevation of Wade to the Lord of Castle Nourne, as Lord Perth retired from his title as part of the ceremony. Tears were in the eyes of both Lord and Lady of Nourne as they saw the couple climb the steps to the top of the stage.

Theresa wore the wedding gown of so many Ladies of Nourne, carefully stored for generations in a cedar chest. Wade wore a leather and cotton suit, made custom for him by the leading tailor of Nourne, accented with silver images of whales, a creature that Wade had fallen in love with on the voyage east and would become part of the new symbol of castle Nourne. Above the whales was a single red rose, showing the continuity of Nourne; a new family crest was borne.

As the couple approached the podium, Phelix stepped forward. He felt his time was coming to an end. He appreciated the opportunity provided by the Order for involvement in the ceremony. The wedding would be the final act of the Order in Phelix's eyes, bringing together the people of so many lands, including from across the Western Sea, into one. The Great Plan of the Teachers was complete.

The couple now faced Phelix and the ceremony began. Phelix spoke as loud as he could to make his voice heard throughout the park.

"Today we burn away the past to make way and to bring forward a new future. Not only do we join together the souls of the two before us, Lady Theresa of Nourne and Wade of Emiliani. (Wade turned to Theresa with a slight smile on his face when he heard the name Emiliani, thinking of Theresa and how she wanted to learn it so badly.)

"From this point in time, all of our history will be as one."

A few minutes before the ceremony began one of the Nomads noticed a large rock with a quartz stripe running through it was turned on the outer wall, somehow, the night before. A coincidence; he couldn't take any chances. Without realizing it, he had stumbled upon Kat's message that the attack was a go. He quickly passed a verbal signal to the others on watch at the gate. The quiet message passed to others on watch throughout the crowd. Hands now firmly pressed on their weapons. As the signal reached Thorium and the others on the stage, they each drew their weapons. Lady Alyce, Lord Perth (now just Perth of Nourne) and Lady Theresa looked on in alarm. The stage was set for whatever was to come. Wade stepped in front of the three of them while his armed friends, weapons out, moved to the front of the stage.

The two assassins began their approach to the stage; their lives were forfeit, however it was a privilege to die for the Myk.

The crowd around the assassins also seemed to surge forward as the armed warriors rushed forward to protect the stage from attack. Followers of the *old ways* rushed towards the stage in chaos as well, unknowingly guided by the force of Kat's mind.

Gar felt something wrong with his brain, a strong presence seemed to make him helpless. He looked upward to Thorium as he fell to the ground as if to say, "its happening."

Thorium's wildcat Tri, as well as Sebastian and Reeds wildcats, got up from where they had been laying behind the others; now alert, their ears back. As Tri's fur stood on end, Thorium fully drew his broadsword from its scabbard. Each of those on stage with him now fully drew their weapons as well. Lady Alyce held her daughters' hand as each drew their long knives from the ceremonial scabbards that each wore. Perth of Nourne stepped back next to the Sage, his limp arm helpless at this side from the injuries he received during the Battle of Erson against the Myk's army. Wade moved to the forefront of the Stage.

The crowds throughout the park and city now realized something was wrong. Double-heads, myk, throughout the park and city drew weapons of their own from under their clothing and there were hundreds of them, guided by a thought placed in their heads by Kat as he left the vicinity of the throngs.

"To the Myk, forward for the Myk!" They shouted as they slashed at whoever was nearest to them. Each was quickly brought down by the Shiaps, Nomads and their wildcats, but not before hundreds were wounded by the crazed myk.

As Kat made his escape, quietly, to the edge of the city, he smiled with his feline teeth. 'The damage is done," he thought. He wore a different coat and hat now than the one he had worn when he arrived at the city.

The assassins now rushed to the stage themselves, unknowingly aided by the remedial double-heads, still unborn, that Kat had controlled.

"We are myk!" they shouted as they ran forward, the short swords that they had concealed in their garments now carried in front of them.

"We are myk!" shouted the White carrying the unborn double-heads as they joined the charge.

Throughout the crowd, the wildcats now charged, creating carnage in the wake, somehow knowing who the double-heads were. Even the double-heads who were not part of the attack, those that had turned their backs on the 'old ways' were torn to pieces by the wildcats. Innocent White, there solely to celebrate the marriage, were killed by warriors, unsure of whom the enemy was.

The two assassins reached the top of the stage, still yelling, "We are myk!" as they slashed out at anything before them. Others of the unborn reached the top of the stage as well, there were so many of them.

Those on the stage stepped forward as one to meet them, Lady Alyce and Lady Theresa each had their arms injured in the melee, before being pulled to the back of the stage by Wade and Mendy, each suffering their own injuries at the hands of the crazed assassins in their attempt to protect them.

Finally, it was over. The two assassins brought down by Thorium and Jamen of Kiln. A deafening silence broke over the crowd. Chants began, slowly at first and gathering throughout the crowd into a crescendo, led by the White. It was picked up and carried throughout the city. "Twror, Twror..." they chanted. Unwilling to allow the horror of the double-heads attack bring an end to their newfound hope.

The warriors dropped their own weapons to the ground now, the horror of what had transcribed vividly in their minds. They looked around at the crowd as the chanting grew. One looked at an innocent White whose life he had taken in the chaos of the assault. Another White, a woman, took his bloodied hand and spoke softly to him as he dropped to his knees and began to cry. He had been a defender of the White in the aftermath of the battle with the Myk's army, standing against the reprisals of the warriors of The Hold. "And now this," he cried aloud.

"He forgives you," she said softly to him. "We all do," she finished, hugging him to herself.

Lady Ruth now stepped forward to the front of the bloodied stage, somehow unscathed in the melee. The wildcats stood on either side of her, still protecting her. She waved her hand to the crowd to silence them and the chanting slowly came to an end, as much out of the emotional exhaustion of the crowd as the action itself.

She now, in a solemn, loud voice, spoke to the crowd before her.

"Yes, for Twror. Each of us here stands for the unity that is Twror. Nevertheless, we must not forget why we are here. It is for the wedding of Lord Wade and Lady Theresa and the formal joining of them and all our lands.

"This tragedy of today we will not and cannot forget.

"However, it is the future that we are here for; let this be the last action of the past. We now must help all that are wounded. Everyone who can help must please help now."

The wounded Wade and Lady Theresa now stepped forward. Wade began to speak. "Let us all together clear this stage and the horror that beset us. Pray together for healing."

At these words, a new spontaneous cheer began throughout the crowd. The double-heads of the myk were removed with dispatch by the crowd, mostly by the White, and unceremoniously dumped without remorse over the wall, to be collected and burned later.

Lady Theresa, along with Lady Alyce, were led back to the Castle for their safety accompanied with the wild cats. The warriors in the crowd themselves solemnly carried to one side the handful of White mistakenly killed. From the Priests of the 'One True God' came spoken words of solace to the warriors and words of peace for the fallen. "In God's name, please pray for all the wounded and dead and for peace in these lands that we will join as one. We must continue to fight for peace."

Later that day, in the aftermath of this tragedy, while there was much to be done, an announcement was prepared from Castle Nourne. Lady Ruth was selected for the announcement. Lady Ruth made her way to the podium, most of the crowd still standing in front of the stage, awaiting some news.

"Today's tragedy will not stop what we have committed too," she began.

The entire crowd of people let out and enormous cheer to Twror, repeating the name repeatedly.

Lady Ruth had tears in her eyes as she began to speak again. "We as one will go on with this precious ceremony on the 'morrow"

The crowd erupted again with a cheer of Twror once more.

Lady Ruth began again. "Please help all of Twror in our recovery. God be with all." Those few words rang true to the people; they had come from every province to show their respect for Lady Theresa and Wade. Now hearing this news gave everyone some kind of hope, everyone joined in who could help to make things as they were before the attack.

Aftermath

At the castle Wade walked back and forth "How did this happen? How did we miss it?" he spoke loudly to his men. "We had gone over and over everything, what did we miss?" His anger showed and the wildcats ears perked up. "I want answers," he was looking at his men with eyes that did not blink.

Thorium spoke, trying to calm Wade. "We had all the entrances with guards; we had the wedding party surrounded with armed guards. There were the wildcats, but we did not look inside our own, our own White that we have lived with in peace. No one could have seen this coming."

Alum was as angry as Wade. "We must be grateful that none of the wedding party was killed. Thorium is right this came within. I have never seen the White act with such anger. It was like they were possessed."

"I agree," said Wade starting to calm down, "I can not put my finger on it but the White I have known would not have attacked us. They were vicious and almost looked as if they were carrying out some sort of command coming from another, another who had control of them. The Myk!" shouted Wade beginning to rant once more. "They're back. I knew it. They have control of the White; we have not done what we set out to accomplish. We have been too slow. The myk have built up more forces."

"Wade," Thorium said loudly. "I know how upset you are, this has been more than anyone should have to deal with, however, we need to make sure before we act. Rest now, Wade, tomorrow there will be your bride waiting for you."

The Ceremony

Lady Theresa and Lady Alyce were preparing for the ceremony. The staff managed all of their clothing, cleaning and repairing what was needed.. Lady Alyce worked to ensure the ceremony stayed unchanged. Deeply affected by the attack, Lady Theresa managed to find strength amidst the ordeal. She and her family had survived this along with Wade and his friends, and she now realized how this entire ceremony was more than just for show. Lady Theresa knew this was for both her parents and all of the people around them, for the people of Twror and the whole Northern Valley. After what happened, she at first wanted to marry Wade in just a simple ceremony with only a few people. Now she understood that the wedding tradition, passed down for generations, was important to her parents and those who came to witness it. 'Yes,' she thought, 'I would not change anything; it is the right thing to do.'

The two ring bearers stepped bravely forward

Wade took the proffered ring, designed with two whales and precious stone from a chain of his mothers that he carried, representing the joining of the two families, and spoke, the tears in his eyes almost choking his words. "With this ring," he said, placing it on Theresa's finger, "I am now yours, my Lady."

Lady Theresa now took her ring that once belonged to her father and placed it on Wade's finger. "And I am now yours, my Lord."

Lady Ruth now stepped forward, now a leader in Twror and among the White. "Let this celebration, this joining of Lord Wade and Lady Theresa of Nourne, begin in its fullest. Let us celebrate this new path to the future. We honor those killed in the tragedy of yesterday. However, today let us show how the spirits of our fallen would rejoice and carry forward the new spirit of this land. This they would want."

Silence spread across the crowd and was noticeable throughout the city. Then once more, the chanting began. This time it was, "To the future...To the future..." The musicians from various regions resumed playing in their symphony written for Twror. Maypole dancing began, a tradition brought to the festivities by the Coastal People, dancing around the poles with their long ribbons shared hand to hand by the dancers. All the people in the park and the surrounding streets shared the food brought from all the lands.

Thul stepped to the front of the stage, speaking to whomever could hear him. Locklear and the rest of the Sage just looked on, not knowing what Thul was going to say. They had welcomed him with some trepidation into the order. And now what?

Thul spoke with confidence. He was no longer the stowaway on *The Proctant* who had talked his way into the good graces of the captain. Like his shipmates, he had gained a new feeling for his place in this new world.

"To the many peoples of this land, in the commemoration of the joining of my friend, Wade to Lady Theresa (he still couldn't bring himself to call him Lord Wade... they exchanged smiles at that) and the unifying of these many lands, I decree that The Hold and its art and treasures from our distant past is now open to all of the people of these lands. The Library will now be open to all whom wish to learn its secrets, not just the select few. These students and scholars, selected from all of these lands, will learn and teach what has been hidden for so long from us all. And finally, a new land, Argonia, will soon be joined and be a part of us."

Milne now stepped forward. Thul had secretly brought him from Argonia to Twror for the ceremony, kept hidden from the Sage, except Chuak, who had aided in Milne's travel.

The two, Thul and Milne, joined their hands and raised them together as the brothers that they now knew they were. "To the future!"

And the crowd joined them, "To the future."

Chapter 6
Massacre in the Myk's Valley

The Jall trader looked around the camp with satisfaction. They had already removed enough of the guano on this trip to make it successful. They just had to keep the caravan hidden from the watchful eyes of those usurpers of the Jall's rightful trade monopoly. Who were these newcomers to think that any but the Jall should have the rights to this treasure? Hadn't they, The Jall, also lost lives in the battle to defeat the Myk? This trade monopoly was given to them by The Teachers and was their right.

They had arrived here two nights before, six ox-driven wagons and a half-dozen from the hold to provide security. They had gone around the mountains and used the northern pass. All worked hard with the shovels to fill the wagons as quickly as possible. All would share the wealth of this *trading* expedition equally.

Already five of the carts were full. They would leave tomorrow night back over the northern pass to the Jall City. A campfire was burning to provide warmth on the cold night of early spring. Its light was hidden from the guards by the mountains of guano and waste that surrounded it.

The waste was an issue, but at least it didn't stink like the still burning fire under what had once been the Myk's Palace. The bones in the waste were mostly deformed, obviously White, and they had been picked free of any flesh before being deposited here along with the warbird's guano and other garbage of the palace. The trader smiled. Even these bones, the remains of those eaten by the Myk and his followers in the Palace had value once ground up. But that was for another trip. The men threw the bones into a macabre pile to one side as they loaded the guano onto the wagons. He'd pick up the bones the next time, the trader thought, and bring an extra wagon to do so.

The bandits (traders in their eyes) were in good spirits. They had just finished off a meal of roasted boar. A nice bonus of the stench of the old Myk's Palace burning was that its smell covered up the scent of their roasted meals each night. The sentries had no idea they were there, except for the ones that had taken the bribes and they didn't matter.

Somebody, however, did know that they were there. Watchful eyes followed the traders every move. More desecration of the Myk; all would pay for this. During the previous week, another half a dozen of the myk had arrived from the south, their second head guiding them here. There were assembled now more than enough to make those trespassers below pay for this sacrilege. Then they in turn would go north to rejoin the Myk. Such was their way now. One would stay behind here in the valley's high walls to gather the next of the reborn to arrive and then guide them north through the hidden ways. The occasional myk escaped their attention and traveled north alone, but most found their way to the Myk through the Myk's valley. Already dozens had passed north this way.

The orders of the Myk had changed. His closest advisor, Kat, had ordered it so. Beginning here, with this group, each party was to create an act of terror on those who had stolen the Land of the Myk. Those below the watchful eyes, they who felt so secure while they stole the property of the Myk, would be the first to feel this new wrath of the Myk.

The traders had little need of sentries around the campfire. Those on duty on the valleys rim, whose job it was to keep these bandit traders out, also worked to keep any dangers away. A small bribe had gotten the Jall into the valley in the darkness of the early morning. Another bribe to the same sentry would get them out of the Valley of the Myk when it was time to leave. The Valley of the Myk, the name had stuck, even with the advent of the construction of the peace memorial.

The Jall traders had carelessly left their weapons in their wagons. What need had they of them under the careful watch of the Northern Valleys sentries? What fear had they here, as they laughed their way into a drunken stupor from the standards of ale they passed between each other?

As the fire burned down, the men tossed the last of the wood they had brought with them in the wagons onto it. They would be leaving tomorrow and would have no more need of fire to keep the spring chill out. Tomorrow night and they would be on their way out of the valley once more. In an hour, the bandit traders were asleep in their bedrolls by the embers of the dying fire.

There were fifteen of them now, all reborn myk. They cautiously made their way down the mountain into the valley below, the Myk's Valley, they told themselves. The sentries above paid them no attention. There had been no attacks, until now at least. With the men below now asleep, this would be a massacre, not a battle. They would all feed well for the journey north. The weapons they gained would be of use in the future, both here for future attacks on the Northern valley and in their preparations to regain all that they had lost.

Each of the Myk carried a weapon as best suited for their needs as possible. However, this was not the time from before the battle against the invaders they had lost, when each myk held custom weapons built for each deformity. These were weapons scavenged, many stolen from waste piles not dissimilar to the one below. They wore no armor. This would be an attack of stealth, not bravery. Small blades would be best to slice open the necks of the humans below. Quiet, silent and efficient and then they would have their feast on the still living flesh of the humans. And the sentries would continue to patrol the rim of the valley without noticing what was transpiring below.

The myk crossed the open space between the jumble of boulders at the base of the hillside and the piles of guano on their bellies using all of their limbs, in some cases five or six. They did not understand why these defilers were stealing the warbird's waste, but it belonged to the myk nonetheless. The last of the myk stumbled briefly, its still immature second head not yet in full control of its body and a sentry not a hundred yards away turned briefly towards the attackers. The myk as a group lay motionless and to the sentry above they just looked like the rocks that lay in profusion on the valley's floor. After a short pause, the sentry turned away and resumed his silent march in the darkness above the valley. The fate of the looters was sealed at that point. The leader of this myk attack breathed a silent sigh of relief and led the Myk forward to the piles once more.

The fire had burned down to mostly embers as the men slept unaware. Only a single man from The Hold, who had been plagued recently with bouts of restless sleep, was awake. He stood by the laden wagons, having a smoke and leaning on a wagon. In the darkness he was nearly invisible, good fortune that stood his alone. Even he, however, stood weaponless.

The myk sneaked into the camp, past the wagons and their oxen, past the unseen trader and slowly, carefully, so as to not make another sound, encircled the campfire. The lone trader who stood now aware of the presence of the Myk could do nothing. To shout a warning would only bring his own death, as well as the other already doomed bandit traders of the Jall. Weaponless, asleep by the dying fire, they stood no chance.

It was over almost as soon as it began and the lone survivor of the massacre could only watch in growing horror at what began next; an assassin of the myk slit each of the trader's throats open. Then the orgy of feeding began. The trader who now lay silently under a wagon had heard the stories. His own brother had survived the battle that had defeated the Myk. However, to witness this feeding frenzy would drive him as near to madness as was possible. He slunk further under the wagon, but could not take his eyes off the feast that he watched.

"To the Myk," one shouted, as he held part of an arm that he had chopped off the trader who withered on the ground held high, still barely alive. The myk were careful with their cuts. The goal was to keep each food source alive as long as possible while its flesh was removed and devoured.

"To the Myk!" the others all intoned in unison. Each held a body part of one of the traders high in his hand(s) in salute.

Legs, arms, hands, these were the first things consumed by the myk in their orgy. However, eyes were especially a delicacy. Each part of the body, finally even the brains and internal organs, were consumed by the myk. To the myk this was not an act of cannibalism. The White, and their successor, the myk, were a higher life form than the humans were. The myk were the superior species and these humans were no different to them than cattle were to the humans. They would leave the oxen. There was plenty here to fill the bellies of these fifteen myk and help them survive their journey north to the new Cavern of the Myk. Human flesh was the only true food source for the myk.

The lone survivor of the massacre lay shuddering under the wagon. Somehow, in the chaos, the oxen had not moved. The memories of what he had seen would remain forever imbedded in his mind. He was found the next day in the early afternoon by the sentries, long after the myk had left the valley. (As was now the order, one myk remained behind, hidden, waiting for the next of the myk to begin the journey north.) The survivor was aimlessly driving a wagon around the valleys floor.

The sentries were initially at a loss for what they had found. Until in his barely coherent ramblings, the trader told the sentries of the massacre and guided them to the spot. Bone fragments and a scattering of skin and hair were all that remained of the feast. The man screamed and started running in circles until caught and held in place by the sentries. The full wagons of guano gave away that this had been a band of smugglers. However, this massacre, this was the work of the Myk.

A sentry shook the man. "How many?" he asked.

"There were twenty of us," the survivor barely stammered out.

"Not you, smuggler," the guard said, emphasizing the word smuggler. "How many of the myk?"

"The myk?" the man said bewildered, "They're all gone."

"We know they left, thief, but how many were there?" the sentry impatiently spoke. The sentry's eyes were now watching the valley walls closely.

"How many of what?"

"The myk, smuggler, how many?" another sentry spoke. Each sentry now gathered at the site of the massacre was thinking the same. "Are they still here someplace in the valley?" He shouted at what had once been a man but was now just a hollow shell after what he witnessed here. "How many?"

"The myk? Fifteen, twenty, what does it matter," the madman laughed at the sentries. "We're dead, all dead," the man melancholy said, sitting down on the ground where his colleagues had died their horrible deaths. "All dead, all dead," the mad man sang in his singsong voice. "All dead, we're all dead," he laughingly sang.

The sentries looked around nervously. This was something new. An armed party of the myk had wiped the smugglers out and feasted on their remains. The myk was not as defeated as thought. Nourne and Twror would have to be told of this. Moreover, the guards would have to be more aware now in the Valley of the Myk; this was no longer the soft duty that they had prepared themselves for.

Chapter 7
The Way North

The Peace Monument, where the Myk's Palace once stood, was starting to take shape. More and more people had come forward to help on the project and the people of Twror had become resigned to the fact that the memorial was no longer just theirs to build. All of the remains of the Palace were gone, tumbled into the gaping hole that had been the Myk's dungeons, prisons and cellars. A foundation for what was to come had begun to fill the imprint of the valley that was once the palace. Under the directing guidance of the Jall, concrete (now used in the Two Valleys in construction for the first time since the Great War) was poured to leave a level surface to build on. Metal rods of great length were formed from the metal scavenged from the Skeleton Cities and laid out in the Jall concrete pour for strength.

"This is a memorial that will last the ages," stated the Jall.

Assembling under a large tent just to the north of the Monument was the party that would soon be striking north to find the reported hidden Cavern of the Myk. After the meeting that Wade had called, with new information on the Myk's spies and the double-heads, it was clear that the menace that was the double-heads was worse than thought. Moreover, with the assignation attempt on Wade and Lady Theresa at their wedding, they made the decision to move one more time against the Myk. However, the question remained, where were the Myk and his misshapen followers hidden? That they were active in Twror was apparent. That the Temple of Hydron was the name of their refuge they knew from Wade's interview with the White family. They knew that it was somewhere to the northeast, from the trail left by the double-heads as they left the northern valley. However, that was all they knew.

A small party would head out in a week to find the cavern and report to the unified people of the South. Then they would send a military expedition. This time there would be no escape for the Myk. Nevertheless, the Myk had spies in the Northern Valley. Double-heads not yet exposed and followers still among the Whites of the *Old Ways*. A trade mission would be their cover, looking for the rumored people of the north that Del had spoken of at the meeting Wade had called. They let it be known in Twror that these people had items of use to the growing Northern Valley and that The Hold and the Jall, once more, would not be awarded exclusive trading rights. Two ox-driven carts carrying trading goods would accompany the party to further the illusion.

As the men gathered for the expedition, they watched the work done on the monument. Rock was being broken by hand using hammers and wedges. Former White and new citizens of Twror carried the rock to the shrinking pit that had been the Myk's Palace. There they separated it into two piles. Some were added to the concrete poured into the hole for the foundation, while the best pieces were set aside for use on the actual building of the monument. The Jall overseeing the construction selected pieces with care. These pieces would cover the face and facade and give the monument its beauty. The Scholars of The Hold's Library gave out the recipe for the concrete used. They mixed the concrete with the unwanted pieces of stone and poured the mixture into the new foundation.

'Soon the foundation would be finished,' thought Thorium, 'and the actual building of the monument will begin.' Already he could see the walls under construction that would list the names of those known to have died on the battlefield. At the top would be Cole; the sole member of *The Proctant* to die there.

As Thorium wandered through what was left of the ruins that had been the Myk's Palace, he could not help but think back to the atrocities that they had found there. Praxton of Pyers had committed suicide there, not far from where Thorium now stood, unable to deal with the sight of what he had so long tried to deny. Thorium glanced in the direction of where Gant had found what remained of his wife; the mutilated empty hulk that no longer contained her soul had died in his arms. How had Gant managed to withstand that grief? It would remain a part of Gant, Thorium knew.

'How many more still remain in denial of what happened here, of what the Myk stood for? How many hidden followers did the Myk still have, maybe even among those working on the monument? Moreover, maybe not just among the White. Many of the Two Valleys, The Hold and the Jall didn't approve of the changes they had brought to this world,' Thorium quietly pondered.

Thorium looked skyward and towards the monument being built. He raised his arms to the heavens and shouted in as loud a voice as he could muster. "I swore vengeance against those that once ruled this land in their barbarism, the Myk and his followers. At this spot I renew that contract once more!"

Thorium's shout drew looks from those around him working here in the Round Valley on the Peace Monument. All knew who he was. All knew that Thorium's vow would bring action. Thorium looked around at those who heard his shout. His only words to them; "I come to this place once more to renew my vow and see the progress of the monument's construction. Now I can return in peace to Erson."

Those around him stood at attention as he walked away from the monument; a hero walking among them.

Under a tent, the rest of the expedition's party was ready to go. All had watched Thorium's vow and knew that this would be no ordinary expedition. The mission would be small in number to avoid suspicion of what it was, however the party more than made up for that with its components. All would be on horseback except for Mendy and Alum who would drive the two ox-driven wagons. For now, each member's horse remained tied to the back of the wagons along with several extra horses. No one knew how long this mission would take and Jamen of Kiln had brought the best from his stables for those without their own mounts.

Unusual by any standard and not remembered to have happened in the recent past, three Sage would travel this road; Gar, Tor and Del the Wanderer whom brought with him his knowledge of the lands and rumors of the North.

After the meeting in Wade's office, two of the Nomads, Reed and Sebastian decided to join the party, along with their wildcats whose job it would be to find and follow the trail of the White leading north from the Round Valley. Even today, five months after the taking of the Myk's Palace, more White males, all presumed to carry the second head, disappeared along the trail they would follow to the desolate North. Somehow, these White seemed to be in communication with the Myk along the way. They hoped to discover how this was possible as well as where the myk hid on this trip.

Jamen of Kiln and Loren of the R'mon's had joined the

expedition as well, each for their own reasons. Jamen to ensure he would see the end of the Myk once and for all. Loren to be close to Reed, his silent protector, with her crossbow slung across her shoulder. His recklessness for a Nomad concerned her. She stayed always in the background so as not to infuriate his Nomadic sensibilities, but always she was close by.

Thorium finally reached the tent of the expedition he would lead. The last to arrive, he walked in with his own wildcat Tri at his side, almost rubbing against him as he walked. Thorium's own protector and at times it seemed his best friend. He exchanged embraces with his shipmates from the Proctant, Mendy and Alum. The two remained inseparable, even in this new land, and their fighting skills remained unmatched. Thorium wished he had Zircon with him, with Zircon's newfound sense of purpose and his long-rifle, but he remained engaged in the Sage's business.

Ten men would set out, with the three wildcats leading the way; an unusual party to those that would look too closely. Too few, too many, time would answer that question.

Several days after the arrival of Thorium, they instructed the wildcats to pick up the trace of the White. They sped ahead, periodically raising their ears to the air or putting their noses to the ground. Sebastian's wildcat, Traveler, took the lead. Tri, the youngest, tended to follow the other two. They were superb trackers, always on the edge of the sight of the expedition which followed them. The wagons plodded along last on the trail. The trail was fairly easy to follow as they left the immediate vicinity of the monument and traversed the Round Valley.

The Round Valley, formally the Valley of the Myk's Palace, as was most of the Two Valleys, were now patrolled on a regular basis since the massacre of the traders from The Hold. Yet even with these increased patrols more acts of violence against the monument and throughout the Two Valleys was taking place by the followers of the *Old Ways* of the Myk..

The mist of the early morning was still in the air as they reached the northern edge of the Round Valley. The trail was clear to the wildcats which pass to take. All spore pointed to the western most pass of the valley's peaks. Thorium's first thought was that the trail would lead through the Eastern pass. The one they took led them towards the

Great Swamp and the home of the Jal-Beast.

The three Sage traveled together near the front of the expedition, whispering among each other. They were heading towards lands that only Del among the known Sage had traveled. Both Gar and Tor spoke with Del about the cloudiness Gar felt in his brain; what it was that could be causing it. Del had only recently returned from his latest travels to the east and felt nothing. The Myk? Something else? It was a concern of the Sage but there was little that they could do about it now. Nevertheless, all three watched for any further changes in his mental capabilities.

Gar seemed especially affected by the malady. His ability had always been the almost supernatural ability to 'connect the dots' without almost any reference points. The Sage as a whole had come to depend on that when it came to questions about the intention of the Teachers for their future. Now he could concentrate on just one thing at a time. It was worrisome to all. Were the Sage finally growing old?

The three Sage started talking about all that had transpired this last year; Thul, the son of Simon and of the Teachers; the defeat of the Myk and the unification of the Two Valleys; Thorium and the crew of *The Proctant*; even Argonia. All seemed foretold by the Teachers, as was expected by the Sage. Nevertheless, there was the wedding, Wade and Lady Theresa, what about that? How did that fit into the plans the Teachers had laid out. It did not and Wade did not. Who, or even what, was Wade? At first an almost footnote to what was happening, a minor character with a minor role. Now, he stood as an unforeseen major player in the drama of their Age; from unknown apprentice seaman to Governor of the Northern Valley and the Lord of Nourne. Could there be other players besides the Teachers or Argonia at work here?

The first day's goal was to reach one of the outposts of the Northern Valley, built of treated swamp logs from the Great Swamp. There were three of these located on the three passes that led from the Northern Valley. Two scouts stationed in each with their warbirds. These outposts were constantly on the watch now for anything unusual happening within their range, especially regarding the Myk.

As the expedition left the Round Valley and ascended the northwestern most pass, the trail became strewn with rock and ruts from the winter's snowmelt and the wagons rate of passage slowed to a crawl. It was because of these conditions that they were using slower ox-driven wagons instead of something faster. They may be slow but they kept moving.

Sebastian and Reed dismounted from their horses and tied them to the back of Mendy's wagon. More comfortable walking than riding anyway they noticed the first signs of unease in the wildcats. They called the wildcats back and had them ride in the wagons. The trail was clear for now and they did not want any White spooked by the wildcats before they could prove useful. The oxen were at first agitated by the nearness of the wildcats. The Nomads seeming ability to calm animals around them seemed to calm the oxen once more.

Snow could still be seen on the higher mountains that surrounded the Valley and although springtime and almost noon, a distinct chill filled the cloudless sky. Patches of snow were in the shadows at almost the elevation of the trail. As they reached the summit of the pass, the reason for the wildcat's unease became clear. A distinct smell, the odor of decaying flesh, reached the men. They secured the wildcats to the wagons with their collars for their own safety and none of the three was happy with that. The men looked at each other as they crossed the summit, the horses barely under control as well. What were they coming too? The scouts had not reported anything unexpected here.

Just past the summit, still partially buried in the snow to one side of the trail, they saw the bodies. There were half a dozen of them, but who they were the men were unable to see from a distance. The stench of the decaying flesh was almost palatable. It reminded Thorium of the stench when they entered the Myk's Palace grounds. Led by Thorium the party continued past the bodies before stopping, both to calm the animals and to relieve themselves of some of the smell.

The three Sage remained at the summit and approached the bodies.

"The smell, we can send a party back from the outpost to check it out," Thorium pleaded with the Sage. Too many memories from the discoveries in the Palace were coming back into his head from it. "This reminds me far too much of the Myk's Palace."

"This is too important, Thorium," Gar said back, dismounting from his horse, his scarf wrapped around his head to protect from both the smell and the cold. Del and Tor joined him. "Go ahead with the wagons; we'll catch up with you."

"Your safety," Thorium objected, pointing to the bodies. "This mission is too important for something to happen to you here."

Loren stepped over to Thorium and took his hand. "Let's go, the Sage can handle this."

Del spoke now, also looking towards the distant bodies. "I have heard too many rumors of the emptiness of the North. The three of us are enough to uncover any clues here and to protect ourselves from any danger. We will join you shortly to keep this trip on track. Go just beyond where the trail bends. That will get you clear of this and yet not be too far for us to rapidly catch-up."

The three Sage tied their horses to a branch near the side of the trail and headed on foot towards the bodies. The rest of the expedition continued on its way on the rugged trail.

The bodies were huddled together in death, as if for warmth. At first, they just saw the six White, obvious double-heads. Then they saw the other two, partially consumed, food for this White party while they traveled. It was from this White 'food source' that the greatest part of the stench came. Obviously, these two were artificially kept alive on the journey and the carrion birds and other animals had avoided them. However, the White with their double-heads, birds had feasted on them as the melting snow exposed the bodies. The Sage removed more of the snow, fully uncovering the skeletons.

The Sage looked over the still partially frozen remains and now, for the first time, saw in the skeleton remains how the second head, now just forming skulls, sprouted from the spine of the White like a tree branch, growing upward, to gain entry to the light in the shoulder area of the White. Tor had thought the second head had been that of a conjoined twin, the two bodies merged as one to become a Myk. In the past they cremated the Double Head bodies when found, in a hurry to destroy the remains and send a message. They had not examined them. Now it was clear that these second heads were something else. They were not conjoined twins, but a true deformation of the White; truly two heads on one individual. On seeing this, Tor wished aloud they had examined some of the dead Myk before destruction. However, none had thought of this.

What could have caused this grotesque malformation of the Whites? Moreover, how could this later, second head, be more intelligent than the first. That was confirmed many times in the encounters with the White. Contamination from the Great War, that seemed clear, guided in some way by the genetic experiments of the Teachers, only now coming to fruition. It did not seem possible that this could have happened naturally. The three Sage looked at each other in silent communication. This would need further discussion, away from the others and in secret. This was not something that the Order was prepared to make public. Meanwhile, what would this mean to their task? The Sage returned to their horses and hurried ahead to catch up with the rest of the party after burying the second heads and their spinal cords, covering up for now this new found secret.

As the party headed down out of the pass at its slow trudge, Reed and Sebastian walked together on one side of the trail, their two wildcats accompanying them. Tri, Thorium's wildcat, patrolled the other side of the wagons while Thorium rode a short distance ahead of the expedition. Loren rode in Mendy's wagon seated alongside him, asking questions of the confederation of him. Always the storyteller, Mendy was happy to regale her with stories of his home. Jamen walked with his horse to the rear of the party, both watching for attack from the rear and for the return of the three Sage.

Barely audible to the others, Reed and Sebastian were engaged in an animated discussion of the future of the Nomads in this newly changing world. Sebastian embraced this change and the Nomads role in it.

"Reed, we can no longer live in the past of our fathers. We bring value to this changing world and must embrace this opportunity to educate ourselves and lead this change."

"Sebastian, we have known each other since boyhood and we are like brothers. That is why we walk this path together now. The Nomads have never shirked from our duty to this world. How many died in the battle so that the Myk could be defeated?"

Sebastian then asked Reed, "What should we have done. Should we have not helped to bring about this change to the world?"

Reed's answer was quick. "Nevertheless, these new ways are not the way of the Nomad. Our way has been the same since the beginning of our time. We survived the Age of Darkness and Ice in this way; above ground, without the shelter of The Hold or the help of the Teachers. We are graced in our ways. Change is for the others, not for us. We are not of the Teachers and must follow our own path in this world."

"But my brother, we have changed when necessary. Just look at our companions, the wildcats. They were not there at the beginning. Wasn't that change good?"

"We were chosen by the wildcats as their companions. They saw value in living with us. The change was not with the Nomad, but with the wildcats."

Sebastian stopped and looked at Reed who also stopped. They faced each other and Sebastian placed his right hand on Reed's shoulder. "Reed," he sadly said, "I feel that there is now a chasm between us, within the Nomad people itself. Soon we will no longer be able to bridge this divide and our people will split in half."

"Then when this trip is over we must return to the plains, our home."

"Or we must embrace this change as one people," Sebastian finished.

Both men continued from that point in silence.

About an hour further along the trail, they reached a smoother road through the low hills and the Great Swamp came into view at times in the distance. The three Sage rejoined the party once more. All rode now on horseback and the pace quickened. The three wildcats raced ahead of the party, enjoying their freedom and staying just in view as they scouted for trace of the White.

The Sage now rode at the back of the expedition and Thorium rode back to them, Jamen taking his spot at the head of the party.

"What did you find, back with the bodies?" he asked the Sage.

"All double-heads, all dead since the winter, frozen to death it seems in a winter's storm and the cold it brought to the pass," Gar answered.

"Is there anything else that we need to know?"

"Tonight," said Del. "Tonight when we read the reports of the scouts. All is not what it seems."

"What?" a perplexed Thorium asked.

"We'll discuss what we found tonight. I fear that this trail has ears," Gar stated matter-of-factly.

Thorium knew how the Sage would clam up at times. They had found something; of that he was sure. He would find out when they reached the outpost. There was no sense pressuring the Sage here for what they knew. Thorium had learned that lesson many times over in his dealings with the Order. He rode back to the front of the expedition and joined Jamen.

'Let the Sage keep their secret,' Thorium thought as he rode. 'I have more to concern myself with. Double-heads in a group, not one or two alone, not a good sign, frozen to death or not.'

"Well?' asked Jamen of Thorium as he rode up to him, not expecting anything new from Thorium; he knew the Sage as well.

"A group of myk; not ones or twos."

Jamen frowned at the news. "Not good, not good at all," were his only words to that news.

As the afternoon progressed, they followed the trail of the White down from the summit of the pass. The trail began to follow a small river through the lower hills that lay just to the east of the Great Swamp. Del had seen maps of this area from the time before the Great War and knew these hills were once part of the Pre-War lowlands. Somehow, during or in the aftermath of the 'Great War' the lands of this continent had tilted. From the lowlands, depressed by this unknown event, the Great Swamp had formed over the thousand years of winter and darkness. From the Pre-War highlands had become the mountains that held The Hold and the Two Valleys, rising above the pre-war plains. He had heard legends on his travels from those that had survived away from this area of great shocks in the land during the Age of Darkness. From the old maps, they must have been caused by this Cataclysm.

Evergreen trees dominated the landscape they now traveled and the spoor of bear, elk, and deer (even wolf) were seen along the trail. The wildcats now traveled close to the wagons and all eyes remained on close watch for ambush. Gar now traveled in one of the wagons, his headaches, this diminishing of his abilities, had grown worse. It was apparent that White traveled all about them, whether in singles or more was the only unknown. However, the number following this trail seemed high.

As they followed the river, they saw large numbers of brownish-red fish swimming upstream.

"Salmon here?" asked Mendy aloud to Loren, still riding in the wagon alongside of him.

"Yes," said Loren, "you are familiar with them."

"Some of our rivers are colored red by their spawning," he enthusiastically replied.

"They are not so prevalent here; however there are some rivers, such as this, where they return in great numbers. None of the rivers that feed the Inland Sea carry them, only those that feed directly to the Western Sea you crossed."

Below them, a single bear was fishing in the river. It stood smaller than any Mendy remembered from home. 'Could he be the same bear that Zircon found had battled the wolves of the skeleton city?' Mendy thought to himself.

Dusk approached as the party reached the outpost. It was made of a large building with a stockade of the Jall's treated swamp-logs. This was the last outpost of the Two Valleys in the northern direction that they were heading. Reaching it reminded Gar that he had been unable to gain the support of the Trader-King to include a Jall on this trip.

* * * * *

The Jall Trader-King had tried to explain to an uncharacteristically impatient Gar that a schism had appeared in the Jall people and his position was too weak to contemplate sending anybody loyal to him on such a mission.

"As schism, what are you speaking of? The Myk still stands before us and you tell me that the Jall are no longer united?" Gar asked in a disbelieving manner.

"Gar, there are many around me who oppose these changes that are happening so quickly around us. For too long we have enjoyed the privilege of our monopoly on trade. Now these outsiders bring change to our lands wherever they tread. And like the White, not all of the Jall and those of The Hold agree with these changes."

"It has gotten that bad, old friend," a now concerned Gar spoke quietly.

"Maybe worse. These are rumors only, but my days may be numbered as the Trader-King. Someone is offering great riches for a venture of which I know nothing."

"All trade goes through you, the missions distributed equally among the clans."

"But there are those outside the clans, Gar, who fear that their share of the trade will disappear."

"No-one would dare to try to depose you. Ignore you perhaps; that has been done in the past. But to try to replace you as King; to what effect?"

"They want to restore the order of before, when trade was held in total by the Jall and The Hold."

"Do you know who is behind this? It seems unlikely a Jall."

"The reports come from the city of The Hold. Someone there stands in opposition to the change we see coming."

'A division among us at the worse time,' Gar thought listening to the Trader-Kings words.

* * * * *

Returning to the future, Gar thoughts continued, 'This mission is too important to change or cancel. The Myk are growing strong again. Nevertheless, what will we find on our return? The Two Valleys and the City by the Lake seem firm in their resolve to move forward. Now the Jall city and The Hold, what would those that oppose the change coming to this world do? What could they do?' Gar only hoped that whatever transpired while they were gone on this mission would not prove fatal.

The post was large and manned on a permanent basis by two scouts from Castle Nourne. The scouts rotated every month on an alternating basis (with two months duty) so that one experienced in this land would always be there. They had their warbirds tethered in a small barn, made not of swamp-logs but of the evergreens native to this part of the world.

Each day one of the two men flew a scouting mission covering an area to the North. However, that range seldom reached one hundred miles and they saw no sign of the Myk, except the occasional spotting of the trail the Whites followed. The spore of the Double-heads was all around them and always leading to the north.

When the party reached the gate of the outpost, the two scouts met them and opened the gate. They led the horses and oxen to a small corral next to the barn where the animals would spend the night. Jamen of Kilne, along with Mendy and Alum, went with the animals to brush out the horses after the long ride and make sure they had plenty of food and water. This could very well be the last time that the horses and oxen could be treated this well on the trip and Jamen wanted to make sure the horses were pampered one last time before the dangers that possibly lay before them.

The rest of the party went inside to a ready common room. A Jall trading party had arrived the day before. With the Trader-Kings warning still on the forefront of Gars mind, he quickly passed word onto the expedition that, at least for this night, they must make sure that no word of their mission or direction is spoken to the Jall. The others understood and as Jamen, Mendy and Alum joined them inside, the word was passed to them as well. For the moment, secrecy was needed.

A fire was burning in a large fireplace and from rotating spits the smell of roast Craul Bird filled the room. To one side of the room large kegs of oak filled with rich barley ale took up a wall. On one side of the Kegs and in baskets woven of swamp-reed, were apples, still fresh from the falls harvest. Blocks of sharp cheese lay on a table on the other side of the kegs alongside bread baked by the scouts in the outpost's oven. To weary travelers who stopped by the post the smells were comforting. To the White, attempted to sneak by unseen, they smells were reminders of the recent past and the lost lands they hoped to regain.

Most of those in the common room this night were with the Jall trading party. Their loud boasts heard across the room as each tried to better the next on the lands they had explored. They loudly announced that they were on the way to The Hold where an unsanctioned trade expedition was to leave. Though Gar listened closely to the words and boasts of the Jall traders, it was apparent that they had no idea of the job, just vast riches promised to all of those who took part.

"I hear that thousands from the unaffiliated clans may take

part," they heard one of the Jall say over the din.

"The riches must be great for the promised reward for all who take part," stated another between bites of the Craul Bird.

"I hear that there is no limit to the number taking part, this may be the largest trade mission ever," a third Jall spoke up.

Gar could just listen with apprehension; this was the discord, the divide in the Jall, which he had spoken of with the Trader-King. For the interconnected community that was the Jall, nothing could be worse than this divide.

'Who was the leader and why was this started at this time,' thought Gar to himself. With the expedition under way, this could not have come at a worse time.

Fortunately, the expedition went unnoticed when they had entered and they gathered in a darkened corner of the common room. The three Sage were able to clear that corner of eavesdroppers and the expedition gathered for the next step. They were anxious to hear from the scouts on what they observed in the direction that they were going. The two scouts made their way to the corner and introductions made.

"We are at your command," the scouts said quietly in unison to Thorium. "Both Sir Wade and Nourne made it clear the importance of your trip." Mendy and Alum quietly laughed at the 'Sir Wade' comment and drew serious looks from the scouts and Thorium.

"Was the need for discretion mentioned as well?" asked Gar. "We do not want to make ourselves known to those already here."

"Of course, Sage, a trading trip to the North."

"Not even that to the Jall assembled here," Gar commanded.

"Do you know the purpose of the Jall," Tor asked.

"Only that they have passed through in large numbers for several weeks on their way to The Hold. I have never seen so many traveling together for a single trade before. Of where this trade lies, except for its richness, there seems to be no answer."

The party looked across the table at each other with some trepidation. There was obviously something amiss that the Sage knew of and were keeping to themselves; first the instruction not to mingle with the Jall and to keep themselves hidden, and now this.

Thorium broke the icy silence at the large table the expedition sat around. "Tor," he looked directly at the Sage as he spoke. "What is going on?"

Tor just looked at him not answering. It was Gar who responded.

"Before this expedition left, I asked the Trader King for a Jall to accompany us on this trip, a medical Jall for emergencies, as well as a trader, to give our story more credence and to enhance the illusion for any of the Myk's spies. For the first time in my long life, a Trader-King refused a request of mine. He mentioned a rift in Jall society and now we hear word of unaffiliated Jall gathering at the request of some unknown person or persons at The Hold. Something that none of the Sage are aware of. I had spoken to Locklear only a few days before I left The Hold and he knew of nothing happening there. Something is definitely amiss. If not for the importance of this trip I would have ordered its cancellation."

"This trip cannot be cancelled. The Myk must be found," Jamen interjected.

"I said almost," continued Gar. "The Myk must come first. But I am concerned about who will lead if this trouble comes to fruition while we are gone."

Jamen spoke almost too loudly, "The council of the Two Valleys will act for the good of all."

"Your council, without you," Sebastian spoke scornfully, "is a bunch of old men and will do nothing"

"Nourne, Wade, Theresa and Zircon; the leadership will come from them. And Locklear remains in The Hold if needed," Gar spoke with quiet force and assurance.

"You put quite a lot of faith in Zircon," Thorium stated as he reached for the cheese.

"He earned that much at the skeleton city of the wolves. Now he must finish his lessons and learn to lead," Gar responded.

"What of the myk? That is the purpose we leave during this perilous time," Jamen questioned the table, redirecting the conversation.

Thorium looked directly at the scouts now, "Tell us what you know, what you have found?"

"Ale first and then our food," Mendy brought up good-heartedly, "It's easier to listen when our bellies are full." All laughed at that, a needed break at the start of a serious endeavor.

"Food and drink for all," Jamen called forth, then more quietly, "we must remain in form for the many ears here tonight."

As the food and drink were brought to the table by Mendy, Alum and Loren (the least likely to be recognized in their party), the scouts began their story of what they had found in the North. Julius, as the more senior, began first to tell what he had found. He had been at the outpost almost his full two-month duty and would soon be returning home to the renewed and growing city of Erson.

"We have been watching the North of here since the fall of the Myk's Palace. I have been here almost two months, our scheduled tour of duty at the outposts. Dudley arrived last month and will assume the duties of the senior scout when my replacement arrives. Each of us takes turns watching the Northern Frontier. One heads out in the early morning and the other finishes his reports from the day before while they are still fresh in his mind. Our scouting lasts the full day, from early morning into the twilight hours. Just before I arrived we lost our first scout. He disappeared without a trace."

"Any idea what happened to him?" asked Thorium.

"It happened the first day we extended our range from 40 miles to 80 miles to the North. No sign of him has been found."

"The Myk?" Thorium almost hoped as he asked the question, though he doubted he would find the cavern so close to the known lands.

"I just don't know," Julius answered. "As we've extended our range it has also increased the amount of land we cover many fold. When I return I am going to ask that a third scout is posted here. It's just so hit and miss right now what we find."

Jamen asked the two scouts after he took another swig from his ale, "Do you plan your routes ahead of time?"

The second scout, Dudley, a slightly smaller man than Julius, now spoke up. "We are instructed to plan our route the previous day after we finish our reports. I have had quite a few of my missions change mid-flight, as happens to us all on the scouting missions. With the increased ground we have to cover, if you think you see something, or even if the weather changes, you can end up dozens of miles from where you planned."

"Go on," Gar said, attempting to gain control of the

conversation while at the same time battling the increased pressure on his mental abilities, "What have you found?"

"We can show you our log books and reports," Julius stated, "Mine are all here from my first mission. When we conclude our tours we return with the logs and reports"

"So what Nourne sees can be up to two months behind?" asked an astonished Thorium. "I thought what we had was up to date." Thorium took the offered reports and began leafing through them.

"Yes, it's been like that since we began," replied Julius, not sure of what Thorium was getting at.

Thorium jotted a quick note to Wade. "When you return, give this to Governor Wade. It requests that all of the reports be picked up on a weekly, if not more frequent, basis. We must have a better idea of what's going on around us."

Julius put the note in his pocket. "I'll attend to the governor's residence first with your note," he said.

"What is directly to the north of us? Have you seen much of the White," Reed and Sebastian asked almost in unison.

"What weapons have you found?" asked Loren.

"As you head north the trail turns and follows the edge of the Great Swamp. We have seen and heard a lot of the Jal-Beast. They seem to be in greater numbers on the Eastern and Northern edges of the swamps lands."

"Even in the winter and early spring?" asked Gar, amazed at hearing this. The Jall thought that their namesake beast was dormant in the winter and never traveled in more than pairs.

"I flew close to several on my second flight," said Dudley. "I think I saw egg nests, but there were too many of the beast to do more than a quick look."

"And that is where the Myk's trail leads," asked Thorium, more than a little concerned. He remembered crossing the Great Swamp from Jall when they first arrived and the close encounter with a pair then.

"We have seen signs of the White along the edge of the Great Swamp, so it seems yes."

"Is there another route that we can take from here?" asked Jamen of Kiln, not anxious to encounter the Jal-Beast himself.

"If you go back to the Round Valley, you take the central pass and it will meet what we think is their trail about one hundred miles north of here," answered Julius, trying to be helpful.

"And if we miss the trail they leave?" asked Reed.

"Then I'm afraid you'd have to return to the edge of the swamp to pick it up again. From the air we lose their trail just beyond the Great Swamp."

"It seems we are forced to take the path before us," Tor spoke solemnly.

"What else have you found beyond the swamp?" asked Gar.

"Something seems to be happening to the north of the Great Swamp. I have found several villages recently abandoned," began Julius. "The population of the north is very small anyway. Not far to the North, winter remains year around. However, in these empty villages we can find no sign of what has happened to the people that lived in them; no sign of where they left to or any turmoil. Both of us have landed in one of these empty places and it is as if the people just one day got up and walked away. They seem to have left everything behind."

"Could this be the Myk, seeking to reestablish his food source," thought Thorium aloud.

"That seems possible," continued Dudley. "But as yet we have seen little sign of struggle and recent tracks show their trail leading further north into the Wastelands."

Julius continued with his accounts, standing to stretch as he spoke. "The bear are now seen in larger numbers, but that could just be the result of the increasing amount of fish in the rivers bringing them close to us."

"But that wouldn't lead to the villages emptying out the way they have," added Thorium.

"I wouldn't think so," said Julius, pausing after finishing a drink.

"What else can you report?" asked Gar.

"That's about it," answered Julius. "A lot of empty lands lay to the north. Traces of the White seem to lead to the northeast from the edge of the Great Swamp and the now empty villages. With our new range, our missions take us to the closest we have been of the 'Blue Lights' the Teachers left behind. We are going to explore them shortly. Perhaps the Myk is using the Teachers former home to hide."

Del brusquely entered the conversation, standing up to add

urgency to what he said. He was drinking the Sage's beverage that he had brought along on the trip and waved his cup spilling some of the 'presso'.

"Avoid the *Blue Lights*. In my travels, I have approached them myself. There are only three of them and their expanse is not great, although the blueness they give out is seen for a long distance. The barrier is not firm. I threw a stone through one (Gar and Tor seemed aghast at this!) and it passed through and landed on the ground inside. I then passed my arm through the barrier. This was several years ago. Though it seemed cool going through the barrier and on the other side, when I removed my arm, it and my hand had the appearance of being burned. It took months for my arm to heal. You can be sure that the *Blue Lights* are not where the Myk is hiding. Nor near them, I would think. I fear that neither the White nor we would survive more than minutes in whatever the Teachers hid behind the barriers.

"I have encountered those people whose villages you now report as empty. A shy people, Gypsies they call themselves. They seem to worship their children. They hide from all. If we encounter them, they would not be a threat. They do use a bow, but of short range and strictly for hunting small game. Many I hear have traveled to Twror. What I do fear is what drove them from their homes if it is how you report. They would not leave their possessions behind willingly and they have no enemies that I am aware of."

"Thank-you for the warnings of the *Blue Lights*, I will post it for future scouts to stay clear and bring it with me to Nourne," Julius responded to the danger Del had laid out. He himself had planned to test the barriers on his last mission.

Del walked away from the table to the fire, warming his hands in its embrace. In his thoughts were the Gypsy people. He knew these people. Their homes and their children were their lives. Where had they gone? Not all had arrived in Twror, in fact very few. What would make them leave? He stood by the fire a long time. None recognized him as a Sage. His clothing was that of a common man and he carried no symbol of what he was.

Del had traveled well beyond the range of the scouts to the North and the East. He had not heard mention of the Cavern of the Hydron until the meeting in Twror. If it was there, either it was a new creation or very well hidden. In one area though, far to the Northeast, in the permanently frozen North, was a range of mountains that he had not explored. They seemed to be new mountains, ice-covered year around; a result of the 'Great War'? It could be so. Del knew from his travels and following maps of before the war that the world had changed in many ways; a result of the cataclysms of that war. The Great Swamp was a result of it, a tilting of the Earths crust. Even now, the Jall in their search for trade, found newly discovered pre-war cities in the swamps; mostly just the sunken remains of the cities, with a few relics not destroyed by the waters or the swamp.

While Del was at the fire, the ledgers and reports of the scouts passed around the table. All asked questions, but the answers were vague at best; the Two Valleys and Nourne just did not know enough of the north. Del returned to the table and the discussions continued well into the night. They decided they would stay an extra day at the post before leaving. That way the Jall party would be gone. They would plan the next leg of the expedition in the day light and leave well rested. Gar finished his instructions to Julius for his return to Nourne. The Valley's must prepare for whatever it was that the unknown person or persons of The Hold were planning.

It was not until three more days after their arrival at the outpost that the expedition left. On the matter of the Jall, and whatever was transpiring in The Hold, they decided that haste was of most importance. Dudley returned to Nourne with the messages of Gar and Thorium and they waited for the reply. In the meanwhile, there were the scout's logs to look over and study. Del made frequent notes of his own for what they had to look forward to on their journey. The Jall party itself did not leave right away but waited one more day for more unaffiliated Jall to arrive. Then they left together as a group. The number that assembled and left this one post was alarming to Gar and he had heard of other assembly locations as well for the Jall who were taking part in this endeavor. What could be the goal that so many were needed?

Any interaction between the expedition's party and the Jall, they left to Mendy and Alum, the least known to the Jall of the party. Del passed himself off as a wanderer who had only joined the expedition in passing. Those known best to the Jall, Gar, Tor and Thorium, stayed in an extra room (fatigue was the story told). Sebastian, Reed and the 3 wildcats searched for spore to show the path of the Whites. They found a lot around the outpost leading toward the Great Swamp and the North, and all along a single trail.

Early on the third day, while Loren and Thorium were saddling the horses (the Jall had left the day before so there was no longer the need to hide) the Nomads and their wildcats spotted a lone White moving slyly along the trail towards the Great Swamp. The White was not yet far from the outpost. Fearing the Myk had discovered the party, Thorium, with Loren close behind, gave chase on horseback, calling back the Nomads. As Thorium passed Sebastian and Reed, he gave the two men instructions to get the party moving as quickly as possible. The rest was over, the pursuit begun.

In the early morning mist, the trail of the White was easy to follow. He seemed to be making no effort to hide his trail. One leg seemed to be dragging behind the other. When they caught sight of him in the distance, he appeared injured, although there was no sign of blood on the trail; a broken leg from a fall? They would soon see, as they were rapidly gaining on the creature. There, in the low hills forest, they came to the White, barely to one side of the trail, lying still.

Thorium and Loren tied their horses on the side of the trail about thirty feet from where the White lay, stomach down, on the ground. They approached the White slowly, weapons drawn, eyes alert to a trap. Loren had an arrow slotted into her crossbow. The White still did not move.

Loren moved to the White to turn it over when Thorium stopped her. "Loren, don't touch it!" he cautioned in a loud voice. Loren stood above the White, scarcely breathing.

"Something doesn't seem right here," Thorium stated with a sense of urgency as he picked up a large stick. Both of their eyes scanned the forest around them.

"A trap?" Loren asked as she backed away.

"Doesn't look like it," replied Thorium as he approached the White with the large heavy stick. With the stick, he rolled the White onto its back. The White's breathing was heavy and shallow.

"It appears to be dying," said Loren without compassion in her voice. To those on the expedition these myk were vermin, to be extinguished.

"So it appears," Thorium stated back to her. He saw the large bulge above the right shoulder of the White, covered by a heavy shawl. He took his blade and cut away the shawl, in doing so uncovering the second head, a myk. That head snarled at them through a still forming mouth. Its first head only slobbered through its coarse breathing.

Ignoring the first head, Thorium spoke to the emerging second head. "You are dying?"

"I fear you not," it snarled, "fear me, for I am myk!"

"You are not the first myk I have encountered. Moreover, I have killed all that I have found. I have no fear of you, myk," Thorium said back, the last bit scornfully, showing no fear of the Myk. Loren stepped back from the sight of the Myk. She had seen them before, but never alive and never this close up.

"We know you," the Myk continued. "We are ready."

"If you know me, myk, then know you are the one that should be afraid." Thorium stood above the myk, watching it closely.

"I do not fear this death. It comes to many of the myk. Those that are not strong enough for what is to come."

"You know we will find your Cavern."

"We grow strong again. We are ready," were the myk's last words to Thorium. The myk closed the partially set eyes of its second head. The eyes of the first head stared vacantly into the air. It's breathing becoming even shallower.

When the rest of the expedition arrived about thirty minutes later, they stopped where Thorium and Loren had tied their horses. The party approached on foot. Thorium and Loren sat on a large dried log from a fallen tree a short distance from the dying myk. Only the Sage approached the myk. Del took his walking stick and nudged the body just below the second head. The first head only continued to drool madly. The second head opened its eyes briefly, looked at the three Sage and spoke its final words.

"We are ready. Our attack will come from where you least expect." Then it died.

Gar had been standing over the Myk, his thoughts more cloudy than before, when the creature before him died. He immediately noticed that the fogginess cleared up briefly with the death of the Myk; a connection between his mind and the second heads. He took his sword that he rarely used and plunged it into the new-borne head. His mind cleared even more, briefly free of what he now knew was the influence of the myk on his mind. Gar now knew with surety what was causing his mental hindrance; the birth of the second heads. Moreover, they could use this as a weapon against the Myk. If he could train and control this hindrance, now that he knew its source, he could detect the myk no matter how disguised. Like the ones they knew were operating freely in Twror. How close it had been for Wade and Lady Theresa. As the cloudiness began again to make its presence felt in his mind he knew another myk or even more than one was approaching.

Now there could be no myk ambush. He could feel them ahead of time.

Gar abruptly turned and walked back to his horse. "Leave it, I have found out much here. We must send warning to Nourne. Now we must continue in haste."

Loren quickly spoke up as she spurred her horse, "I will take the message to the outpost and catch up," and she began galloping back to the outpost.

The expedition remounted and the wildcats called to the wagons from their prowling to ride and rest. The trail was clear going forward.

Chapter 8
Edge of the Great Swamp

It was eerie how quiet the dense forest had become. They were still following the trail north to find the Myk. In addition, they were still finding telltale signs that the White males, double-heads in various stages of development, were still using the path they followed. They had caught one on the trail not two days before. When the Sage tried to question him, he had fled into the Great Swamp, not a quarter mile to the West. They could hear his screams from even that distance as the denizens of the swamp consumed him.

'Did the Myk hear his screams as well', thought Gar, whose mind cleared a little with the White's death. Part of the message he had sent back with Loren was his ability to sense the myk.

Thorium had expected to hear the loud cries of the Craul Bird this close to the northern edge of the Great Swamps. In the South, there were times you couldn't hear the person next to you talk, over their loud cries. Here, nothing and no signs of the slow moving tree snakes as well, known to travel great distances from the swamps edge.

The lack of Bear and Elk spore bewildered Gar. Further inland, the day before, it had been everywhere. He had expected the Bear to be their chief nemesis on the way north.

The Wildcats were uneasy.

It was on the second day of traveling along the edge of the Great Swamp that they all heard the roar, then a second and a third; the Jall-Beast. It was rumored that they made the northern portion of the Great Swamp their home but that had never been confirmed. Jall parties sent to explore the Northern reaches of the swamp seldom returned intact. They spoke of the great numbers of the Jal-Beast at times.

In the direction that they were moving another roar was heard. The three wildcats stood motionless in their tracks. Reed was the first to notice them. He motioned his wildcat into the wagon and the other two followed its lead.

"It seems it is time to leave this trail. We passed a fork a few hundred yards back. That is the way we should travel for now."

No one disagreed.

The party was now led by the two wagons with the others following close behind on their horses. They reached the new trail, of crushed timber and grass, and followed the ominous trail. None wanted to consider what manner of beast had made this trail. It did seem to lead them away from the immediate danger.

They heard another roar closer, behind them in the swamp, followed by another roar, further to the northeast, but away from the Great Swamp, from the direction they were heading. The oxen and horse became more agitated by the moment and it took a great deal of effort to control them. It was Sebastian and Reed that calmed them with the inherent ability they carried.

They came to a partially dry creek bed that crossed the trail. Thorium didn't hesitate to make a decision. They had to get off the trail they were on, quickly.

"Upstream, everybody help the wagons." To his cat Thorium he called, "Tri, stay calm, stay in the wagon." The cat seemed to understand.

The men dismounted, tied the horses to the front of the wagons with the oxen, and all, man and beast, worked to get the wagons over the smooth stone of the creek bed. At times, the water was ankle deep and slippery. Sebastian almost lost his footing and he fell under a wagon wheel before Thorium grabbed him and pulled him upright. The roars were getting closer, behind them and to one side.

They reached a short bend in the creek bed and the cover of some large boulders to one side of the creek that enabled them to hide from view of the trail below them. Thorium ordered the men to halt. He knew that the Jal-Beast limited vision would help them. However, the Beast hearing was acute.

"Everyone stop. Make sure the animals are quiet. Muzzle the oxen and horses." Muzzles had been brought along for each horse and oxen. Gar had insisted. Now Thorium knew why. "Reed, Sebastian, keep the wildcats quiet as well."

"Quiet all," Gar repeated in a soft commanding whisper.

On the trail that they had left, the Jal-Beast had reached the creek bed. Over sixty feet tall, it stopped and turned its giant head up and down the creek bed, the giant's razor teeth in its mouth reflecting in the sun. Its tiny eyes seemed out of place on its immense head. The men of The Proctant had seen one before briefly, in their first trip from the Jall City to The Hold, but this view was clearer. This was the first time Loren or the Nomads had seen one. Reed held Loren close as she shivered at the sight. Sebastian concentrated on keeping the agitated wildcats silent.

The short arms of the Jal-Beast surprised the men. While its claws seemed limber enough to grab them, what good were they when they didn't even extend beyond the giant head? To grasp and hold, they guessed.

The men breathed a sigh of relief as the Jal-Beast resumed its path on the trail, its mammoth legs, like tree-trunks, and finally its long tail helping to further break down the trail with its powerful swings from side to side as the Jal-Beast walked.

The decision now was which way to go. It would almost be impossible to follow the path they had been on at the edge of the Great Swamp. However, that was where the trail of the White led. Moreover, to further accentuate their problem, Gar could feel the presence of White around them.

The White hadn't eaten in days, trying to stay ahead of the party from the old lands of the Myk that seemed to be following him. He had to reach the new lair of the Myk its second head told him. Reach the Myk and be reborn.

The dangers of the Great Swamp were all around him. His hairy feet were nibbled on when he had entered the water to avoid a Jal-Beast. Apparently, the fish hadn't cared for his taste and left him alone after the first few nibbles. Nevertheless, his bloody feet had brought new, larger predators towards him and he had to get back onto dry land to continue. The White now followed a trail made by the Jal-Beast. This was dangerous but this White was fast and quiet. The trail enabled him to put more distance between himself and the pursuers.

He hadn't slept for longer than he hadn't eaten. The White found a dense thatch of brush, undisturbed, not far from the wide trail. He had already learned that the giant beast wouldn't stray from the path. He wasn't sure where he had learned that.

'A gift from the Myk,' his second head told him.

The White made a sleeping nest more than fifty feet from the trail. The Jal-Beast may stay on the trail but their long tails could still reach thirty feet on either side of it. The White needed sleep. He was still far from the lair. The second head told him there were three or four weeks of march left. He would need many stops. And food.

The sound of human voices in the distance woke up the White. And the Sage, his second head could feel them. He had gotten used to the roars of the giant Jal-Beast, but these voices were more dangerous to him. He had slept longer than he had expected and now the humans were in front of him. The White heard the beast roars; a pair. They seemed to be behind the humans on the trail. 'Even better', the second head told him. 'Let the beasts destroy the humans, then we can travel without worry.'

The White rose from his sleeping position, stretching his long arms. His hunger for live flesh was almost overwhelming. 'Leave something for me,' he thought as he waited for the expected attack by the beast on the human party.

The White followed the beast trail a good distance behind them. 'Don't worry,' the second head told him, 'they hunt by sound and can't hear you if you are careful.' The White was unsure but the second head now controlled his actions. It was almost fully mature.

He crossed a shallow creek bed, the beasts well in front of him, but what had happened to the humans? There was no sign of an attack; they seem to have just disappeared. 'Don't worry about that. They are near by; the Jal-Beast must not have caught them yet. They are hunting them.'

'The Jal-Beast?' questioned the White.

'That is the Great Swamps beast's name,' answered the second head.

'How do you know such things?' asked the White of the voice inside his head.

'They are a gift of the Myk. Keep going, you must be reborn.'

The White kept going further along the trail, watching the Jal-Beast pair in front of it a good distance ahead and no longer worrying about what may be behind it.

The two Jal-Beast had traveled beyond the creek bed as the expedition discussed how best to travel North.

"It seems the path that we were traveling remains the best path to find the Myk," Jamen stated, not happy with his conclusion.

Thorium had been watching the trail from the top of one of the boulders, a better vantage point than the others had.

"A White," he spoke aloud to himself. "We are on the right path it seems." He hurried back to the others and told them what he had seen.

"Not just a White, but a myk, fully mature,' said Gar. "My mind is now clearly cloudy."

"Then we must follow the myk that follows the Jal-Beast," Jamen said, preparing to leave. "He will lead us to their cavern."

"The Jal-beast ahead is not a danger now. We follow on foot. The animals remain muzzled and all pull the wagons. Keep the wildcats inside the wagons. We can afford no mistakes here," commanded Thorium.

"Remain in the carts," Reed ordered the wildcats as they prepared to get up and leave the wagons to follow the White. He reattached their collars to the wagon.

"Everybody, quickly now, we have to turn these wagons around and follow the White before we lose him," Jamen said as he reached the lead oxen to turn him around. Back down the creek bed and then onto the Jal-Beasts trail to wherever the White would lead them next.

Nightfall had come to the White as he followed the Jal-Beast pair in front of him. Just ahead the Jall-Beast moved away from the main trail to a point some distance away. There they stopped and seemed to lay down to rest. 'Strange behavior,' thought the second head.

The White moved slowly and carefully past where the Jal-Beasts had left the trail, and then he moved quickly along the trail in the twilight.

'Where are the humans,' thought the White.

'Keep going,' said the voice inside the Whites head, 'there is food ahead.'

'Food, the humans,' the White excitedly thought.

'No, but alive and nourishing. Move quickly now, to the left, a nest. Can't you smell it?' said the voice.

'Yes I can, what is it?' answered the White as he rushed towards the nest.

'The nest of the Jal-Beast, it's unattended and the eggs are ripe for hatching.'

'Jal-Beast?' thought the White.

"Its nourishment you need for the trail ahead. We have far to go to be reborn.'

The White moved more quickly now, hunger impinging on its judgment. Instinct was taking over.

'Carefully,' said the voice.

The White practically stumbled into the nest, cracking an egg as he fell.

'Quiet,' said the voice, 'one egg and we must hurry away.'

"There is no Jal-Beast around," said the White aloud. He picked up the cracked egg he had fallen against. It was over two feet long and very heavy. The White brought the egg down hard on a rock on the ground. It broke open with a loud 'CRACK!' sound. He quickly picked up the still forming Jal-Beast and began to eat it, but not before the small creature opened its mouth and emitted a low cry.

'Hurry, you fool!' said the voice of the second head. 'Silence it, we must go!'

With a quick bite with its sharp teeth, the White silenced the creature. The White finished consuming the Jal-Beast and then picked up a shell fragment that contained some of the eggs fluid and drank that.

"Hurry! We must go!" the second head now shouted aloud, forcing the words through its still forming mouth. The White ignored it and in its hunger, the second head now had no control over the White's body. The White finished the fierce creature and moved to a second egg.

"Ignore the egg, we must flee," the second head screamed, its cry muffled beneath the sheath the White wore as a garment. In a panic it tried to assume control of the Whites body once more, but in the confusion and lust for food, it could do nothing. It just wasn't dominant enough yet. The second head did manage to drop the egg. It hit the ground and cracked open with a slight noise. This egg was more fully developed and the tiny Jal-Beast it had held stood up briefly and emitted a cry.

"Too late," screamed the second head.

"Too late for what?" answered the White.

"Look behind you and run!"

The White didn't have to look. He could feel the breath of the Jal-Beast above him. Nor could he run. The Jal-Beast hatchling had grabbed hold of his leg with its already sharp teeth. The end came quickly as the two Jal-Beasts and the hatchling tore the White apart. Briefly, the body was reborn as they crushed the first head. In its last act, the Myk sent its alarm to the lair of the Myk. "They are coming"

The forest had thinned and changed since they had left the vicinity of the Great Swamp. Pine forests had replaced the leafy trees near the swamps edge. The trail of the Myk still led northward, but now it veered away from the Great Swamp to the northeast as well.

They had been fortunate to escape the Jal-Beast with the loss of a single wagon and two of the horses. They tied the two oxen, now extra, onto the back of the remaining cart. Jamen of Kilne cringed at the thought as he remembered the sight of one of his prize horses crushed in the jaws of the Jal-Beast. Still alive as it was eaten, the horse's plaintiff cries for a savior as it was swallowed, tail first by the beast, were heard. The horse's cries ending as the Jal-Beast jaws clamped down on the horse's body. This had been a horse that Jamen himself had raised from a young colt. It had been one of Jamen's son, Raymond's, favorite horses to ride. His son had pleaded with him not to take it. Nevertheless, he, Jamen, had wanted the best horses for the expedition. To give them the best chance to succeed, he had told himself. Had he been wrong to take this horse, now lost, on the trip?

The second wagon was left behind with the faux trading goods they no longer needed. Speed was necessary to outrace the Jal-Beast, slower on the ground to their good fortune than in the water.

The other lost horse had slipped its ropes, tied to the back of the wagon, and in its panic at the nearness of the beast, had run swiftly away from the swamp into the forests. Perhaps it had survived and would find its way home.

In the final commotion of their escape from the Jal-Beasts attack, near the beast's nests, they had captured a White, more than happy to jump onto the fast moving wagon and escape with its life. This White had witnessed the death of another White, caught eating the eggs of the Jal-Beast and not so quickly devoured. The expedition had heard the Whites cries in its death but had been fortunate enough to be far enough away not to see it. The rescued White was still shivering from the sight. That, the death throes of the White, had been the noise that had brought the Jal-Beasts onto their trail. The White cowered in the wagon, its second head not yet developed enough to have any affect on it or communicate.

It was the White, in the end, who helped them escape. He pointed out a barely visible trail that angled off from the swamp and provided firm footing for the wagon, now pulled as rapidly as possible as Mendy and Alum were able to drive them, trying to get the most out of the oxen. The wildcats remained in the wagon as well, staring at the White, their collars affixed to the inside of the wagon on leashes for their own protection. The Nomads had not wanted to attach the leash, but they understood the necessity. As Thorium had followed the eyes of the White, he had caught the almost invisible markings of the new trail, left for the Whites to follow by those that had come before.

For now, clear of the Great Swamp and its Jal-Beast, the way was open. What to do with the White was another matter.

Clear of the swamp the wildcats were once again released from the wagons to follow the trail of the White. Gar's head remained mostly clear, the one immature brain of the White's second head not yet strong enough to affect him. Gar still felt vagueness though. There was more White around them in the distance, with mature second heads, *myk,* that did bother him. Ahead or behind it was hard to tell, and they seemed few in number. Meanwhile Gar could learn a lot about the Myk and their effects from this immature second brain.

They began to climb the low hills to the Northeast on what appeared to be an old pre-war way. It was still mostly unbroken pavement, just a few ruts to avoid. This was not a frequently traveled way, except by the White. It was narrow though as it climbed along the river's valley. When they came to a long bridge across the river below it seemed none to safe.

"Send the White over first," Jamen suggested as he surveyed the bridge that they must cross. "He will show us the best way across, then when he gets to the other side we finish him."

"It may have use for us yet," Gar spoke up. "Keeping it alive for now is not a hindrance except to me. And I can continue to learn from it."

"The Myk have crossed this many times," said Thorium, sitting on his horse and looking across the gorge. He watched the wildcats cross without issue, then sit and wait for them on the other side.

Thorium took command of the crossing. "We lead the oxen across one at a time. The bridge is smooth, we save one oxen to pull the wagon across. Unload the wagon of everything. We carry our needs across in small loads. Lead the horses across, one at a time as well. We'll make camp for the night on the other side."

Everybody immediately got involved in moving the expedition carefully across the worn bridge. There were small holes in the bridge's surface they found as they crossed.

"Mendy, you have bragged so many times about your fishing skills, can you catch us anything fresh for our meal tonight?"

"There are so many fish in these rivers; you can almost catch them by hand. Just keep the wildcats away or they'll eat their share and ours," Mendy laughed. Sebastian looked at him in amazement. 'It seemed the more danger these people are in, the more they laugh,' he thought to himself.

"You catch the fish, the wildcats will behave," he seriously answered Mendy.

It was a slow deliberate process for the expedition to bring everything across the bridge. It was longer than they thought and detours had to be made around dangerous points on it. One of the horses almost went through the bridge as a piece of it gave way, rusted metal giving way at its feet. Only the alertness of Jamen saved it for the journey ahead; its only injury, a minor cut on one leg.

"Be careful," Thorium reiterated from where he stood halfway across, leading his own horse. "Even the parts that seem safe may not be." Reddish orange rust could be seen through the bridge and it discolored the concrete.

The wagon was the last thing to cross, guided by Alum on foot and pulled by the last oxen. Even empty this was a lot of weight and

Alum anxiously guided the ox and the wagon, looking for the best path to follow. More holes had been made by those in front of him, some large. At one point in the crossing a piece of concrete and metal from the bridge started to give way under one of the wagon's wheels. As the wagon limped over the small hole that it made, a much larger piece gave way behind it. Cracking could be heard in the bridge. Alum raced ahead, fearing the worse. The ox pulling the wagon needed no prodding here and crossed the remaining distance with the wagon, instinct taking over. They had to catch it on the other side, the ox wanted as far from the bridge as possible. As the wagon reached the end of the bridge and solid ground again, a large chunk of the bridge gave way and fell to the river far below. This bridge's days were clearly numbered.

As Alum and the wagon raced across the remaining distance of the failing bridge, Reed and Sebastian were beginning the job of setting up camp for the night. They were in their element here. This is how they lived, never in one place for long, frequently just a night. Two tents were assembled, one for the Sage and one for everyone else. These were large Nomad caravan tents, high, dark colored, resistant to the rain and the wind when tied securely to the ground. There was plenty of room in each for the party and their supplies. A large fire started cracking between the two tents. There was a lot of loose dry wood laying about to gather to keep it going and Loren had created a circle of stones to keep the fire in place. A small fire was started in the center of each tent, venting through the circular hole in the top.

In the nearing of twilight, Mendy, followed by Alum, made his way down to the river, following a steep animal trail, probably created by the local bear population to fish. The fire would keep any curious bear from the camp (that and the scent of the wildcats), but the two men would have to keep an eye out for them as they fished. Mendy was thinking aloud how this bear trail meant this would be a good fishing spot. Alum wasn't as sure as he kept looking around them in the gathering darkness of the gorge.

Mendy carried a large fishing rod and line from the outpost. It was provided by the scouts for the expedition. Somebody who had stopped for a rest at the post had left behind the set-up. Mendy could only admire the pole and everything that he was given; complete tackle for any river fishing. The person who had left it behind had had too close an encounter with the bear along the rivers and decided that fishing wasn't for him. "Give it to somebody who can make good use of it," he had told the scout in charge at the time. It had sat, forgotten, in a corner of the storage room when Julius remembered it just before the expedition left.

When they reached the bottom of the gorge and the riverbank, Mendy assembled the rod and reel while Alum looked for bait.

"What do we use for bait?" Alum asked Mendy, not an angler himself.

"Look for worms, bugs, wrinklers, anything will do here I think." Mendy looked out over the wide shallow river and could see the fish jumping clear of the water to catch the early evening bugs. "The moon is full for us. Alum, this is perfect."

Mendy reached down by his tackle box where he saw a large black and red beetle and he picked it up. He put his hook through it, trying not to squish its soft shell. He didn't know what kind of bug, it was but he was pretty sure some fish would love its taste.

One cast and a quick strike. A large fish on the line, like a trout but differently colored than what he was used to back home, was on the line. "When I bring it to land, don't let it get back into the river. The fish will try to escape. We should have brought a basket or net to put them in."

"I have my rope I always carry," said Alum, trying to be useful here on the muddy riverbank, patting the small cord he kept with him.

"When I have it landed, put the rope through its gills. We'll use your rope as a fish line. Then, while I'm after the next one, tie the rope to a branch and put the fish back into the river. That'll keep the fish fresh until we leave."

"How long do you figure to stay," Alum asked Mendy after they had the first fish on the line."

"With the fish out there, until your rope is full," Mendy said back re-baiting the line with another of the beetles that seemed to be all over the riverbank. "They love these beetles, try to catch some more and this won't take long."

"We'll eat well tonight and give the wildcats a feast for their hard work at the same time," Mendy grinned as he landed another fish. "Close to five pounds and I see even bigger. The Gods are smiling on me tonight."

A bear ambled down to the river on the opposite bank to fish. Alum looked at it alarmed.

"Don't worry, buddy, there are plenty of fish to keep us both occupied. He won't bother us."

An hour and a dozen fish later, the two men began the hike back up the embankment to the camp above. And true to his word, the first fish Mendy caught was the smallest. They had to call for help to get up over the last of the trailside with their haul.

When Thorium saw the number and size of the catch, he gave Mendy a hearty slap on the back. "I'll never question your fishing boasts, again," he laughed.

After the feast of the caught fish and ale from a keg, the men called it an early night. Sebastian and Alum gathered what remaining wood they could in the darkness of a cloudy night and replenished the fire. Enough to keep their neighbors away during the night, they hoped. Then all but the Sage made their way to the large Trader's tent, found their space, rolled out their bedrolls, and lay down for what they hoped would be a quiet evening from the days exhaustive travel. The White they secured with them in the tent, tied with rope to a corner and given an extra blanket for cover. The White, still traumatized from the encounter with the Jal-Beast, did not provide much resistance. The three Sage gathered in their own tent to discuss the expedition with a pot of their 'presso. The fire roared into the night, contained only by the rock border of Loren. The Sage talked privately, content that if they spoke in a low voice the others would not overhear them.

Chapter 9
The Way of the Teachers

Several hours into the evening's rest, Reed, lying awake next to Loren and unable to sleep, quietly arose, wrapping a blanket around his shoulders for warmth. He looked down at the sleeping Loren, smiling at her, but unable fully to understand her; they seemed as one to him, but could she ever truly enter his world. Her world he wanted little part of, could they make their own world, together? He frowned at that thought and stepped softly to the entrance of the large tent.

The fire still burned brightly with the larger logs Sebastian and Alum had added to it. There were still a few sizable pieces of wood lying near the fire. There were few sparks and little smoke from the dry wood burning in the fire. 'The two men had done a good job of selecting the night fuel,' Reed thought to himself as he breathed in the smell of the burning wood. Its smell was pleasant to him, reminding him of the fires built in the encampments on the plains. He added the remaining wood to the fire and prepared to return to the tent and he hoped, slumber.

Gradually, infiltrating themselves into his personal thoughts, voices crept into his hearing. Whispers in the night, it was the Sage, awake, still talking. 'What could they be discussing at this late hour,' Reed thought. 'All needed rest for the next days travel.' Reed's ears, trained since birth on the plains to pick up any sound that may prove dangerous, focused in of the words of the Sage. It never occurred to him that these were words that he shouldn't hear.

"The time of the Teachers, when the Order was first formed," Gar was quietly speaking to the others, in a whisper he thought none but the three could hear, but clear to Reed, "the Teachers tried many things. We know of their experiments."

"I remember well those early days," said a pacing Del. "It was our job in those early days to watch over their successes."

"And their failures," added Tor. "Not always a pleasant task."

"But they always meant well for us. They saved the planet for us," Gar said with a sense of urgency.

"That's true," Tor replied, lighting his pipe. Reed could smell the sweet smoke of the pipe coming through the smell of the burning fire as he crept closer to the Sage's tent to hear more clearly what was being spoken in secret.

"We must remember that they cleared the skies of the radiation," Del spoke before once again taking a seat on his blanket. "Yet they left the skies darkened, for a thousand years they told us. A lesson for us to learn from they said."

"Yes, they cleared the skies and the land, or at least parts, of the radiation. And they cleansed the DNA of most survivors, as they did those of The Hold," Gar once more defended the Teachers efforts.

"Look how they created the Jall and gave us the gift of long life." Tor took a sip of the 'presso as he spoke. "They created much good for us."

"And yet," Del continued, always contrite about this part of their duties, "they left many untouched. To see what would happen."

"Their experiment with the Two Valleys has always been a concern of mine," Tor slowly added, warily, his pipe in one hand, his cup of 'presso in the other. "To keep silent over what they did has not been easy."

"Genetic manipulation, to bring out the best in this they said," Del stated.

"More survived than would have been possible above ground," Tor continued. "But to cleanse the DNA of the Southern Valley and enhance the mutations of the Northern Valley?"

"That brought us the greatness of Nourne," Gar stated.

"And," Tor continued for him, "the White and the double-heads of the Myk. Didn't they tell us of their coming?"

"Could they have known the outcome of their experiments, centuries ago?" asked Del, standing once more, agitated over what they were saying.

"It seems certain now," said Tor, putting down his empty cup, "otherwise, why the warning?"

"The Hold protected the Valleys; the Jall gave the world trade once more, a grand experiment and the rest of the world..." Del was saying, sitting and then standing once more, "... the reasons for my travels, to discover and unravel just what the Teachers have done."

"More good than bad, I would wager," said Gar, once more the defender of the Teachers.

"Did they manipulate even our friends from across the sea?" Tor questioned.

"It would seem, through Simon, how else would they have appeared here now at this crucial time. What powers was Simon given before his *exile*? We have seen much in Thul that we have not encountered before, the seed of the Teachers inside him, his DNA." Gar spoke, more loudly than he wished.

"To finish that thought what of Simon. Was he truly one of us, or an experiment, or even something else?" Tor added.

Reed had heard enough of the Sage's conversation. Hearing and understanding to his limited ability, Reed returned to his blanket next to Loren, angry at what he had heard. He put his arms around her form and tried to sleep. Much of what he heard was beyond him, but he understood one thing plainly. The Myk were the fault of the Teachers. That was clear to him. The Nomads had done their job. If the Teachers had made mistakes, why couldn't they fix their mistakes? Why put this life on these people? If they, the Teachers, made themselves like a God, why not make creations happy in their world? In the morning, he would leave the expedition with Sebastian and return to the Northern Valley to take his people home. They would no longer have a part in the deception of this world. Loren in her sleep drew him close to her. 'She will understand and return with me,' he thought to himself as sleep overcame him. But deep inside he knew that wasn't true. The gulf between their worlds was too deep to cross. This night would be their last. He held her tighter, a tear in his eyes.

The Sage conversation continues late into the evening.

"Argonia, The Hold, across the sea and the confederation, it seems that the Teachers experimented much with our past," Tor spoke aloud.

"To make this a better world, that was always their goal. Without them would any have survived?" Gar stated.

"That is the thought that has kept me true to them. Even Phelix in his darkest hour has remained true, because of that one truth," Del spoke, almost sadly. "The burden that we have had to carry at times has been almost more than any could bear."

"The connection that I have to the Myk now seems certain. A gift of the Teachers I would guess, in preparation for what is to come, if I can learn to use it?" Gar now spoke excitedly.

"You were always the strongest, Gar" Del added, "It seems that the Teachers made a wise choice, if this is indeed a gift from them."

"At least, even now, it tells us if they are around and in strength," Tor spoke in urgency.

"The hindrance is weak, almost gone. Just a few on their way to the cavern it seems, and none developed as the one we found dying." Gar said, matter-of-factly, taking another sip of 'presso'.

"And when we find the cavern?" Del asked of Gar.

"You may find me helpless at that time, I'm afraid," Gar solemnly replied.

"There must be a way to block the hindrance, to use it against the Myk," Tor spoke directly to Gar, pointing his hand upward. "The Teachers must have given you some clue, some tool, to be able to use what you have discovered within yourself."

"I will try to remember something. It's to bad Locklear isn't hear. He recorded and remembers more of some things than all of us," Gar said before walking from the tents entrance where he stood looking out at the night to where his blankets lay on the earth. "Time for rest."

Reed had a troubled sleep lying next to Loren under the large Nomad tent. He had heard much, understood little, but what he had understood he didn't like. That the Myk were the creations of the Teachers made him even more distrustful of the Sage Order. Dreams, nightmares and troubled sleep plagued Reed throughout the night. Reed woke up several times shivering, not from the cold, and each time Loren pulled him tighter. He would tell Thorium what he had heard when the two were alone. Both what he had overheard and that he was returning home. Thorium he trusted. Thorium would continue on and do what was right. But he, Reed, would return to Twror and lead his people back home to the South. The war was over for him.

The fire was roaring once more as Reed stumbled out of the tent in the chill of the morning air, the last to awaken after his difficult sleep. Alum had hot cakes cooking in a large fry pan and Reed could smell the pot of 'presso the Sage were heating. It was the smell of the Sage's beverage that brought Reed fully awake. He had made his decision and needed to find Thorium.

As Reed approached the logs set up as benches around the fire everybody was in good spirits. Even the captured White showed little fear of his captors. Loren waved Reed over to her where she was holding a plate of the hotcakes and plump blackberries she had picked earlier in the morning when she had awoken.

Reed walked over to Loren and plucked several of the berries she offered off the plate. "I have made a decision," he stated matter-of-factly. Loren was used to his coarse ways and only smiled at him.

"Oh," she said. Maybe it was this basic element attracted her to Reed.

"Where is Thorium, I must see him now," he asked her.

"I saw him go to see the Sage in their tent. I think he wanted to plan the next few days. What's this decision, Reed?" she added as she reached for his hand.

Reed lightly stroked her hand, and then turned to go to the tent of the Sage.

"Your decision?" she repeated her inquiry of him.

"I'll tell you before I leave," he bruskly replied, only turning his head slightly towards her.

"Leave," Lorne stated as she stood up, alarmed.

Reed only said, as he turned back to the Sage's tent, "After I see Thorium."

As Reed approached the tent he heard the voices of Thorium and the Sage talking quietly about the journey ahead of them. Del seemed alarmed by the stories they had heard of the Northern People and their apparent disappearance. Reed pulled the tent flap to one side and entered, unannounced.

Gar was facing the entrance when he saw Reed enter. "Reed, just the person to help us decide our next step."

"I came to speak to Thorium. I give no more trust to your Order." Reed continued to approach Thorium who turned to face him.

"Reed," Thorium reached out for Reeds hand, but the gesture was ignored. "Why the anger?"

"I have things to tell you, Thorium. You are still my friend. The

Sage and their Teachers are not what they seem," Reed said in a solemn voice, looking squarely at Thorium as if the Sage were not in the tent. "There are things I heard."

The Sage looked at each other in alarm, what had Reed overheard and when? They had spoken of so many things in confidence amongst themselves. Things others couldn't know.

Gar spoke aloud at Reed, "What are these things that you say you know?"

Reed looked directly at Thorium's face and placed his hand on Thorium's shoulder. "My ways I know are not yours. But you I trust to do what is right. Today I return to Twror and take my people back to their father's lands."

"Leave, why?" Thorium seemed astounded at Reed's action.

"This battle, this war, is not that of my people. It is the war of those and their creations," Reed answered, pointing at the Sage.

Tor now spoke up. "What is this claim, Reed, that we created the Myk?"

Del seemed taken aback by the accusation. "What and when did you here this?"

Reed now turned to face the three Sage. "Last night I couldn't sleep. I got up to sit by the fire and add wood to keep it burning throughout the night. I heard voices, late at night, from your tent. Do you deny that your Teachers created the White as an experiment? That you knew of the coming of the second heads, of the Myk?"

"Is this true?" Thorium asked point blank of Gar.

"Yes, he replied, "but..."

"This death and suffering was brought on by the experiments of your Teachers?" Thorium continued bluntly.

"They did much good," countered Gar, once again finding himself the defender of the Teachers, good and bad. "Their *experiments* were to better us, to prepare us for the future. They saved mankind, cleansed the air after the 'Great War'."

Thorium himself was now growing apprehensive as well about the Sage and their Teachers. Not always trustful of the Sage Order already and their endeavors, Thorium wondered what other secrets from the time of the Teachers they kept hidden. "Who were these beings you call your Teachers?" he declared at the Sage. "They, whose directives you continue to follow long after they have left us. Were they the creators of the Myk, and who knows what else? What gave them the right to play God with us; did their experiments on us bring them joy?"

"Yes, that is part of who they were, our Teachers. They loved to experiment. But it was always their desire to save us, to make us stronger," Gar voiced his defense of the Teachers.

"To save us from whom?" Thorium asked in a loud voice.

"Ourselves," Tor expounded at Thorium and Reed. "We would have destroyed ourselves already if it wasn't for the work of the Teachers."

Del now walked over to the others and joined in the animated discussion. "I have always had my own questions of what the Teachers have done. That has been the reason for my own travels throughout this land. To uncover more of their secrets, not all of which they told the Order of. Good and bad, I have never questioned their motives. Neither through ambivalence nor Greed, they saved us and have prepared us out of a sense of duty."

"Prepared us for what?" asked Reed, not backing down from the Sage and his accusations.

The Sage looked a little bewildered by the question. In their following by rote everything given by the Teachers, they seldom questioned the reasons. They accepted, even Del, the de facto reasoning that everything the Teachers did was just for the survival of the human race. There had been in the background as the justification of their experiments; to prepare man. To prepare man for what had not been questioned; Just survival or something more? None of the three answered Reed's challenge.

"As I thought. My people have done their duty in this. We helped defeat the White and prepare the town of Twror. Now it is time for us to return to our homes. Your ways are not ours," Reed stated as he prepared to leave the tent.

"But the Myk, the threat remains!" exclaimed Thorium. "Your people are still needed."

"I trust you, Thorium, to do what is right and necessary. You carry none of the dishonor that is the Sage. But my part in this is done," Reed answered, pausing before lifting the tent flap and exiting.

"Does Sebastian know of your decision," Thorium asked Reed.

"Not yet. I thought it best to inform you first. We are a free people and he has the will to do as he wishes and thinks best."

"What of Loren?" Thorium continued to question Reed.

Reed's anger now flashed briefly at Thorium over this, to him, a question of person and honor. That anger passed just as quickly. These people of their Confederation were not as the Nomads. However, they carried their honor well. With sad eyes, he turned to Thorium, put his hands on the man's shoulders, and finished his words to him. "She will not understand, that I fear. She will continue on with you. I can no longer protect her. You, my friend, I ask that you do that for me."

With that Reed turned and left the tent. As he lifted the flap on the way out, he heard Thorium in a loud voice say, "I will, my friend, I will."

Thorium now turned to the Sage. "What other secrets do you have that will costs us the friends we need in what is to come? Tell me now, what you can, and then I'll decide whether this expedition goes further."

"You will decide," Gar said, surprised by Thorium's tone. "What you do now has been laid out long ago by our Teachers. What choices you have are limited."

In his mind Thorium thought, 'The audacity of the Sage'. He managed to keep his temper mostly under control. But he was in command here, not the Sage, and it was time to show that.

"My will is my own, Gar. The decisions I make are my own and not yours. I make those decisions on the information I have at the time. Those were your Teachers, not mine. This part of the world is yours and, as many have insinuated, not mine. I have led your army, defeated the Myk and forced him to flee. With what I know now, that should be enough. Tell me why it is that this expedition should go forward or it ends here, now. Then you and your order can deal with the Myk and his followers, created like you, by your Teachers."

"But the words of the Teachers?" Tor now said, with fear that all that had been accomplished would now fall apart without these men.

"The words of your Teachers are not mine," was Thorium's crisp response to that.

"What of Thul and Wade? Would you abandon them now as well?" asked Gar, trying to turn the conversation back to Thorium and his duty.

"How dare you speak to me of duty. Already, to save you and this land from the White, I have lost friends to this enemy, your Teachers creation. I have led people to their death to defeat this monster that they, your Teachers, so casually left behind. Now! Before I leave this tent and return to Twror myself with those I lead, why should I continue with this fight of your Teachers creation."

Thorium looked at each Sage in turn. None looked directly back into his eyes. So many secrets they kept, so many things that they had been warned by the Teachers not to divulge to any. Now this; the prophesy of the Teachers at the point of collapse. Finally, Del approached Thorium, looked directly into his face, put his hand on Thorium's shoulder as Reed had done, and said in a solemn voice, "I will tell you what I can. Then you are the judge of whether we have been right in our faith in the Teachers."

Thorium shrugged Del's hand off of his shoulder and resumed his seat opposite the Sage. He motioned Del to sit next to him, now fully in control of the situation, and simply said to the Sage, "Begin. When you are done we'll see if it was enough."

Del sat in the offered seat and began, looking directly at Thorium and ignored the looks of Gar and Tor. "Back in the beginning, just before the 'Great War' that destroyed so much of the planet, the Teachers came upon our world in their travels. They saw what was happening, what was about to happen and could do little to stop it. They tried. Were there other forces at work? That question can never be answered. The Teachers saw enough good in the planet to save what they could. They were not however, omnificent.

"They had not months, nor even weeks to work. They had but days to accomplish what they could. They found what the technocrats were trying to accomplish on Argonia, on which you have heard other survivors from your ship had landed. The Teachers built on what they had found and throughout the world built a series of Holds like the one you have visited. We don't know how many were attempted, but from the words of the Teachers we know that many were attempted. Most we fear were never finished. I have yet to find even one in my travels to the east. There just wasn't time. People, knowledge, treasure, whatever could be saved was transported to these holds. Argonia was left to itself as it was already prepared to survive what was to come."

"I know most of that. And it says nothing of why the Teacher created the Whites and who knows what other ungodly creations," interceded Thorium with skepticism of the Teachers nobility.

"Let me continue, more will become clear," Del said, standing and beginning to pace as he spoke again. 'How much to divulge' he thought to himself. When he looked at Gar and Tor they seemed to be saying, 'whatever is necessary'.

Del looked directly at Thorium and began again, "The Armageddon came quickly. The 'Great War' was over in hours, minutes even, a religious fever that destroyed the entire land of those that launched it. Weapons beyond our grasp, containing the power of the sun, launched at their so-called friends and enemies alike. A counter-response destroyed what little remained of their lands. Throughout the world these weapons were used in their entirety. A force so great the entire mass of the land moved and changed. Our inland sea became separated from the ocean you crossed, and the Great Swamp and the mountains of The Hold formed as the lands bowed from this force.

"Few were saved below ground. Most who survived remained in the open. The skies were covered by clouds of contamination and dust. Without doing something, few would have survived. So the Teachers cleansed the sky of the waste of the war. However, the dust was allowed to remain in the sky and with it came the one thousand years of winter. Perhaps as a reminder to us of what we had done. But the human race survived.

"The Teachers watched those that remained above ground through the Armageddon and saw genetic change and damage to the DNA that makes each of us unique. So they began a cleansing of this DNA. But not all of the mutations were bad. So their experiments on us began. But they knew so little of us. Their study of us before the 'Great War' had been too brief. Still, their goal was to make us better."

"Better than what," challenged Thorium.

"Better than those who had come before, those that had almost destroyed our world. They began their study of our damaged DNA. How could they know, but through trial and error, what was the best determination of what they hoped to accomplish," continued Del.

"And the White, they thought those best?" questioned Thorium.

"They truly didn't know, at least in the beginning," explained Del. "So they experimented, to determine the best result."

"You're still not convincing me," stated Thorium, preparing to stand.

"Wait," said Gar, "There is more."

"Tell me then" responded Thorium.

Del began speaking again. "We don't know what happened in your lands once the sky was cleared of the contamination, but we know what happened here. In outlying areas the people were left to their own devices; the R'mons, Shiaps, Nomads and the like. Also the DNA of the animals was allowed to develop on their own, with a couple of notable exceptions, the Wildcats and the Great Wolves. We know from what the Teachers have told us that both were experiments; to increase the intelligence of these creatures that had been mans companions.

"Here, close to The Hold, other experiments were made, as under as controlled conditions as the Teacher could arrange. The Northern and Southern Valley's, few in number, were who they chose to experiment with. In the Northern Valley mutations were not excluded, they were enhanced. In the Southern Valley, any imperfections in DNA that may cause mutations were removed. In doing so the two peoples grew apart over the thousand years that The Hold remained closed."

Standing now, Thorium once again brought up the question, "And they, your Teachers, had this right to play God?"

Gar now spoke up, "No, not to play God, to learn about us, to study us, to make us better."

"To study us! Were we but lab animals to them?" Thorium clearly upset demanded an answer.

"From their studies they created the Jall, their symbiots, the Gators, and other wonders that you will see around us," Gar finished.

"It wasn't until it was too late in the experiments that they realized the monster that they may have created in the Northern Valley," continued Del. "Then they were forced to leave us, for what reason or reasons we do not know. But they left us the warnings so that we could be prepared. And the created to tool to unify us and defeat the White, and its evolved masters, the doubled headed Myk."

"Us, you mean that we are that tool, left by the Teachers, but how?" stated Thorium as he once again sat down.

"It seems certain now that Simon had instructions that we of the Order knew little of. And your arrival now, with the son's of Simon, confirms so much for us," Tor stated.

"Sons, I thought that just Thul was the son of your Simon," exclaimed Thorium.

"The Teachers spoke in the plural when they mentioned the *savior,* Tor said quietly. "We at first thought the second was you," Tor finished matter-of-factly.

"Me!" answered Thorium, standing once more.

Tor continued, "While you are the Uniter the Teachers spoke of we of The Order agree, we have no doubt that the second son of Simon arrived on the shores of Argonia, to finish its path as well."

"Two sons of Simon, on *The Proctant,*" Thorium said in a calm voice, almost defeated. He looked up, "And I am your Uniter?"

"That seems true," said Gar, looking into Thorium's eyes.

"And Erson, Nourne and the White?" Thorium asked.

"Two sides of the same coin. All carry significant mutations. In those of Erson and Nourne it has created a people of higher intelligence, nobility and honor, all of the virtues the universe holds most in awe," replied Tor.

"And the White then, the leftovers, all that is lacking in man," Thorium added snidely.

"No, not all of the White, but at the extreme is the Myk, with its high intelligence and lack of any virtue. Without one there could not be the other," Gar responded.

Thorium got up to leave. He was finished with what the Sage had had to say, his decision made. The Sage looked on anxiously. What would the verdict be of Thorium?

"Prepare to break camp. We continue on as soon as we are loaded," said Thorium.   'Did he really have a choice' Thorium thought to himself. Like Reed had said, it was up to him to do the honorable thing, to make things right. He left the tent to get the expedition under way once more.

While the discussion continued between Thorium and the Sage, Reed was seen leaving the tent by those having their morning meal around the fire. Reed was obviously upset as he headed straight for the fire and the others.

When Reed reached the others he looked at each in turn, last facing Loren and Sebastian, sitting together, and announced in a loud voice, "I am leaving the expedition. Who chooses to go with me and return home?"

There was a collective gasp and almost simultaneously, Jamen, Loren and Sebastian asked, "Why are you leaving? What happened in there with the Sage?"

"Last night I overheard a secret of the Sage," Reed started. "I have never trusted them and now I know why. I came north with my brothers to support our cousins to the north. I have no regrets over that. But with what I have heard I can no longer take part in this unholy war and I return to Twror to take my people home."

"Home?" Sebastian asked. "Twror is now our home."

"For some, maybe, but I will lead home those who wish to return to our lands. I hope there will be many," Reed spoke looking at Sebastian.

"What did you hear? You must have misunderstood," asked Jamen of Kiln, wanting to calm Reed's manner and give pause to his leaving.

"Misunderstood! I misunderstood nothing. The Sage confirmed all I heard," Reed angrily replied to Jamen.

"What did you hear, Reed?" asked Loren in what she hoped would be a comforting voice to Reed. Her voice inflection seemed to have worked as Reed calmed visibly as he turned to face her.

"The Myk are a creation of the Teachers. The Sage has known this all along. Part of the Teachers experiments with the people of the Two Valleys. The Sage denied nothing. They knew." Reed left nothing out.

Jamen rose to his feet on hearing this. His people were those of the Southern Valley. "I always felt that there was some inherent difference between the peoples of the Two Valleys. They mingled together at the City by the Lake, but in those that remained in the Southern and Northern Valley's the differences were apparent; the nobility of Nourne and the depravity of the Myk, both transcending, good and bad, anything that has come from the Southern Valley.

"But whatever their creation or creators, we have a job to finish or none of our peoples will be safe from the evil that is the Myk."

"My job is finished here. I trust the judgment of Thorium to continue with what is best," Reed quietly said to the group. "The Nomads return home, their task completed."

Sebastian was of mixed feelings as he stood and approached Reed. "Reed, my brother, I understand your feelings of betrayal. I feel them as well on hearing your words. However, these people are my brothers as well now. It is a new world that we are building together and our people are an important part of this. We can't abandon this mission we now follow."

Reed's voice and manner displayed for all to see the sadness he now felt as he replied, looking once more at each of the others around the morning fire. And Loren he thought to himself, what was she to him, more than a lover, more than a friend. He saw from her face that she didn't understand. Their eyes could barely meet. "I return home, brother and lead out people home as well," he finally spoke directly to Sebastian.

"And those that choose to remain in Twror, to build it into the city that it will become?" asked Sebastian, his eyes locked on Reed's.

"All of us, we the people of the land, have the free will to decide in turn our fates. Those that remain will become of Twror, not the Nomadic people of the *land* and out Fathers," replied Reed, matching Sebastian's stare.

"Do we not remain as brothers even still?" questioned Sebastian of Reed.

"The people of Twror and we of the land will always be of brothers. But my time is done as part of this," Reed answered.

Sebastian clasped arms with Reed. "Then go in peace, my brother. Lead those who wish to return to the home of our Fathers. But I ask you this," Sebastian turned serious with these words. "Let those who wish to remain and become part of Twror know that they remain as brothers of the land, cherished by our Fathers as are all of those of the land."

"I promise, brother." With these parting words Reed turned from the morning fire and left, joined by his wildcat at his side. As he left the warmth of the fire Loren got up from where she had sat, listening to the good-bye, and hurried to catch him. For a brief moment Reed thought that she was joining him. That moment was brief. He knew that her part was to remain in the group and continue the search for the hiding place of the Myk.

"No good-bye for me, Reed?" she asked, no tears in her eyes, her head held high as she knew that Reed would want. Any tears would come later when she was alone, Loren thought to herself.

"This is not good-bye, Loren, my friend, our lives will cross once more," he said very stoically.

"Forever without emotion, Reed, we have been so much."

"We remain as one, completed," he answered Loren, taking her hands in his. "Now, for this brief time, we follow separate paths." He turned and left her, walking briskly away.

Reed's wildcat briefly brushed against Loren, her hand running through his fur as she had done countless times. "Take care of him for me," she said quietly to the cat. "Sometimes he thinks that he is more than he is." The wildcat looked up at her, seeming to comprehend her words and give acknowledgement of them, then moved swiftly to join Reed on the hike back to Twror and then the return to the home of his Fathers.

'We will meet again,' thought Loren as she returned to the fire. The men had a hard time looking at her as she regained her spot by the fire and began eating again.

"We must hurry to break camp and continue our pursuit," was all she said.

Thorium rejoined those by the fire shortly after Reed's leaving the camp. This was his expedition he told himself before he spoke to those seated before him. The Myk may have been a creation of the Teachers, but he had a job to do, Sage be damned.

"I suppose you have all heard what Reed discovered," he asked the expedition's party around the fire.

"We heard," said Jamen.

Mendy and Alum looked at Thorium, what was coming next?

"I understand Reed, he is my brother. But we are all brothers now and have a duty to the others," Sebastian spoke for the group finishing their morning meal by the fire. "When do we go on, to find and destroy this Myk?"

"We travel now; quickly, fast and light. Free the oxen; there is good range for them here. We leave the wagon and travel only by horse. Share what we need among the horses," Thorium ordered.

"It's a good thing I brought the extra horses," said Jamen now arising from the log he had finished his meal seated upon. "And the White?"

"Tie him to a horse, he may prove useful yet."

"The tents are too heavy for the horse," Loren stated to Thorium.

"Then we leave them and anything else too heavy for the horse to carry, responded Thorium, now fully in charge of the group. "We sleep in our bedrolls now under the stars."

"When it rains?" asked Mendy.

"We pack a single tarp that we all can share.

"Will the Sage like that?" asked Sebastian.

"They are just one with the expedition now, no more equal than the rest of us," Thorium gruffly added.

Chapter 10
A Vast Emptiness

As they prepared to break camp, Mendy and Alum walked over to where the four oxen were grazing.

"If we leave them behind, they'll just be food for the bears," Alum mentioned Mendy with more than a little concern for the Oxen.

Mendy had started unloading the wagon. A lot would have to be left behind if the horses were not to be overloaded.

"You know, Mendy, the four oxen pulling the wagon together isn't that much slower than us using the horse as pack animals and we wouldn't have to leave much behind. Just leaving the Nomad tents would speed up the oxen. And we're leaving those tents anyway."

"You heard Thorium, Alum. We travel fast and light," said Mendy as he added to the pile to be sorted among them from the wagon.

"I bet if Thorium and the others saw how much we have to leave behind, Thorium would change his mind."

"He's already in a bad mood, Alum, do you want to push him. His talk with the Sage must have gone very badly," answered Mendy.

"Can you believe what Reed said, the myk being the outcome of their Teacher's experiments? And Reed going home, the look on Loren's face," spoke Alum as another armload went into the pile. Meanwhile the others were adding their own effects as the tents and the campsite were broken down. The Sage still hadn't left their own tent and sounds of disagreement were coming from it.

Jamen looked over at the growing pile of goods that lay on the ground. "Too much will have to be left behind. We don't know how long we will have to travel to find the Myk."

Alum looked over at Jamen from the now nearly empty wagon. "Talk to Thorium, Jamen. How much time will we really save, overloading the horse and living off of the land?"

Jamen looked over at Alum, then the pile. The horses that he had brought were for riding, not carrying supplies. They weren't pack animals. 'Does Thorium know the difference?" thought Jamen to himself.

"I'll talk to him," answered Jamen.

A little over a mile away Kat sat, his back to a tree, trying to see and hear what was going on in the camp through the still forming myk held captive by the party below. It was still too unformed to give Kat everything he wanted to know, but it was enough. He now knew with certainty that a sage could feel his presence and that of the other myk. In addition, there was dissention in the human's camp. Kat watched as one of the Nomads left with his wildcat. He didn't know which, but that didn't matter. Should he tell the one who ruled them, the Myk? No, but this played into his, Kat's, hands. It was time to contact his ally in The Hold and put their plans into action; tearing apart this fragile alliance put together by these strangers from the sea.

Kat smiled his sharpened teeth and stretched out the claws from his feet, no longer confined to human boots. It was almost his time, when the myk, the White, would grow strong again.

The pile of goods on the ground by the wagon was bigger than Thorium expected. The travelers were trying to split it up as evenly as possible but a lot would have to be left behind. Thorium still had no idea how long they would be gone. The extra horses were having the heavy blankets the Sage had brought put over their backs before loading. But even Thorium could see these horses were not bred to carry large loads. Speed against expediency, the tough choice Thorium had to make as their leader. Thorium saw Jamen look his way and waved him over.

"How long until we are ready to go?" Thorium asked Jamen who was overseeing the loading of the horses. How much each horse could take was Jamen's decision..

"This is slow, very slow. The horses I brought were for riding great distances. They weren't bred to carry freight. If I had known we would be abandoning the wagons I would have brought pack horses."

"Can they do the job?" Thorium questioned Jamen as he watched the makeshift loads put on Jamen's prize horses.

"Yes, but they can only carry light loads, a mans weight, any distance. They were not bred to carry more than a rider and his requirements. Alum has an idea I think you should listen to," Jamen stated, showing concern in his voice for the horses.

"Alum, huh, I hope that it is a good one. But oxen just can't pull a wagon fast enough."

"But the four oxen, yoked together, with the heaviest that we don't need left behind, could," Jamen said as he spoke to Thorium of Alum's thoughts.

"Oxen are unwieldy enough with just two to a wagon," was Thorium's reply. "Two harnesses and they're liable to just pull against each other as often as together."

"Alum says that he can make a dual yoke from the harnesses we have for the oxen and spare wood from the cart. Then he could drive them as a single ox with one harness."

"A dual yoke, he can do that?" asked Thorium.

"He says he can with Sebastian's help. Then the wagon can travel faster for extended periods than the over loaded horses would be able to." Jamen's heart was breaking as he saw the loads placed on the over burdened horses.

Thorium looked at the ever-shrinking pile of goods (still a lot there) taken off the wagon, the already overburdened horses, and then at Alum, Mendy, and Sebastian. Each was trying to help decide the priority of what to take and what to leave behind.

Jamen spoke again, "As we travel the horses will have to rest more often with the loads they are carrying and for longer periods as we go forward. We'll have to walk much of the way."

"Thank-you, Jamen," Thorium spoke as he shook Jamen's hand. "Sometimes I need to hear from other voices, so that decisions change. Reload the wagon; just leave the canvas tents behind. That will lesson the load a lot. We'll save your horses for now. Have Alum and Sebastian prepare the yoke. And we tie the White to a spare horse."

Jamen smiled as he turned back to the wagon and the pile of goods. "Reload the wagon and prepare the dual yoke and oxbow. We're leaving in an hour," he shouted to the three men at the wagon.

From his distant view of the expedition, Kat saw the humans first unload the wagon, overload the horses and then reverse the process. Were they going on as he had planned or were they turning back? Just what was happening there? Communication with the White (not yet a myk) was almost impossible. He had to move on quickly. Things were in motion and he still had his part to play. The answer back from The Hold had been an affirmative. The crisis would begin. And the Myk would have time to grow strong again. 'Under the leadership of myself,' Kat, thought to himself.

Kat turned away from the expedition and walked to his living 'food source'. The legs would be the last to go on each of them. The two partially consumed Nomads, drugged with the special chemicals of the myk, rose to their feet, a rope tethering them together, and followed Kat north and east. One wouldn't last much longer. 'Two days at most,' Kat thought. Then he would have a feast on what remained of the Nomads and rest. The trip ahead was long and there was plenty of 'food source' in the woodlands ahead.

It took Alum and Sebastian a little longer than a hour to make the double yoke oxbow harnesses for the four oxen. In the end, they had a secure harness so that they could pull as one. While the two men finished the yoke, the wagon was reloaded by the rest from the pile and the horses. Very little would be left behind; just the two large Nomad tents and a few incidentals nobody wanted. The trading goods had already been dumped on the trail when the second wagon had been lost. Removing the tents alone saved several hundred pounds the oxen wouldn't have to haul.

At seeing the tents left behind, the Sage were not happy and quickly voiced their displeasure to Thorium.

"One tent for all, we have the lightweight tarps we'll still be carrying. The weather will get better as we travel; summer is coming. And there are other things more important to carry," was Thorium's reply. "Put your goods on the wagon before they are *forgotten*."

By late morning, the party was on the move. The White captive was securely tied to a horse, though it seemed he was in no hurry to escape. Why should he? The food was human food, but he could survive on it and they were moving in the direction he wanted to go. Besides, he had understood enough of Kat to know that it was his duty to the Myk to stay with the expedition. Moreover, as he matured, the link with Kat would become stronger.

The way they followed remained pitted and rough. However

Thorium was very pleased with the speed they were making. With Mendy and Alum driving them, the four oxen were working as a team. Sebastian and Thorium's wildcats were given free reign to roam now and scout the terrain around them. Del knew of few direct threats to them in these woodlands they were heading into. The bear and the wolf would give the wildcats a wide berth, and the people of the woodlands, they called themselves Alsatians, lived in small villages and were mostly harmless. As they set forth, Gar felt a lessoning of the pressure on his brain. Fewer myk around, or as Gar thought most likely, one of great power was moving away.

Gar thought to himself, if that was true, maybe his curse could be used as a weapon. If he could maintain a constant pressure, identify this one myk from the background of lesser myk, he could use this interference to guide them in the direction they needed to go.

The expedition traveled rapidly along one of the old ways from before the Great War. Severely rutted, overgrown in places, even the occasional oak tree pushing tall through the concrete; it was still quicker than the alternative of following the dirt trails of the animals and the people of these northern woods.

Gar felt the pressure on his brain continue to lessen as the way led north and then back towards the west. As they traveled, the way crossed another leading east-west. Gar didn't hesitate to suggest that they move to the eastern leading path. Thorium was happy to take the suggestion as it at least gave them some hope of finding the Myk in the wilderness of the north. The party, led by the oxen-driven cart, moved to the new way, now heading in a northern and eastern direction. As they changed direction, within the hour Gar felt the pressure increase. They now knew that they could follow the course of the powerful myk Gar felt.

So did the White prisoner.

Through him so did Kat, who smiled his sharp teeth. The days of the Myk in his cavern were numbered.

The time of Kat and the renewal of the myk was getting close.

Kats ability to reach his colleague in intrigue in The Hold was growing tenuous with distance. He would try for a last message before he reached his fortress where his destiny was waiting.

First on to the cavern of the Myk.

As the expedition followed this new way, the forest grew denser and began seriously to impede them on the way. The pace slowed as they often had to choose which path to take, the way almost completely overgrown now. Although the concrete remained in places it had almost become a bigger obstacle than the trees and their roots. The wildcats now stayed near the wagon without being commanded. All of the riders on horseback also stayed within sight of the wagon. The presence of the myk seemed to be growing. This was the land of the Alsatians, a people that Del knew well from his travels.

A clearing was found where the way divided once more and a camp made for the night. They were a week removed from their camp at the bridge and the rivers edge, and the setting up and breaking down of a camp in these woodlands had become mote. They should have encountered the Alsatians by now, Del insisted. Was this the land of empty villages as reported by the scouts at their most distant reach?

A lone elk, its imposing rack on its head exceeding seven feet, stood between two trees staring at the men.

"Do we need food?" Thorium asked.

"We have fresh meat for another week," answered Alum, in charge of their commissary.

The elk continued to stare at the men, unafraid.

"A magnificent beast," Sebastian spoke. "It's well that we have no need for its flesh."

All around the fire, started in the late afternoon as the camp was set up, the party seemed in agreement to let the beast live.

Loren smiled at the elk and that seemed to be what it was waiting for, only now turning and leaving. *'A messenger from Reed,'* thought Loren.

The empty village was the first that they had actually entered. By now, Del had become a close confidant of Thorium as they jointly led the expedition through the wooded forests of the North. Where were the people? Their homes were rough looking but very habitable, made from the local forests wood. They entered a home on the edge of the village. No dogs, no birds, no animals of any kind greeted them from the vicinity of the village. The door was unlocked. Children's toys were scattered about the main room. A table was laid out for a meal; the food now cold and rotten. Where were the people?

Sebastian sent the two wildcats out to scout the vicinity of the village. They returned a short time later. It was apparent that they had found nothing. Del had no answers. He knew these people well, but this?

Thorium was sitting on a log in the center of the village. Like the home, it was built of rough hewn logs. He called Del over to him.

"Tell me about these missing people, Del."

"They call themselves the Alsatians. It's what this land was called before the 'Great War', Alsace. Not really a primitive people, they keep to themselves and lead a simple life, not unlike the Nomads that way," Del began as he sat next to Thorium on the log.

"Their villages are small, never more than a few hundred people, and they travel and trade frequently between their villages, each village having its own specialty to give to their culture. With this trade amongst themselves they have little need for outside discourse.

"They are supreme hunters with their bows, a good as any I have seen. And they are very unique in one way. They still manufacture their own steel tools, not from the recycled remains of the skeleton cities, but from small ore mines they still operate in their lands. These may be the last operating mines in this part of the world."

"Why would they abandon their villages? Disease, war, or something else?" Thorium questioned Del.

Del responded, at loss himself for why these villages were being emptied. "I am not aware of any plague in this region. And of war, they had no enemies."

"Something happened, something drove them from their homes in a hurry," Thorium spoke, looking at Del for his response.

"Like the Gypsies they value their children above all," Del continued. "They would do anything to protect them. But why would they leave their homes in mass?"

"There must be a clue here someplace," Thorium finished as he got up from the log.

Sebastian found the first signs of the distress that had led to the abandoned villages. He noticed the captured White was getting agitated and sent the wildcats out further in the direction of the furtive glances of the White.

Sebastian, Mendy and Alum were talking not far from the White when they heard a commotion from the direction that the wildcats had been sent. They heard a scream and a voice calling out. The three men rushed to the direction of the scream, weapons drawn, not sure of what the wildcats had found. Loren was rushing across the village, her crossbow loaded, as the rest followed behind on the race to the scene.

With their greater speed than Sebastian and their lead over the others, Alum and Mendy were the first to arrive, Sebastian close behind. They found the wildcats mauling a group of Whites, feasting on a meal withering on the ground before them. The Whites didn't have a chance, though three of the four had pronounced double-heads protruding from their shoulders. Before Sebastian could pull the wildcats from the White, all four were dead.

"I have never seen the wildcats attack like that without orders," Sebastian said as the others arrived, defending the actions of the wildcats. "Something provoked them."

Thorium had witnessed first hand when Tri had defended him, the controlled actions of the wildcats.

Del, who had arrived shortly after the fighter, now spoke up in the wildcat's defense. "They were provoked, look here."

Del was standing by the remains of the Whites meal. He reached down and picked up an object from the ground. A toy, as they had seen in the house that they had entered earlier. "They had arrived too late to help the children of this village, but they remembered Twror and took their revenge."

Loren walked over to the remains of the children, took one look, and retched all she had eaten that day. "The myk, in their exodus... they are eating..." she was unable to go on with her words.

Loren was interrupted in her effort to speak by the arrival of Gar. He finished Loren's thought. "They are living off of the villages of the Alsatians who are helpless before them."

Thorium spoke again. "These people are fleeing from the myk. We must be close. We must hurry now. The myk must be made to pay for these atrocities that they have committed. We spend the night in this village and then move on early in the morning. Find a building with a corral for the animals. I don't like the look of the clouds gathering overhead."

Thorium walked over to Gar. "Gar, didn't you feel those White?"

"I felt the pressure," Gar answered, "but I still have a lot to learn of my abilities before I learn to identify the myk around me.":

When the group returned to the center of the village where they had left the White captive tied up, the two wildcats nervously began pacing near the captive White.

"And the captive?" asked Jamen.

"Keep him tied securely; there are probably other White around. He led us to that group." Thorium answered Jamen then he looked towards Gar.

"Yes, most definitely, yes," Gar answered the unasked question. "Quite a few of them I can now feel. We must take care."

"Everybody in the building tonight," Thorium ordered. We stand a full nights watch, especially over the livestock in the corral."

Alum spoke up now. "I saw a large barn on the far side of the village. It should be big enough for us and the animals."

"Better still, lead the way." Thorium was now in full command mode. Danger was near. He could *feel* it.

The people of this village were gone. '*Had any survived?*' thought Del. These were a peaceful people, so many were friends of Del. Now they were being destroyed by the *reckless* behavior of the Teachers. 'Yes,' Del thought, 'they had done so much good and saved the human race. But that was balanced out by the harm that they have caused with their experiments, a few of which only now bearing out their results.'

Chapter 11
Wilfred, The lost Sage

A small brick forge, with its chimney leading up through the roof, was in one corner of the barn. Its tools and its axe lay next to it. They all thought aloud about their uses for it tonight, food and heat. Alum and Mendy took it on themselves to gather as much firewood as possible. Large amounts were stacked up outside the barn; mostly dry.

Already the first signs of the coming storm were appearing. The wind was picking up and a light rain was beginning to fall.

Sebastian and Jamen led the horses and oxen into the barn and placed them into empty stalls on one side. They found several cattle in one of the stalls, survivors of whatever had happened here. Thorium, Loren and the Sage looked through the wagon, now inside the barn for anything that they would need for the night.

As the storm picked up, Thorium and Sebastian called their wildcats inside. They had been pacing around the barn, nervous over what they smelled in the air. The two wildcats lay together just inside of the barns only entrance, always on duty as sentries.

Gar's mind became more clouded, not from the mind of power that he had held before and could now identify as Kat, but by the sheer numbers of myk that surrounded the village. Were they now the hunted and not the hunters?

The storm hit the barn in all its fury several hours after the sun set. The barn shook with the immense power of the winds. The roof rattled as if it would fly off and the door flew open. It took all of them to set it closed, now with an extra beam holding it in place.

There were several leaks in the barns walls which they covered with whatever they could find. They were thankful that the large cut logs that covered the roof remained in place, although the number of leaks increased over the night, largely in just one corner of the barn that the men avoided during their sleep.

The storm lasted for two days, during which they stayed dry and warm from the fireplace-like forge. They had food and beverage and each in their own way appreciated the respite from their march to find the Myk's cavern. For now, their worry of the myk disappeared.

On the late morning of the third day the rain finally came to a stop. They all walked to the barns door and opened it. What they found when they opened it was the last thing they expected. Myk weapons, in all of their strangeness, lay about the plaza in front of the barn. There were a lot of them. And with those weapons, laying dead and dying, were dozens of myk; all double-heads.

One man stood alone in front of them, his army standing around him in a semicircle, facing towards them; the Alsatians.

The man spoke loudly to the dazed men as they staggered into the light, weapons in hand; was this a new foe, or was it a friend.

"It's about time you came out. This was over quickly an hour ago. You're among friends."

"Wilfred, alive!" Gar exclaimed loudly. He had seen Wilfred carried away by the force of the Teachers over 500 years earlier. How had he escaped?

Wilfred held one myk captive with a rope around the prisoner's neck. "Are you ready to see the last one killed?" Wilfred asked almost gleefully.

Thorium stepped forward, "We need information."

"Who and what are you?" Wilfred stated to the expedition. He already knew but he still went on the offensive. He had expected to find just the myk raiding party, not the three Sage and their party.

"You know us well," Gar spoke to Wilfred.

"It's been a long time, Gar," Wilfred said quietly as he nodded to the other two Sage.

The three Sage looked at Wilfred, thought killed by the teachers, with suspicion. 'More secrets kept from us', thought Tor. Gar had been the last to see Wilfred when he was taken away.

"Perhaps it is best if we continue this inside," spoke Wilfred in a voice used to giving commands that the Alsatians would follow. He motioned for the myk to be saved for now. They placed him with the myk that the expedition already held. The expedition sat on the ground, surrounded by the Alsatians, just looking at each other and then the Sage. Tor's look to Thorium was enough to tell the men to be careful.

"Come, come. Your men will be safe," Wilfred spoke directly to Gar, upset at the hesitation of the three Sage. "And we'll be out of sight of any prying eyes of the myk," Wilfred half-laughed.

"You know of the myk!" Tor exclaimed in surprise.

"They breed and spread like mice. I have brought my people chosen closer together and further north to protect them."

"The empty villages we passed," questioned Del, wondering to himself how he had never encountered or even heard of Wilfred. The Alsatians were even more secretive than he had thought.

"Yes. Now come inside, the three of you. I, the *Son of Odin*, grow impatient with my former friends."

Wilfred turned and walked to the closest hut. He opened the door and held it so the three Sage could enter inside. Tor looked back at the expedition one more time, as if to say *be alert*. They didn't need the warning and held their weapons firmly beside themselves, an arrow notched in Loren's crossbow.

Inside the large hut Wilfred stood tall before the three Sage, in regalia befitting a king. A hat, more a crown than the hood that the Sage wore, covered his head. The staff he carried was be-speckled in gems. He wore a plaid kilt, green and red, with loose woolens around his torso. A bronze handled short sword was attached to his wide belt with an ornate scabbard at his side.

'*The Son of Odin*', Gar thought, 'what madness is this?" This was the grandeur that had led the Teachers to take away the then (and now?) dangerous Wilfred.

The four Sage walked into the dark interior of the hut. A fire burned in a brick oven in one corner of the room, providing heat but little light. A table and chair stood near it, a candle lit there for light. The table and chairs were all rough-hewn. Wilfred led them to the table and the four Sage sat down around it.

Wilfred's man-servant, whom had been stoking the fire, walked over to Wilfred. "Do you have any orders, my Liege?"

Wilfred looked over at the other Sage and asked them, "Did you bring any of the beans? It's been a long time since I drank any of our brew." Wilfred was casual in his behavior, as if nothing was out of the normal.

"Yes," said Tor before the others could speak. "Already ground, do you have any hot water?"

"On the fire," Wilfred answered. He spoke a few quiet words to his man-servant who then walked over to the brick oven and brought back to the sage a pot of hot water. Del brought out a packet of the ground beans from under his tunic, handing it to Wilfred. Wilfred added a careful amount to the pot.

"It may be bitter, the beans are getting old."

"Even bitter it will be a sweet tonic for my parched brain," Wilfred laughed, seemingly free of worry. "A ladle and four mugs," Wilfred called out to his man-servant, who hurried to get what his master had commanded.

After each Sage had drunk their fill in silence Gar spoke up, trying to bring lightness to the unspoken words that haunted each of them.

"So how has the *Son of Odin* managed to survive for so long?" Gar half laughed.

Wilfred glared at Gar in a menacing fashion. To challenge or make jest of his linage was a crime for his people. Gar, Tor and Del exchanged brief glances. This Sage was more dangerous than they had first thought.

Tor quickly interceded. "No offence was meant, old friend. It's a natural question, even to one as esteemed as you."

Wilfred relaxed and sat back in his chair, almost tipping it over before catching himself. He laughed as he sat back up, his hand now loosely resting on the surface of the table.

"It's good to see you all again. Together we will fight the menace that is the Myk." He raised his mug high in a toast.

"To the Teachers in their infinite wisdom," Wilfred called out.

The other Sage raised their mugs in toast as well, somewhat fearful of what Wilfred had become.

"To the Teachers," they all called in unison; all the while they exchanging knowing glances with each other.

Outside the rest of the expedition was gathered together at one side of the town square. They had so far been allowed to keep their weapons. The Alsatians had heard of the wildcats and looked at them in both fear and admiration. They had tried to order the expedition to order the wildcats into the barn with the livestock, but it was clear that neither would leave the side of Thorium and Sebastian.

It was mid-spring and still very cold in the north. Large ice sheets still covered much of the very northern lands. A large bonfire was burning in the center of the square. The expedition, now sitting on logs, on one side, while the Alsatians remained sitting on the ground in a large crescent facing them.

Thorium sat with his old shipmates. Loren and Sebastian sat on another log close by. All were silent as they listened to the chatter going on among the Alsatians. Alum quietly cracked a joke at Mendy's expense. It drew a soft laugh from Thorium and Loren. Sebastian only gave Alum a serious glare. The Alsatians looked on at the laughter with more suspicion.

The two captured myk sat tied up a short distance to one side. The wildcats kept looking their way and the myk trembled in fear. They had both seen first hand what the wildcats were doing to myk found in Twror.

Thorium motioned over to one of their (captors?) and called to him. "Do you have any food; we haven't eaten today and are hungry."

The man just looked at him without comprehension. The language these people spoke was different from the common language spoken by the expedition; more guttural and harsh.

Thorium pointed to his mouth and belly and the man seemed to understand. He pointed to where a bear was roasting over the fire. A meal to be shared by all it seemed.

A woman walked over to the expedition. Here in the north, as like in the south, women fought alongside men for survival.

"Who speaks for you?" she said in a barely understandable voice. "I speak your tongue."

Thorium stood up and slowly approached her. "I am Thorium and lead this expedition."

He had barely gotten his words out when she jumped back at his approach. It occurred to Thorium that at no time since their initial contact with the Alsatians had any approached within six or eight feet of them.

"Stay your distance," she commanded. "It has not yet been determined if you are friend or foe. Or if you are a member of the *One True Race*."

"We come in friendship," Thorium interjected. "We are here to find and destroy the Myk." Thorium made sure not to get any closer to the woman and after speaking took a step back.

"That is to be determined. I am Gertrude, right-hand of our King, Wilfred, Son of Odin." She stood tall and powerful at this proclamation.

"Who are the *One Race*?" asked Alum.

Gertrude seemed surprised at this question. This raised more suspicion in her mind about these people. "The *One Race* is the chosen people. If you ask such a question you must not be of the *One Race*, she straight forwardly answered.

"Who decided the chosen people?" asked Thorium, pushing for the answers they needed.

"The Teachers chose the *One People*, as taught to us by our King Wilfred, he of the long life."

"We too are of the Teachers," Thorium stated to her. "Don't we travel with three of your King's friends?"

"That is to be decided as well. Food will be brought to you, do not approach the fire. You remain neither friends nor enemies. That is to be decided."

With that, Gertrude quickly turned and walked away, her harsh features catching the sun breaking through the clouds.

"Questions and more questions, and here we go again, more questions than answers," Mendy glumly spoke.

"Do you remember when we first arrived? We encountered Gar...or at least his image," Alum added.

Thorium laughed at the memory. "An eternity ago it now seems. And the way Zircon attacked the image."

They all laughed at the memory, even Jamen, Loren and Sebastian whom had heard the story many times before.

"Always it seems that we are in the center of things," Alum stated matter-of-factly. "The prophesies that we never heard of seem to guide us."

"So it seems," said Thorium, walking back to his sear as he saw bread and meat being brought to them, "guided by the prophesies of the Teachers that we never knew, equals with the Sage that we had never encountered. It seems that our confederation and this world are awakening from a 2000-year slumber.

"Even without knowing all this, we were guided, unseen, by Simon," Alum finished the thoughts of all.

The three of them, Thorium, Mendy and Alum, now friends, glanced at each other. Whatever was going to happen next, they had each others backs.

Thorium looked down at Tri and scratched his back. "Guided and never alone' were his thoughts.

It was just past noon when the four Sage came out of the dwelling. Tor was the first to speak.

"Load up the wagon, we're heading north with Wilfred and the Alsatians," Tor announced to the expedition.

"North!" Thorium was surprised at that.

"Yes, north," Tor repeated to the group. "Wilfred has *invited* us to rest, before we go on, at his home, the Danegold."

Thorium and the others picked up on the inflection in Tor's voice. This was more an order than an invitation. And they were in no position to fight the Alsatians right now.

All of the myk expedition worked to load the wagons and they re-hitched the oxen to the wagon. This gave Thorium a chance to talk to the Sage.

"So, is Wilfred friend or foe?" Thorium asked the Sage.

"Right now, we really don't know," answered Del.

Thorium looked directly at the Sage and stated. "You were in there a long time."

"Remaking acquaintances, but we have to be careful. One wrong word can set Wilfred off," Gar quietly mentioned.

Thorium spoke again. "I met his wife, Gertrude."

"His wife?" Tor questioned.

"She seemed that and his second in command."

"So how far do we have to travel?" Loren asked.

"We'll be there by nightfall," Del answered. "It's in a small valley and caverns just to the north of here. The Alsatians there survived the winter in the caverns before his arrival, though Wilfred says that there were very few remaining when he found them."

Everything was quickly loaded and they headed north. The expedition rode in the oxcart or on horseback. The Alsatians moved quickly on foot. Only Wilfred and Gertrude among them rode on horseback. The two of them rode alongside the Sage. The wildcats ran close to Thorium and Sebastian who rode horseback at the front; the wildcat's eyes up and alert.

As the four Sage rode together they spoke back and forth with each other. Wilfred was primarily asking questions about what had happened in the south in his absence. He was especially interested in the Myk War and the new confederation of peoples.

"That was the goal of the Teachers," Wilfred stated. "But they didn't have to do that with the creation of the White and the double-heads. One strong leader among the Sage could have done it, with a lot less pain."

"And who would lead us?" Gar asked. "We have always followed the Teachers instruction as a council."

"The strongest," Wilfred answered, "perhaps I."

Not liking the direction of the conversation Gar spoke. "How much farther do we have left to travel?

"Not far," Gertrude spoke up for Wilfred, the first time she had spoken since they had left the village. Nevertheless, the three Sage had seen how attentive she was to the conversation. "Then you and your party can rest until it is time for you to continue your journey."

Though Gertrude's voice seemed friendly, there was something off about it. Wilfred looked at her as if she should not have spoken. The three Sage exchanged anxious glances. Tor thought to himself, 'could this be something that they could use to there advantage. Was Gertrude becoming too independent for Wilfred's liking?'

The party continued to amble along in awkward silence. Del rode closer to Wilfred and quietly spoke. "I think that we can all take a little break from the travel. We have been making good time and you can tell us more about your story."

"A break," Wilfred exclaimed. Then he spoke in a quieter, calm voice. "Yes, you have traveled far and need one. My story; my people know it. Perhaps it's time for you and your party to learn it as well"

They came to a stop at the next clearing, the oxen and horses tied to one side. The Alsatians gathered with Gertrude in a group near the wagon and shared in its dried meat. Alum and Mendy started a small fire on the other side of the glade, close to the Alsatians, but not too close. There was still danger around, though Gar felt nothing of the myk.

Mendy and Alum brought out some flat bread that they had baked in the barn and dried fish from their own supplies. The Sage brought out their pot and brewed some of their 'presso, now almost gone.

Sebastian and Thorium found near the glade small logs and placed them, with the Alsatians help, around the small fire. The expedition all engaged in small talk about their expedition so far, trying to cover their nervousness about the situation.

Del spoke to Wilfred once more. "So Wilfred, tell us your story. How you came to be among the Alsatians, without sign or word from you for all these hundreds of years."

Before starting, Wilfred called over Gertrude and told her to get the Alsatians moving to their valley to the north. When she hesitated, he ordered her to lead their people back home. The expedition all saw the hesitation in her voice and maybe, just maybe, and little bit of fear and trepidation in her manner.

Wilfred, after she had led their people away, looked at each of the expedition in turn, with an almost solemn look on his face. Then he began his story in his calm voice that the other Sage were happy to hear. Perhaps here in his story there would be a clue to Wilfred's behavior.

Wilfred began his story.

"I had to leave the Hold, for my own good and peace of mind. I knew of the Teachers experiments in the Two Valleys and voiced my opposition to them."

"The Teachers said that they destroyed you," Gar said. "I saw them carry you away."

"Somehow I was able to cloud their minds and escape."

"Cloud their minds? How?" Tor asked.

"At that time I wasn't sure," was all that Wilfred said about the subject.

"I could have followed Simon across the Western Sea," Wilfred continued, "and then what? Play second fiddle to the one sage who could challenge me for control. That wasn't what I sought out. It is what the Teachers wanted. To drive away the two strongest Sage who might challenge them so that they could continue to lay out their plans for our future."

Wilfred looked at each of the Sage in disdain. "We could have stood up to the Teachers, if the Sage had stood up together."

"Under your command?" Del pointedly asked. "I spoke against the Teachers as well, one reason that I wandered so much of the frozen north. However, I never forgot who I was and often returned to the Hold. However, they did good as well, we can't forget about that. And we were important to the future of man."

"A thousand years of winter that they could have stopped. How many died because of the Teachers? How many died so that they could pursue their plans for the future of mankind?" Wilfred practically yelled to the expedition as he looked at them one by one.

Wilfred calmed down again and looked at the other Sage as if to say, 'I'm Okay.'

Gar spoke now in his quiet firm voice. "Continue with your story, Wilfred."

Wilfred now continued. "If I traveled to the south the Teachers would have sent you to follow me. If I traveled to the east, that's where they still lived. So I traveled to the north."

"Thorium broke in with his own question now. "Could the Teachers have let you escape, to further their plans in the north?"

Wilfred considered the question for a moment. "I had never considered that. To be used by the Teachers without my knowledge. It seems doubtful, but it is something I must consider now. It would be shocking if this was true."

"Continue, Wilfred," Mendy spoke. "You hold us in suspense."

"Yes," Wilfred began again. "To the north then I left the Hold and the Teachers; to oppose the teacher's experiments.

"I passed through the passes to the north of the hold on foot and wrapped in furs to hold off the bitterness of the cold. Not even the layered furs that I wore could hold off the bitterness that I felt, both mentally and physically.

"'Damn the Teachers and their 1000-year winter' I shouted to the sky.

"Wood became scarce to make fires at night and the skeleton remains of the prewar cities towered above the ice. And this was summer. I cut down the green wood that I found in those cities where the ground was sheltered from the ice. I used the fire-starters that I had wisely brought from the Hold. I sought shelter many times in the remains of those cities. What a world it must have been before man's stupidity brought an end to their world. Small animals remained somehow in these cities and I was lucky enough to bring down an elk, which I dried the meat of and it provided me several months of food. I also found wild fruit and berries in these cities."

Gar interrupted Wilfred there." Why did you keep going, what drove you on? I can't imagine the suffering you faced."

"I couldn't stay for long in any of them, in fear that the Teachers (or you) would find me. Suffer I did. But I couldn't let the Teachers win."

"Win?" Tor said.

"There was another way, not the Teachers way, and I was determined to find and learn what that way was. That was my mission and that is what drove me," Wilfred stated matter-of-factly.

"Continue on," Thorium said, "I find this fascinating."

Wilfred looked at Thorium with a hint of (respect? Friendship?) something. Thorium, himself, wasn't sure what the look meant.

"To north than I traveled, to find a lost people to lead out of their wilderness, this hell that the Teachers had allowed to happen.

"Across the ice fields I traveled, always facing to the north, to the Danegold that we as Sage heard rumors of.

"I found a shoreline and continued along it. Fish to eat, however there were also serpents I had to fear, worse than the Jal-beast our Teachers had created from the past. Several times, I barely escaped them with my life. Fortunately, they never traveled very far from the water.

"Finally I found my people, hundreds of miles across the ice to the north. They called themselves the Alsatians from times past. There were only a few hundred left and I found them barely alive. A small valley, sheltered from the worst of the ice, and a series of caverns, that is what they called home. Here they had lived, on lichen, small animals, and mushrooms since the Armageddon.

"The Teachers had to know something of them and did nothing to help them."

Wilfred stopped here to catch his breath and Del asked, "What if the teachers only recently had discovered those people and directed you to them through their strange means."

"Again, with maybe I was a tool of the Teachers. Even if I was, their inhumanity drove me north. No, I refuse to believe that I was a part of their plans that I opposed."

After a sip of his now cold presso, Wilfred continued to the men that he held in the rapture of his story; a rapture that he lived for. "

"It was months or even years before I found my people, the Alsatians. Time had lost its meaning in my travels north. The Alsatians were barely alive as a people, I found them hiding in their caves when I approached and entered the valley.

"As starving as they were, they overcame their suspicion of me, a stranger and welcomed me into their valley as a friend. I had to do what I could for these people, survivors somehow, of the scourge of the Teachers.

"There were several streams that ran through this little valley and they teamed with fish. Whether they feared the fish, with their superstitious ways, or just lacked the skill to catch them, I didn't know. I caught several of them for myself with a fish trap that I built along the shore of one of the streams. I started a small fire and cooked the fish on rocks that circled the fire. The Alsatians smelled the cooking fish from their caverns and came out to investigate. As they saw me get ready to eat the fish they rushed over to me and knocked a fish from my hand. Their language was strange sounding, but now I understood. The fish in the past had become poisonous. I was certain with the passage of time that the fish were now safe to eat. I had eaten many on the coastline without becoming sick. I reached for another fish, and before they could knock it out of my hand as well, I took a bite. They all drew back as if I was crazy. I finished the first fish and began the second without showing any signs of illness. A few of the bold Alsatians now approached me and watched as I finished a second fish for my famished body. I could feel the energy of the food coursing through my body. Several of those now motioned that they would like to try some. I gave them what was left of my first catch and they tried them, not without a little trepidation. A new industry was born for them as those few brave people now motioned the rest to come eat the fish. I left to check my nearby fish trap and found over a dozen more trout of good size in my trap. I gathered those up and added them to the rocks around the fire. The Alsatians now all gingerly tried the fish, finishing all that I had caught. I looked on with amazement at the good order they showed, none going back for more until all had had something to eat.

"Overtime, we extended this fishing to the coast, not more than a few days march away.

"As I explored this region where these people had survived I found strange ruins towering above the ice. The Alsatians called them the home of their Nordic Gods and said I must have come from there. In their strange tongue, which I was rapidly learning, wild rumors rapidly spread about me.

'He never ages...'

'They sent him here to save us...'

'He must be a God...'

"I embraced this as a way to teach them and lead these Alsatians from their hell.

"Several hundred years passed and I truly became the *Son of Odin* to these people. Our village was now a thriving town and food was plentiful. The ice had receded beyond the valley. I placed greenhouses through the town and filled them with the fruit and grains from the seeds I gathered in my journeys.

"I almost returned to the Hold once, but I quickly changed my mind. I saw all of the activity around it. I was surprised that I was not spotted, but the Sage who would have recognized me were few and I was long forgotten in the memory of the people there.

"As the ice melted between Danegold and the coast, disaster struck us.

"We were a peaceful people. The only weapon we had was small hunting bows and knives.

"Coastal raiders, slavers, attacked one of our fishing parties on the coast. Of the eleven on the trip, only one returned, injured; the rest killed or taken prisoner to sell as slaves. I am a peaceful man; we of the Sage are all inherently so. Nevertheless, as you showed in your victory over the Myk, we do indeed know how to fight.

"Our hunting bows would become long-bows. We had plenty of ash growing to make the bows straight and strong. I taught them to string the bows with the tendons of the game we killed for food. The tips changed from stone to primitive metal tips. I had taught them to Forge 100 years before. With that, our blacksmiths competed with each other on how to create Swords from the knives that they had created up to that time. Long and short swords, they shared their techniques with each other, all the while creating better and better weapons for us.

"We weren't quite ready when the first small party of raiders found us and approached our valley. However, even with primarily just the hunting bows, we were able to drive them away. Now they knew where we were. Next time they would come in force.

"Training began in earnest with our new weapons. Some weapons in training broke at first use. Our blacksmiths learned even from these mistake and no shortcuts were taken after that. Our archers were already good, especially the women, and the best, the strongest, were given the longbows first. And as each longbow was cured and formed we became stronger.

"We would be ready.

"Several months later, we were prepared. A fishing party, aware of the danger the raiders brought us, spotted the first; dozens of ships and their warriors. However, they saw no sign of archers, to my great relief. The fishing party rushed back to tell us what they had seen.

"There was only one approach to the valley from where the raiders landed. That position in the valley had been prepared; firing pits in the valley's walls for our archers, a series of staggered walls, over six feet high, with no two openings through them lined up. You can see the remains of these today to the northwest of the town, at the opening of the valley. I will take you there.

"When they arrived, they found strong positions before them. I am sure that's not what they expected. They marched in loose groups through several of the staggered openings in the walls. We remained hidden.

"Then I gave a signal from a watchtower that we had built hidden in the forest. From there I had a clear view of the battlefield. I released a falcon into the air that had adopted me and called me its friend. That was to signal for the battle to begin.

"My archers on either side of the valley opened fire almost as one, at the sight of the falcon, at the enemy below. Most of the raiders fell with that first volley. A second volley was in the air even before the first volley had found their marks. The raiders now ran in disarray, those few that remained. Our swordsmen now moved forward in unison from behind their walls. In view now of our enemy, the raiders fled in further disorder. As brave as the swordsmen were, I glad they had to do nothing more than chase the survivors down. One on one against veteran fighters we would have lost many souls here.

”We were never bothered again by the raiders or anybody else. Not until the Whites, and then the myk appeared in the north.

"We now blossomed and flourished into the city you will soon see before you.

"Over time the people of the Danegold (as I named this city) told me of stories that I had discounted at the time. Then I found ancient papers, preserved from time, on one of my explorations in the north. I was eventually able to mostly decipher them. There was something important to the east. That confirmed the stories that the Alsatians had told me so long ago. This was not the 'Blue Lights' as I first thought, the stories placed them far to the north and east for that. There was something else; a lost Hold; caverns like here; or something else. I didn't know. However, I'll tell you what I was able to determine before you leave us.

"I created this society from nothing. They were dying. Now I bring them into the future with my words and deeds.

"That is enough of me for now. It is starting to get late and its time to continue to my home."

To the Danegold they traveled now, the three Sage in the wagon to better speak with each other. Thorium, Mendy and Alum now rode at the front with Wilfred. Alum and Mendy peppered him with questions that flattered Wilfred's sense of vanity and Thorium encouraged their questions. The wildcats roamed on each side of the men, alert for any scent of danger.

Chapter 12
The Alsatians

They reached the city of the Danegold and it rivaled any city of the south; stone-paved roads; wooden buildings three and four stories tall; an aqueduct bringing to the city water from a river to the north; a sewage system that rivaled the one of The Hold.

Tens of thousands of people now lived in this secret society, hidden in the valleys and ice of the north. Both the descendents of the people that Wilfred first found and many whom had since made refuge in this valley; especially with the advent of the Myk. All of them of the *True* people, none with the deformities of the White or the myk.

Statues stood in abundance throughout the city; all of their Nordic gods, especially Wilfred, son of Odin and their savior.

Dozens of greenhouses spread throughout the city containing grains, vegetables and fruit trees. There were stables of livestock, as expansive as the Southern Valleys. Giant Elk (somehow domesticated?) stood corralled, along with small horses, rabbits and their kittens, cattle, sheep and goats. They the men samples of the cities cheese as they entered the Danegold.

The Alsatians were short, stocky and hairy. Their guttural language was both easy and hard to understand. Wilfred had introduced as much of the common language as he could. However, the Alsatians stuck with many of their most important words.

As the expedition approached the city, they saw a hunting party arrive back into the city carrying several large sea snakes over twenty feet long and a giant flying lizard, all brought down with the composite bows they carried.

Not all of the Alsatians, they were told, lived within the city. Many lived in small family groups of ten to twenty people in the surrounding valleys, their superstitions keeping them out of the city. Wilfred bragged about this. He expanded on their fear of disease to keep the Alsatians isolated and under his (benign?) rule.

The Alsatians they encountered were a fearless people that worked together as one and Wilfred was the glue that kept them together. Repeatedly Wilfred had proved that he had the right to rule them and that he was the true Son of Odin.

The expedition traveled closely together as they entered the city. None wanted to be separated from the others. The question remained heavy on their hearts; were they the guests of Wilfred, or were they his prisoners?

Just before Wilfred rode ahead into the city he spoke to the weary travelers. "I have preparations to make for your unexpected arrival. I will leave Gertrude with you while I ride ahead to tend to your needs."

"Gertrude," he called over to her. "Please find suitable housing for our *guests*."

"As you wish," she obediently answered.

Thorium spoke up to Gertrude on the matter of their housing. "We prefer to stay together. If you have an inn, that would be fine."

Wilfred gave a strong glance at Gertrude's direction before riding off.

"I don't think that will be possible," she said to Thorium. "We don't have inns here as we allow no visitors."

The expedition's members just looked at each other on hearing that. Thorium thought he saw some apprehension in Gertrude's eyes when she answered him.

Once Wilfred rode out of sight, Gertrude rode over next to him. "I'll do what I can. I think that there is an abandoned house on the edge of the city. I will bring you there. But Wilfred may be angry at that." Thorium could hear the worry in her voice.

Tor now asked Gertrude a question. "Do you so fear Wilfred?" He had also seen fear in her eyes.

"We all do, yet he is our savior."

"We must tread carefully here," was all that Thorium added.

"Yes, you must," agreed Gertrude.

Shortly after the expedition settled into their new abode on the edge of the city in a small but usable house, Wilfred arrived.

"This will just not do," Wilfred stated matter-of-factly. "The Sage do not live in such squalor. It will be fine for the rest of you but Tor, Gar, and Del; you must come with me. I will give you quarters in my own home."

Del spoke up for the tired expedition, hoping that his natural bond with Wilfred over the Teachers activities remained. "Wilfred, my good friend, we welcome you offering us rooms in your home. But may we rest here first?" Del hoped for a delay in their separation. "We have come a long ways, very quickly, chasing the myk and are only now resting. Perhaps a day or two here before we join you?"

Wilfred looked briefly perplexed. He was used to his every order being followed without question. He had expected his offer to be immediately accepted. His anger briefly flashed; in a moment, it was gone. Wilfred briefly thought it over. Del hadn't said no.

"A day or two is fine. That gives me time enough to prepare my home for your arrival; no longer though."

"Of course," Del answered, looking briefly at the others. "We look forward to your accommodations."

With that brief exchange over, Wilfred turned and left the small wooden structure that was the expedition's home (prison?). They couldn't help noticing the small group of the Danegold's warriors sitting just a short distance from the house.

After food and beverage was brought to them, they all gathered around a large table in the main room to enjoy it; a wide selection of meats, fish, fruit, berries, vegetables, bread and cheese from the stables and greenhouses of the city.

Mendy, after eating his fill, leaned back in his chair. "Best meal since our journey began," he laughed.

Alum joined in the laughter, almost falling back in his chair with his guffaws, his chair was caught by Sebastian who was walking behind him to refill his ale.

Loren now stood up as well and began speaking in her serious tone bringing the brief bout of levity to an end.

As she began talking, she walked to the fireplace, warming her hands and then turning back to the table. "So, is he our ally against the Myk? Or is he something nearly as bad? The Alsatians, including Gertrude, live in fear of him. She admitted as much to us. Is this an idyllic Eden or something from hell?"

Sebastian started speaking then, as he reseated himself at the table. "I have seen the dread in these people's eyes in whomever I encountered"

Tor now stood, holding a cup of the Sage's brew, made from

the last of their beans. He walked towards the fireplace and then back. They could all see that he was in deep thought. Finally, he began. "We must be careful and keep our tongues and wit about us. Even in this house, we must be wary of Wilfred. Somebody could easily overhear us through the windows or doorway. In two days he expects to split us up, when his invitation for the Sage to live in his home comes to fruition."

"That is also an opportunity for us," Del stated, setting down his mug of ale. He looked at Thorium for his thoughts.

Thorium, having finished his bird leg and wiped his hand, spoke once more, in a quiet voice, as to be not overheard by any eavesdroppers outside. "An opportunity, yes it is. You, Sage, you can keep Wilfred occupied while the rest of us study the city for our... escape."

"Escape?" asked Tor.

"Yes, escape. I doubt that Wilfred will freely let us go. This is important; the three of you must study Wilfred, his strengths and any weaknesses we can use. Ply on his vanity."

"We can do that," replied Tor.

Thorium continued, looking around the table at each of them. "Mendy, Alum, the two of you always seem to make friends wherever we are. Mingle; find out about these people."

"You got it." "Consider it done." The two of them answered together.

"Sebastian and Loren, the two of you have the toughest job. We need to know the best route out of here. Sebastian, tell the guards that the wildcats need exercise. That they don't want the wildcats to become bored. Instill some fear of the wildcats in them, but not too much. If the wildcats get their exercise, they are just big kittens. Any excuse you can come up with to search out the south and east of this city."

Thorium looked over at Loren. "Maybe you can join a hunting party and check out things to the north and east.

They both nodded in agreement with Thorium.

"And what about you?" asked Alum.

"I will try to get closer to Gertrude, find out the real story here. There is much more underfoot than it seems."

"What about me?" asked Jamen of Kiln.

"We don't know what they will do with our belongings if we are all gone. I need you to stay here and watch over them," Thorium told the disappointed Jamen.

They continued talking into the night in their quiet tones. Finally, with the sharing of thoughts and instructions complete, they all settled down on the warm beds their hosts provided for a well-deserved good night's sleep. The next few days would be busy ones for all of them.

The next morning, they were all aroused from their sleep by an early morning pounding on the door of the small house. The two wildcats paced back and forth in front of the door, growling. The door was locked, closed on the inside by a small beam of wood attached across the door.

Sebastian was the first to awaken and move to the door. He heard shouting through the door.

"Open the door, on the word of Wilfred. We demand that you open this door." The loud procrastinations were barely understandable with the coarse accent that they were shouted in. However, those inside got the message.

Quickly Thorium and the rest joined Sebastian at the door. All carried their weapons in their hands, a habit in their journey in search of the Myk.

"All-right, we'll be right there," Thorium called back through the door. He wasn't going to open it until they were ready for whatever was coming next. All stood back from the door, weapons drawn, in the clothing that they had worn to bed the previous night. Mendy was still yawning from his awakening. Loren was standing in the back, an arrow notched in her crossbow. Mendy's yawn became contagious and they all started yawning before they all broke out in laughter at the ridiculousness of the situation; all half-dressed, yawning with their weapons in hand.

Finally, Thorium held his hand up and they all quieted down. "We have to be ready for anything," he calmly voiced to them.

The three Sage, properly dressed now in their cloaks, joined the group at the door, the last to arrive and their own weapons out.

"Open up the door on the orders of Wilfred."

"The orders of Wilfred," Del quietly asked.

"So it seems," answered Thorium. "Is everybody ready?"

All nodded their heads. Thorium slowly removed the plank from the door, stepping behind it as he opened the door up.

The two men carrying plates of food almost dropped there cargo, seeing through the now open door the weapons pointed in their direction. They had only been ordered to bring food to Wilfred's friends. On seeing the plates of food, the band inside the house all broke out laughing once more. Mendy and Alum set their weapons on the table and hurried to help the two outside with the food that had been brought, both on the plates in their hands and in a small cart they had pulled to the door.

Thorium clasped the two men's arms as they left. "No hard feelings... We have been through a lot."

The two men just looked at the party inside the house and sighed as they left. 'Strange customs,' they both thought. 'But they are friends of our God.' As the two men left, one turned back with final words for these strangers. "Wilfred does not allow locked doors in Danegold. There is no danger here."

The expedition just looked over each other with the same thoughts. 'No danger here! Just how dangerous is it for us here for us?'

The two wildcats, returning into the house from their business outside, lay down in front of the fireplace, purring. Sebastian brought each of them their own plate of meat from the larder they had been brought.

After they all finished the morning breakfast, the day's activities began. Mendy and Alum left first, to scout out the city and try to get a reading on the Alsatians.

The first thing they noticed in their walk-about was how solemn the people seemed; almost sad. No laughing, no smiling, just a touch of melancholy the people seemed infected with wherever they looked.

Sebastian left next, with the two wildcats at his side. He walked with them to the edge of the city. There, at the undefined limits of the city, two sentries accosted him.

"Halt, you must go back, you are not allowed to leave the city," they ordered him in their guttural speech that Sebastian could barely make out.

"My wildcats," he smiled back at them. "They must hunt everyday or they get restless."

"You cannot leave the city, you must go back," they repeated.

The two wildcats, acting their part with an unspoken look from Sebastian, approached the two sentries and rubbed against them. The sentries jumped back at this.

"You must go back!"

"Right now my two wildcats are calm and happy. You have nothing to fear from them. It will be another story if they not allowed to hunt and find fresh game to eat. They may have to do their hunting here, instead. Do you want them to become angry?"

As if on queue, the wildcats looked at the sentries whom had backed off and emitted a low growl.

The sentries looked at each other. Finally one spoke. "You will return soon?" he asked.

"In a couple of hours, and the wildcats need to hunt every day."

"Everyday, Wilfred will not be happy," they said anxiously.

"Then let no one tell him," Sebastian finished.

The sentries looked aghast at this suggestion. Then they looked at the wildcats and each other once more.

"You will tell no one?" the tallest asked Sebastian.

"No one, I promise. You can come along and watch the wildcats hunt if you wish," Sebastian offered in a friendly way.

At that, looking at the wildcats once more and then quietly talking to each other, the tallest sentry (apparently the one in charge) answered, "We'll wait for you here."

Sebastian casually strolled past the sentries, a smile on his face. The wildcats joined him on either side. 'Yes,' he thought to himself, 'they needed to exercise and hunt. But so do I, hunt for a good route to escape the Danegold.'

Loren left with Thorium to find Gertrude. Jamen of Kiln stayed behind to keep an eye on there belongings. Loren hoped to get permission to go on a hunt to the coast; to reconnoiter the northern passes to the city.

They found Gertrude, with some help of the locals, beginning to inspect one of the hundreds of greenhouses scattered throughout the city. These were the major source of the cities nutritional needs; Gertrude had made it her job to inspect them as frequently as possible.

This agriculture was her true passion, as Thorium and Loren quickly noticed, bringing a rare smile to her face as she spoke about them.

"Wilfred says that we grow the most diverse crops in the world," she happily said.

"That wouldn't surprise me," Thorium responded to her. "The variety and quality of the food here far surpasses where I am from or anything I have encountered in my travels."

"This is quite a system," Loren added, truly admiring the greenhouses. "This is something that I need to bring back to my own land."

Sadly, it seemed, Gertrude spoke to Loren, almost a tear in her eyes. "You will never have that chance. Those who come to the Danegold can never leave it. Even our warriors are from those who have been here for generations. Newcomers stay in the Danegold. So are the orders of Wilfred."

Thorium and Loren were alarmed by this response from Gertrude, however each kept their composure. Loren used this as a way to segue way into her request to join a hunting trip. "Gertrude, as I am unable to leave, I would like to make myself useful."

"Wilfred, himself, will assign each of you your tasks in the city. He informed me of this," she answered.

Loren continued, as if not interrupted. "I was considered quite a good hunter where I am from. Can I join a hunting party tomorrow? We saw your hunters returning with the giant serpents they hunted as we entered the city. I would love to join a hunting trip for such a creature."

"Hunters are usually men here," Gertrude answered pointedly. "I understand that you come from a different land and your ways may seem strange to us here. You will adapt to our ways. You said that you are a great hunter." Loren didn't correct her statement; she just listened intently to Gertrude. "That does seem to be your best use for the community. A party is leaving to the south tomorrow morning to hunt bear. It is dangerous, but I will arrange for you to join it."

"To hunt bear in the south?" Loren was disappointed.

"First you must prove yourself there. Only the best hunters hunt the sea serpents. That danger is extreme. We have lost many hunters who have gone after them."

"I understand, Gertrude, thank-you," Loren responded. At least she would be able to explore the region to the south for their escape plans.

"And a job for me?" Thorium asked.

"Helping me inspect the greenhouses, that would be a good job for you," Gertrude smiled at Thorium. "You would have much to learn, however I will gladly teach you. I will ask Wilfred of this. I have much to discuss with him considering your people. Duties must be assigned."

"I would be honored to work with you," Thorium answered her. A blush seemed to come from Gertrude's face, though it quickly disappeared. "Does Wilfred review every decision that you make?" he quietly asked her.

Gertrude seemed taken aback at the question, her mood quickly changing to a dour one. "Wilfred, our God and Savior, reviews every decision that we make here. We would not be here now without him." She seemed saddened as she spoke the words, even a little defiant, but wary.

"I apologize," Thorium quickly answered her, taking her hand in his. She made no attempt at first to remove her hand. "I think that we should go now. I look forward to seeing you tomorrow and hearing Wilfred's decision about us."

As he turned to leave, Thorium felt Gertrude give his hand a slight squeeze.

"The two of you are free to visit the greatness of our city. I will see you both when the sun rises in the morning. Loren, I will take your request to Wilfred tonight."

"Can you also request that Jamen of Kiln also join us? From what I understand, he is a great hunter as well."

"I will do that for you," Gertrude responded, relieved that Thorium and Loren were not the couple that they had seemed. "I will take you both to the hunting party; be ready Thorium," she smiled. "I will have jobs for each of you in the morning as well. I look forward to teaching you our ways."

The expedition gathered again that night for their evening meal. Sebastian and the Sage were the last to arrive, Sebastian exhausted from his hike with the wildcats. The meal provided for them once again boasted of the best that the Danegold had to offer. They brought an elk stew to them. It contained many of the different vegetables grown in the city's greenhouses. Herbs were used that none of them had tasted before.

Alum and Mendy, their hunger quenched by the stew, began their story of the day first. They had never before failed to make friends in any of their journeys. Here they hit a brick wall.

"I just don't know what to think," Alum started. "We did everything we could to be polite, respectful and friendly. We didn't try to get to close to them physically, but nothing, just a vague distancing of themselves by the people of this city."

"I know," Mendy added. "We could see terror in these people of this city; no smiling no laughing, no nothing."

"They knew that we are the friends of Wilfred, that news of our arrival had spread," continued Alum.

"Yes," Mendy took his turn. "We were treated as guests, but with a certain aloofness I don't get. We were both given a hearty lunch that was delicious, like all of the food here. Servants of Wilfred, who tracked us down, brought it to us. However, we ate alone. No one joined us to ask any questions about where we are from, no children asking stories from us. In fact, I don't even remember seeing any children. That alone was strange to me. Usually, children are the first thing we notice when we visit different lands. Even in the Northern Valley there were children playing; none of that here."

"That's right," Alum stated. He looked over at the Sage, sitting together at the table. "Since when do the Sage have servants?"

"Any idea of what they are thinking," asked Tor. "And none of the Order has ever had a servant, which is very unusual. However, it fits in with what we found in Wilfred's home. Continue your story."

"It was hard to figure out just what these people are thinking," Alum answered.

"Just the fear and distrust; No inns, no food vending, no cafes, nothing to bring the people together in groups; just Wilfred's statues and places of worship," Mendy finished.

"Places to worship Wilfred, this is worst than I thought. Wilfred now must truly believe that he is a God," Thorium exclaimed as he got up from his seat to get another mug of ale.

"We were invited to a service in a few days by one of Wilfred's servants. It was almost like an order. The only real interchange we had with anybody in the city. Once we came to the worshipping session, we would become one with the people here. It sounded ominous," Mendy inserted into the conversation. "We can expect no help from these people. They fear their God too much."

"When I tried to talk to a few of them about the myk, with several of the friendliest ones we saw, they became more fearful and suspicious. They did, however, know of the myk and the atrocities the myk have committed," Alum added.

"We did learn one thing," Mendy said.

"What was that?" asked Thorium.

"There seems to be a common thread in what few stories were heard or overheard; a hint of a Hold to the east. And that Hold maybe the home of the Myk."

"A Hold in the east, Wilfred hinted at such when we spoke with him today."

"Anything else?" Thorium asked.

"Several times weapons were drawn against us. We went into the city without our weapons as you had suggested," Mendy said.

"Weapons drawn against you," Gar said aghast at the idea.

"Nothing happened, Mendy confirmed. "Those who drew weapons on us were talked down by those in the crowd."

"It wouldn't surprise me if it was all staged. I never felt threatened," Alum finished the story.

"Staged?" Thorium asked aloud.

"That wouldn't surprise me from what we have learned," stated Del. "From our visit to Wilfred's home, really a palace, that wouldn't surprise me at all."

They all sat quietly for a few minutes, taking in what they had heard so far. Was everything they had seen so far been nothing but a charade by Wilfred for their benefit?

Finally, Sebastian set down his mug of ale and began to tell the others of the day's activities.

After recounting his encounter with the sentries at the entrance and his initial explorations of the cities environs, he finished with," I traveled over 16 miles distance from the city to the north and the east. I managed to climb a relatively high peak and got a good view of the city and the surrounding lands.

"An aquifer from the north brings water into the city. I haven't seen anything like it before."

Loren added, "We saw several of the pools where these aquifers ended in the city. They bring in most of the water for the greenhouses. There is definitely no shortage of water here. The fountains go continuously, fed I'm sure by that aquifer. "

Sebastian continued after taking a drink from his ale. "I saw no sentries or patrols in my travels. That surprised me. Just the sentries I spoke of at the edge of the city. My guess is that Wilfred feels secure enough with his security here. Nobody who discovers this land is allowed to leave, keeping his secret safe; no patrols, which may be spotted by outsiders, are necessary."

"That would confirm my thoughts that we are prisoners here," Thorium said. "We must make our plans to escape. What else did you find out, Sebastian?"

"There is a passage just to the east of the city that is snow and ice free. It leads to the northeast, is unguarded and not patrolled, barely a two-hour walk from the city. If we can reach that unseen, we should be clear of any search by Wilfred for us."

"Our escape route?"

"So it seems. One last point, I saw almost no game in my wanderings of the hills to the east. The hunting parties here have done too good of a job, it seems."

"We'll need supplies then. I think Gertrude will take a chance and help us with that."

"We'll plan on being on horseback, then?" Jamen asked.

"We'll have to see what happens tomorrow to decide that. We still have a lot to learn to finish our plans," Thorium finished.

Thorium now began to discuss what he and Loren had discovered in the walks with Gertrude in the city. "First off, outside of Wilfred and Gertrude, there appear to be no leaders among them."

"That's right," Loren interjected. "And I got the distinct feeling that those who bring up some sort of disagreement with Wilfred... disappear."

"Disappear?" asked Tor.

"Yes, the people are so superstitious here; to them the people who voice displeasure with their God just disappear."

"Kill squads... I have heard about them in some cultures I have visited in my travels," Thorium angrily stated. "The worst of the worst."

"And you think Gertrude will help us, knowing that she could *disappear*?" Gar asked.

"I'll come to that," Thorium continued. "Wilfred gives his orders to Gertrude who passes them out into the city. The people have no direct interaction with Wilfred, unless it's a war party with select warriors of his; like the one that met us. The entire city works under her commands."

"And the death squad, too?" Gar asked.

"No, I don't think she has anything to do with that, she fears it.

"Tomorrow we will all be assigned jobs in the city. Pretend to go along with these plans. We all must learn as much as we can before we finalize our plans. It all must happen tomorrow night."

"So soon," asked Mendy.

Gar answered that question. "I fear that in two days we will be dispersed throughout the city and will have little opportunity to congregate like this again and talk freely amongst ourselves. And the death squads... that is a worry."

"Tomorrow night then it's agreed," Thorium stated. "We have much to do in a short time."

Loren spoke now. "We are free to explore the city, however we cannot leave it. The religion of Wilfred and his Nordic Gods reigns supreme here. This is a cult of fear and repression."

"I think Gertrude understands that much," Thorium added.

"I will be joining a one-day hunting party to the south to hunt bear, "Loren stated. "We will leave in the early morning. I asked that you join me on this, Jamen, and Gertrude agreed."

"I'll be happy to do so. I was bored all day, just sitting here, watching over our meager possessions. I have nothing to report; no threats to take our weapons and a wonderful mid-day meal that was brought to me," Jamen of Kiln reported.

Loren finished her story of her and Thorium's journey through the city with Gertrude. "I think that Gertrude would like to be friends with us. She acts so differently when Wilfred is not around. I am confident that would she help us, if she could do so secretly. I think she fears what Wilfred is now doing to the city. She sees her own fears in the eyes of the people of this city. Thorium, I think that is up to you tomorrow. She seems drawn to you."

"I noticed that," replied Thorium. "A two-sided sword; she wants friends, change. Nevertheless, her fear of Wilfred is great. We need to be careful. Sage it's your turn."

Del began. "Our meeting with Wilfred was much for show, I think. He had us escorted to his main room, trophies of his journeys lines the walls. A large round table was placed by the fireplace which had a roaring fire."

Tor spoke now, "His servants greeted us at the doorway and escorted us in. Sage do not have servants. We are the servants of our people."

Del continued. "He motioned for us to join him at the table. It was covered with plates of foods, all that the Danegold has to offer."

"I couldn't help but notice the passageway we were taken down to reach the main room walls were covered with portraits of Wilfred and others. I saw none of Gertrude."

"Probably his Nordic Gods the way they were painted," said Del.

"While he didn't outright say that we could never leave, I think that was implied in much of what he said," Tor worriedly said.

"We had a long talk about his travels," Del started once more. "He spoke glowingly of the lands around the Danegold. He is especially proud of how far to the east he has traveled. Well beyond my own travels. And he spoke again of his secret to the east, although he didn't specify what he had found."

"Yes," spoke Tor, "he seemed to want to keep us in suspense about that."

"We have but little time I fear,' Gar concluded. "I could see in his eyes, his control has to be absolute. The madness was there."

"Yes," Del and Tor concurred, "Wilfred has truly gone mad."

Thorium now looked over each in turn. "Sleep well tonight. It maybe our last good nights sleep in a while."

They got up the next morning to begin the days planned activities. Their morning meal had been brought to them the night before; batter for pancakes, berries and a special surprise for the crew of

The Proctant, maple syrup, a rare treat for them even back home.

"Where did you get the syrup?" Mendy asked the Alsatians who brought the food to them.

"It is a special gift from Wilfred for all of you to enjoy. A raiding ship we captured and destroyed carried several barrels of it. I am told that this is the last of it."

"Tell Wilfred that we are honored," Thorium replied to the Alsatians, truly grateful for such a treat. 'The raiders must have traded for it,' thought Thorium.

All gathered around the common table for the meal, attempting to keep the conversation light. However, mostly silence surrounded the table. They had a lot to do and much of it dangerous.

About halfway through the meal, Gar spoke aloud to everybody with shocking news. "I don't know how, but my mind is stronger now. Something in the valley, I just don't know. Our myk prisoners are no longer causing any cloudiness as before. In addition to that, I can clearly pick up in the distance the myk mind of power. It is definitely Kat, as we suspected. His minds power, I can feel and it is stronger than belief."

"The melee at the wedding, could he have caused that?" asked Thorium.

"It seems very likely now. It was so out of character for the emerging double-heads to behave like that. Kat must have somehow placed a thought that controlled them into the emerging heads. I can feel him in the distance; I know which way he is traveling."

"Will this newfound strength remain?" Thorium asked Gar.

"I don't know," Gar sadly replied.

"Know need for sadness, Gar. We now have a powerful weapon to use against the Myk. And we know who our unseen enemy is."

"That knowledge is powerful indeed," Sebastian said as he looked at Gar. "Perhaps, you are a tool created by the Teachers to counter the power of the Myk.'

"Perhaps," said Gar.

All gathered their thoughts on this news; an enemy that they could now identify and follow. If they could escape Wilfred's grasp of them in the Danegold.

Loren and Jamen of Kiln were the first to leave the relative safety of the house in the early morning. The hunting party banging on the door shortly after they had finished the morning meal drew their attention.

"Go, hunt, now!" was all the leader said before he turned to lead the party out of the city. He seemed to care little whether they joined him or not. The two from the expedition hurried to catch up with them.

Loren and Jamen of Kiln had a hard time keeping up with the hunting party. They traveled rapidly on foot; six in the hunting part plus the two *friends of Wilfred*. They moved into the southwest, a hilly, thickly forested region south of the Danegold.

As the hunting party moved south, Loren and Jamen of Kiln thought, 'Not a good direction for the escape,' confirming in their minds the decision to escape to the northeast. That was also the direction that Kat was heading, they had learned had from Gar.

"Are we hunting for bear?" Jamen asked.

"No, the lead hunter said back. "This is the season for Elk hunting."

"Oh," said Loren.

Elk were plentiful throughout the forest and it was shortly after the midday sun was overhead that Loren bagged their second. The hunters were impressed by her accuracy and range.

"Only two," asked Loren.

"Wilfred only allows two kills a day, so that the herds remain strong," was the answer she received.

"A good thing," Jamen agreed.

After the second kill the hunting party set up a temporary camp to eat the midday meal they brought along with them; dried meat, cheese, fresh baked bread and ale.

"You certainly eat well in the Danegold," Loren stated to the hunter who seemed in charge.

"Wilfred provides for us, as he has done since his arrival from the land of the Gods."

Loren and Jamen nodded in agreement.

"After our meal, we butcher the elk here," the lead hunter said to the two visitors. "We, all hunters, are trained to butcher our kill."

"Here?" asked Loren.

"Yes, are you fearful of this task?"

"No, just surprised it's not done in the city like at my home."

"We leave that which we cannot carry for the scavengers here in the forest. Such does Wilfred teach us. With the two of you we will be able to carry more."

After the meal, as promised, the hunters began the process of butchering the two elk. Loren and Sebastian could only look on at the skill it was done with. Every time they tried to help, they just got in the way. Finally it was finished, the meat cut into large roast of a size they could carry. All of the innards were left for the scavengers of the forest.

Once the meat was distributed evenly, they began the long march back to the city. There the meat would be stored in a refrigerated building, kept cold by ice brought back to the city from the north.

It was Mendy and Alum's job to repeat what they had tried the day before; to try to make friends among the Alsatians and learn what more they could. They left shortly after Loren and Jamen of Kiln, after cleaning up the mess on the table from the morning meal.

Mendy and Alums day in the city was very brief. Once again their attempts to make friends in the city failed, although they didn't meet the open hostility of the day before. After a little more than an hour, they returned to the small house and began preparations for the escape. They had saved food from each meal and now began to carefully wrap it. None knew how long this food would have to last, although they expected to be able to hunt along the way.

The Sage had a difficult assignment, one they were not entirely happy with; to flatter and keep Wilfred convinced that they were all prepared to stay. Before the Sage left for their meeting with Wilfred, Thorium held a brief meeting of his own with them.

"You don't trust us," stated Gar.

"I don't trust your ability to deceive Wilfred," declared Thorium. "Do you have your questions prepared? We must keep him off guard. I'm still not sure how my day with Gertrude will go. She is a strong woman and seems to like us. However she lives in a state of fear."

"We are concerned as well, that Wilfred may be able to pick out some of our thoughts," answered Del.

"Then it is even more important that the three of you concentrate your thoughts on the questions of how we can best be part of the Danegold. He must be fully deceived, any hint..."

"We understand that," Tor interrupted. "The success of our venture depends on it. If we fail..." He didn't have to finish the sentence.

"If he found out our escape plans I have no doubt that we would be made to disappear," Gar plainly stated.

Shortly after the Sage left for their meeting, Gertrude arrived. She invited Thorium to join her in her rounds of the greenhouses. "Wilfred has approved of your learning the greenhouses." They left walking side by side, Gertrude almost smiling as they left. "May I join you," Sebastian said as he hurried to catch up to the pair.

Gertrude looked him over as he caught up. "If you must, Wilfred has not yet decided the best job for you. You left your wildcats behind?"

Thorium answered for the both of them. "We decided it was best for all if the wildcats remained in our quarters for now. Mendy and Alum will be able to take care of them when they return."

"A wise decision," Gertrude matter-of-factly stated. "You will both be great aides in the *future* of our city," she smiled at them both, but mostly at Thorium.

Both Thorium and Sebastian noticed the slight inflection in her voice. Then they noticed the bruises on her face. Thorium stopped walking and looked closely at her. He and Sebastian could both see the dread in her eyes. Thorium took her hands in his. "Wilfred," he asked.

She quickly pulled her hands away. "Somebody might see."

They all walked together a short distance to the nearest greenhouse. Nobody was inside. Once inside Thorium again clasped her hands in his, Sebastian standing close beside her. This time she made no effort to move away.

"Wilfred did this to you," asked Sebastian bluntly. She looked briefly at him and then turned away, ashamed.

"Yes, I displeased him. He is our God. I must do as he asks or be punished."

Thorium was blunt now. "He is no God, no more than

Sebastian or me. The teachers gave him long life, just like our Sage who accompanies us."

"Yes, the teachers. Wilfred has spoken of them to me. I know that he is no God. But he breathes fear throughout this city. He has his secret ways…" Her voice trailed off.

"We have all heard, already, the whispers of the disappearances."

"He has warriors, like on the party that found you, loyal to an extreme. They do his bidding. Any sign of disobedience and that person is made to *disappear*. We are powerless and do his bidding. He allows no other leader."

"Was he always like this," Thorium asked.

"No. When he first found me he was quite good. There was no fear, just respect of his wishes. The people here still believe he is a God."

"Found you?" questioned Sebastian.

"I was from a near-bye village. Over twenty years ago he found me and brought me here. At the time, I thought he loved me; he did. He married me and made me his Queen. Then he started to change."

"And now?"

"I fear this madness that has come to overwhelm him. I fear for myself," she touched her face as she spoke this. "And I fear for the Danegold. I do not know what to do. I am powerless to stop him." Her face briefly brightened up, along with her voice. "You, you can stop him. Yes?"

Thorium and Sebastian looked at each other. Then they looked at Gertrude, standing proud, but starting to cry.

"You can help us, please," she cried out to them.

Thorium pulled her to him, holding her as she cried. A decade of torment within her emptied itself on his shoulder. Sebastian stood next to them, watching the door. "Something must be done before we leave," Sebastian said aloud.

Thorium now spoke, once more taking command of a situation as it changed around him, his strength coming through once more. "We act tonight, before we leave."

"Leave," Gertrude stated. "But you cannot leave. Wilfred will not allow it. He watches you at night with his special warriors."

"That is news to us; they have kept well-hidden," Sebastian said alarmed. They had seen a few 'sentries out in the open. However, nothing of these special guards Gertrude spoke of.

"We still act tonight, with Wilfred's orders," Thorium stated plainly. Then he explained his plan to the two of them. It was drastic, but it had to be done. And he would do it himself; he could not ask this of another. Gertrude and Sebastian both nodded at him in agreement. Gertrude just looked at him when he finished. Thorium could feel her hand squeeze his.

"I see no other way. For my people it must be done so," she sadly stated. There were tears in her eyes.

"I think that you should stay away from Wilfred until it is time. He may see inside you what we have planned. Can you arrange our meeting through one of his servants" Thorium asked her, now holding both of her hands, looking at her tired eyes.

"Yes, I think that is best. I will send a servant. I will tell Wilfred there is a distant greenhouse I must check. I will meet you and enter with you when you arrive tonight. Yes that is best."

Thorium could see in Gertrude the pain she carried from the decision.

"He was a good man once," she briefly cried into his shoulder. Then she stood straight once more, wiping her tears with her one hand while continuing to hold Thorium's with the other. "It must be done. For the Danegold, it must be done," she quietly repeated to herself several times.

The three of them continued to inspect the greenhouses together. They shared their midday meal. Anything else would have raised unwanted questions. However, they were silent through most of their day together. It had to be done, but…

Just before they left, a few words were spoken, well within hearing of two of Wilfred's special warriors.

"A meeting with Wilfred then, tonight, right Gertrude?" asked Thorium.

"Yes, I will arrange that. To discuss his plans for your people in the Danegold," she answered. "I have a lot to inspect. I will meet you tonight and bring you to Wilfred."

"You will prepare for the meeting." Sebastian cryptically asked her, not happy with their decision as well, but seeing no other way.

"Yes, I will *prepare* everything," she regretfully said. It had to be done, for the Danegold, for her, but she carried her pain quietly inside her.

With that, they parted in the late afternoon sun. Gertrude to continue her inspections in the city until it was time, Thorium and Sebastian returning to the house to discuss their plan with the others.

When the Sage arrived at Wilfred's home (a palace really), one of his servants was waiting to meet them. "Wilfred has prepared rooms for you. He requested that I take you there. He will join you later. He has last minute duties."

The servant escorted them to a wing of the palace; three bedrooms, a common room with one wall covered by bookshelves holding a large library of printed books (Where did he find those?', Tor thought.), a small kitchen and a fireplace in the common room. The whole thing was very comfortably set up.

Del spoke to the servant as he left. "Thank Wilfred for such comfortable quarters."

After the servant left and the door closed behind him, Gar asked the others. "So what do you think?"

"It seems that Wilfred has plans for us," Del answered as he sat down by the table in the middle of the common room.

"So it seems," replied Tor, examining the books on the shelves of the room. "So it seems."

The wait for Wilfred wasn't long. Gar had just started eating an apple from the tray of fruit on the table when Wilfred walked in, unescorted. All three of the Sage stood up from where they had been seated when he walked in.

"No need to stand, enjoy the fruit. We are all friends here," Wilfred stated.

"It is good to see you doing so well," Tor said in a friendly tone to Wilfred. "And our new accommodations are beyond our expectations."

"I am glad that you are all pleased. We have much to accomplish now that we are all here together once more; to the last of the Sage."

"The last of the Sage," queried Gar.

"All that are important to the future," Wilfred laughed.

"Where did you find such a library?" asked Tor, truly impressed.

On one of my journeys to the east; I hinted at such a place when we traveled to my city from where I found you."

"A Hold?" asked Gar.

"Yes, alas unfinished. However, I salvaged and brought here what ever I could carry. It took several trips, each more dangerous than the last. That was several hundred years ago."

Tor, holding one of the volumes, spoke to Wilfred, "I don't recognize the language."

"It was new to me as well. I have had but little success in translating it. I gave up on that over 100 years ago. But I kept the library, hoping to one day unlock its secrets. Maybe now, together, we can do that.

"A job for us then?" asked Del.

"Yes," Wilfred answered. "I think that is a very good job for the three of you."

"This Hold to the east, you could find it again?" asked Gar. "Perhaps we can travel there together."

"In the future, yes, but not right now. Now I fear that it is home to the Myk," Wilfred wistfully answered.

"Then we must travel there at once," Del responded.

"Always impatient, I remember that in you," Wilfred answered him, looking right through Del with his eyes. "In time, when we are ready. Right now, I am content to destroy what myk I find in my domain. Those prisoners you brought, they must be destroyed. The Myk can find the Danegold through them."

The three Sage could tell from Wilfred's tone there was no sense in going any further in that direction in their talks. Nevertheless, a Hold in the east, Del was somewhat shocked at the confirmed existence. There had always been stories of other Holds, unfinished, built by the Teachers in the waning moments before the Armageddon that almost destroyed everything. Now Wilfred confirmed it.

Wilfred continued, "I still have much to teach you before we can take on the Myk. He grows powerful I fear, in the east. And I must protect my people here, first."

"We have things we can teach you as well," answered Gar. "I

can detect their mind of power and we know who it is."

Tor looked at Gar as he made that statement, wishing he had kept that a secret. They were getting off course now and getting too close to their plans. And if Wilfred detected anything amiss. Tor quickly steered the conversation back to the Danegold.

"The study of this library would be wonderful, indeed, 'Tor said. "There must be other things that we can do as well to help this city grow."

"Perhaps," Wilfred quietly answered, getting up from where he had sat to approach Tor and the bookshelves. "Teaching, that shall be your jobs," he exclaimed joyfully. "I have done what I can, but with your knowledge the Danegold will be the crown of the world."

"We can leave then, to return then to The Hold and get teaching aides?" asked Gar, once again getting perilously close to their real goal.

'No, you can never leave, never leave," answered Wilfred stoically.

Del Sensing how close Wilfred was to detecting their secret moved the conversation once more to the Danegold. "Well, then," asked Del, "If I cannot leave, perhaps I can be your aide and help Gertrude give your instructions to the city?"

Wilfred seemed alarmed and agitated at that. He began pacing the room. "No, I am God. Gertrude is my right arm. You can never leave, never leave," he kept repeating that last part.

Alarmed at Wilfred's actions and words, Del spoke again, trying to calm Wilfred. It seemed to work. "Wilfred, we only, in making Danegold our home, want it to be the greatest city in the world."

"Yes, indeed," Wilfred softly said. "But I sense some deliberation in you."

'This is dangerous,' thought Gar and he sought to relieve any of Wilfred's suspicions. "We are here to help you," he said to Wilfred. "You are the greatest among us."

Wilfred sat at the table once more. Tor remained standing by the bookshelves. Gar and Del leaned back slightly in their chairs. Each was ready if this went bad with Wilfred, although none was sure what they could do.

"Do you have any more of the brew?" Wilfred now calm, asked them.

"Unfortunately no. We finished the last of it during our evening meal. We couldn't help it, the food was so good."

Wilfred answered in his melancholy voice. "The food, yes, we eat well here. But no more brew, so sad, so sad…" He looked at the three of them. "Yes, with you three here I will travel to the south to get more. None would recognize me. Yes, I think so. Soon."

"And one of us can go with you," Del asked hopefully.

"Oh. No. You can never leave. None who come here can ever leave."

A servant knocked on the door. He brought the midday meal for the Sage, trays on a cart of the finest foods the Danegold produced.

"Now we eat," said Wilfred. "I remember those early days, when there were so many of us. And now, how many survive?" he asked them.

Tor answered carefully with what he said and not mentioning Thul. "Not many; the four of us, Phelix, though I fear he is close to the end, Chuak, Locklear, Vlad and Tuck. That's all now."

"And Simon," Wilfred asked anxiously, his head picking up.

"No word from him since the Teachers sent him into exile."

"Yes, Simon and myself; the two strongest. Teachers could not control us. With us their experiments could not be continued."

"The Teachers told us that you were destroyed and Simon sent into exile. That was so long ago, we thought that you were gone," Del said.

"Yet here I am, now a God. My rule is just and strong. I am supreme above all in what I build here. You may eat your meal now. I have much to ponder about the three of you." Wilfred almost carried a smirk as he said the last of his words. "You are free to wander the city, but you must return here tomorrow. Do not try to leave. I have given orders as such. Do not betray my trust. Yes, I must ponder this, your fate." Wilfred left after these last remarks and the three Sage were left sitting at the table.

The door closed behind Wilfred and Tor motioned for the other two to join him by the bookcases. He spoke in a low, quiet tone. "He has truly gone mad."

"And dangerous," added Gar.

"Do you think he suspects our plans?"

"No," said Del, each speaking in a whisper. "He is now filled with paranoia and has grown truly dangerous. Could Wilfred be as bad as the Myk?" he said once more, reopening the question of the previous night.

"I think the answer now, is yes." Tor spoke. "It is time to finish this meal and return to the house. Our time is very limited here I fear."

"Carry with you what you can, back to the house, especially the bread and the cheese. Who knows what we will find when we leave," added Del.

They finished their meal undisturbed and returned to the house, carrying several bags of food with them. The guards only watched as they left the palace, heeding to Wilfred's orders; they had the freedom of the city, but like all others, they could not leave.

Upon arriving back at the house, they added their stores to what Mendy and Alum had saved and gathered up. The extra bags they brought helped with that.

"How was Wilfred?" Alum asked them.

"More dangerous than we thought," Del stated before the three Sage retreated back to their room for rest and discussion. A Hold in the east, what was to be thought of that.

"More dangerous than we thought," Mendy repeated. He and Alum just looked at each other, exchanging their worried thoughts, and then finishing their preparations for the escape.

The expedition gathered for their last meal in the Danegold before the escape attempt. They made their most of the delivered feast, devouring it. All had heard Sebastian mentioning Wilfred's secret warriors watching the house.

"Our last meal," said Mendy quietly.

Over the course of the meal they discussed their day's findings. Loren and Jamen of Kiln both confirmed that the low mountain pass to the northeast was their only escape path.

Mendy and Alum confirmed once more the fear in the eyes of the people. They heard new whispers of the disappearances. They themselves witnessed one of the disappearances. Coming around a building they saw a group of warriors gather up three of the city's dwellers. They saw them try to flee the warriors and heard their shouts of innocence. The warriors roughly tied up each of their now captives and dragged them away. They discreetly followed them a short distance to an alleyway. There, to their shock, they saw the warriors execute the townsfolk and dump their bodies into a wagon. As they got into the wagon they turned back to the entrance of the alleyway, leaving the bloodstains behind. Mendy and Alum hid in a doorway as the cart drove by with the dead bodies and the warriors. They heard the warriors brag that the *strangers* would be next.

Everybody at the table just sat in a moment of silence, hearing the horror of their story.

The Sage now spoke of their meeting with Wilfred.

"He has gone mad, if he was ever very sane," Gar added to the conversation. 'We all should definitely fear him."

"How do we escape with them watching us? That's just the excuse they need to make us disappear," Alum asked.

"Wilfred will lead us out," Thorium stated firmly.

"Lead us out?" Del questioned.

"Not only will he be leading us out, he will also be joining us," Thorium finished.

Thorium then laid out the plan to those around the table as he had to Sebastian and Gertrude in the greenhouse.

When he finished Del asked solemnly, "Is there no other way?"

They all just looked at each other around the table. Nobody came up with a better idea and none liked the idea before them. Silence filled the room.

"Anybody?" Thorium asked hopefully. Nobody answered his question. He stood up from the table. It was time to go. He looked over each member of the party in turn. "Be ready. If this goes wrong…" He didn't have to finish the words, they all knew. The entire party stood and watched in silence as Thorium left the house.

Then Loren spoke, reaching for her crossbow. "Let's be ready, just in case."

Thorium slowly walked down the city streets in the early evening air. There were very few of the cities dwellers on the street which made it easy for Thorium to spot the three warriors who followed him; his watchers. Thorium just smiled at their clumsy attempts to stay hidden. 'Maybe I should just ask them to join me,' Thorium laughed to himself. His watchers acted with alarm at the laugh, but they drew no closer.

As Thorium approached the ornate entrance to Wilfred's palace, his watchers drew back. No guards were posted there, Gertrude made certain of that.

She met him at the door. She patted her side as she approached Thorium, indicating the plan was a go. She loudly called to the three watchers, "You can go home now, Wilfred's orders."

When they hesitated to leave she started to approach them. "Do you dare defy the orders of our God!" The three men quickly turned and left.

When Gertrude was standing next to Thorium, he whispered to her, "Anybody still inside."

"No, Wilfred feels he has no need for guards inside and the servants have left for the night."

"Good," was all that Thorium said as they walked inside together.

"Wilfred is waiting for us in his main room."

"Destiny awaits us then," responded Thorium, his nerves as calm as ice over what needed to be done; quick and fast, there was no other way.

They walked together to the main room of the palace; Gertrude first, Thorium walking behind her. He could feel the attraction and trust between the two growing. Would Wilfred notice this in his madness?

Wilfred was standing near the fireplace in the main room when they entered. My friends," he said as he turned to face the two of them. "Come stand by the warmth of the fire. I understand you have concerns about the responsibilities of your people. You want to be sure that your people are treated fairly. I can assure you that they will be."

"Yes," said Thorium to Wilfred. "I have concerns about how they can best serve your city." Thorium passed Gertrude as he spoke those words. His hand outstretched as if to shake Wilfred's hand. The tile floor was polished and Thorium seemed to slip. Gertrude reached over as if to help Thorium catch his balance; she passed him the blade she had concealed in her clothing. The rest was over in a second, as Thorium slipped the blade into Wilfred, just below his heart.

"Why?" Wilfred asked, knowing he was dying. Wilfred slipped to the floor.

Gertrude had turned away as Thorium slipped the blade into Wilfred. She now dropped down to her knees, cradling him in her arms.

"Why?" he asked again as Gertrude cradled his head in her arms.

"It was your time, my love," she openly cried. "You did so much for us. Now it is your time to rest."

Wilfred spoke first to Gertrude. "I do love you," he softly said.

"Yes" she whispered back to him through her tears.

"Do not cry for me," he whispered back as his breath was beginning to leave him. "I knew that my time was at end. With the arrival of the Sage, I knew this end was coming."

"Yet, you did nothing?" she asked her dying husband.

"Everything I did was for you." He seemed almost sane now, in the end his sanity returning with his dying breaths. "Everything I did was to get us to this point in time." He could barely speak now, his voice getting hoarse.

Wilfred weakly motioned for Thorium to approach him. Thorium got down on one knee next to him and Wilfred spoke. "I put know blame on you. You did for your people as I have done for mine. There is no hatred between us. Go east now, find the Myk."

Wilfred looked to Gertrude. "Go now, and lead our people," he spoke once more to her.

And then to Thorium, his last words weakly spoken. "Watch out for betrayal among the Sage. They are not…" and he died in Gertrude's arms.

"Betrayal, by whom." The two just looked at each other, neither happy, each just glad, as painful as it was, it was over.

They remained on the floor next to Wilfred's body. Gertrude watched as his eyes glazed over in his death. She continued to caress his head and brush his hair from his face. She held him tight for a long time, Wilfred's still eyes looking at her.

Finally she spoke to Thorium who had one arm around her. "He is at peace now," she tearfully said. "I knew that he had gone mad, but I could do nothing… The city lived in fear, but I could do nothing…but what could I do alone…" her voice trailed off."

"It's OK. You did what you could for your people," Thorium said quietly to her, tears in his own eyes. "He seemed to know what was coming. He made no move to try to stop me…"

She put her arms around Thorium, hugging him tightly, the tears still streaming from her eyes. "The death squads… they answered only to him… I couldn't stop them. If I had tried…"

"I know," Thorium said as he held her close. "It's over."

"Yes," she cried a last tear. "Now I can remember him with just the good that Wilfred did for my city… Just the good."

"We must prepare Wilfred," Thorium said as he rose to his feet. "I grieve with you Gertrude, but we must hurry."

She looked up at him, trying to gather what strength she could from him, finding a little. "I will miss the good that he brought to our people. Who will lead us now?"

"You will, as Wilfred said. And the people will think he is with you. He will still be their God. Wilfred himself will just be on another journey, with us."

"Then I will see you again," she forlornly asked Thorium.

"Soon I hope," he answered.

"I have a cart prepared for your trip. It is in a large room that leads to the street. It is fully loaded with supplies. I told those who prepared it that it was for Wilfred's next journey. I was not lying, it seems now. Two oxen are attached to the cart for your journey."

"I am sorry it had to happen this way," Thorium sadly said as he looked into Gertrude's eyes. This was something that he would have to live with for the rest of his life; no honor here, just a necessary death.

Gertrude was the strong one now, as Thorium stood trembling slightly. "I will get a blanket and fresh clothes for Wilfred," she said. "You must cleanse his body. He must go on this journey as benefits a God, as the savior of his people."

Thorium nodded in acknowledgment and when Gertrude had left the room he removed Wilfred's clothing from his still body. Thorium moved the body to a clean space near the fireplace. With warm water from the fireplace he pulled the body next to, he washed Wilfred's body of the blood, his penance for the crime. The blood had emptied from his body and stopped. It was a *good kill*, quick and painless. However, Thorium felt anything but good about it. 'It had to be done,' Thorium thought, 'for the good of the expedition, for the Danegold to prosper and for Gertrude, whom he was beginning to love. But could she love him now?'

Gertrude returned with the blanket and fresh clothing for Wilfred's body. When Thorium reached for the clothing to dress Wilfred's now pale body, Gertrude stopped him. "This is for me to do," she sadly said, tears in her eyes once more. "This is my time to say good-bye." She began dressing Wilfred in his finest clothes.

"We will mark the spot where we bury him. A memorial will be built there for him. He saved your people from the wrath of the Teachers, no matter the madness that consumed him in the end."

Together they carried Wilfred, now fully dressed, and placed him upright in the seat of the wagon, the blanket wrapped around him as if he was asleep.

"I will go with you to your people, "Gertrude said. "I will have to give orders to those that watch the house."

That was all that was spoken as they sat on either side of Wilfred's upright body, Thorium at the reigns. They pulled up to the house at the edge of the city where the expedition waited with uncertainty.

Gertrude, getting out of the wagon, called out to the warriors watching the house, "Come here quickly, I have new orders for you."

The warriors assembled together, unsure of the fully loaded wagon and Wilfred sitting on its bench. Mendy and Alum had taken Thorium and Gertrude's spots on the wagon's bench, Wilfred fully seated upright between them.

"You," she motioned to two of the warriors. "Bring these people their horses from the stable and their equipment. And bring extra horse for our God."

When none of them moved she ordered, "Go!" They left for the job she assigned.

The warrior in charge approached her. "What is this?" He motioned at the full wagon and Wilfred sitting in it. As he started to approach Wilfred's body, the party paused; could this be it.

"Halt!" Gertrude shouted. "How dare you approach your God while he rests? I carry his orders to you."

The warrior, as if by rote, having obeyed her orders so many times before, returned to his spot and the expedition breathed a sigh of relief.

Sebastian and Jamen of Kiln loaded the last of their belongings onto the cart and Thorium stood with the three Sage. The warriors arrived with the saddled horses. The expedition quickly gathered and mounted the horses. There were six extra; Gertrude tied them to the back of the wagon.

"Wilfred requested these six so that he could ride as well," she said in a loud voice for the warriors to hear.

Thorium took the reigns of his horse and walked over to Gertrude.

"Thank-you," he said.

"Thank you," she responded. "I know it was difficult for you."

"It had to be done. And the myk prisoners?" Thorium asked her.

"They will be spared, I have work that they can do."

They both wanted a closer good-bye. Thorium could see love now in Gertrude's eyes. However, with the warriors watching, that was the best that they could do.

Thorium mounted his horse and Gertrude turned to the warriors still standing there.

"Wilfred now leaves with his friends on his next journey."

The senior warrior spoke up again, "Alone he travels. That's seems wrong. Let him speak to us now."

"He goes with his friends, not alone. He has left me alone in charge as he goes on his journey. He rests now from his long day. Do you dare to question me, before the eyes of your God? Perhaps I should waken him so that he can see your disobedience."

"No,' he responded in his unquestioned loyalty and he backed up to the rest of the troop.

"Listen then, all of you. Wilfred travels to find the Myk. You all know of that menace. He travels with this strong party. Return to your barracks. Stand watch for the myk. They fear us. I will give you new orders in the morning."

Gertrude then turned and walked back to the city after one long glance at Thorium, the warriors following behind her.

Thorium turned his horse and rode to the front of the

expedition, leading them out of the Danegold, a wildcat racing ahead on either side. They knew the direction that Kat was heading; Gar's hold on his mind remained strong.

Chapter 13
Abandoned Villages

They traveled northeast now, the over-laden oxcart moving slowly on one of the old, broken concrete roadways. Del often saw signs of people, but nobody remained in the villages they passed through. Once again, Gar's headaches started getting worse. There were myk around them; a lot of them.

Gertrude provided them with a large cache of goods on the oxcart. As promised by Thorium, Wilfred led them out of the Danegold himself, seated upright in the wagon between Mendy and Alum, a blanket tightly wrapped around him. Once clear they would give him a proper burial and mark the spot well, for the future monument Thorium had promised Gertrude.

They saw large elk on either side of the byway. They seemed to be the dominate species here; very few signs of predators were seen.

In a grove just beyond the valley they escaped through, they buried and said their good-byes to Wilfred. They cut down a large tree and fashioned a crude memorial for the Sage. It would have to do for now.

Two weeks out of the city and one week from the supply cache Gertrude mentioned where they restocked the wagon, they encountered the first indication of the presence of the myk in this region.

A small village, a few huts, was just off the way. A hut in the village was under siege by a dozen or so myk. From the cries coming from inside one of the huts the expedition could tell there were men, women and children trapped inside.

Thorium and the expedition did not hesitate. Loren notched an arrow into her cross bow and pulled out several more to have them handy. Thorium, Jamen and Sebastian charged ahead, with their wildcats right there with them. Their swords were drawn; one captive was all they needed, no mercy shown to the rest. The three Sage followed close behind and Mendy and Alum drove the wagon forward.

The myk were so preoccupied with the fresh food inside that they did not notice the expedition's attack until it was too late. Loren took out two of them with her cross bow from the charging oxcart. The wildcats took out another three before the riders even showed up. The rest fled, but Thorium, Sebastian and the wildcats quickly caught them.

Loren, Mendy and Alum went to the barricaded hut where the survivors hid. Loren called out loudly, "It's over and you can come out now." A single soul peaked through a boarded-up window.

Mendy saw the eyes peaking out and slowly walked up to the window. "It's safe now," he quietly spoke.

The door opened a little bit and a man looked out. He saw the party with the three Sage on horseback. He walked out cautiously, as Thorium and Sebastian returned with the sole myk survivor, pulled behind with a rope around his neck. The two wildcats, seeing the man in the doorway, approached quietly, their tails down, almost purring; more villagers to protect, just like in Twror.

At first the man feared the wildcats; nevertheless he let them approach him. He had seen through a window slat how they had attacked the myk and stood bravely at their approach. Both wildcats brushed against him and then lay down on either side. The door opened wider and half-dozen children rushed out to pet the wildcats. They showed no fear of the wildcats and rested their heads on the soft fur. They felt safe for the first time in days as they fell asleep against the wildcat's bodies. The wildcats just purred contentedly. Seeing the children rest so serenely, the rest of the villagers came out, six more in all.

Mendy and Alum started a small fire and prepared enough food to feed them all. These people spoke a different language than the Alsatians, not as guttural and more flowing. Del recognized who they were; the Gypsy people that he encountered on his travels. He addressed them in his imperfect Gypsy dialect, striving to convey that they were friends and that the upcoming feast would celebrate their triumph over the myk.

They stayed a full day with the Gypsy family, sharing their food with them. It was a large extended family with six small children. The children couldn't leave the wildcats alone. The wildcats themselves seemed content laying on the ground with the children climbing on them.

Thorium and the Sage met at one side of the village together.

Del was speaking in urgent tones.

"We can't just leave them here. They would be butchered by the next myk party to come along."

"We just aren't equipped to bring along families like this," Thorium spoke in an agitated voice. They were too far from the Danegold to send them to Gertrude and Thorium *knew* they would be butchered if left behind, just as Del said.

"Thorium, they have a small ox-wagon of their own. I saw it on the other side of the hut they were in. Their oxen are still there, the myk never seems to bother with livestock. They could travel with us in their own wagon. It wouldn't really slow us down much. And they would be safe with us," Del pleaded.

Thorium understood that these people had no choice. It seemed fate once more was forcing him in one direction.

"Del, tell them that they can travel with us. However, it is important to inform them of the potential danger. We travel to find the Myk and it will be dangerous."

Del walked over to the man who had first left the hut to greet them. He spoke in his halting Gypsy dialect with him, explaining their mission. The man, Elijah, walked over to the other three men in the family. They conferred briefly among themselves before entering the hut where they had previously taken shelter. When they returned to Del, each man carried a hunting bow and a quiver of arrows, with a long-bladed knife strapped to their hips.

Elijah talked briefly with Del, informing him of their decision.

'We will go with you. We are proud and brave. We will join you in this crusade."

Del just looked at the man and what he now knew were the man's sons and smiled. These were indeed the gypsy people he knew.

Del returned to Thorium and the Sage while Elijah and his sons prepared the family to travel.

"It seems we have an army now."

Tor spoke up now. "Do they know the risks?"

Del responded proudly, "They know of the myk only too well. It is because of this they are joining our 'crusade."

"Crusade?" asked Gar, hesitantly using that word.

"Yes, crusade. To rid the world of evil that is the myk. That is their word for our expedition," Del answered.

"A word like any other," Tor said. "Used and misused throughout history."

Thorium just looked at the Sage and just sighed. They were at war with a terrible enemy and the Sage were discussing semantics. "We travel once more with the lost people of this world. That seems to be out task in life now, to bring safety to these people."

The Sage looked at each other in turn. "The Teachers prophecies are coming true," Tor said. "From the lost of the world will come the end of the myk."

That night the entire expedition slept in the village's huts, a roof over their head for the first time in weeks. The Gypsies gave the Sage, whom they recognized from their purple robes one hut. The rest of the party spent the night in another. Despite being in close quarters, they were comfortable and protected from the night-time rain that had accompanied them throughout their travels.

The gypsy family knew of Del from the stories the clans told amongst each other when the clans gathered for trade. It was late in the night when the last of the family drifted off to sleep, listening to Del tell stories of his travels in the north.

Early the next morning the entire camp arose, awakened by the smells coming from the meal Mendy and Alum were preparing in a fire-pit. The two built it in the middle of the village. They prepared their own version of the feast that was prepared for them in the Danegold, thanks to the incredible larder of goods Gertrude had provided them; sausage, fruit, jams, bread and cheese.

The Gypsy family first drew back from the meal; Del had to assure them that the morning meal was for everybody. Elijah was the first to step forward and accept a plate of food that was offered. He smelled it carefully; there were new sensations to his nose. Once he sat down to eat, his three sons' wives served plates for their husbands and then for the children. The wives took their own plates last. The food was such that they had never eaten before and before long each had a second plate of food they were consuming, greedily.

After the morning meal was finished, Sebastian and Loren hitched up the two ox driven wagons and prepared them for travel. One of the gypsy women began loading what few possessions the family had onto their wagon, giving special care to the children's toys. The other two women got the children ready to travel and loaded them onto the cart as well.

The women and children of the family planned to ride in the wagon, with its canvas cover, while the men walked alongside. Thorium walked over to where Del and the Gypsy men were conversing. Each of the men held their hunting bow high as Thorium approached. Thorium nodded in recognition of their bravery and spoke to Del.

"We can't have them walking, that would slow us down too much. Can they ride in their wagon?"

"That's not their way. And besides, their wagon is full of the women and children."

"Can they ride a horse?"

"I'll ask," said Del, turning to ask the men that question.

"Yes, we know about horses. We are a poor family and only own the oxen that pull our wagon. We can ride though."

Del relayed this to Thorium who called over to Loren and Sebastian. "Bring four horses here for our friends to ride."

Loren brought the four horses to the men after saddling them. "It still leaves us with three extras. Gertrude was very generous to us when we left," she smiled at Thorium.

"Yes, she was," Thorium replied, holding back the blush, or at least attempting to, as he remembered their good-bye.

The group departed from the small village in the late morning. Thorium and Sebastian, Jamen of Kiln rode ahead with their wildcats. The Gypsy wagon was next, with the men now on horseback riding alongside. Next came Mendy, Alum and Loren in the expedition wagon, driven by the two oxen. Despite their absence from the Danegold for several weeks, it remained nearly full due to Gertrude's generosity and the provisions provided by the supply depot she had informed them about.

The Sage rode in the back, discussing the events of the trip to find the Myk and how they tied into the Teachers prophesies. Finally tiring of this, Del rode up to Elijah and began speaking with the Gypsy men.

The eldest spoke for them all.

"These are my three sons, Goliath (Del couldn't help but notice his huge size, a giant indeed), Hezekiah and Kalos."

"Strong names," Del answered.

"We are a strong people, but scattered we can do little against the myk. Now we will grow strong with you."

"Grow strong with us?" Del asked Elijah.

"Others of our village, who hid from the myk attack, saw you. We were not alone in the village you entered. We stayed so that they could flee. Now they travel to other clans. Many will join you, you will see," he smiled.

Del thanked him and rode up to the front to give Thorium this news.

"It seems that you truly will have an army once more to command."

"What?" Thorium asked Del.

"Word of us is spreading throughout the Gypsy villages as we speak. It seems this family we saved was not alone in the village. Many were hiding from the attack in the forest. They saw us and what we did to the myk. And they know of me."

"An army?" Sebastian himself asked.

"Expert hunters and brave, we won't be alone as we travel following Kat."

Several days further along and more Gypsy clans had joined the expedition. Entire families in wagons and those that owned a horse rode them. Each brandished their hunting bows as Thorium and Del led the caravan. Each wagon joined the back of the caravan. Del would ride to each clan as they joined, giving them his greetings. Those on horses now rode on either side of the caravan, their bows at hand.

Sebastian and the group watched in awe. This did slow the caravan down slightly, but not enough to annoy Thorium, who himself could only watch his column grow.

On the third day out from the Gypsy village they had rescued, one of the Nourne scouts was seen in the air above them. The scout, realizing it was an expedition, flew down to meet them. Thorium rode his horse over to him and the scout spoke first.

"Sir, I almost didn't recognize your party. I am Tiberius. At first, I thought it was just a large Gypsy caravan. We have seen a lot moving to the south, fleeing the myk. But this is moving in the wrong direction, towards the Myk. Then I saw your wildcats and knew it was you."

"My army," Thorium replied smiling. "It seems that these people have decided to join our quest against the Myk. We are lucky you spotted us."

"Wade increased our patrols and assigns now four scouts per outpost. Another outpost was added to the north. I fly from that one."

"Have you seen much of the myk?"

"We have observed scattered groups moving towards the north and east."

"Anything else I should know?"

"We have also seen scattered bodies of dead myk."

"Dead myk," Thorium exclaimed.

"Yes, dead and dying of no outward cause. One was brought to a Jall doctor; a disease he thinks. Wade instructed us to report any bodies we find but to leave them in place."

Alarmed Thorium now asked, "Are there any dying besides the myk of this disease?" He remembered well how just a few short years previously a disease had swept though his own homeland. Thousands had died before it was brought under control.

"I am happy to report that no others in the two valleys have come down with it. Several White have died of it, but when examined they were just immature double-heads, myk."

"That is good news as well. We found several large myk groups and defeated them. We have a prisoner. Can you take him?"

"I am afraid I can't carry another on my bird. It is still just a juvenile. Your army grows large," Tiberius said, looking over the large caravan following Thorium. "It seems the people follow you wherever you go."

"My army, what it is. Nevertheless, as Del has remarked, they are courageous people. Do you have news for me of our new Confederation," Thorium asked, concerned by the news they had learned at the beginning of their trip.

"Not good news I am afraid. It seems all the south is in motion once more. More and more of the Jall with thousands from The Hold move against Zircon in the Wolf City."

"They are moving against Zircon," Thorium asked, his fears realized.

"Yes. A large army now assembles outside that city to attack. All the confederation is moving to aid him. Do you have news for me, sir?"

Thorium remembered Wilfred's dying words to him and he repeated them to the scout. "There is a Sage to beware of, all is not as it seems. This is too important to wait," he added. "You must fly directly to Wade with this information."

"A Sage to beware of…who?" the scout asked. "One who travels with you?"

"No, one who was left behind by us," Thorium answered.

"But that can only be…"

"Yes, it could only be one. You understand the urgency."

"Yes, I fly at once."

As the group continued their journey to the northeast, following Kat's trail, they were joined by an increasing number of gypsy clans. The caravan was now over a mile long. The Sage continued to ride in the rear. Along either side of the caravan were several hundred of the horsemen with their bows, enough to keep any myk from getting too close. Due to his age and being the first to contact the expedition, Elijah was in command of the Gypsies, with others deferring to him. Thorium, Jamen and Sebastian were in the front, with their wildcats serving as scouts.

It was at the beginning of the third week from the Gypsy village that they found their first signs of the dying myk. Or rather the wildcats did. Both stopped in place, just ahead of the caravan, ears and tails up. Sebastian rode up to them while Thorium, with hand gestures the Gypsies now understood, brought the caravan to a halt. The Gypsy's horsemen now spread out on either side of the wagons. The wagons tightened together, now two abreast. The Sage rode up to the front where the expedition's wagon was and waited for orders. Loren notched an arrow into her crossbow while Mendy and Alum took their own weapons out. Jamen, on his horse, drew his own weapon and his eyes scanned the forest around him. Everyone was thinking the same thing; was the Myk going to make a stand here against them.

Thorium, once the wagons had all stopped in the double line, rode up to Sebastian. Del came riding up to them quickly as well. The forest was near the path at this point, an ideal location for an ambush.

Del reported to Thorium, "The Gypsies are ready."

Thorium looked back at his *army*. They were prepared and unafraid. He asked Sebastian, "What do you think?"

"They found the scent of something. I have only seen them act this way around the myk."

"Del," Thorium asked, "ride back to Gar. I need his *seeing* now. I need to know how many myk are around us?"

Del rode back to the other Sage, already on their way to the front of the columns, and all three rode up to where Thorium, Jamen and Sebastian sat on their horses, eyes scanning all around them. The wildcats still stood very still, quiet and alert. Jamen rode back to the Gypsies to give them any aid they needed in what was coming.

Once Gar had ridden up to the front of the caravan to join Thorium, Thorium asked him bluntly concerning myk around them.

"How many myk are around us now? You were supposed to give warning if there were a lot of them."

"I feel very little of their presence. My mind remains clear," Gar answered defensively. Had he lost his ability to detect the myk he worried? "Just a few scattered in the distance around us. And I can still feel Kat very clearly. He's still moving in the same direction as before."

"Then what is waiting for us," Thorium asked those around him. "Another Wilfred?"

"I don't think so," Tor said calmly. "Sebastian, give the cats leave to follow the scent and we'll follow them. I don't think that there is any real danger here."

Released, the wildcats slowly moved into the forest to one side of them, following the scent. The riders followed closely behind. It was about 100 yards in from the way that they found the source of the wildcat's agitation; over 30 dead and dying myk double-heads, with their weapons, lying helplessly on the ground. Even the wildcats could sense their dying and moved no closer. Only Thorium and the Sage approached the myk in front of them.

One of the myk, its second head fully grown and the scar showing the removal of its primal head clearly visible, tried to stand, its weapon in hand. It staggered and fell back to the ground.

The Sage held back from approaching the myk. However, Thorium rode up to the now quivering myk who had tried to stand. He quickly identified this as the disease that the scout had mentioned. He dismounted and walked over to the myk.

"We are myk!" It tried to stand once more and fell back to the earth, helpless before Thorium.

"Do you know who I am?" Thorium asked the myk.

"Yes, we know of you. We are myk. We are prepared."

"You planned an attack here?" Thorium asked the myk.

"Yes, we are many. We know."

"The Myk sent you?" Thorium continued his interrogation.

"Yes," it proudly said. "I die for the myk."

"You all will die it seems," Thorium callously replied.

"There are more, we will be ready," it tried to bravely state.

Thorium just looked down at the dying myk scattered around him. He rode back to the others. "We have nothing to fear here."

"The disease?" Tor asked.

"Yes."

"Then the Teachers did plan for their rise," Gar stated.

Thorium ignored the Sage and started back to the way and the caravan.

"We'll check the other side of the way as well," he called back to the Sage and Sebastian. "Del, tell the Gypsies we drive two abreast on the way with the wagons and close together. The disease spared us here, but the Myk knows that we are coming."

Del rode back to the Gypsies, passing on Thorium's orders. He had to reassure several of the clans about the myk that were found. He rode past Jamen on horseback when he reached the Gypsies. Del told Jamen, "Thorium wants you to stay in the back and help watch out for the myk."

"This disease, it is safe for us?" Elijah asked.

"Yes," Del confirmed. "The Jall report it only affects the myk, those with the double-heads."

"Good," Elijah responded. "We will remain vigilant. Perhaps not all are dying of it."

Elijah called several of the riders over to him and in turn passed on Thorium's orders. These horsemen in turn spread the orders throughout the caravan. The horsemen now spread out in pairs on either side of the wagons with a small group now riding at the back of the convoy with Jamen.

The remaining four at the front of the caravan, Thorium, Sebastian, Tor, and Gar now rode behind the wildcats as they followed the scent of the myk on the other side of the way. They found two more camps of dying myk, each group armed with weapons, about forty in all.

"They were prepared for the ambush. If the Gypsies hadn't slowed us down by two days, if they hadn't joined us…" Gar said aloud, his voice trailing off in conjecture.

"Yes," Thorium stated, looking at the dying myk, some trying but no longer able to stand. "Two days ago, without the Gypsies, we would not have stood a chance against these in battle."

"I would have spotted them," Gar said emphatically.

"Yes, you would have. But would it have been in time."

"The teachers prophesy still follow us," Tor said.

Thorium once again disregarded the comment regarding the Teachers, feeling uneasy with the recognition that many of his actions appeared to be influenced by strategies established long ago. He was tired of being at the forefront of these prophesies. He rode back to the caravan with the others.

"Forward, we make camp on the way at nightfall."

Del had returned from his meeting with Elijah.

"Del, you are now my captain for matters concerning the Gypsy people. How are they doing with this news of the myk?"

"I understand, my relationship with these people is strong," Del said. "It feels good to be among these people again. They understand the disease will not affect them. And it seems that all of the clans of the Gypsy nation are joining us.

"More have arrived?" Thorium asked amazed at the news.

"Even as we waited a dozen more clans have joined us."

"Their entire families?"

"Yes. That is how the Gypsies travel. Elijah rides to each clan as they join the caravan, giving them their instructions. He is now accompanied by several other elders who are also riding among them, maintaining order. There is real order among them."

"I have seen that in their horsemen."

Thorium gave his Captain of the Gypsies, Del, more instructions to pass on about their encampment for the night. Del rode back to meet with Elijah and the other elders to pass on the instructions.

That night, hundreds of Gypsy wagons camped along the way. Cooking fires were roaring, roasting the food that they had brought. Clans mingled, intermixing. None of the clan members could recall such a large gathering in their collective memories. Mendy, Alum, Jamen and Loren wandered through the encampment in the avenues laid out by the wagons. They couldn't believe the friendliness and order. Oxen were gathered in small herds for safety, horses tied to the wagons, being fed and groomed by the riders not on duty, watching the shadows in the forest around them for any danger.

All the traveler's bellies were soon full of the exotic foods of the Gypsies. Sebastian walked among them with his wildcat as if he was back with his own people, the Nomads. These people were very similar to his own. Many stories about the wildcats have captivated the young Gypsy clans once again. The children interacted with the wildcats, which lay quietly and purred, providing a sense of security to the children once again.

Chapter 14
Prelude to War

Kat lay flat on high hill looking down at the party below. Their 'search for trade' hadn't fooled him and his spies. Kat's spies were everywhere and not all were of the White. Certain Jall were a great source of information. He thought back to how he first learned of the discord.

* * * * *

It was shortly after the wedding of now Lord Wade and Lady Theresa. Kat smiled his feline smile from under his oversized hat. As he had expected, the assassination attempt was a complete failure. Wade and Theresa had escaped the bungled attempt unharmed. Security measures now tightened throughout the Northern Valley. And Kat couldn't be happier. The Myk's plan, that Kat had co-opted, was leading to results that only Kat wanted. The days of the Myk's reign were coming to an end. Then it would be Kat's turn to lead the myk. In the upcoming peace, under Kat's guidance, the myk would have time to grow again in their new home under Kat's guidance. Their new home, as chosen by their future Myk, was carefully hidden from those who opposed him; a relic of pre-Great War splendor. Then…

As Kat wandered the stolen lands of Twror he heard the grumbling; malcontents, very few in number but of great interest to him. There were those, it seemed, in the conquering armies who were no happier with the current state of affairs than were the followers of the *Old Ways*; these malcontents were, in Kat's mind, were the only way for the higher evolution of the myk to survive.

The strangers who had come from across the sea had brought their own ways with them. Who were they, then, to dictate the laws and rules of this land? Let them return to their own lands or die here. These were the sentiments Kat heard from a handful of people in his wanderings through Twror. 'Could there be a larger discontent that he could harvest?' thought Kat.

Free trade these newcomers had decreed and the Jall had lost much of their claimed trade primacy. Those whose clan wealth was already established welcomed these changes; there were still riches for them to gain. However, those unaffiliated to the top clans suffered.

When Kat first heard of this he thought, 'What folly'. A great many of the Jall and from The Hold had taken part in the battle against the Myk. Kat's unexpected ally, his *friend* in the very heart of The Hold, reached out to Kat and explained it all.

Control was being lost in The Hold and the Jall City. This same changed that had driven the Myk and his followers into hiding was wrecking havoc here, in the lands of this Confederation, as well. New players were taking the place of the old. Power and control is never relinquished without a struggle. The collapse of the *faux* trade war that they planned together would bring this out into the open. There were those that didn't want to give up their hold on this power and they would do whatever they could to keep it. Even in the Two Valleys this resentment was lying just under the surface. It was only the threat of the Myk that was holding these people together.

* * * * *

Kat had left Twror two weeks earlier, following the expeditions path to the great swamp. He wanted no part of the way through the Round Valley and the increased security there. He had long memorized the path to the Cavern of the Myk. That was a piece of brilliance by the old Myk (Kat had to admit) to refer to that place as a cavern.

But first and foremost importance to Kat's plans was a meeting with his ally from The Hold. It would be a shock to all of Kat's enemies if they knew who this person was.

They met a short distance north of the Round Valley, in a small secluded house that the myk used as a safe house on their way north. Kat was already seated, with a roaring fire in the fireplace, when his ally arrived.

"Were you followed?" Kat asked.

"No, I am sure of that," his ally answered. "I have the good fortune to be able to travel anywhere I choose without suspicion."

"That is the one reason I trust you," Kat responded with sarcasm. "If they only knew…"

"May I have a taste of my brew? I brought some fresh roasted bean for us to enjoy."

Having become accustomed to the brew from his several meetings with his ally, Kat responded affirmatively.

"How are things progressing on your side?" Kat asked the man across the table from him, sipping his brew.

"Very well I think. This Trade war will bring further suspicion among our enemies. How about your mission?"

Kat replied slyly, his feline teeth now fully developed and exposed. "I too experienced the expected; failure. When I return I will use this against the Myk. Then I will become Myk and there will be peace, led by myself and you."

"That is the plan."

"And those from across the sea?"

"They will be dead or they will flee," the visitor and fellow conspirator said.

"And the rumor of Argonia?" Kat asked.

"Argonia will become irrelevant," his ally reassured Kat.

"To peace," toasted Kat, raising his cup of the brew.

"To peace," Kat's ally repeated before putting his cloak and hood back on before exiting the house.

And each thought to themselves, 'Peace, until I grow strong enough to destroy you.'

As Kat left the house and traveled north he thought to himself, 'let them look all they want for the *cavern*. The hints all pointed to the wrong place and in the wrong direction. His new home was a relic from before the Great War, its tunnels and buildings left somehow intact; an unfinished Hold. Within the complex was a still working nuclear reactor, a tribute to Kat's God, Hydron; that which gave them their shape and form.

Kat caught up with the expedition north, a week after his meeting with his ally. He had briefly lost touch with it (or at least his spies had) shortly after the expedition encountered a Jal-Beast. He was told that the expedition was made up of ten people and the three Sage, along with three of the despised wildcats. Now he counted only the three Sage and six others in the party. Had the reports just been wrong? This gave Kat some degree of concern.

The party was moving in roughly the right direction. Kat was dismayed by that. What had corrected their course?

That accursed Thorium rode in front of the expedition with Gar. Kat would have to be careful; either would recognize him, even after his rebirth, on sight. His teeth and eyes would give him away. Kat worked to loosen his effect on Gar's brain.

Peace; that was the promise that his ally had given Kat. If this expedition was to become somehow *lost* and if the attacks by the myk in the round valley should end, this peace would be insured as the old masters of the land assumed once more their hold on these lands.

Only the sickest of the myk made their way to the Myk's new home. Kat made sure of that. He and his emissaries intercepted the strongest of them, those that seemed at least partly immune to the disease that was ravishing the myk, and redirected them to the real cavern, his unfinished Hold. These, the strongest of the myk in mind and body would grow undisturbed, not in the Myk's *cavern*, but in their new home, far to the north and east of the Myk's hide-away. Kat had already taken from the Myk what breeding stock and food-source that he could secrete away. When the expedition discovered the Myk's cavern, with no myk survivors, they would report that the Myk danger was over. Then the expedition's members would be made to quietly (Kat hoped) disappear. After that Kat's ally would consolidate his grasp on The hold and assume control throughout the Two Valleys, The Hold, and the Jall Kingdom. And Kat and his secret followers could grow undisturbed in the north, in peace. Peace; until they were strong enough to regain all of the lands they had lost. And maybe a little bit more.

Who would survive the expedition, to report back the end of the Myk. Not the Sage, they would have to die in the North to give more freedom of action to this ally. Thorium, too, could not be allowed to survive. The woman, one of the others, one would be enough to be allowed to escape. It would be staged and blamed on the people of the North. The gypsies and their puny bows would be the perfect pawn. The bows were an easy weapon to find, there were plenty of them in the villages that the myk had ransacked in their quest for food-source. Just one survivor of the gypsies bows. In addition, a few gypsy bodies would be left behind for effect; a waste of good food-sources, but important for the design of the plan.

As Kat watched the expedition move, he was shocked to see a pure myk, as yet primitive with his two heads, being held captive in the wagon. Should he attempt to make contact with him? Best not, but the captive may yet prove useful to Kat.

One of those wildcats (Damn those creatures!) turned toward where Kat lay hidden in the distance. Discovered? Kat knew that the wildcats possessed a strong sense of smell. Then, as Kat prepared to move to a more distant vantage point, several birds darted out from the underbrush beneath Kat on the lower slope of the hill Kat hid on. The wildcats saw them, hesitated, and then turned back onto the trail that they had been following.

Kat followed the expedition for several more days as it traveled north before he turned east to where his own lair lay hidden in a distant skeleton city. He needed more time to finish his work and destroy the Myk. When it was time, one of his spies, a myk loyal to Kat and not the Myk, who understood his mission well, would allow himself to be *followed* to the cavern of the Myk. Those that searched for the Myk would only find death there; the end of the Myk. The final part of his plan was the elimination of this expedition. On the way back to Nourne from the Myk's cavern the expedition would be attacked (Staged by those loyal to Kat) by the gypsies with the one survivor allowed to report that the Myk threat was no more. He, himself, would take care of the wildcats. He could easily best any three of them with his own claws.

Kat watched as the expedition moved out of sight over a rise in the land. Then he turned to his food source, two well selected and *treated* Nomads and he chose an arm for dinner. There were other parts that he would have preferred to eat; however, his food source still needed to walk. Kat as yet had a long march ahead of himself.

At the beginning of his travel north shadowing the expedition Kat saw the sick bodies of the White double-heads off to one side of the trail. He left them there as markers, helping to lead the expedition where he wanted it to go. Now he was once more searching for them. The trail double-backed in places, but he found no sign of his avowed enemies, until now. What had happened in the North in the weeks that

Kat had lost track of them?

Finally, Kats curiosity got the better of him and he contacted a myk prisoner that was held by the expedition. This was a different myk than the one he saw them with at the start of the expedition. No matter, he contacted the prisoner with his mind. This was a mature myk and he had no trouble making himself known to the myk. He knew that this would infringe on Gar's mind, but he didn't think it mattered. Let Gar have a worse headache.

"Tell me," he commanded the myk. "Tell me what has happened in the North."

"You are in danger," came the mentally whispered reply. "He knows that you are near-bye."

"They can't know," insisted Kat. "I am hidden, tell me what happened."

"A Sage in the North, I am sure of that. You are in danger. He knows of your fortress in the north."

Kat sat down and thought to himself. 'A lone Sage wandering the north, how could that be?' He knew of Del and his spies told him Del knew nothing. Was there another Sage that he left unaccounted for? The thought of this gave Kat pause.

"Tell me," Kat demanded of the myk prisoner. "Tell me who this Sage is and what he knows."

"Gar knows, he recognizes you, run!" the myk practically shouted with his thoughts at Kat. "Run!"

Kat looked down at the party a great distance away. His eyesight gave him details at a distance. Somehow, it was true! He saw the two wildcats (only two now?) and Thorium on horseback turn his way as Gar pointed into the distance, toward where Kat lay hidden. They were coming his way.

"Run, master," the prisoner shouted mentally and verbally, screaming to Kat as Tor plunged a blade into the prisoners heart. This was something that Kat could understand. They had kept the myk alive solely to catch him. And the trap had been sprung.

Kat ran, his great speed putting distance between him and his pursuers. He left his food source behind. A waste, but it would help to confuse the wildcat's pursuit and the expedition would stop to attend to the bodies. Kat wasn't ready to confront them. It wasn't time. Kat fled, kicking off his useless boots, with a speed that not even Thorium's horse could match. They had seen him, which he was sure of. Or at least Thorium had. It mattered not and this would help convince them that the Myk cavern that they were traveling towards was the true home of the myk.

Chapter 15
The Trade War

Twror

Gant looked out of his now finished second floor apartment at the park below. They were still cleaning up after the wedding and its aftermath. The stonewalls would remain in place; a memorial to what had happened and what was to come. He had heard the warning from the Sage of a pending civil war through Castle Nourne. He watched as a legion of the Twror assembled below to march to the aid of Zircon and the Wolf City. Already over 200 warbirds had left. Now this mixed legion, White, Nomad and refugees from all the far lands, was getting ready to march. It bought a tear to Gant's eyes. He wondered how this war was possible. So much good had happened since the foreigner's arrival, but now this.

Zircon was a hero to the people of Twror and another legion was preparing to march south as well to aid the Two Valleys and if necessary, march on The Hold. It was from the Hold that the rumors of war had originated from; so many willing to march, and if necessary, die to aid Zircon.

Gant sat back down in his chair, almost weeping. When would the dying end, wasn't there enough for everybody?

With the gathering of the armies the Trade War was now inevitable. It seemed that it was Nourne, Erson and Twror (with the Nomads) arrayed against the Two Valleys, The Hold and the Jall. Gant watched as the first column from the R'mon's arrived to aide Zircon. They would march through Twror, taking the Northern most pass to reach Zircon. He watched as they marched without any apparent fatigue. King Gunther of the Raff's joined the march through town as well. Now a part of this new confederation, he saw that there was little time to hold it together. The Coastal Peoples were rumored to be streaming north as well, their leaders seeing the value in trade for their seafood, to satisfy craving these new northern people had for it. These scattered people were the final piece of bringing resolution to the Crisis. They had refused to give the traders from The Hold and Jall the exclusive rights to the trade between themselves and the north.

It was the richness of this trade and the trade of the *Treasure of the Myk* that led to this war. The hold and Jall wanted it all, refusing to make way for the new.

There was enough for all, but the greed of the traders threatened to pull the new Confederation apart. Where was the Jall-King in all of this? How had he let this happen. There were too many factors at work here and Gant just didn't understand half of it.

The Confederation's armies continued to gather and march below as Gant took a final look down. How would all of this end? He thought of Mara again. Will he be joining her sooner than he thought? Gant got up from his chair and left his office. There was so much left to do.

The Wolf City

Zircon stood on the highest point of the ravine that the way passed through on its way to the Wolf City. It was here that he had first met the Emperor Wolf. Here he had found an unlikely friend. His horse, Traveler, now well used to the scent of the wolves, stood patiently close behind. The Emperor Wolf sat on his haunches next to Zircon, his (lieutenants?) close by. All watched what was coming from the South. An army was moving against them.

Zircon had heard from the Sage almost two weeks earlier that rebels from The Hold and the Jall City were preparing to take the Wolf City for its resources. They promised him that all of the Confederation would come to the aid of the Wolf City. However, up to now no reinforcements had arrived. The wolves stood no chance on their own.

Late afternoon arrived and Zircon rode Traveler to a high point a good distance to the South. There on a high point he could see the armies arrayed and marching against them. There must have been thousands. What chance did the wolves have standing up alone against them? Nevertheless, Zircon would not leave the Emperor Wolf and his Tribe. He would stand and fight, and if necessary die, alongside the wolves

Zircon rode back to the Emperor Wolf and together with the Wolf army all returned to the city to a well-prepared feast. Man and wolves carried the same thought. A tidal wave of steel was marching towards them. If they were meant to die, let it be on a full stomach.

The elderly she-wolves gathered up the pups too young to fight and brought them to the walled enclave on the far side of the city. That would be a last stand for the wolves, if that became necessary.

Early evening and they all heard a commotion to the Southwest. The Emperor Wolf's head and ears rose up. Scouts hurried back to the Emperor Wolf to sound an alarm. Zircon took one look at the Emperor Wolf, jumped aboard Traveler and raced towards where the commotion came from. Close behind raced one of the Emperor Wolf's lieutenants and a small pack of wolves. 'Was this another army set to oppose the wolves?' was Zircon's thoughts as he raced. He had all but given up hope of any reinforcements coming. After all, this was just a city of wolves, no matter how intelligent they seemed.

Zircon, in the lead, saw them first; camels. That could only mean one thing. The Shiaps had arrived to give aid. 'Would more be arriving as well?' Zircon's next thought was, 'how could he make the wolves understand that these were friends.' The Emperor Wolf's lieutenant seemed to understand Zircon's thoughts. This had happened before, but Zircon had just passed it off as coincidence. 'Could they read my thoughts, at least some of them?" The Lieutenant motioned for the pack to stay back. Only he approached with Zircon.

The Shiap leader, Ra'Shone, now rode forward ahead of the troop to meet Zircon. He had never met Zircon, but word of Zircon's exploits had long reached the ears of the Shiaps. He would gladly follow this man into battle. As the two men met on their steeds; the lieutenant held back a little and sat down to await the outcome of this meeting.

The two men dismounted and silently trod to meet the other. Finally, Ra'Shone gave Zircon a bear hug. Ra'Shone stood as a giant next to the large Zircon.

"Are all of you Shiaps also giants?" was the first thing out of Zircons mouth. He laughed and Ra'Shone laughed with him. "I am glad you are here what-ever your size."

Ra'Shone now spoke in a loud voice, a voice that commanded respect. "All that have answered your call are as such. All have rushed to join a man that they could follow into war. We think much of you, Zircon."

Zircon could only stand and look eye to eye with Ra'Shone.

Ra'Shone motioned to where the lieutenant sat. "And are these for whom we fight?"

"Yes," answered Zircon simply. "Come meet one of their leaders".

Zircon walked over to where the wolf sat patiently awaiting him. He sat down next to the wolf and motioned the hesitant Ra'Shone to the other side of the wolf. Ra'Shone, fearful of none, so he thought, sat down on the other side of the wolf that did not move. He saw Zircon rub the neck of the wolf and he did the same. An alliance was born of the act. The wolf's smooth tongue briefly brushed against the face of Ra'Shone. A friendship was borne as well.

"Are they all as such?" asked Ra'Shone.

"This is one of the lieutenants of the Wolf-King."

"And we fight for this Wolf-King?"

"Him and his Tribe."

"We stand with you, Zircon, but to fight for wolves. At home the wolves are the killers of our herds. How are these any different? I see their tremendous size, but…"

"This Wolf Tribe is unlike any other wolf that you will meet. You know of the Teachers. And you know of the Wildcats and their relationship with the Nomads."

"Yes," Ra'Shone responded. "I know of these things."

"These wolves must be a creation of the Teachers as well. They have a city and a society that rivals in some ways our own."

"That I will have to see," Ra'Shone grinned. "A city of intelligent wolves, that I will have to see."

"When we get back to the city, I will introduce you to their King" Zircon said. "They seem to understand our words or our thoughts. I'm not sure how that really works, I am just getting used to it myself."

The rest of the Shiaps arrived, their camels leery of the scent of the wolves. Ra'Shone signaled his men to dismount and approach the wolves. They did so singly and in small groups. The rest of the wolves now joined the macabre scene. Only the camels stayed back.

"How many do you bring?" asked Zircon in a moment of quiet, marveling at the scene around him.

"Over 500 have answered your call," boasted Ra'Shone, "and all giants as me." Once again he laughed a hearty laugh and Zircon couldn't help but join in. However, in his mind, his only thought was the size of the army he faced. 500 brave fighters, he knew that they would stand with him to the end. This alone was not enough. 'Would more be arriving?' They had little time.

The wolf who had been seated between the two men seemed to understand what was being spoken. He looked up at Zircon and then Ra'Shone. He stood then and seemed to say to the two men, 'When you arrive my Emperor will be ready to receive you.' Both Zircon and Ra'Shone understood the thoughts as if the wolf was truly speaking with them. Then the wolf turned and raced ahead with his small pack to alert the Emperor of men's arrival.

"Did you understand it?" Zircon asked Ra'Shone.

"Yes, but how?"

They all remounted and began the swift ride to the city where the Emperor Wolf awaited them.

Upon their arrival at the gate to the city, The Wolf-King sat waiting for Zircon and Ra'Shone. The two men approached the Wolf-King who sat on his haunches. No other wolves were around. The Wolf-King looked at Ra'Shone from head to foot, appraising this man who had come to help.

As Ra'Shone approached the wolf, Zircon held back. Ra'Shone looked back at Zircon. "Aren't you coming with me?"

"The Wolf-King wants to meet one on one with you. He'll take you on a tour of their city so that you can see what you are fighting for."

"You know that, how?"

"He told me," Zircon answered matter-of-factly.

"More wonders?" Ra'Shone laughed. "Take me to your city," he said to the Wolf-King.

The Wolf-king turned and together the two entered into the city that Zircon had made his home after that first trip.

Dusk had fallen over the Wolf City when the next contingents of relief arrived. First came the R'mon and their crossbows, mostly women, the leader of which Zircon had met in the battle for Nourne. With her came a legion of 250. Also, close behind, were King Gunther of the Raffs with 500 archers of his own. They were met at the city's entrance by the wolves, one of whom had hurried to get Zircon. Friend or foe, the wolves would take no chances.

"Welcome. So few, but those that are here are friends. The Emperor Wolf will meet you shortly. Fear not of the wolves. You may make your camp to the far side of the entrance. The Shiaps have made theirs on the other side."

"We are alone then, in providing aid?"

"So far, it seems."

"Others are on the way. Twror should be here soon. In addition, with them comes Nomads, those without their own wildcats. There was much talk of the wildcat's reactions to the wolves so they thought it best to leave them behind to watch the northern valley. Much is happening throughout our newfound confederation of peoples. A trade war has broken out. Even in the City by the Lake. We marched the long way to get here.'

"A Trade war? What could have brought that on? I thought everything was settled."

"The Hold and the Jall City brought it on. It's rumored that the Jall-king is held prisoner somewhere in his city. More help will come in time, but we must hold until then."

In the early morning, the first help from Twror arrived, over 1,500 loosely formed troops. However, ill trained as they were, how much help would they provide? Of great help, Zircon saw with them several hundred of the Nomads. Their leader he did not know, but with them, he now had three corps he could depend on. Would that be enough?

The next morning broke clear and windless. The first of the invaders had passed through the ravines that led into the city's plain. Wolf Assassins had attacked throughout the night where they could, bringing some panic to those of The Hold and the Jall-city. However, they were few and the army they faced so large. It did bring hesitation, though, in the invader's army who failed to advance at once towards the city.

Just pass the ravines the invaders stopped to organize. There was no one person in command. All thought this would be a painless city to take. In the night, however, dozens had died of the silent attacks. Now before them were primitive earthworks, thrown up overnight by those that had arrived to aid the Wolf City. A confab was needed before they could advance into the city. Who and what lay arrayed before them. Not having the answers made them uncertain.

Zircon looked on from a high tower still standing at the edge of the city. He had a great view of what was assembling before them. The reinforcements hurried to build up what earthworks they could, but did they have time. Time, it was always about how much time they had. A trade war with the Wolf City as the prize. That meant for days they would be on their own with what few reinforcements that could arrive. Who was he to command the armies? Finally, he reached a conclusion and called each of the corps leaders to his side at the entrance to the city. The Emperor Wolf sat with them as well, seemingly to understand every word.

Once all gathered, Zircon began with his blunt language. All had been given tours of the Wolf City by the cities Wolf-King. All had been amazed by what the wolves had accomplished in their evolution. "Truly a creation of the Teachers," the R'mon leader spoke aloud. All understood the seriousness of the battle before them.

"A trade war has begun and it seems that we stand here alone before an army that outnumbers us many folds. If there are any who wish to leave, now is that time." Zircon stopped here and waited. Finally, after a long pause and none getting up to leave, Zircon spoke again.

"Our only hope is delay; we cannot carry the war to them. However, we are strong here. They cannot attack us but from in front. To march around the city would take days. As such, here are my suggestions. You have all come to join me in the defense of the Wolf City, but in leading an army such as this, I have little experience. I call on each of you to help conceive our defense.

"First, the Shiaps, we know little of how your camels will react in combat to the presence of the wolves. Of the wolves themselves, you have no fear. I suggest you form on our flank to the right. From there you can harass the enemy and keep us from getting flanked."

"Your vision is wise," spoke Ra'Shone. "We well cover you from there until the end."

Zircon now turned to the R'mon and Raff's corps. "There is a slight rise on the left of the cities entrance. From there your archers can reach the battlefield to come. I suggest you cover the left flank from there. Perhaps we can channel the attackers towards it to so that you can wreck more havoc upon them."

"As you wish, Zircon, but we do not mean to be mere onlookers in the battle to come. When the time comes you well find us stalwart on your left, advancing if necessary."

"Thank-you."

Finally, to the people of Twror and the Nomads he spoke. "In the middle then you must stand; those with experience in war alongside me in the front. Those without we hold back at the cities entrance, to rush any breakthrough, a tough job for any of you."

One of the Twrorians, a White, moved forward now. "You protected us from those who seeked to destroy us. We have met your friends, the wolves, and many have paid a visit to their city. We stand by you now, in our freedom, so that we may pass on our freedom to those whom you now protect."

One of the sect of the *One True God* now spoke, with reverence. "May God grace us victory upon this battle to come."

The Emperor Wolf now looked at Zircon as if to say, "What of us, in this our city that we stand to defend. What of us?"

Zircon looked at his friend, the proud Emperor Wolf and spoke; in words he hoped the wolf would understand. "You are our rock, upon which they will throw all of their might against us. You must attack where you can, breaking apart any attack that seems too strong for us. You cannot meet them individually, but can only meet them in mass."

The Emperor Wolf seemed to understand and went to his lieutenants sitting not far away.

"Now we prepare. Breastworks need to be built, a fortress in the plain for our foes to break against while we hold."

Each leader now went back to those that they had brought into this battle, each to prepare for what was to come in their own way.

Zircon returned to his tower, to see what waited before them.

And the wolves gathered in mass in front of the entrance to their city.

The Library

Thul sat at the desk in his office. For a change his thoughts were not on the new computer connection to Argonia. There were undercurrents throughout The Hold and the outlying areas. A crisis was coming as the *old guard* refused to accept the changes that were coming to these lands.

Thul had a pretty good idea who was behind it. However, knowing and proving were two different things. With the three Sage he could depend on up north searching for the Myk, he was on his own. Thul knew that it was up to him to secure the library, to bring the traitor to light and quell the revolt in The Hold.

The Northern Valley was secure in what was happening; Twror, Erson and Nourne remained strong. That left the Southern Valley and the City by the Lake. How would they break in the battles to come? The final revolt of The Hold and the Jall was simmering just below the surface. The massacre in the Round Valley of the Myk had set the stage for that revolt.

Thul's first thought in what was coming; protect the Library and the treasures of The Hold. The scholars could be trusted to follow him. However, they were scholars and not soldiers. He recalled those who had been working in the Northern Valley; they were on their way now.

Thul had to bring the scholars together without his hidden enemy knowing until it was too late. A traitor among the Sage; the three Sage in the North had refused at first to believe it. Nevertheless, it could be no other.

A special lecture from the Teacher, Thul knew that would do it. He had given several of these since the connection to Argonia, bringing the scholars up to date on the latest news. Now he called another. Let his opponent remain a secret for now. The traitor never attended these lectures anyways. However, this time there would be hints; just enough to make his opponent curious, a curiosity that would bring him to Thul at the right time.

Word passed quickly throughout the Library and The Hold. Every scholar hurried to attend it; a *special* learning session from the Teacher. What would he be presenting to the scholars this time? Thul had never used the word *special* with his lectures before. Thul didn't have to make this lecture mandatory; no scholar was going to miss it.

Locklear heard of this lecture and the word *special* attributed to it. He could only shake his head. There was nothing unusual about these lectures; Locklear had even attended the first one. However, the timing of this conclave was off-putting to Locklear. And the word *special* to describe it, that was new.

"What is this pretender up to this time?!" Locklear practically shouted from his desk. 'I'm needed elsewhere and now this,' he thought to himself.

Locklear paced back and forth in his office. Everything was going as planned. Thul; he was the wildcard in all of this.

The scholars assembled in the Library's largest lecture hall. Everyone attended; this was something that Thul with his rumor passing made sure none would miss. All were curious as to what new wonders their Teacher, Thul, would pass on to them. Only a few weeks earlier Thul had reported on the discovery of Argonia. Had Thul found a connection to another new land?

The lecture hall quieted as Thul entered through the lower level door. Expectations were high, as Thul wanted. Thul surveyed the scholars sitting in rows above him. The lecture hall was almost at capacity. Thul hadn't realized just how many scholars there were. Only three doors led into the lecture hall, two above and the one Thul entered through at the bottom of the hall. Once all were seated and quiet Thul motioned to several of his closest scholars to secure the three doors. Even at this, the assembly found nothing unusual. To them Thul must have found something truly extraordinary to share.

Thul looked over the hall and began to speak, in a low tone that carried throughout the room. He barely needed his microphone. As Thul began to speak, he held the scholars in rapture. Slowly he explained what was happening there and elsewhere. The Confederation was in danger of collapsing. The bud of that revolt was in the library. Someone who they all knew well was directing it and it was up to them to stop him. Thul carefully presented his suppositions and what he knew. Questions came from the scholars and he answered them as best he could.

"A Sage turning against us?"

"How?"

"Locklear?"

"Why would Locklear do this?"

"What can we do?"

Finally, Thul brought this to a conclusion. "I will bring Locklear to justice myself. You, my friends and scholars have a far more difficult and dangerous job to do. The Library, just reopened, must be closed and protected at all cost. Then together we must move to protect the treasures that The Hold possesses for all of us. We cannot expect much help from the Hold. We know that many throughout the land are with us. However, the cost could be heavy."

The scholars looked at Thul now with grave concern. They would do what was necessary. However, they were scared of what was to come. Thul walked slowly up the right-hand aisle and looked at each scholar as he walked by them.

"It is time," he quietly spoke as he had the doors reopened. "It is time."

The scholars solemnly followed Thul out the doors, each in their own way knowing what they had to do.

Finally, Locklear's curiosity got the better of him and he hurried to the lecture hall to find out just what was going on. He arrived and found the doors locked; that had never happened before. Locklear looked through the door's window to see Thul beginning to speak. He could tell that the lecture hall was packed. Alarmed, Locklear began to walk away quickly.

"Where to go," Locklear spoke aloud to himself. He had to find out what was going on. His office, No, he would find out nothing there. He went then to Thul's office which he found unexpectedly unlocked. Locklear looked on with suspicion before he went in. He needed answers and here he would find them.

"How dare this man from across the sea take possession of the Library of The Hold," Locklear spoke aloud to himself as he entered Thul's office. "I have spent over 1000 years protecting this place. Thul has no right to command the library. A DNA sequence, how does that compare to my time at the library." It was time for Locklear to reassert his control.

Locklear sat down in Thul's comfortable chair behind his desk.

He feared that the end of the era of the Sage was coming to an end, so few remained now.

He opened the top drawer of the desk in front of him. A small notebook inside seemed to stare at him. Calderon's notebook; how had Thul found it when he was unable to? Locklear had murdered before to protect his dominion; Calderon did not stand alone in that regard.

Now Thul; he needed to stop Thul before it was too late, before he became too strong.

Locklear took the notebook in his hand and to return back to his office. On his way there, he stopped by a shop and picked up a cup of the hot brew. He needed the 'presso to calm his nerves. He sat down for a moment to plot his next move.

Thul and the scholars; could he break Thul's hold on the scholars or was it already too late? He had witnessed through the lecture rooms window the hold Thul held them in. They revered him. It was too late for Thul to be stopped that way.

He had murdered before.

Thul; the conspiracy, everything was going according to plan except Thul. The Confederacy was on the brink of collapse. The attack on the Wolf City would end it. It didn't matter who won the battle, the damage to the Confederacy would be done.

Thul must be stopped, but how?

Locklear needed to send a message to the leader of The Hold. The Hold's leader was not happy with the prestige that he had lost do to the failure of The Hold's soldiers at the battle and the emergence of the Confederacy. The Hold's leader would send his soldiers to the Library, Locklear was sure of that. And Thul will be banished, or more likely killed defending it. And Locklear would be clear of Thul's death as he retook control of the Library.

When Locklear reached his office, he called his personal aide to his side. He wrote a quick note to the leader of The Hold and handed it to his aide. The aide took the note and hurried away to deliver it himself.

The aide rushed past Thul just as Thul was entering Locklear's office, unannounced. The assistant intentionally averted his glance from Thul as he hurried away. Thul noticed that as he entered the office. 'Something is fishy here,' he thought to himself as he approached

Locklear seated behind his desk.

Locklear had just sat down after expressing to his assistant the importance of the need for haste in delivering the message when Thul entered. He wasn't ready as yet for a confrontation with Thul. He wanted that to come later.

Thul looked at Locklear as he approached the desk. He thought Locklear looked nervous. Thul suspicions were only highlighted by the way Locklear's assistant practically sneaked out of the office.

As Thul approached him, Locklear tried to assert himself. "How dare you enter my office unannounced?" Locklear did his best to sound offended by Thul's action.

Thul just stood at the edge of the desk. He seemingly towered over the now fully seated Locklear. Locklear now wished that he had remained standing when Thul entered the room.

"Just sit there and listen," was all Thul said.

Locklear, who had begun to stand up, was taken aback and sat back down.

"I have some questions for you," Thul continued unabated. Thul remained standing over Locklear as he continued. Locklear now felt truly worried.

'Is it already too late,' Locklear thought to himself. 'Was Thul now sure of himself?'

Thul now pulled a chair to sit opposite Locklear. He sat down, never taking his eyes off Locklear's face. His first question caught Locklear off guard as Thul intended.

"What really happened to Calderon?"

"That was so long ago I scarcely remember," Locklear quietly answered, trying to gather his thoughts.

"But you knew of his dictionary. The teachers must have helped him." Thul saw Locklear in possession of the notebook on his desk. Locklear tried to hide it, but it was too late.

"You were in my office and went through my desk!" Thul stated with the full force of his voice.

"Yes, as the head of the Library that is my prerogative." Locklear answered angrily.

"You are no longer in charge of the Library," Thul calmly stated back. He reached for the notebook as Locklear tried to pull it back.

"That notebook is mine, Locklear."

"Here," Locklear said as he pushed the notebook into Thul's outstretched hand. Locklear now hoped to stall the inevitable. "Thinking back, yes, I'm sure that they did."

"So, you were threatened by Calderon," Thul calmly accused Locklear.

"Not at all, of course not," an agitated Locklear replied. He didn't care for this line of questioning. 'How much of the truth does Thul know?'

"He died mysteriously," Thul stated.

"Yes, it was an unfortunate accident."

"I have been studying the Sage of the past," Thul calmly said. "The Order of the Sage was pretty big at one time. Quite a few died *mysteriously*."

"Sad but true. So few of us are left now, so many died in those early years, so many accidents happened as we worked to bring the future from the past."

"Locklear," Thul paused, "quite a few died of mysterious circumstances around the same time as Calderon. How do you explain that, Locklear?"

"Accidents happen, Thul, it's as simple as that."

Thul looked Locklear firmly in the eyes. He studied Locklear's body language and his tone and as he did so he learned the last of the truth that he had been seeking.

Thul knew that he had to stop Locklear. .

"One final question before I go, Locklear. Did you kill Calderon and the others?"

Locklear's blank stare after the question finished the truth for Thul. The unspoken answer was…Yes.

Thul just stared down Locklear as he stood up. He knew that he had to act fast. Without a further word, he turned and walked out.

Thul stopped briefly at an unused office, not far from Locklear's own, and jotted a quick note on a piece of paper.

As Thul returned to the library he stopped the first scholar he saw.

"Yes, Teacher," the student asked.

"This note must get to Nourne as quickly as possible. No

delays."

"I go at once, Teacher. I can ride a horse and will take it there myself without stopping."

The scholar hurried away without another word. Thul, himself, rushed to the Library as fast as his feet could carry him. As he passed each scholar, he sent word that all scholars were to return to the Library; with weapons, whatever they could carry.

"With weapons," so many asked as the word was passed.

"Yes, we have but little time."

Thul reached the final door, now open for all, to the Library itself.

'Our last stand will be here,' Thul thought to himself. 'Will Nourne arrive in time?'

To the scholars around him Thul now spoke. "We will stage our defense where it is narrow at the outer doors." Thul looked at the faces of the scholars around him. These were but the students of the Library. Too young and too old and none was trained in fighting. Thul stood alone in that moment; however, he couldn't show his fear to the scholars.

They gathered in the hundreds around Thul, some carrying just a stick or a cane. Nevertheless, Thul was their Teacher and they would stand with him against the coming threat to the end.

Rumors began stirring about Locklear. As Thul marched to the outer doors with the scholars, more arrived by the minute.

They passed Locklear's office; empty. Where had he gone?

In front of the outer doors, the scholars began building a barricade with anything that they could find. The corridor was ten feet wide here with a polished stone floor. They heard a commotion near the entrance of The Hold. Thul sent two scholars to find out what was happening. One returned an hour later, an arrow in his abdomen. His dying words, "They are coming."

"Keep building up the barricade, anything that you can find. Throw it on the pile. We'll set fire to it when we retreat."

"Fire, won't that engulf us as well?" asked a young scholar.

"It will slow their advance. The fire will not go beyond the stone wall and floor here. It *will* give us the time we need to gather everything into the Library." Thul spoke with confidence and those around him stood strong with him. 'But what hope did they really have against a well armed, well trained foe,' he thought.

"How many of you have any martial training?" Thul asked the throng around him. They could all hear the army marching down the hallways. And they continued to stand strong.

Four scholars, with their bows, raised their hands. A dozen more raised swords to the sky.

"The rest of you, retreat to the inner doors. Stand by to close those. Pull out everything from every office and throw it into the hallway to slow them down. Take whatever treasures and writings from the offices as you can carry back with you." Thul now pointed to a small group of women. "Strip Locklear's office of anything you find. Tear it apart. Break into his cabinets. I want everything. If you need help, grab others to help you."

Thul turned to all of the scholars, "Locklear you are the cause of this," he shouted in his heartfelt grief.

While Thul and his small band stood tall at the barricade in the outer hallway, the rest hurried to carry out Thul's orders. They ransacked office after office as the scholars took anything that could be of value with them. The offices could be fixed up again once the conflict was over. They looted Locklear's office of everything in it. The scholars figured that Thul could sort out what he was looking for in time. The scholars emptied out everything of value in the offices to take back with them, every desk, chair, table or cabinet they could move was strewn into the hallway, only a narrow passage left behind for Thul and the others to stage their retreat. Thul and the defenders could make their way through it, but the shieldmen of The Hold would have difficulty traversing it.

The scholars in retreat were well clear of the outer corridor when the shieldmen finally made their appearance. Thankfully, for Thul and his small band, only a couple of archers were among them.

Thul now gave his orders. He was no longer the shy traveler who had talked his way into the Captain's ship in what seemed now so long ago. Like the others of *The Proctant*, he was now a leader among these people, his people; the scholars. The hallway where Thul chose to make his stand was barely ten feet wide and their barrier stood over half of the corridors ten feet of height.

"Archers, aim high to the ceiling. Let your arrows skim it. That way they will fall among the soldiers. Once you have used up all of your arrows, hurry back to the inner door. All that we can hope to do is slow them down."

The four archers now pointed their bows down the hallway. Each only held ten or twelve target arrows, but anything at this point would help. They didn't bother aiming their bows; they just shot the arrows high down the hallway at the on-coming shieldmen.

As the first arrows arrived over the shieldmen's heads they stopped their march. This was not something that they had expected to find. They were told that they were just facing a few disgruntled scholars who were weaponless. The scholars could hear their arrows dropping among the soldiers. In just a few minutes the scholars had loosened all of their arrows at the shieldmen. However, before their own retreat from the now burning barricade, they had the privilege of hearing more than a few explicative's coming from the shieldmen as the arrows made their mark.

The scholars carrying their swords had begun piling loose paper into the barricade. As the archers had finished their last flight of arrows and begun their retreat to the inner doors, Thul gave the order to the last of those who stood with him.

"Light the barricade and prepare to begin your retreat, slow, steady and facing our foe. We must give the other scholars time to ready the inner doors."

First one part and then another part of the barricade burst into fire from the burning paper. The fire had not yet consumed the entire barricade when the shieldmen now rushed the barricade, to pass through it before it was entirely ablaze. The shieldmen's archers, few in number, let loose one volley and charged themselves at the towering barricade that blocked their way.

"Steady now," Thul told his small band in as brave a voice as he could muster as the shieldmen approached. "Keep lighting the paper and fan the flames."

As the volley of arrows from the shieldmen came over the barricade, one of the students, Jhon, was hit in the shoulder. He only looked at Thul as if to say, "I'm OK."

When the shieldmen came within 25 yards of the barricade Thul gave his command. "Slow backward retreat, together now. It will take a while for them to get through the barricade." The barricade was now fully ablaze, although the fire itself had weakened it in places. "We must stand and stop any individual shieldmen who get through it."

For the sake of Thul and his small band of resistance, only one shieldmen broke ranks and charged ahead, looking for personal glory in the fight. He charged blindly through the now smoke-filled hallway. Thul and two others dispatched him to his ancestors, but not before each were injured in the brief ruckus.

When they had retreated 100 yards from the barricade, turning a corner in the corridor, a young, fleet scholar rushed forward to Thul and his handful of now injured men from the inner doors.

"We are ready," was all she had to say.

"Now we hurry," Thul ordered his beleaguered men. "We race back to the inner doors in pairs. Paulo, you and I will be the last to retreat. Don't lose your footing, any of you. Paulo, you and I will throw anything remaining that we see into the path of the shieldmen. Now go!"

And they hurried, with Thul the last to enter the inner doors, just ahead of the now charging shieldmen. The inner doors sealed against the onslaught. The Library was safe; these doors of the Teachers could not be broken down.

They were safe from attack, but also trapped. When would help arrive?

Nourne

It had been two weeks since Wade, now Lord Wade of Nourne, had received word of the coming rebellion and Trade War from the Sage who were on the expedition north. With Thorium gone in search of the Myk, it was up to Wade and Gant to figure out the counter-stroke.

And now, but three days earlier, he had received warnings from his scouts that the rebellion was on the march against the Wolf City.

Wade had sent word immediately upon receiving the information from the Sage to all of the newfound members of the

Confederation. Already contingents from the R'mons and the Shiaps were moving to aide Zircon. However, more help was needed.

More forces were arriving in Erson and Twror on a daily basis to aid Zircon and to move on The Hold. Along with the latest detachment of the R'mon were a new people, ready to join the growing confederacy and help.

They marched from the East and called themselves the Phoenix. Over 1000 strong they marched in a formation they called a phalanx and bragged that their army could not be beaten. They were led by three generals: Nicholas, Elias and Tobins. Each phalanx was 300 soldiers. 1 archery regiment of 100 archers was led by Iris, the huntress.

An army from the Coastal Peoples would arrive shortly through the Southern Valley, avoiding the area around The Hold. There they would be met by Raymond of Kiln, Jamen's oldest son. Raymond promised 1000 riders to move against The Hold.

His army was coming together, but where was it needed the most. Wade wished that he had heard back from the Jall-King, but he seemed to have disappeared, taken prisoner by the rebellious clans of the Jall. The Wolf City had to be defended; Wade would march there; a combined force of Nourne Riders and the warbirds who would arrive first, followed by their second contingent from the R'mons with their new ally; the Phoenix.

However, in the midst of this, two questions remained for Wade. The City by the Lake, what would they do? And the army assembling in the Southern Valley, where should they move.

The council of the City by the Lake was torn and dysfunctional by the strife. Several members supported The Hold, their traditional ally. Others supported staying neutral in the coming conflict. A third faction now arose in the city. The young people of the city, their wishes so often disregarded by the council, tried to make themselves heard. They had led the City by the Lake's army against the Myk. And in turn they had received nothing from the council. They now supported the new and growing confederation of nations and now they demanded to be heard in the council.

The two councilmen who supported The Hold tried to send their army south in support of their ally. A mutiny now threatened the military of the City. None of the council knew which way that mutiny, if it happened, would break; a thing of worry for Wade.

Wade sent a message to Raymond. It was brief. March to the City by the Lake and end any insurrection there.

Shortly after Wade sent his message to Raymond, he received the young scholar in the Castle that Thul had sent. He had been flown by warbird from the City by the Lake to Castle Nourne. However, as speedy as his trip was, it was still two days since he had left the Library.

A third crisis had formed in the coming insurrection. First, the Wolf City had to be spared. Then the City by the Lake needed to be neutralized. And finally, the Library had to be rescued. This meant his army had to be split three ways.

And where *was* the Jall-King? He had to be found.

Wade called his generals together to assemble in Erson. Those from the Southern Valley arrived by warbird to avoid for the moment the City by the Lake. In his mind the Wolf City had to come first. More armies from throughout the confederation and their friends were assembling in the plains between Erson and Twror. 'Would the need for armies never end?' thought Wade. All the armies assembled on the field of two battles against the Myk agreed on a plan. They would move through the northern valley to Wolf City, each at their own best speed without, they hoped, of being spotted by the spies of The Hold. To arrive in pieces to defend the Wolf City would be better than moving at the slowest pace and reaching the city too late, and seeing the city fall before their arrival.

The Castles Knights on their warbirds left first, speeding during the night to Zircon's aide. Every ox-cart that could be commandeered now carried the tired foot soldiers of the Phoenix, worn by their quick march to Erson. The ox-carts were slow but they could reach the Wolf City without stopping and give the weary soldiers a much needed rest. The archers from R'mon rode on horseback to join their colleagues there on any horse that they could muster. They didn't have time to wait for Raymond's promised horses. There was no time for anybody to wait.

The remaining volunteers from Erson and Twror would march on foot to the Wolf City. They would take the middle pass, the shortest route, but the one to be most likely spotted by The Hold's spies. To

Wade that would accomplish two things; his better troops could march, unimpeded by the loose order of the civilians going to help Zircon in his conflict. And it would feed The Hold false information about just who was marching to Zircon's aide.

The scholar from the Library was given a place to rest by Lady Theresa. Lord Perth and Lady Alyce prepared to travel to the City by the Lake on foot with their small guard. They insisted that any carts, horses, or warbirds were needed to transport the armies for the coming conflict. Wade was eventually able to convince them to travel by wagon. "One less wagon won't slow us down and you are needed to convince the council of that city." With hesitation Wade's, now in-laws, agreed to the wagon.

"We will do what we can to convince the council there not to support The Hold in this," Lord Perth assured the worried Wade.

Wade now delivered a new message to Raymond during their confab in Erson. Send half of the army of the Coastal Peoples to the City by the Lake for a show of force. The rest of the armies assembled in the Southern Valley needed to move to The Hold and relieve Thul and the scholars in the Library there.

Orders were left for any newly arriving armies. For those in the Northern Valley, Gant was to direct them immediately to the aid of the Wolf City. Those in the Southern Valley were to move directly against The Hold.

By now Reed had returned back to Twror. His first thought was to lead his people home at once. Then he became aware of the increased activity in the city and the armies assembling on the plains and advancing from there. "What new devilry is this," Reed thought and he moved quickly to find Lord Wade.

Reed met with Wade in Erson, as the army Wade would lead was beginning to march. He entered Wade's command tent with his head held high and his wildcat at his side. Wade welcomed him happily, not yet aware of Reed's decision to return home with those of the Nomads who wished to return with him.

Both men clasped arms and hugged; their friendship long since set.

"Reed, you're a welcome sight in this time of need. Have you come to lead your people?" Wade asked, not expecting the answer he received.

"Yes, friend Wade. I congratulate you on your wedding. And now I return my people home. At least those who wish to return with me."

"Return home…" Wade stammered. "We need you here."

"Tell me what is happening. I see the armies marching, against the Myk once more?"

"The Hold and the Jall are moving against Zircon in the Wolf City. We are marching to his aid there. And The Hold has moved against the Library. Zircon and Thul need our help," Wade almost pleaded. He needed all of his friends in this time of trials.

"Fear not, Lord Wade," Reed stood tall and smiled. "I do not leave my friends in a time of need. Thorium and the others can take care of the Myk. I, however, will no longer take part in the travesty of the Sage."

"The travesty of the Sage," Wade asked confused.

"That is for another day," answered Reed. "How can I best help you?" he simply asked.

"My armies are moving to aid Zircon and Thul in the Library as we speak. Unexpected and new friends our coming to join our Confederation as well."

"As to be expected," stated Reed. "This Confederation of the peoples is a good thing. We Nomads will remain a part of it."

"That is good to hear, Reed. Already Nomads have joined the march to the Wolf City to aid Zircon."

"What is this Wolf City that Zircon defends?" asked Reed, seeming somewhat incredulous at the term Wolf City.

"Zircon was sent by the Sage to scout a city in the west."

Reed spit on the ground at the words the *Sage*. "I do nothing for the Sage."

"Let me continue," Wade spoke again, unsure of the reasons for Reed's now scorn of the Sage. "Zircon found a surprise there, a highly intelligent breed of wolf. I have been there myself on a visit. They have a highly evolved well-organized colony there, maybe as well organized as our own cities. They are led by their Emperor Wolf. I have spoken, I guess that is the right word, with their King. He seems to understand every word we speak and somehow, I understood him as well. That city is rich in the metal we need and they are in need of the food that we can provide. A trade has developed between the Northern Valley and the Wolf City.'

"And the Jall do not like this trade?"

"The established clans do, but not the others."

"Such is the madness of the Jall and The Hold. I hold no respect for either. I join the march then to aid my friend, Zircon."

Looking eye to eye with Reed, Wade now spoke directly to him. "Not all of the Jall stand against us Reed. The Jall-King opposed this action by so many of the Jall's independent clans. But he has disappeared."

"Have they killed him?"

"Gant and I talked about this. We don't think so. It's just not their way. We need him, Reed, to bring an end to this insurrection. We've lost touch with many of the Jall-Kings supporters as well. We need to find him."

"You wish me to do this," asked Reed, cautiously, "to find these friends among the vipers who have turned against us?"

"Yes, Reed, we are so divided in our forces right now, I can spare but a few. With your ways, I hope that you can find and rescue the Jal-King."

"I go at once," Reed quickly replied. "How many may I take, this will be a dangerous thing to do in the swamps that surround their city."

"Boats will await you on the northwestern edge of the swamp. A guide will take you there. You will be guided by Jall whom remain loyal to our new confederation."

"The Jal-Beast?" Reed asked, unafraid.

"I am told that they live on the eastern edges of the Great Swamp."

"At least that is good news. These *loyal* Jall, they can be trusted?"

"Yes," Wade answered. "Plan on about 50 of your people and their wildcats, that's about all the boats that we can command can hold."

Reed shook hands with Wade one more time before he turned to leave the command tent to gather the men he would trust on this mission. "Consider the Jall-King saved."

With events unfolding quickly around them, the council of the City by the Lake finally made the only decision that they could. The two councilmen who supported the insurrection were placed under house arrest. By acclamation of the people of the city two new members were chosen; both young, both pro-Confederation.

The council was still split, however there was now no chance of it joining The Hold. The council voted seven to two against fighting The Hold. By the same seven to two they voted to remain neutral. In what was to follow the military was told to stand down.

One general refused the order to stand down. Alexandre, staunchly pro-Confederacy, the youngest of the City by the Lakes generals, declared his allegiance to the Confederation.

The council received this news while simultaneously learning that the army of the Coastal People had arrived at the cities outskirts. In a rare show of unanimity, they refused to declare Alexandre's action a mutiny. He fought for the Confederation, not the City by the Lake was their reasoning. Several days later, with the Coastal People's army fully into the city's limits, Alexandre now assumed control of the combined armies. They began their march to The Hold and then the Wolf City, now 25,000 strong.

Everything that could be was now in place and now in motion.

Wolf City

Zircon looked over the field of battle before him. There were thousands of the Jall and The Hold camped in the hills on the city side of the ravines. If they attacked now the defenders would have little chance.

Zircon looked over his own army arrayed in the city's defense; still so few. He was told more would be arriving. Would they arrive in time?

The Emperor Wolf continued to meet each army's commander as they arrived. After the meeting the Emperor Wolf escorted each of them into and around the city. All were amazed by what these wolves had accomplished. They were even more amazed that they could communicate with the Emperor Wolf.

Another 250 of his Shiap friends had arrived. They now numbered over 750. But how would the camel riders, a light cavalry, do against the wall-shields that they faced. They were brave and a strong force on the right, but… There was always a but with each troop as they arrived.

On his left were the R'mon archers and the first contingent of foot soldiers from Nourne and 500 of the Knights on their warbirds, even now scouting from the air. Those not in the air, scouting, a handful at a time, were stationed several miles distance from the city. Out of range of the enemy's archers, but close enough to respond where needed. These were the best that Castle Nourne had to offer. Wade himself had started calling the airborne warriors knights after warriors from before the Great War. Even with these they were far too few.

The citizen army of the Northern Valley, those that came to Zircons aid of Erson and Twror continued to trickle in. Their number now exceeded 10,000. But all were untrained. They asked no question of why Zircon protected these wolves, although many started their own communications with them.

Zircon had a job for them, a job they could do well. Trenches were being dug by them and the dirt thrown up into a breastwork, in some places already over 6 feet tall. Metal from the city was dragged out to help reinforce this wall and stockade they were building. It would be high enough and long enough to force the attack over it. Zircon and his commanders hoped this would allow the archers the chance to repel a central attack, while at the same time hiding the true strength of the defenders.

The archers of the Jall and The Hold were Zircon's main concern of those troops facing him. Neither the knights on their warbirds nor the Shiaps on their camel would stand a chance against them. So far nobody had come up with an answer for them.

"Why do they attack us," the Emperor Wolf seemed to ask Zircon, both looking out the tower's window at what was assembled in front of the city.

Zircon could only look over at him sadly. "It is the greed of some men."

There was hesitation as well in the camp of the invaders. More had arrived during the night there as well and they now numbered over 10,000 soldiers, evenly split between the Jall and The Hold. They numbered over 1000 archers as well.

However, without any cohesion, leadership and no idea of what faced them beyond the breastworks being thrown up in front of them the entire army was frozen in place.

One leader was chosen from among the Jall and one from The Hold. And neither could agree on a strategy. They sat across a table from each other with a crude map drawn up between them.

"We need more warriors; they still outnumber us. I received a report that several thousand reinforcements arrived last night for them and all top soldiers, the Jall commander Antoine stated firmly. "Where are the promised shieldmen of The Hold?"

The Holds commander, trained in warfare, unlike the Jall's who was elected by the clan participating, just dismissed the Jall's, foolish in his mind, concerns.

"What reinforcements they received are nothing; a handful of warbirds, camel riders and the poor of the Northern Valley. Nothing there can withstand an assault if we go now."

"I will not order the Jall forward until we outnumber them. We did not expect an army before us, just the damn wolves. Last night some of my officers were killed by those silent assassins."

"We strike now!" The Holds commander Swartzell demanded.

"We wait!" Antoine demanded in turn. "Where is the rest of the giant army of The Hold that we were promised?" he asked again.

And so it went on deep into the night. Another day of just camping in front of the city as each side saw more reinforcements trickle in.

The Hold

After a full day of forced march from the Southern Valley and the City by the Lake, the combined armies of Alexandre and Raymond converged on the city that had sprung up around The Hold over the centuries.

They cautiously entered the city, not knowing what to expect. As fortune would have it, the army of The Hold had finally left for the Wolf City just the night before to reinforce those who had previously marched against it. 25,000 shieldmen, they would arrive at the Wolf City in three days. The generals of The Hold's military had not expected a quick response to their actions against the Wolf City. Fewer than 250 of the now defenders remained. As the armies of the Confederation entered the city, the handful of shieldmen and security left by The Holds officers withdrew to the entrance of The Hold. Here there were fortifications that they could hold until the attack on the Wolf City was over.

The combined armies of Alexandre and Raymond moved through the silent streets of the city, its residents hiding behind closed doors. They needed information; what had happened to the army of The Hold. Alexandre knocked on the door of a merchant he knew in the city. The merchant, peeking through a window and seeing who it was, opened his door.

Alexandre was brief. "Where have they gone?" he asked the merchant.

"All march on the Wolf City," he answered, somewhat afraid.

Alexandre could fear his trepidation. "You have no need to fear us. You and I, we remain friends."

"Not the armies that march, your…"

"We go to aid our friends. Did any stay behind?"

"A few," the merchant said. "They await you at The Hold. My son…" the shopkeeper cried.

"I will try to spare those that remain here against us. They don't march on my friend. How many?"

"Fewer than 300, mostly young and new volunteers, like my son…"

"I will do what I can," answered Alexandre soberly. "I will do what I can."

By early morning the combined armies arrived in front of The Hold; forces from The City by the Lake, the Southern Valley and the Coastal Peoples. They set up a camp in clear view of the defenders, showing the size of their forces. Alexandre, Raymond and Lorenzo of the Coastal Peoples all agreed that a massacre had to be avoided at all costs if The Hold was to remain part of the new Confederation.

As dawn broke Alexandre rode up to the fortifications in front of him, alone, carrying a flag of truce.

"I call for a parlay," he yelled out to the sentries at the gate.

A young sentry called down from an embankment to one side of the gate. "Wait here."

The sentry hurried back to his own camp to find their commander, also young. All were shieldmen just beginning their training, unprepared for real combat.

The young commander walked through the wooden gate and approached Alexandre, unsure of himself.

"I stand before you with 10,000 well-trained shieldmen and their archers," the young officer blustered as Alexandre approached him, now also on foot.

Alexandre put his hand forward to shake the young man's hand. Both were about the same age, although Alexandre didn't know him. The officer of The Hold reluctantly took it.

"I am Alexandre. I command the forces that you see before you. We make no effort to hide our strength from you."

"I am Jules, commander of 10,000 shieldmen."

Jules," Alexandre said in a friendly tone. "You are brave, I see that. But I also know that the army you have is less than 300 men, all new recruits."

"But… But… I have…"

Alexandre didn't let him finish. He put his arm around the shoulder of his fellow officer and spoke in a stern voice now. "I know what you have. We are going to enter The Hold and free the Library. Do you know that it is under siege?"

"The Library, no…" Jules stammered. "The Library?"

"Yes, and we are here to free it."

"I don't understand. We were told to stay here and protect it."

"My friend, Jules, you need to lay down your arms."

"I cannot do that. We must protect, with our lives if necessary, The Hold and the Library."

"Protect them from who, Jules? Those that march on the Wolf City or those that march to protect it."

"We stand firm here," Jules stated aloud.

Frustrated, Alexandre now tried to calm the young officer he faced. Bloodshed had to be avoided here. "Then you will die here. There is no need for that. Do you know of the new Confederation?"

"Yes, my father speaks well of it."

"Those whose orders you follow are trying to destroy it. Even now the Library is sealed behind its doors. The scholars are hiding behind those doors, fearful of the leaders that you follow."

"A civil war?" Jules asked, scared of the thought.

"Yes, if that is what you want. It can end or begin right here. That's up to you. However, we are here to prevent that and free the Library from its siege. What is it, Jules, peace or war?"

Jules looked over at the giant encampment in front of him. He knew it would be a massacre if he tried to stand up to it. A civil war wasn't something he wanted as well.

"I surrender my army to you," the crestfallen Jules said to Alexandre.

"Have your army return to the city, leaving your weapons behind."

Alexandre remounted his horse and rode back to where Raymond and Lorenzo stood watching.

"We have peace here; they have wisely surrendered."

"Thank the Gods," a relieved Raymond said.

"Today we march to relieve your friend, Zircon," Lorenzo added.

"Yes, today we march, only a day behind the Shieldmen of The Hold."

The last of The Holds warriors slowly marched through the encampment of the soldiers that were positioned against them. The army of the Confederation could not believe how young they were, some only ten or twelve years old, forced to bear arms by the conspiratorialist.

Two more things happened that day before the army resumed its march. Alexandre and Raymond reached the Library's solid doors. As they came through the hallways of The Hold, the destruction they found was almost beyond description; little remained but the floors, walls and ceilings. It took a while, but by banging on the doors they finally got the attention of those hiding inside. Thul arrived at the door. He put his ear to it and heard the clamoring from outside. And he recognized the voice of Raymond, whom he had met on a visit to the Southern Valley.

The door opened, slowly in case it had to be quickly reclosed, and Thul stood at the opening. The exchange was brief but emotional.

"You are free."

"Thank-you."

And the two men clasped arms.

The second thing that happened was more poignant. In the city built up around The Hold, a young man, hardly more than a boy, approached his father's store. He timidly knocked on it. When the door opened, the two, father and son, rushed to each other and embraced in a hug that lasted a good while, both men and boy crying and laughing at the same time. Alexandre had kept his word to his friend.

Wolf City

The Sun broke through the early morning clouds; an ominous red sky shown through the clouds. The camps of the city's defenders were awakening to the smell of their cooks preparing the day's food. New stores of food were also being provided to the Wolf City, whose females spread the hunter's fresh kill throughout the city.

Zircon was standing by the strange door they had found on that first trading expedition. The mark of the Teachers was clearly visible on the door. Zircon still held on a chain around his neck the key that the Sage had given him. The key was a polished piece of petrified wood another scholar of The Hold had told him. Was it time to open the door? Gar, himself, told Zircon that he would know when to open it.

"Not yet your time," Zircon spoke aloud to the door.

One of the Emperor Wolf's lieutenants found Zircon and loosely grabbed his hand and pulled to get Zircons attention. Zircon looked over at the wolf and clearly heard in his mind, "follow me."

Zircon hurried on foot after the wolf and reached his tower. Climbing to the top he saw the Emperor Wolf looking out its window. When Zircon looked out, he saw the armies of the Jall and The Hold positioning themselves for battle. The period of calm was over. A storm of metal was about to hit the Wolf City's defenders.

Zircon looked over his own forces arrayed below him. Now he had a strong defense in the middle. There were the new arrivals, the phalanxes of the Phoenix, well-rested after traveling in the ox-carts and wagons of the Northern Valley. On his left were the men of Nourne and the archers of the R'mons. The knights with their warbirds remained in reserve, ready for battle from their own staging area a mile east of the city.

Also in reserve were the people of the Northern Valley, Twror and Erson, a citizen's army, who had answered Zircon's call for help, holding whatever weapon they had collected from Erson's armory. Among them were hundreds of hunters with their bows that Zircon hoped to make good use of.

On the right were the Shiaps, strengthened overnight to over 1000 proud warriors, their camels safely staged a good distance behind their line of force. The initial battle would be fought on foot by them.

Still, Zircon could see the size of the army opposing them. They were still outnumbered by better than five to one. How could they hold on?

Antoine and Swartzell, the commanders of the armies facing the Wolf City, stood beside each other, some distance behind their assembled armies. The Jall soldiers, mostly untrained traders, stood on the left and The Holds veteran shieldholders stood on the right. Over 2,500 more shieldmen had arrived overnight and the two generals were told another 25,000 were on the way.

Antoine looked over at Swartzell. It was time. Swartzell gave a runner a note to carry to the archers. It would begin with them.

By mid-mooring Zircon's army was in position to receive the attack. Vastly outnumbered they depended on the R'mon archers and the hunters to blunt any attack. The wolves, under their Emperor, patrolled behind their human allies. They seemed to understand their part well; to stop any breakthrough by the opposing army.

Zircon positioned his men well beyond the entrenchments and barricades the people of Twror and Erson had built up in the two days that they had to prepare. Neither was as deep or as high as they had hoped. However, it would still slow the shieldmens advance.

Zircon's commanders, Shiap, Nourne, R'mon, Phoenix, Erson and Twror assembled with Zircon in front of the opening to the Wolf City. The Emperor Wolf was there as well with his lieutenants. They, the wolves, appeared to listen and understand every word that was spoken to and around them. And they understood that these humans were their friends.

"The middle must be held", Damien, the leader of the three Phoenix generals stated. "We claim the right to the middle."

None argued with Damien; that would be where the greatest strength of the attackers would fall.

As they discussed further their defensive positions a Shiap rider came hurrying up to the commanders.

"Sirs, it appears that half of their army is moving towards us."

Zircon and the others were alarmed by this development. They expected the charge to come squarely against the middle or the lightly held archer's position on the right.

Zircon called over the commander of the warbirds and their knights. "We have to know what they are doing, your scouts?"

"On the way, sir."

Zircon was still having a hard time coming to terms with others calling him, sir.

Quickly two of the warbirds went aloft. One was hit and tumbled to the ground by the now constant storm of arrows coming from their attackers; rider and warbird both dead.

The other made it back to the command tent, the warbird having a difficult landing; one arrow had torn through a wing.

"Quickly the news," Ra'Shone commanded, almost shouted at the rider as he dismounted his hurt warbird.

"It looks like the entire left of their army, all Jall, is moving against the Shiaps," the scout reported.

Ra'Shone just looked at the others around him. "We will do what we can."

Zircon looked around at the others. To weaken any of their positions would lead to a collapse of all of them. The Emperor Wolf lightly tapped Zircon's leg and looked up at him. He didn't speak but everybody there understood his words. "We understand. We will go there. The Shiaps are our brothers as are you, Zircon."

Zircon brushed the neck of this friend. "Do you understand the risk? Can you fight alongside the camels?"

Ra'Shone answered the second part of Zircon's question. "We will fight on foot here. Our camels are of no use against armored foes. And I welcome my brother wolves in this combat."

The Emperor Wolf just looked up at Zircon and Ra'Shone and then the others and he seemed to smile, his teeth showing. They all hear him speak, "Yes, we fight for our home." The Emperor Wolf then walked over to Ra'Shone and sat up in front of him, his lieutenants on either side. He seemed to say, "We are at your command."

"Ra'Shone, it looks like you have your reinforcements."

Ra'Shone knelt down in front of the Emperor Wolf and reached over to scratch the wolf's neck. The Emperor Wolf in turn raised his paw and put it on Ra'Shone's shoulder, his tongue brushing Ra'Shone's face. He stood again, facing Zircon.

"These are for whom we fight. We will be honored to have them at our side. For this battle to come we will fight on foot, our camels secured in the rear. Let our foes try to defeat us with such powerful friends."

With that, Ra'Shone mounted his camel and rode out to command his flank of the defense. The Emperor Wolf and thousands of his pack followed shortly behind. Zircon watched the tribe hurry to keep up with the Emperor. A bloody fight was in-store for them and Zircon feared for their leader.

The center of the line would hold with the legions from Nourne and the Phoenix, with Erson and Twror in support. The R'mon archers and the hunters with their bows would do what was necessary to turn back that attack. Would the Shiap and the wolves be able to turn back the Jall attack with over twice their number? Zircon looked up to the sky and prayed to his God. "Give us our hope on this day."

The attackers could see little of what was happening beyond the defender's barricades. All they knew was that over 10,000 arrows would soon fill the sky as their archers launched continuous flights of their arrows beyond the barricade. They had no idea that the defenders stood in mass just beyond the barricade and, with Zircon announcing the archers moving forward, they had raised their shields to the sky, harmlessly deflecting the arrows to the ground. They suffered almost no casualties from the storm from the sky and runners now collected the forest of arrows that had fallen to the ground and stacked them for their own archers, the hunters of the Northern Valley, to use.

Half-way to the earthworks the attackers split into two sections, the Jall moving rapidly on the left against the Shiaps. There they expected an easy victory and quickened their pace in that direction. That in turn fully exposed the left flank of The Holds shieldmen. When Damien heard this from the warbird scouts, he saluted quickly to Zircon and almost ran to his troops, stationed several hundred yards away.

"Phalanx, to the left march," he ordered his army. As one, his well-trained troops side-stepped to the left, turned 90 degrees and quick-marched to a position on the left of the breastworks built up by Twror and Erson. Their own archers stood just behind the three phalanxes and prepared to launch their own flights of arrows at the attacker's unprotected flank.

The hunters from the Northern valley now spread out behind the warriors aligned in front of them. Each archer had their own quiver of arrows, plus stacked alongside of their positions, the stacks of arrows the runners had collected from the aerial assault of The Hold's archers.

"We hold our fire until they reach the top of our barricades. Then we fire at will," was the order the Huntress gave and it was passed along from archer to archer until the entire corp had heard it.

The archers of the R'mons moved to the top of their ridgeline themselves, standing even with the earth works that had been thrown up almost overnight before them. When the attack was within their range they would move to the top of the earthworks and let their own arrows loose on the unprotected right flank of the attackers.

"What of us?" asked the commander of Nourne's warbirds.

Zircon looked over at him. To send him into this battle now would be suicide against the archers of The Hold. He had no idea how many arrows they still had in stock. Those archers would have to be disposed of first.

"You are to stay back. Watch our right. If your help is needed there then that's where you must engage.

"Yes, sir," he answered as he returned to his airborne knights.

The army of The Hold marched forward, shields held to the front, one sure step in front of the other. Against the Myk they had broken and run. Now 6,000 strong, they would march as one and destroy the enemy before them.

It took the shieldmen two hours to reach the earthworks and stockades before them and as yet no response came from the defenders. Had they fled the battle before them? They could see nothing over the loose dirt, metal and wood thrown up before them.

They began the short climb up and over the obstacles placed before them, their ranks starting to separate from the tight formations that they had marched in. More separations between them began to occur as they climbed over the mounds in front of them. Gaps in their shield wall began to form. They reached the top of the barricades, still unopposed, over 1000 of them at the tops with the rest pushing them closely behind. Then they saw what was arrayed before them.

This wasn't just the peasant army they thought they would face. Over 1000 archers stood plainly in the distance, ready to unleash hell on them, piles of arrows stacked alongside each archer. And in front of the archers, stood over 2000 strong, shieldmen of Nourne and the phalanxes of the Phoenix. It was apparent their own archers had had no effect on the enemy in front of them.

The fuselage of the arrows began. Before one flight had arrived the next was in the air. It seemed that the sky was dark with the airborne terror that was unleashed against them, devouring the Shieldmen that had made it to the top of the earthworks.

All that had reached the top now tumbled down the front of the earthworks. And now the arrows began falling from the sky on the ranks of shieldmen that had not yet reached the earthen mounds in front of them. The ranks that had reached the top came to a stop. And now the arrows front their right, from the R'mons cross-bows began to find their mark. Once again, as before against the Myk, The Hold's finest turned and fled the battle in front of them, through their own camp as they raced in headlong fear, Swartzell watching helplessly as his troops fled to the safety of the ravines.

Only when they reached the 25,000 coming from The Hold to join them did they stop, ashamed and embarrassed by their flight.

The new arrivals looked upon them with scorn. "You let villagers do this to you," they laughed at the crestfallen, broken troops.

"Its not just villagers," they tried to say.

None listened and the new arrivals marched into their camp beyond the ravines in front of the cities defenders.

'Tomorrow they will see what The Hold is made of,' they thought.

On the defender's right, things didn't go as smoothly. The Jall quick-stepped and reached the Shiap's line in under an hour. They had lost touch with their colleagues on their right. Their only concern was the thin, loosely formed ranks of the camel-riders, now on foot, in front of them. Once they were only a few hundred yards from the defenders they charged, unhindered by the shields the men from The Hold carried. Into the line of the Shiaps, out numbering them over five to one, they charged. The Shiap did what they could to defend against the attack but there were too many of the Jall fighters. They stepped back in retreat, giving no quarter, but they were devastated by the attack.

Then the wolves, led by their Emperor, joined the attack. The wolves had split themselves into three packs, each numbering over 500 wolves. And now they counter-attacked as one, hitting both flanks and the front of the Jall lines. The Jall hadn't expected this; a cohesive attack from the wolves they knew populated the city. It was now sword against the claws and fangs of the wolves. And the wolves gave no quarter.

Ra'Shone, himself wounded in several places now rallied what remained of his Shiap fighters, now halved by the initial Jall charge. Back into the center they charged, fighting along side their wolf brothers-in-arms. And now it was the Jall line that began to break.

As the Jall lines began to reform, inflicting heavy casualties upon the wolf attackers, a new force struck them from the air. The knights of Nourne, seeing where they were needed from their airborne position circling the Wolf City, now attacked the Jall from the air, their long-hooked lances creating devastation among the Jall attackers. And now it was the Jall's turn to run from the field of battle; the wolves and the Shiaps too hurt and tired to give chase.

Ra'Shone fought alongside the Emperor Wolf in the final moments of the conflict, each giving far more than they received. Each defending the other from attack as they pressed their own. Too late Ra'Shone saw the blow coming from behind at the Emperor Wolf. A Jall they both thought dead rose up behind the two. He plunged his blade deeply into the side of the wolf before Ra'Shone took off his head with a single blow. Ra'Shone now stood in shock as the Emperor Wolf fell to the bloody field of battle. He could see the wolf's wounds were severe.

"Here," Ra'Shone called out to several Shiaps that stood near him. "Help me carry the Emperor from battle."

The Emperor Wolf's Sire, who was also fighting alongside his leader, also saw the Emperor fall. He gathered the other wolves around their Emperor to protect him. Any Jall that moved around them, wounded or otherwise was quickly dispatched, by the wolves. Few Jall would live to see their homes again.

Ra'Shone signaled to a Nourne knight to land beside them. "We need the doctors here to this battlefield quickly. And we must get the wolves Emperor to safety at once."

The knight quickly understood what had happened. He leaped from his warbird and rushed to the Emperor Wolf's side. "I can stop the bleeding here, but he needs help I can't provide. My warbird is unhurt. Once I stop the bleeding, I will carry this *man* to the doctors of the R'mons. They have set up a hospital inside the wolf's city. Help me bandage his wound."

The knight removed his knife from his waist band and knelt beside the Emperor Wolf. The Emperor's Sire growled at the knight, fearing he intended to inflict more pain on his father.

"It's OK," the knight spoke to the Sire. He himself had visited the Wolf City almost everyday since his arrival. He understood that the wolves could understand what he said. "I need to remove some hair by his wound to stop the bleeding."

The Sire sat down on his haunches. "I understand," he *spoke*. "Do what you can for my father."

Ra'Shone sat down next to the Sire. "Your emperor is one of the bravest I have fought with."

"Thank-you," *said* the Sire. "You must save him if you can. He is beyond our own help."

"I will do what I can," replied the knight, shaving the Emperor's hair from near the wound. Then he tore off a piece of his clothing and matted it into a ball. "Hold this on the wound," he told Ra'Shone. "This is the worst of his wounds. The rest can wait. I must hurry him back to the city."

The knight tore long strips from his garments and wrapped them tightly around the wolf's body. "I hope this will stay until I get him to the hospital."

The warbird was skittish around the wolves but stayed by his knight's side. The knight looked at the Sire. "You must move your pack away from my warbird. It will be hard enough to load him on my warbird."

The knight brought his warbird next to where the Emperor Wolf lay wounded. He kept a tight hold on the reigns. "Ra'Shone, can you lift the Emperor onto the back of my warbird. I must hold my reigns tight. He is not happy." The knight struggled to hold the warbird in place with the scent of the wolves all-around. The warbirds were used to the scent of the wildcats, but this was something new.

Ra'Shone called over several of the Shiaps that had gathered around them. "Help me gingerly, carefully load the Emperor on board this warbird."

To the knight Ra'Shone now spoke. "Once he is on the warbird, how do we hold him in place?"

"Put him on the front of my saddle. I have cord there for when I carry a passenger, to hold them in place. We can use that to hold the Emperor in the saddle. I will ride behind him."

Ra'Shone now spoke to both the Emperor Wolf and his Sire. "Do you understand what we are doing? This is the fastest way to get you to safety."

"I understand," the Emperor Wolf *said*. "I will do what no other wolf has done before. I will walk in the sky on your warbird."

The Sire spoke now as well. "I will run to your hospital and see my father there."

Ra'Shone spoke to the Sire. "The battle here is won, so many lost their lives. Now we should all be proud. We have held the line for your city."

"I will send for more help for the wounded here," the knight called down to Ra'Shone as he rode into the air with the Emperor Wolf tied securely in front of him.

Ra'Shone looked over the battlefield. Dead and wounded lay all about the field of battle. Even now those Shiaps who could stand were collecting the dead and transporting the wounded, wolf and man, to safety back at their camp. Wolves and man that were wounded but could walk, sometimes helping each other, slowly withdrew from the battle field to tend their own injuries. A thousand of Jall dead lay about the battlefield. No thought was given to them. Once the dead and wounded of the forces defending the Wolf City were taken care of, then Ra'Shone would take care of the dead of the Jall.

"Let them see the folly of their war," Ra'Shone told those around him.

One of the wolves Lieutenants approached Ra'Shone. "You need to tend to your own wounds," the wolf's mind spoke to Ra'Shone. "You bleed in many places."

"As do you, my friend," Ra'Shone answered. Both stood side by side, ignoring their own injuries, as they saw the last of the wounded carried off the field of battle.

The Jall City

Reed and the fifty Nomads he had chosen, along with their wildcats, were met in Erson by loyalist of the Jall-King. Reed shook hands with each of the Jall who would lead him through the swamp. Each said the same thing to the other, "We stand with you."

The Jall leader, Claude, spoke directly to Reed. "It's a full two days mach to where the boats are waiting."

"Then we must make haste to free your King," was Reeds quick response.

Their route took them to the northern edge of the Great Swamp. They moved without fear of The Hold's spies in this part of the land; they were busy watching the passes to the north.

In the distance, as the party reached the edge of the Great Swamp, they could hear the roars of the Jal-Beasts. Both Nomad and Wildcat were nervous at the sounds of the beast. None had encountered one before, but they had heard the stories.

Claude spoke to the Nomads, almost laughing at their fear. "The beast lives on the eastern shore of the Great Swamp. What you hear is miles away. We have no fear of them where we will be crossing the swamp." Reed and the other Nomads looked at Claude sheepishly; if he showed no fear, neither would they.

It took the full two days to reach the promised boats from Erson; a dozen of them, with their polemen, waited to take them to the Jall City.

"Those you leave us with," Reed asked Claude, "can I trust them?"

"All remain loyal to our King. They will guide you safely and quickly to our city. Most that are dangerous to you have left to join the attack on the Wolf City for its riches." Claude looked closely at Reed one last time before he added, "Bring our King home. I fear for the future of the Jall without him."

The two men clasped arms as Reed in his bluntness said to Claude. "I go to free your King and to help my friends."

"You are but half a day from the city here. Be safe my friend."

The Nomads and their wildcats gingerly boarded the boats. One boat tipped over in the boarding, spilling man and wildcat into the water. The wildcats drenched in the swamps water refused to reboard the boats.

"We will wait for you here," one of the Nomads, whose cat refused reentry, said to Reed. "This is good dry land to camp."

The remaining forty Nomads, their wildcats and the three dozen polemen moved out from shore in the shallow draft boats. It would be a quick and silent trip to the northern edge of the Jall City and a wharf the loyalist held.

Reed looked back over his people in the boats. Then he looked forward as the polemen guided their boats through the maze of reeds that was the Great Swamp. None of his people could hope to make it to the Jall City or back without the help of these men and their boats. The boats reached the edge of the city and their wharfs early that evening. New guides now took the Nomads deeper into the city.

"Where are you taking us?" Reed asked one of the guides as they turned a corner on the wooden avenues that rose just above the swamp. He noticed the woman was unarmed.

"We now know where our King is being held."

"How many in the city stand against us?"

"Most left the city to join the march against your friends. There are fewer than 100 well-armed soldiers of The Hold guarding the building where they hold our King. The shieldmen of The Hold have always been our police and protectors."

"Only 100 from The Hold, not a fair match it seems," Reed mused.

She seemed to misunderstand Reed. "We will do what we can to help, but that is so many."

"I fear them not," Reed confidently answered her concerns. "We are more than enough for ten times that number. He looked over the Nomads and their wildcats that had joined him on the mission. "100 times that number could not defeat us."

She looked at him with a combination of fear and trepidation. Then she looked over at the wildcats, standing in place alongside their Nomad. 'Yes,' she thought, 'these are more than enough.'

"Are there any others that we need to fear here" Reed asked her.

"Our trading clans have never invested in a military or police of our own. Those that remain in the city either don't care about the situation, and there are many of those, or they support our King."

The Nomad's guides led them to a tower, low and broad, that rose from a giant pool of clear water. In the light of the tower Reed could see a handful of The Holds warriors lazily standing watch on the roof. There was no road or bridge to the tower.

"How do we reach them," Reed quietly asked the leader of the guides. He knew her name now, Gwen. She reminded him in her bravery of Loren. His thoughts of Loren made him smile. Soon he would find a way to join her again.

"You smile before battle," she softly spoke to Reed.

"I think now of another, brave like you. She is part of me now."

"She is a Nomad, like you?"

"No, she is an R'mon, hunting on the trail of the Myk."

"I will wish her well in my dreams," Gwen answered. Then she pointed to over 20 small boats sitting on the water's edge.

"Those will take us there?" Reed asked.

Reed had heard the stories his friends of *The Proctant* had told about their first visit to the Jall City; boats that would fly to the tops of the buildings.

"Yes, we will guide the boats with our minds. That's why there are so many of us here to help. It takes a lot of mental strength to move an object, especially like these boats when loaded. Those of us here will have little strength for days. Most of the Jall have this ability but can only move small items before weakening."

"That's why we do not see a lot of your abilities in the world?"

"Yes. Most tasks are easier to do without the aid of this power."

Reed motioned to his men and their wildcats to board the boats. Over a hundred Jall now stood with them on the boardwalk before the giant building. Once all had boarded the boats he ordered the Nomads, "Keep a tight leash on your wildcats. We don't want them jumping off." Ropes had been provided on each boat to hold their passengers on board them.

Reed spoke once more to Gwen. "We are ready."

Almost as one the boats began to silently rise above the waters. It seemed to take mere seconds for the boats with their Nomad riders and their anxious wildcats to reach the roof of the building. The wildcats, happy to leave the boats, were the first to reach the roof, leaping off the boats before they had even touched down. The Nomads quickly followed as the boats touched down on the roof.

It was almost over before it began. Over two dozen shieldmen of The Hold were on the roof. Feeling themselves secure from attack they mostly just talked with each other, each trying to outdo the next with their exaggerated stories. Most of their weapons lay stacked in a pile. Unprepared as they were, the wildcats quickly overpowered them. Not all were killed; most meekly surrendered the moment the wildcats appeared.

"Put them on the boats," Reed commanded. "Let Gwen and her people deal with them."

All but one of the prisoners was placed, weaponless on the boats. Once the prisoners were loaded, Reed signaled down to Gwen and the prisoners were transported back to the boardwalk. The Jall quickly manhandled them out of the boats, no longer fearing them, and sent the boats back up to the roof.

Reed now stood over the one prisoner left on the roof. His wildcat stood above the quivering prisoner.

"Where do you hold the King of these people?" he demanded of the prisoner.

The prisoner acted brave and defiant. Then Reed's wildcat approached him and put its face in that of the prisoner, opening its mouth wide.

"He is in a small room in the basement. I don't know which one for sure," he practically screamed in fear of the wildcats.

Reed and the other Nomads laughed heartily at that.

"Place him in the boat, another for Gwen. We split into parties now; 10 Nomads and wildcats in each group. There are four ways into the building. Each party takes one of them in. Their King is down their somewhere's. We must find him."

The Nomads and their wildcats split into their four groups, each heading for one of the entryways from the roof. If they expected a fight, there wasn't. As each party encountered shieldmen of The Hold, at the warrior's first sight of the wildcats they surrendered. Weaponless they were marched up to the roof where Gwen and her people now awaited them.

"It is as Reed said. These *proud* warriors refuse to fight."

Finally, a prisoner was captured who knew where the Jall-King was hidden in a small corner room in the basement of the building. Reed was given the task by the other Nomads of opening the door. This was his mission, given to him by Wade and Gant, and it would be his honor to finish it.

The door was locked with no key in sight. That was no issue for Reed. While the wildcats looked fiercely on, two of The Holds soldiers were ordered to force the door open. Each shattered their weapons, but they finally forced it open.

The Jall-King sat on a small bench on the far side windowless room, unchained.

"You are free," was all that Reed said to the Jall-King.

"What has happened? I was taken late at night," the Jall-King exclaimed, hurrying to the door.

"Your people march on my friends," Reed answered.

"March on your friends?" the King asked, confused.

"They march to claim the riches my friend, Zircon, found. All of Zircon's friends march to his aid."

"Where is this happening? Take me there."

"First, I will have you taken to Gant. He will decide what is next for you. He sent me to find you. Wade marches against your army."

"That is not my army. Tell me your name, please."

"I am Reed of the Nomads, friend of the Confederation and the Wolf City."

"Reed of the Nomads, take me to Gant. Something must be done to stop this madness."

"Yes," Reed said. "Something must be done. The killing must stop."

Later that night, several warbirds of Nourne, awaiting Reed's signal from the Jall City, alighted on the roof of the building that had held the Jall-King prisoner. One of the knights walked over to Reed after landing.

"Over so quickly," he asked.

"Yes, once again the soldiers of The Hold show they have no stomach for a fight they start. This man," Reed indicated the Jall-King, "must be taken at once to Gant in Twror."

"That will be done." The knight motioned over to one of the others with him. "Take this man immediately to Gant."

After the Jall-King climbed onto the knight's warbird and was loosely tied on, the warbird took off. "Hang on," the knight said to the Jall-King.

The knight standing beside Reed asked if they needed any help out of the city.

"Once our friends here in the Jall city have no need for us, they will take us back. Our wildcats and your warbirds…" Reed trailed off as he answered the knight.

"I understand, you do not wish to abandon them here."

"They are our family," Reed answered him. "And they won the battle here, not us."

Wolf City

Zircon received very little sleep the next few nights. Casualties among the Shiap and the wolves had been heavy from repulsing the Jall attack. The Jall were decimated as a fighting force. Those that could, maybe half, fled to the safety of The Hold's encampments, but at what cost? The Emperor Wolf rested in his city, gravely injured leading the counter- attack that had broken the Jall's will to fight. Zircon now spent most of his time at the side of his friend. The R'mon doctors had placed the wolf on a comfortable cot (Jall doctors were on their way), but the doctors held out little hope for the Emperor Wolfs recovery.

Wade had arrived that morning with the rest of the army of Nourne; over 1000 of their own shieldmen and the remaining members of the Castles airborne knights on their warbirds. Another 1000 from Erson and Twror arrived as well, shortly behind Wade's army. However, what hunters with their bows from the Northern Valley had already arrived, placed behind the fortifications or foraging for the food necessary to keep the Wolf City and the army fed.

Shiap reinforcements continued to trickle in throughout the day and night; it seemed the whole Shiap nation was marching to the aid of the Wolf City. Ra'Shone had sent back word that this was a cause worth fighting for.

Scouts arrived from Nourne as well with word. The remaining armies that had gathered in the Northern Valley, just north of Erson on the Rose Hill plains, were now on the move as well. However, they were still two to three days away. With them as well was another phalanx from the Phoenix. Wagon and oxcarts were doing their best shuttling troops forward to speed up the reinforcements, emptying and returning as quickly as they could. Fresh ox and horse were supplied at each end of the trip in a shuttle.

Wade had assumed overall command of the armies, much to the relief of Zircon. Each commander, as they arrived with their army, put those forces in pre-selected areas where they could do the most good. With the reinforcements, archers were now assembled on each flank as well as the middle. All new arrivals were given tours of the city by the Emperor Wolf's lieutenants so that they could see what they were fighting for. None could believe what they saw in the city, the organization and the communication with the wolves. All understood the importance of preserving this place.

Wade, looking out of Zircon's tower, could see the remainder of The Holds army arrive and assemble in their encampments. Would they attack today? Wade didn't think so. The invading army was not yet organized for attack. 'How much time did they have,' he thought. 'One day, maybe two.' Outnumbered still better than three to one, Wade would continue to do what was necessary to defend the Wolf City.

Wade came down from the tower to find Zircon. He had much to discuss with him concerning the upcoming battle. As Wade walked through the city he saw the terrible sight of the wolf pack carrying injuries, many severe, and being attended to by the doctors of the R'mons. Jall doctors were needed here and quickly; the wolves as a fighting force was done. It was up to man, now, to save this city.

Wade found Zircon where he thought he would, at the bedside of the Emperor Wolf. Two R'mon doctors were attending the Emperor Wolf when Wade arrived. He saw Zircon sitting on a chair next to the cot that held the wolf; the Emperor Wolf's head on a crude pillow that Zircon made of clothing for him. Zircon saw Wade as he came in and waved him over.

"We need more doctors, Wade," Zircon quietly spoke.

The Emperor Wolf tilted his head up and looked at Wade. They had met before, 'another friend among the humans.' "Is the city safe?" he seemed to ask Wade with his mind.

"Yes," Wade answered. "And more arrive to protect it…"

"My tribe, so many hurt…" the Emperor Wolf's minds voice fading as he spoke.

"You should be proud of your tribe. The stories the Shiaps tell of their valor is the stuff that makes legends."

"I am…" the Emperor Wolf whispered.

Wade now spoke to all of those present. "I have received word from our scouts. The Jall-King is freed. He is sending Jall doctors here now, on warbirds to tend wolf and Shiap injuries. They should be here by nightfall."

Zircon looked up at Wade. "Is any more help arriving?"

"I am told the City by the Lake, the Southern Valley and the Coastal People march but a day behind The Holds Army," Wade answered Zircon. He then turned to the Emperor Wolf. "You have many friends among the humans. Please don't judge us by the greed of a few."

"I don't, friend," the Emperor Wolf whispered.

Zircon looked up at Wade again, optimistic for the first time of their chances. "We have a chance then."

"A very good one if we are given the time. The Southern Valley riders are swinging to the south of the armies that face us. They should arrive tonight to join the Shiap. And the Shiap's numbers grow by the hour."

"A brave people, the Shiap."

"I have met Ra'Shone and he commands my respect."

"Are the armies arrayed as they arrive?" Zircon asked.

"As you laid out and the breastworks and fortification the people of Twror and Erson build have become formidable. All who wish, and that is most of those who arrive, are visiting this city and seeing its wonders. They are amazed as I was when I first visited here."

The Emperor Wolf seemed to smile as he looked up at Wade while hearing this.

Wade now asked Zircon, "Have you visited the *Hold* here lately"

"Just yesterday." Zircon brightened up a bit at the mention of his discovery. "It's not yet time to open it."

"What do you think you'll find?"

"All that I can think is that it will be something unexpected given all that's happened to us in this land."

The emperor Wolf now spoke, clearly yet still softly. "That has always been our duty, given to us by those who created us, your Teachers. And we have grown strong in that duty." The Emperor Wolf seemed prouder than before as he spoke these words.

Wade and Zircon just looked at each other at this news. Zircon immediately thought back to the words that Gar had given him, 'something important will be found there.'

Wade started to ask the Emperor Wolf a question, but he had fallen back asleep.

"Let him rest now," one of his doctors told the two men. "Rest is what he needs. I'll notify you if anything changes. Right now, you both have things to do."

For reasons Wade and Zircon failed to understand, for two days The Hold's army remained in their encampment with little sign of movement.

Nourne and The Phoenix, now 2500 strong, now manned the middle, mostly untouched by the combat so far. With them were the hunters and their bows, trading off hunting for food and duty standing with the soldiers. Their quivers were full and large stacks of arrows, many scavenged from The Holds failed attack, stood next to their positions.

On the left were now assembled over 1000 R'mon archers with their crossbows; positioned on the low ridge, waiting behind their new earthworks, thrown up by the citizen army of Twror and Erson.

There were now over 15,000 from Erson and Twror and more arrived by the hour. Untrained and unproven in combat, they were there for their hero, Zircon, and took pride in the building of the earthworks and fortifications their armies would fight from.

The Holds archers had attempted to slow the building of these works. However, a phalanx of the Phoenix stood close by, using their shields for the workers to hide under. With each flight of The Holds flights of arrows, tumbling safely to the ground off the shields of the phalanxes shields, more arrows were collected by the runners for their own use by the defenders of the city. Finally, The Hold's commanders ordered an end to the bombardment and the workers worked unimpeded.

On the right over 1000 riders from the Southern Valley had now arrived to join the Shiaps. The Shiaps had been almost overrun on the first day of battle; only the wolves and their counterattack had saved the Shiaps from destruction. Now the Shiaps engaged in that first battle were having their injuries attended to by the doctors of the R'mon's and the newly arriving doctors of the Jall.

Raymond and Ra'Shone both visited these brave fighters. Although many suffered only minor injuries, most suffered more severe ones and were through in the engagement.

However, on the right, besides the newly arriving Shiaps and their camels and the riders of the Southern Valley, one more army arrived to aid the defenders of the Wolf City. Answering the call from Ra'Shone and the Shiaps, their long-time friend and ally the Franco's, led by their General Alaine, arrived. Over 500 strong, their cavalry carried, besides their eight-foot lances, single shot rifles, not much more primitive than Zircon's own. With the continuous flow of new Shiap arrivals, over 3000 cavalry now stood on the right.

From Castle Nourne, for Zircon's own gun, over 200 rounds arrived: not much, but maybe enough for Zircon to make a difference. He could easily reach the battlefield before him from his tower.

What wolves that remained uninjured of the tribe's fighters were ordered back into the city. They had done their part on that first day. There were growls of disobedience from many of the wolves. Finally, they came to understand and were given orders by the Emperor Wolf's Sire himself, that they were the last line of defense for the city if their human allies failed.

Such was the army that faced over 30,000 warriors of The Hold and the Jall.

The next day, now the third since the initial assault, Zircon and Wade called a meeting of all of their commanders in the city where the Emperor Wolf lay dying. Each in turn, as they entered the room, paid their respects for him. All had heard the stories from the Shiaps how he had led the counterattack that saved the right. The Emperor Wolf's Sire, who would assume the leadership of the tribe upon his death, sat next to the Emperor Wolf and acknowledged each commander in turn as they approached his father. He raised a paw to each, saluting in his own way their courage and much needed help. Each knew that, aside from the untrained citizen army, they were outnumbered better than three to one, maybe even worse than that. All they could do was pray to their Gods and fight to the end. There would be no surrender here.

Each commander knew his job now. And each returned to prepare their armies for the assault they knew would come the next morning. The armies opposing them were positioning themselves for that attack. Before they left the side of the Emperor Wolf, he *spoke* to each of them in turn, thanking them for their help in preserving his tribe.

Zircon and Wade left the side of the Emperor Wolf last. He asked them, "Will my city be saved?"

Zircon answered the Emperor Wolf one last time as he knelt alongside him. He could see the wolf's time was coming to an end. He stroked the wolf's fur as did Wade, kneeling on the other side of the bed.

"We will hold your city and our friendship will last an eternity."

The Emperor Wolf laid his head back on the pillow Zircon had made from his clothing. He could smell Zircon's scent on the clothing. His breathing was now heavy and labored. He looked up at Zircon and brushed his soft tongue against Zircon's close face. "Thank-you, my friend," he seemed to say. Then his eyes grew vacant as he died in Zircon's arms.

Zircon and Wade continued kneeling next to the bed for several minutes. Finally, the new Emperor Wolf, the Sire of their friend and now the leader of the tribe, nudged the two men in turn with his nose.

"There will be time to mourn my father when this is over," his mind spoke to the men, his friends as well. "Now is the time to prepare for what's coming."

Zircon and Wade both stood. The doctors started cleaning the stains of battle from the old Emperor's fur. Both were openly crying at the loss of their friend. Tears were openly flowing from their eyes as they left the room to prepare for battle. Promises were made that had to be kept. The new Emperor Wolf, head held high, walked beside them.

The next morning, as expected, it began. First the sky darkened by the thousands of arrows from The Holds archers filled the air. Flight after flight was launched as quickly as the bows could be reloaded. The arrows sailed over the earthworks into the assembling armies of Nourne and the Phoenix. Shields were raised skyward to deflect the arrows; however, more than a few still found their mark. The cries of anguish from those hit filled the air. The citizen army turned and ran at the sight of the darkened sky. They had no defenses against such an onslaught. And then it was over, the skies clear. The defenders looked around at each other and then reformed. Hundreds were dead or injured and the doctors from the Jall and the R'mons moved quickly to take the injured to the field hospitals set up beyond the range of The Holds archers.

From his tower vantage point Zircon was able to see the whole field of battle before him. He had seen The Holds archers move forward and had signaled down to the troops below as a warning. The warning arrived just in time to prevent carnage among the soldiers of Nourne and the Phoenix. Now Zircon could see the troops of The Hold and what remained of the Jall move forward, this time the Jall in a support position behind the three large shieldmen formations of The Hold; one to the right, one to the left and one moved straight ahead. Zircon signaled down to his runners below; prepare for the assault, archers forward. The citizen army of Erson and Twror reformed in the middle. The wolves anxiously paced in front of their city.

The signals Zircon used were brought to the armies defending the Wolf City by the Phoenix and were quickly embraced by the commanders. Scouts on horseback rushed the commands to each flank of the defenders.

The sky filled once more in darkness; this time it was the archers of the defenders as each army of The Hold reached the range of the woodsmen archers.

Warbirds filled the sky, those of the Jall on their own warbirds recklessly charged forward in the air, only to be brought down by the hunter's bows of the peasants they underestimated as a fighting force. What few remained returned back to the camp of The Hold. This battle would be determined on the ground.

The arrows of the hunters of the Northern Valley fell mostly harmlessly to the ground at the feet of The Hold's shieldmen marching one step forward at a time, their shields held aloft, protecting them. At two hundred yards that changed. Now the archers from the Phoenix and the R'mon crossbowman let loose their barrages. These were not mere hunting bows with a high arch depleting their power before they arrived. These were the power of the crossbow and long bow; short-range straight flights, that carried the full force of their archer's bows. Shieldmen began to fall by the hundreds, but now close to the barriers in front of them and their lines almost undiminished they double stepped it forward. On the other side of the earthworks the soldiers of Nourne and the phalanxes of the Phoenix locked shields and arms to prepare to meet the charge that was coming.

The archers, by now, had finished most of their flights in the center and the left. On the right the hunters and their bows were moving in front of the mounted forces of the Shiaps, the Southern Valley and the Franco's. Against them marched over 6,000 shieldmen moving confidently forward against the defenders in front of them. Once again the arrows of the hunter's bows fell mostly harmlessly to the ground and the shieldmen moved confidently forward.

As the shieldmen approached the hunters let loose the last of their flights of arrows and then scampered behind the mounted troops of the defenders. Each force prepared to make its charge; the Shiaps against one flank of the advancing soldiers, the riders of the Southern Valley to hit the other. Only from the sides could they hope to defeat the shieldmen before them; to charge straight on would be suicide. Now only the mounted horsemen of the Franco stood in front of the marching shieldmen.

At two hundred yards the first volley hit the shieldmen, not arrows, but the fire of the 500 rifles aimed at them. Every three minutes a new volley hit them. The shieldmen began to charge, but they started staggering off-balance as they tried to step over their fallen comrades. Their lines became disorganized, wavering. Fifty yards now from the horsemen and their lines now were completely disorganized, no longer protecting the sides of the man next to them. And then the Shiap and Southern Valley hit each flank. There was chaos in the shieldmen's lines and they were hit from every side. Still the rifles of the Franco discharged their fire. A new weapon commanded the battlefield and the shieldmen began to fall back, evenly at first, then in a mad rush to the rear, their lines crumbling as they fled. The riders paused their attacks and just watched the shieldmen flee. It was over in minutes. As Ra'Shone, Raymond and Alain viewed the battlefield they expected to see thousands of the shieldmen dead on the field of battle. They saw very few. The lines of the shieldmen had broken and fled with very few casualties amongst themselves. The defenders even fewer. Once again, the valor of The Hold warriors proved a myth.

Raymond looked over at the other two generals and asked, "Do we pursue?"

Each of the other two generals just nodded their heads, no.

"The power of The Hold was broken this day," Ra'Shone added in response.

In the middle things were dicier. Even with the casualties inflicted by the archers of the R'mon and the Phoenix, over 10,000 reached the breastworks thrown up before them. As they reached the crest of the barriers the archers unleashed the last of their bows and prepared to meet the charge on the flanks of the defensive line with the citizen army. The shieldmen were unwavering in their line and moved only forward at the center of the defender's line.

Help for the defenders now came from the sky. With each side's archers fully depleted of their arrows the sky belonged to the warbirds and their knights. They pin-wheeled out of the sky with their long scythe-like weapons, reaching downward to strike. They wrecked new carnage on the attackers.

The few remaining warbirds of the Jall tried to help, but weakened from their premature charge against the hunter's bows, they could do little more than watch.

At the top of the earthworks and just beyond the warbirds struck. As they struck the warriors of the phalanxes began to move forward themselves, to meet the attackers at the earthworks. With their discipline and drive they met the shieldmen of The Hold at the earthworks and held firm.

The soldiers of Nourne moved to place themselves alongside their brothers from the Phoenix, but there were just two many making it over the breast works. Holding for over an hour, the defenders line threatened to crumble on both sides while the middle held strong. Even the strength of the phalanxes was not enough as they were pushed back, yard by yard. The citizen army of Erson and Twror tried to stem the attacks on either side, but they fell back in turn. The Nomads now moved forward to protect the flanks with their wildcats and some havoc was wrought on each side where they struck. But there were just too many of the attackers.

As the human troops began to fall back to the city's entry, the wolves, under their new Emperor Wolf, prepared to add what they could to the defender's effort.

Zircon, using the last of the ammunition provided for his rifle, felt now the city was lost. Would salvation arrive in time?

It was Alaine on the right who saw first the danger of the collapsing middle. He called over Raymond and Ra'Shone. "Make sure that those before us continue to flee and do not reform. We ride to the middle where our guns our needed."

"We ride with you," Ra'Shone shouted to his men.

"Against that mass of shields you would stand little chance. This is a ride only we Franco's can take."

With that he turned and led the charge of the Franco cavalry into the left of the shieldmen attack at the cities entrance. At 200 yards they stopped their charge and the shieldmen there turned to meet them.

"How much do each of you now carry," Alain asked his men. None had more than a dozen rounds.

"Then we make each round count," as he turned towards the shieldmen and fired his own gun that signaled in turn his own men to begin the attack. 500 rifles now fired and reloaded as one. And, like on the flank, the shieldmen had no defense for the rifles. Those on the flanks turned and fled. And as they turned the middle of the shieldmen line began to stagger as bullets flew into them from the side as well.

Zircon, out of ammunition for his rifle, saw it first as he charged down from the tower, even before the scouts in the air. Coming over the ravines to the east were the armies of The City by the Lake and the Coastal Peoples.

The Hold had kept no reserve; they had thrown everything at the Wolf City. The Coastal People's army arrived in the Holds encampment first and quickly overran it. The Hold's archers tried to defend the camp, but without arrows for their bows, they were quickly overrun. Once past the encampment the two armies (City by the Lake and the Coastal People's) split apart, attacking the rear of The holds army in a pincer movement.

With The Hold's army now under attack front and rear, what remained of the Southern Valley's riders and the Shiaps rode in from the flank. The R'mons on the left unleashed the last of the bolts from their crossbows and charged down the hill.

Alexandre and his Phalanxes, almost untouched in battle now drove forward as one, pushing the shieldmen back over the earthworks. The soldiers of Nourne collapsed the flank they were facing and The Hold's shieldmen started to panic.

Erson and Twror now added their weight to the battle and the defenses of The Holds army folded away, the battle turning into a route. Zircon, looking at the battlefield before him couldn't believe his eyes at what was happening. After four hours of battle all the armies of the Confederation, along with their new friends and allies now encircled The Hold's and the Jall soldiers. The airborne knight of Castle Nourne commanded the air as the warbirds of the Jall landed to surrender.

As the allied troops slowly tightened their circle around the soldiers they faced, the shieldmen of The Hold began to throw down their arms. They surrendered in mass to avoid the extermination they otherwise faced.

The remaining Jall, and there were still several thousand, grouped together. Traitors to their Trader-King they retreated to the center of the battlefield, standing alone with nowhere to go.

A poignant quiet took place over the battlefield. Zircon, Wade, Raymond, Ra'Shone and Alexandre, all carrying wounds from the conflict, gathered together at the front of their armies. Terms of surrender had to be determined. The parties were split over any reprisals.

"We cannot allow this to go unpunished," Raymond and Alexandre jointly said.

"The punishment must be such that the Confederation remains intact," was Wade's enjoinder.

As the Generals in command tried to hash out the terms of surrender The Jall-King arrived with Reed on warbirds. They quickly joined the conference of the victors.

The Jall-King spoke first. "I cannot allow those that fought against me, those that imprisoned me, to return to the Jall City."

"Where can they go then?" asked Wade.

Lorenzo of the Coastal People spoke now. "In the inland Sea there is an island, yet raw and almost untouched since before the Great War. There is valuable material there for trade, marble of great beauty. I suggest exiling those of the Jall who took part in this battle, and their families, to this island. It will be tough for them in the beginning. However, we will give them what they and their families need to make this island a success."

"How does that strike you?" Wade asked the Jall-King.

"That is agreeable to me. How will they travel to this island?"

"We will supply them the transport ships to arrive there," answered Lorenzo. "They will pay for their transportation with future goods in trade."

"And the Army of the Hold," asked Ra'Shone.

Reed now gave the telling answer to that question. "The Hold's shieldmen are now a relic of the past. Twice they have folded in combat. Let them throw down their weapons here and return to their city in disgrace. That should be enough for them."

"And The Hold then remains part of the Confederation?" asked Zircon.

"Yes," answered Wade. "And invitations will be extended to all that fought here."

Damien now happily spoke up. "We came to this land to defend your Confederation. My people see the value of the friendships gained here today. I am authorized to formally request membership in this good thing."

Alain spoke quickly following Damien. "We of the West, the Francos, friends of Ra'Shone and the Shiap people also request to join this growing thing. Let us all live in peace as one."

Zircon himself now approached the general of The Hold and the leader of the Jall. Standing with the new Emperor Wolf at his side he presented the terms of surrender. The generals looked at Wade in defeated tones. Then they looked at the giant wolf standing alongside him. Into their minds the wolf spoke. "Why did you attack my city?"

The generals were dumbfounded and almost fell to their knees. They easily understood the words of the Emperor Wolf.

"Well." Zircon asked. "Do you accept these terms?"

None of the invaders had a choice. Each lay their weapons at the feet of the Emperor Wolf, turned back to their troops and walked slowly back to them in disgrace.

The defeated army of the Hold began the long march back to their city, weaponless and crestfallen. Their days of glory were past and they had no future.

The wolves now surrounded the remaining Jall who still stood defeated, but defiant.

"We do not accept this exile," many cried out.

The Wolves now began to approach these humans who had killed their Emperor and so many of their pack. Only the fierceness of the Emperor Wolf and his lieutenants kept this, so far, from becoming a massacre.

Zircon now approached the Jall himself. He was tired of the killing.

"You have a choice here today, men of Jall. A choice you did not give the Wolf City. Stay here and die at the hands of the wolf pack or accept your exile."

"What choice do we have," their leader spoke aloud as he looked all around them at the eyes of the angry wolf pack, "We accept."

Zircon sat in his chair in the tower that he now called his home. The Jall-king had ordered the Jall to repair and reconstruct it to its former glory as part of the penance before they left on their exile to the island of marble.

The new Emperor Wolf, Sire of the Emperor Wolf that had been Zircon's friend and died protecting his pack, watched closely as two wolf pups climbed all over Zircon's lap. These pups were his; sired shortly before the battle to protect his city had taken place.

The new Emperor Wolf carried his own scars from battle. One foreleg was damaged enough that he walked mostly with three legs. An ear was gone and he carried a scar across his head. The injuries came as he was protecting his father, the old Emperor Wolf, in combat; he and Ra'Shone arriving too late to save him.

The pups were good for what ailed Zircon. He quietly mourned his friend. This Wolf City would be his home now.

There would still be more adventures for Zircon he knew; a world to discover and the Myk to find.

Nevertheless, here would be the place that Zircon would always return to in the future to find peace.

Chapter 16
Argonia Reborn

Sarah had given in to the realization that she would soon be dead, thrown off the cliffs edge to the rocks below; a wasted sacrifice to the false gods of the High Priests.

She looked over at her older brother. At least he would live on and help spread the fruit of the tree of knowledge. Maybe he would be successful in making her sacrifice the last. Too many virgin daughters died below on their final journey to satisfy the beliefs of the Priests.

Sarah was a member of the Sect of Knowledge. This alone would have been enough for the Priests to declare her a heretic who must be killed. To preserve Argonia they would say. To keep the power of the Priest King and the ignorance of the people was the truth.

Sarah glanced over at her uncle on the edge of the crowd. He had introduced her and her brother, Michael, to the forbidden sect. He had shown them both the power of truth. Now her time was measured in minutes, not years.

"The time will come when we will be strong enough to overthrow the Priest King and his cult. To restore Argonia to its rightful place under God," her uncle had said.

"When?" Sarah and Michael had asked in their youthful spirit of the now.

"Soon," was all that he was able to tell them.

Sarah could see the anguish in her uncle and brothers faces as she stood and faced the Priest King in just a light cotton cover, made from the ball of White cotton twine she had played with as a child not so very long ago, before her parents died in the accident.

Her father had been felling trees for a new temple when the Priests called for her mother and sent her with a message to her husband on the far side of the island. That was the last time Sarah and Michael had seen either of their parents alive.

"An accident, they fell to their deaths," was what the Priests had told them. "Your father was cutting a tree too close to the edge. He slipped and your mother fell trying to save him." That was the official story, the Priests story. However, Sarah and Michael had learned the truth from their uncle who adopted them.

After their induction into the Sect of Knowledge, they learned that their parents had also been members. A slip of the tongue and they had been found out. It was the Priests goal to capture them together and then use their children to find more of the Sect. It was the way of the priest's cult that they killed heretics in secret after they divulged as much as the torture could provide. Accidents set an example for those of the Sect that remained in secret; a way to keep the general population of Argonia from knowing of the Sect of Knowledge and its strength. As none of the others of the cell that Sarah and Michael's parents were part of disappeared, their uncle thought that the two had indeed gone over the cliff together. Not in an accident, but a joint suicide to protect their children and the Sect.

The Priest-King approached Sarah now and callously tore shift from her body. "You go now to Zacar as Zacar brought you into this world." He leered at her breasts and naked body as he picked Sarah up and raised her over his head, only steps from the cliff's edge.

"Sarah," her uncle cried out, unable to stop the madness.

"Revenge," were the words of her brother under his breath, not daring to speak the Truth.

Many members of the Sect were in the crowd, over half if they had known their actual numbers. However, each cell remained invisible to the others, protection against the watchful eyes of the Priests.

"Halt," came a call from the back of the crowd. The men of *The Proctant* stepped forward as one. This was something that none of them could just stand by and watch. "Put the girl back down," another of the crew called out as the ship-wrecked crew came forward. They had heard of these sacrifices on their arrival in Argonia. Their appearance had caused one to stop. Now they moved forward as a group to face the Priest-King.

"Who are you, strangers from the sea that surrounds us, to interfere with our reverence to our God?" one of the priests asked the shipmates.

A mummer rose throughout the crowd. At first just a few and then more and more of the crowd began yelling "Put her down!" The roar spread throughout the crowd. As the roar increased, the Sect of Knowledge members began to understand that they were the strongest now. The shipmates took the girl from the Priest-king's arms and he fled with the other priest from the crowd. A cheer went up through much of the crowd now. The revolution had begun.

The shipmates quickly surrounded the intended sacrifice victim, Sarah. Her brother Michael and uncle Victor also rushed to her side. Victor took off the cloak he wore and put it over the shivering Sarah's shoulders to cover her.

The villagers now began to separate into two groups; the Sect of Knowledge gathering around Sarah and the crew of *The Proctant* and those that remained true to the Priest-king and Zacar moved towards the village. Each side looked at the other with growing suspicion.

"You will bring down the wrath of Zacar on us," was heard among the followers of their god.

Neither side carried weapons. Those were forbidden except for the priests. The crew now carried theirs, gathered by each of them when they heard that the sacrifice would take place. Only Milne was missing among the crew. Where he had often gone to remained a mystery to the crew as Milne kept the secret of the cavern to himself.

Slowly a new group, a handful of villagers, approached the crowd around Sarah. Milne was with this group.

"Milne, where have you been keeping yourself?" asked Niob, in nominal command of the crew.

Milne, Altur and Kristof looked around at the size of the group of villagers that surrounded Sarah; many fold more than they had believed belonged to the Sect.

"I have much news for you. But first we need a safe place for these people."

"We are safe here," Boron spoke to Milne. "The priest-Kings have fled and we have the only weapons."

"They will be back with whatever weapons they possess," Kristof said to the group.

"We have weapons from before the Great War," Chuak said to Boron. "If some people come with me we can collect those weapons. They were protected in metal boxes. Milne…"

"Who are you?" Niob asked the tall man in his dark blue Robe.

"I am Chuak, the Sage of this island."

"The Sage?" Bell asked a little bewildered by Chuak.

Milne now took the lead. "I'll go over all of that later." He pointed to Victor and the others around Sarah. "I assume you are all in the Sect of Knowledge?"

"Yes," answered Victor. "We had no idea that there were so many of us. Most of the village it now seems."

One of the villagers, Stephen, continued on with what Victor said. "It was a secret; we thought that we were very few."

Sarah spoke to the crowd around her, collecting herself in a loud voice. She held her uncles cloak tightly around herself. "The other villagers are not our enemies. They must be spared."

"And if they choose to fight us. The Priests have weapons," one of the Sect of Knowledge called out to her.

Stepping forward Lute said loudly to the crowd. "We can handle the priests. And you outnumber their followers." He looked at the other crewmen. "We will deal with the Priest-King."

All the crew nodded affirmatively.

As the two groups, villagers and crew started to separate, Milne now once more stepped forward. He turned to Chuak, Michael and Victor. "Gather a dozen of the villagers you know and follow Chuak. He'll take you to our cavern."

"Cavern?" Michael questioned Milne.

"Yes, the cavern. Gather what weapons are held there. Maybe if the Sect is armed, the followers of Zacar will back away."

The villagers just looked at one another, still amazed by how many there were of them. Michael and Victor pointed to a dozen people they knew well.

"Follow me," Chuak said to the handful Victor and Michael gathered. "We will not hurry. The cliff-side trail is very dangerous."

Niob now took charge of the crew. "We must be ready for anything, whatever the priests can do."

While the villagers stood together *The Proctant's* crew drew around Niob and Milne, each anxious about what they had just started on the Island. Niob turned to Milne, "Tell us what you know, but just a quick summary. We don't have much time and a lot of this that has happened seems…strange; Priest-Kings, the Sect of Knowledge, and where have you been. We have scarcely seen you since we arrived here."

Milne began his story; of being contacted by the Sect of Knowledge; the cavern and its computer, the teachers and their Sage, and finally visiting the Northern Valley for Wade's marriage.

"What?" Bell asked incredulously. "Wade has married a princess?"

"Yes, and Thul and I are brothers, a generation apart. Our father was Simon, sent to this part of the world by the Teachers."

"Who are these teachers?" Samuel asked.

"A short answer is they were visitors from the stars who arrived just before the Great War. They did what they could to save the survivors. They worked at times with the original people who came to this island just before that war."

"This is beyond me," Boron exclaimed. "I am a man of science. And you tell me that people from another world saved man from its stupidity."

"Yes," said Milne, stoically. "I have seen proof of their existence in our past."

The crew of *The Proctant* looked at each other a little uneasy at all they heard. A tool of the Teachers; Kristof had told this to Milne and he now told the crew in his story.

Kristof himself now began speaking. "It seems that your voyage was preordained by the Teachers. Having Simon's two sons in your crew is astounding. And whatever lands you have touched have brought positive change. In the land where I am from the people are now unified as one by the leadership shown by your Thorium, Wade, Zircon and the others.

"Zircon, a leader?" Niob questioned Kristof.

"Yes, he was the final piece to bring our lands together as one."

Now the crew looked at each other even more amazed. Thorium and even Wade they could be seen as leaders; but Zircon. All remembered him as the disturbed malcontent who kept to himself.

"I have seen this change in Zircon, myself," Milne now added to the story. "At Wades wedding he stood with me a changed man, his arms still healing from the burns he suffered trying to save a burning family."

Niob once more took charge of the situation. "Time for us to get back on track. Lute, Bell, you still have your rifles I see."

"Yes," both men answered.

"Bloodshed must be avoided; but I fear the priests won't allow that."

A young priest approached Niob. He was alone and hadn't fled with the Priest-King and the other priests. He had stood to one side as the priest-King had attempted the sacrifice. "I am of the Sect of Knowledge, as was my father whom the priests killed. I was taken from them as a young boy and made a priest. I do not fully agree with the Sect on many things, but I know the Priest-King and his followers are wrong. I have read parts that remain of our Holy Book and I see where our priests have faltered. It is not the Sun that we should be worshiping, nor Zacar, but the son of God. And I see now in the work of the Teachers that they are part of this.

"My name is Paul. The Priest-King and many of the Priests will not surrender to you," he pointed to the crewman as he said this. "They know no other way. I have a small hope that a few of my fellow priests will follow me. We have much to teach the villagers that follow Zacar."

"Take me to your Temple," Niob ordered the young priest. "We will move now, quickly, before they can recruit their followers in the village against us."

"Follow me," Paul said as he began to walk a trail along the top of the Cliffside.

Niob next spoke to Kristof before he followed Paul and his crew. "Keep the Sect of Knowledge here, safe."

The crewmen now marched as a unit behind Paul; Lute and Bell carrying their loaded single-shot rifles.

Chuak led the villagers that came with him down the narrow pathway in the Cliffside to the cavern below. He stopped at the turning stone and explained to each its danger. Once all were safely past the stone, he led them through the curtain of air at the caverns entrance and into the cavern.

Sarah was part of the small group. As she passed through the curtain of air, she immediately felt the warmth of the cavern. She noticed equipment around the entrance, still running and finally the computer with its screen. As the rest filled in their exclamations were all the same.

"How long has this been here?"

"How did you keep it secret from us all?"

Sarah pointed to the computer screen. "What is this, who is she?"

The woman on the screen looked out at her. "My name is Amelie. I am a scholar from the Library."

Sarah looked on mystified as did the others. This was technology long since lost on the surface of the island. Chuak walked over to the screen and spoke to Amelie. "It's begun here."

"Do you need help? I can call for Thul."

"No, it seems like our Teachers foretold. Once more the strangers from across the sea are creating what is necessary for change to happen."

"I await word for Thul and the others."

"Thank-you, Amelie. I will call you when it's over, stay at your station."

"I will stay, Sage."

Chuak now turned to the villagers that had accompanied him into the cavern. "We have work to do. Once our revolution is over, we will bring word of what's here to the surface. Follow me."

Chuak walked to the back of the cavern. There, against the wall, were stacks of metal boxes. Chuak broke open the rusty lock on the first one. All that remained was rust, rotted wood and bits of plastic scattered throughout the box. Another box was opened, the same thing. All the boxes as they now rushed to open them were in the same condition; the weapons rusted and rotted from the millennia of storage.

Chuak was disappointed, but also strangely relieved. Without these weapons perhaps, just perhaps, more villagers would be spared.

"Its time to return to the surface," he told the villagers with him. "We'll be needed there. "

As Sarah remained sitting at the computer screen Chuak called to her as well. "Come with me Sarah. When this is over, I promise to explain the computer to you.'

The scholar on the screen, Amelie, smiled at Sarah. "I look forward to seeing you again, Sarah."

The villagers now followed Chuak back up the trail in the cliff face to the surface and their comrades above.

Paul led the crew of *The Proctant* along a path to the Temple of Zacar. The crewmen recognized some of the coastline from their aborted attempts to land.

In the distance they sighted, as they rounded a grove of trees, the temple; not high but still imposing.

"How many wait for us there, Paul?" Niob asked.

"No more than twenty priests and the Priest-King. The number of priests is limited to twenty-one, a holy number to us."

"Will they fight?"

Paul just put his arms forward, palms out. "I don't know. Many are friends. I just don't know," he solemnly said.

"You wait here. You have done your part."

"Thank-you," Paul said and he retreated to the grove of trees.

To his handful of crewmen Niob gave his command. "We move on the temple. We only fight those who fight us. Lute, Bell just try to injure the priests; arm and leg shots. The Priest-King is our goal."

The men now moved forward in a line towards the Temple, in clear view of the Priest-King.

The Priest-King and his priests all came out of the Temple. Each carried a long, pointed wooden shaft, each one tipped with metal. The Priest-King carried a short sword as well; useful against the villagers, not so useful here.

Niob stopped moving forward as did the other crewmen on either side of him. "This can end without bloodshed," he called out to the Priest-King and his priests.

"Die infidels," the Priest-King shouted at the crewmen as he led the priests forward against the lightly armed (so he thought) crew. His priest far outnumbered the men before him.

The Priest-King called out to Paul, standing in front of the stand of trees. "You will die for your sins here."

Niob looked over at Lute and Bell. Each had their rifles aimed at the leg of an adversary. A difficult shot but each was confident.

"Fire one shot and reload. We'll see the effect."

Each fired their rifle and two priests crumpled to the ground, wounded.

The priests halted their advance and several of them drew back.

"What devilry is this?" the Priest-King shouted into the air. "Zacar will protect us. Forward my priests, know that God is on our side."

Most of the priests moved forward together once more, closing at a fast walk on the crew of *The Proctant*.

"One more shot from each of you," Niob ordered, "to wound and not to kill."

Two more shots and two more priests crumpled to the ground. Now half of the priest stopped their advance and drew back. The Priest-King just looked at those priests with fire in his eyes. In his madness he drew back and threw his spear, striking one of the retreating priests in the back, killing him.

The Priest-King now turned back to face the crewmen, standing almost alone. "We fight for our God," he screamed as he and the remaining two priests charge the crew of *The Proctant*.

Niob looked over at Lute. "A kill shot, the Priest-King," was all he said in a stoic voice. Lute's shot rang out and hit the Priest-King in the chest, bringing him to the ground, instantly killed. All but two of the priests now began to run back to their sanctuary in the Temple.

The remaining two priests, upon seeing their Priest-King fall to the ground, dead, made a suicide charge at the crew, their long spears leveled before them. Bell brought down one with his rifle. Boron deflected the spear of the other and brought him to his knees with a non-lethal blow to his back.

Paul came forward from the stand of trees. It was over. The reign of the Priest-King was done.

Milne turned to Paul. "It's up to you now. Do you need our help?"

"I think not," Paul answered. "Thank-you for your grace, only two had to die. Now I will work to teach them the true meaning of our Holy Book."

Paul walked forward, arms outstretched, "You are safe now, my brothers."

The followers of the Sect of Knowledge now moved as one into their village, unsure of what had transpired at the Temple. Those that followed the Priest-King cowered before them. Sarah moved to the front one last time.

"You have nothing to fear from us. You are our brothers and sisters, fathers and mothers, uncles and aunts. We are all from one family here."

Both sides stood uncertain in their groups. Sarah, still just wearing the cloak her uncle had given her, stood in the middle, between them.

Kristof saw them first, coming through the fields of crops almost ready to harvest; the crew of *The Proctant*.

"Its over," Milne called out.

And it was truly over on Argonia. The cult of the Priest-Kings ended and a hope for a new start for the island.

Chapter 17
The end of the Myk

Since leaving the site of the planned myk ambush, Thorium continued to lead the expedition to the east. The direction they moved was almost due east now with the ice shield of the North clearly visible only a few days ride north of their route. It seemed that the ice extended further to the south as they moved east.

They now followed a wide ancient way of the past; overgrown through much of it, the way provided the caravan an easy pathway for their travels.

Hundreds of Gypsy clans were now part of the caravan, their wagons carrying their wives and children with whatever property they possessed. This had become a great crusade for the Gypsy people against the terror of the myk that had devastated their communities.

The men were now all on horseback. The Gypsy riders now numbering in the hundreds, continued to fan out in all directions. After seeing what had so narrowly been avoided, Thorium made sure the riders maintained constant communications with the caravan. A sort of word and hand gesture language grew quickly between the common speech of the expedition and the fluid language of the Gypsies. Together they found much in common between the two languages.

Gar kept his mental awareness of the myk's minds in sharp focus. There always seemed to be myk around them. The myk's minds were weakening; possibly a sign of the disease inflicting them before they died. As the caravan traveled east, they encountered more of the dying myk, as well as the remains of those already dead. The Gypsies just left the bodies where their lay; a fitting ending to the suffering they felt at the hands of the myk.

Always in the distance, Gar could feel Kat's presence. And Kat's mind remained strong.

A week's travel from the intended ambush, the path split into a northeast direction towards the ice and southeast away from it. Here at the junction the influence on Gar's mind seemed to come from two directions. To the south was a large group of myk. To the north was

Kat and just a few myk. Gar met with Thorium as they debated which way to go.

"Thorium," Gar spoke, "Kat must be able to *see* my mind as well as I can see his."

"And what does that mean to you?" Thorium asked, stroking his chin as he tried to decide which way to go.

"It means that he is trying to lead us away from the Myk's cavern. Why else would he move away from so many myk?"

"He fears the illness that has taken so many of the myk." Loren responded.

"Regardless," Gar countered, "doesn't that indicate that our course to travel should be directed southward. That must be where the Myk's cavern lies."

"That makes sense to me," Jamen added to the conversation. "And it is the Myk's cavern that we seek."

"To the south then, we follow Gar's lead," Thorium proposed to all those around him.

"Yes," they all agreed as one.

"We find the Myk!" Sebastian shouted as he raised his fist to the sky.

Everybody joined in with his shout and his salute to the sky, expedition and Gypsy alike.

"To find the Myk!" All the Gypsies carried the shout the length of the caravan as they broke camp to prepare for the trip down the southern byway.

On a low mountain in the distance, Kat did indeed pickup Gar's thoughts. His deception had worked. He had brought the expedition close enough to the Myk's cavern that they could now find it on their own.

They would find the Myk and his followers dead or dying in that cavern. They would return to the two valleys with the information that the menace of the Myk was over. There would be no further planned ambush though, as much as Kat hated to admit it. The Gypsies joining the caravan had ended that dream of his.

Kat would remain free in his northern Hold in the ice that he had found. Those myk who remained immune to the disease, like Kat, would find there way there in one's and two's, guide by Kats thoughts.

Food source, mostly Gypsy was alive and secure for them in that Hold. They would reproduce, by force if necessary, and provide the slave labor and sustenance Kat and his followers would need to grow. Already the first litters from the females were close to arriving; several from Kat's own seed.

The myk would grow once more under Kat. Someday they would get their revenge.

Locklear had by now joined Kat on the march north. 'A useful idiot,' thought Kat. He could still be of some use. There were still some books that he could read the secrets of for Kat. And when his usefulness was done, he would be added to the food source.

Kat smiled as he marched north into the icy wastelands. They still had weeks to travel to reach the Hold. There was just Kat, two myk and Locklear. The gypsies they brought along, tied with ropes around their necks, would provide the nourishment that Kat and the myk needed, kept alive through the drugs Kat carried. Locklear could survive on the food he carried, and if it wasn't enough. Well, he really wasn't needed anymore anyways. A Sage as food source, the idea intrigued Kat.

Locklear could only march in silence, struggling to keep up with the others, disgusted by the sight of the myk feeding.

'What have I done,' he thought.

As the expedition and the caravan moved to the south, they spotted several more of the skeleton cities around on either side of the way. Far to the south they began to see the strange blueness in the night sky of the Teachers abode when they were on the planet.

As they gazed at the blueness at night, each of the Sage had the same thought. 'Will the Teachers return someday?'

The number of dead and dying myk that passed along the way continued to increase the further south they went. Gar's hold on the thoughts of the large group of myk ahead grew stronger with every mile. Meanwhile, his hold on Kat's thoughts grew weaker. He heard Kat's thoughts on Locklear as food source and passed it on to the other Sage.

"A fitting end," said Tor without remorse.

Another week's march to the South and Gar rode up to where Thorium, Jamen and Loren rode point.

"We are getting very close now, I can feel them. Hundreds of myk very close. And I think I can pick up the thoughts of the Myk himself as well."

"How strong do they seem?" Thorium asked the Sage. "Do we need to call in the riders?"

"I feel hundreds of them, but all seem extremely weak, including the Myk himself. I think that they are all dying of the disease."

"What do you think, Jamen, I value your judgment here," Thorium asked.

"I say we call in the riders. The space here is big enough with plenty of visibility for an encampment. We should have the Gypsies wait here for word from us. The rest of us will head to the cavern. If what Gar feels is correct, the nine of are enough."

"I agree with that," Sebastian now spoke up. "From here the wildcats can lead the way to go and we can follow close behind on horseback, weapons ready for any surprises."

Tor added his voice to the conversation. "They are close now; even I can feel their presence."

"We travel light, close behind the wildcats," Thorium gave the command. "The Gypsies will make their encampment here. We leave in the morning."

One of the Gypsies riders, close by, heard the command and relayed it down the now two mile length of the caravan.

That night the entire Gypsy encampment on the trail of the Myk knew the end was near. Campfires were lit and meals prepared. The gypsy music could be heard throughout the encampment. Thorium and Del traveled the length of the encampment well into the evening, greeting each Gypsy clan in turn. The men all raised their hunting bows in salute to the two men.

"We will be ready," were the words the two men heard from every clan. "If you need us, we will be ready."

Thorium truly had his army to take on the Myk, brave and fearless, ready to take on the challenge if needed.

And Thorium prayed that they would not be needed.

The next morning all arose early, the anticipation of the end of their crusade in the air. The expedition was all on horseback within an hour of awakening, meals in their bellies, following the wildcats out of the encampment. Another skeleton city rose in the distance, their destination.

Thorium, Sebastian and Jamen rode in the front, close behind the wildcats. The three Sage rode in the middle. Mendy, Alum and Loren brought up the rear, watchful for any myk who might try to attack them from the rear.

They traveled over a very small way, almost entirely overgrown, on a pathway the myk going to their leader's cavern here must have made. Near the apparent entrance to the city the riders stopped and the wildcats passed nervously a few dozen feet away. Dozens of dead and dying myk lay before them, strewn about the entrance into the city; if there to defend their hidden cavern, they were now of no danger to the expedition.

"Well,' Thorium told the party around him, "we travel on foot from here."

"I can feel the Myk," Gar quietly said. "He is very close and very weak."

The wildcats prowled around the dying myk near where they dismounted. Even the wildcats showed no taste for the myk they smelled.

As the party entered the city, two myk tried to stand, to impede their entry. Each stood only for a moment before collapsing back onto the ground.

Tor spoke aloud as they rode past the myk who had tried to stand. "It seems the Teachers had a fail-safe for the scourge of the double-heads after all."

"Yes," Gar added. "They have served their purpose in unifying our lands as one people."

"Your Teachers, "Thorium spoke with a little anger. "To bring us all together you say, but at what cost... at what cost...?" his voice trialing away.

"Over here," Sebastian called back, ahead of the others as he followed the two wildcats.

An entranceway was seemingly carved into a pile of the metal ruble of the city, blocks and sheets of metal placed to support its roof. There were no more myk to be seen, however a door blocked their access a little ways in.

"Another Hold of the Teachers?" Sebastian asked the Sage.

"The door is wrong," answered Del. "And it's rusted though in places. I think it was just thrown up here by the myk."

"That's the direction we need to go," Gar voiced.

Jamen gave the door a solid kick and it gave way. Just inside was a series of steps leading downward into the darkness. Each of the Sage now stepped forward and pulled out their light shafts to show the path ahead.

A little over 100 yards into the tunnel, the expedition could see light just around a turn. As they reached the turn the tunnel opened up into a large open space with channels running the length of it on either side. Mendy walked over to one of the channels and looked down into it; rusted metal from the partial remains of the trains that used to run through it.

At the far end of the open areas sat the Myk, dying on a throne made of metal fragments from the city. Around him lay over twenty scattered myk, all dead, and to one-side two breeding females; one with her newborns climbing over her. Next to the Myk's throne was the remains of several gypsies; his food source.

"The end of the Myk?" Alum asked.

"Yes," said Thorium trying to smile without success.

"What do we do with these," asked Sebastian, pointing at the females and the litter.

"We can do nothing for them," he sullenly answered.

"The children," Loren exclaimed. "We can't just leave them here."

Thorium looked back at each of the others, then at the two breeding females; they were now just barely human and the second one was clearly pregnant.

Del approached Thorium. "The Gypsies will take them."

"We need to bring the children and the two women to the Gypsies then," Loren pleaded. "Let them show them the love they deserve."

Thorium went over in his mind everything he had been through since the mutiny. So much here that had done was out of necessity, now this.

"Gather the children and the women. We'll do as Loren said."

All left the underground room with the two women and the young infants, except Thorium and Jamen who remained behind.

"We just can't leave the rest here like this," Jamen said.

"All are dead or dying, what do you suggest?" Thorium said, feeling anything but warm-hearted towards the dying myk.

"What can we do?" Jamen just shook his head as he said it.

"Nothing," Thorium said, turning and leaving the Myk's Cavern, Jamen close behind.

"What about the two Gypsies here they kept as food. Shouldn't we return them to the Gypsies to mourn?"

"OK," Thorium sadly said as he walked over to gather one of the Gypsy's bodies in his arms. Jamen gathered the other in his arms.

The nine returned that late afternoon bringing the two females and the children, five in all, to the Gypsies along with the two Gypsy bodies. The Gypsies quickly embraced the children, four near normal.

"We will embrace them as our own," Elijah said. "My clan will adopt them all, women and children."

"Thank you," said Loren, crying as she handed the child she carried to Florence, his daughter-in-law.

"The two, whose souls you saved by bringing them here, we will bury here and say our prayers for them. Thank-you for returning them to us."

That night another celebration broke out in the Gypsy camps; a celebration of joy and new beginnings.

"Tomorrow we head home," Thorium said to the expedition. He turned to Del. "The quickest way, we have been gone a long time."

"The quickest way is past the blue lights and then the Two Valleys," Del answered.

"How long," asked Loren, thinking of Reed.

"Less than a month if we have a wagon or two."

Elijah overheard Del. "You can have three if you need more."

"Two will be enough, thank you."

"What will we find when we return?" Jamen Pondered.

"Change, we can be certain of that."

"Kat?" Gar asked.

"That's for another day."

Three weeks later the expedition reached the Northern Valley through the Eastern Pass.

Twror was alive and boisterous. The Jall seemed to be trying their hardest so that the short lived Trade War would be forgotten. The central park was alive with a late fall festival.

The travelers' arrived almost unnoticed. It was Pluto who recognized them first, as the party entered an inn at the edge of the growing city for a meal.

"You're back," he exclaimed as he rushed over to them, "The Myk?"

"Gone," said Mendy as he embraced Pluto, "all gone."

"The city?" Jamen marveled at it size.

"It is now the capital of the Confederation."

"The capital?" Thorium asked.

"Yes, and even yesterday a new people from the north applied to join.

"The North?" Thorium brightened up.

"Yes, Gertrude, I briefly met her in passing," Pluto said. "She said she is a friend of yours."

"Gertrude," Thorium said. "Where is she?"

"I think she is with Sir Wade at the new Capital building."

Thorium just turned and quickly left the Inn leaving the others laughing a happy laugh.

"Did I miss something?" Pluto asked.

"Thorium has finally found his home," Loren answered.